The War of Souls is over, the three moons once again rise into the skies, and the gods of magic have returned.

But wild sorcery runs rampant in the world, and the future of magic, the very future of Krynn, remains in doubt.

Dalamar the Dark and Jenna of Palanthas, leaders of the black- and red-robed wizards, must restore the Orders of High Sorcery to their proper status in the world.

But an insane sorcerer is corrupting the legacy of magic for his own destructive ends. . . .

From the icy wastelands to the south comes a young woman, barely more than a girl. She is frightened and unsure, sent on a great quest for reasons she does not understand. Is her innate strength sufficient to restore the ancient orders and allow the Wizards' Conclave to gather once again?

The first of the post-War of Souls novels, *Wizards' Conclave* promises a thrilling journey to a fantastical world rich with danger, magic, and all the unusual creatures and races of the best-selling DRAGONLANCE world.

THE WIZARDS' CONCLAVE

Douglas Niles

WIZARDS' CONCLAVE

Cover art by Daniel R. Horne
First Printing: July 2004
Library of Congress Catalog Card Number: 2004101048

9 8 7 6 5 4 3 2 1

US ISBN: 0-7869-3351-8
UK ISBN: 0-7869-3352-6
620-17571-001-EN

U.S., CANADA,   EUROPEAN HEADQUARTERS
ASIA, PACIFIC, & LATIN AMERICA   Wizards of the Coast, Belgium
Wizards of the Coast, Inc.   T Hofveld 6d
P.O. Box 707   1702 Groot-Bijgaarden
Renton, WA 98057-0707   Belgium
+1-800-324-6496   +322 467 3360

Visit our web site at **www.wizards.com**

CHAPTER
1

THREE GODS

When the War of Souls ended, the gods of magic returned to their own cosmos together with all of their immortal kin among the pantheon of Krynn. For long years they had dwelled in banishment, their world stolen away by the treachery of the late and unlamented Dark Queen. Their world had been bereft of godly magic for decades, and all were cognizant of the fact that there was much work to be done. In the time-honored manner of gods—and mortals as well—they immediately began to flex their respective might in competition with their fellows.

Each returning god, male or female, master or mistress of major or minor creed, had, of course, a somewhat narrow scope of interest. Zeboim turned to the seas, the briny landscape of her nearly limitless domain, while Sargonnas reveled in the martial splendor of his minotaurs. Shinare gently nudged her worshipers toward a restoration of the trade and commerce that was her lifeblood and joy. Reorx spoke to his dwarves, his basso voice thrumming up from the bedrock, reaching the stocky mountain folk through dreams and clerics, urging them to set aside their clannish differences, and to apply themselves jointly to the advancement of the race. Some gods worked for the cause of good, others for evil; while the neutral gods strived to maintain the ancient Balance that had long been the most stable force in the world.

The three immortal cousins who were the gods of magic each had distinct plans, schemes, agendas. Yet they shared a closeness that was foreign to the other gods, a connection no other immortals could know. In their guises of black, red, and white, they embodied evil, neutrality, and good. As moons, they once again waxed and waned in the skies over the world. Two of them were visible to the eyes of men, while the third—the black moon—remained an unseen presence that was, nevertheless, keenly potent.

The gods of magic knew that, during the decades of their absence, foul sorceries had arisen among the mortals. This wild sorcery was an affront to true magic power, an abomination in the eyes of the gods. Yet it lurked and grew and swirled throughout the world, a blanket of corruption cloaking the land and—an even greater abomination—clouding the minds of the wizards who might otherwise have welcomed the return of their ancient lords. Each god of magic yearned for a return of true arcane power, and each set about restoring the faith, and the powers, of loyal followers.

Nuitari, the black moon, sent a summons to the world of Krynn, commanding his practitioners to once again take up their spellbooks and potions, to plot and scheme for the furtherance of the Black Robes among the lands of dragons, men, and all the lesser peoples of the world. Those followers were ordered to restore the glory of that mighty order, a glory revealed in the fear it provoked in the souls of all the creatures of the world.

Nuitari's female cousin, Lunitari the Red, likewise sent out a call. The Red Robes were to gather in her name and await her commands. She would organize them and grant them her favor, and they would once again be a force upon

Krynn. The message went to all corners of the world, thrumming with power and truth: the Red Robes must awaken and arise, seizing their crucial position astride the fulcrum of the Balance, striving for prominence and mastery among the Orders of Magic and the councils of men.

Even Solinari, the gleaming perfect circle of the white moon, felt the competition, the resurgence of power, and the threat to his primacy presented by the foul pollution of wild magic. Solinari knew the nature of his ambitious cousins, and understood that might must be met with greater might. So he, too, directed his attentions toward the world, and made to pull the wearers of the White Robe into a council of magical power, a meeting to allow them to plan the future course of true magic in the world. Evil and apathy were the threat, and the stern guidance of the white wizards was needed to hold the world on a steady path.

But Solinari's command, like those of Nuitari and Lunitari, went unheard in the world. The magic users were scattered; those who survived were uniformly elderly—since they had, by necessity, completed their training in an earlier age—and the gods of magic were unable to draw them back into the fold.

"It is the curse of the wild magic," observed the god of black magic, when at last his fury settled enough to allow reflection. "It runs rampant in the world, drawing those who have talent away from us and toward its own ruinous ends. It is corruption and betrayal, and it bars the way to our full return."

"I tried to battle this wild magic," said Lunitari. "But it was a force too strong; it turned me back at every angle, every corner. I could find no chink in its arcane armor. And it has seized the souls of those who would otherwise raise us to our deserved glory."

"Nor could I reach into the world as I desired," admitted Solinari, though perhaps he was not as surprised as his cousins. "For more than thirty of Krynn's years, the forces of wild magic have grown in power, while our own faithful have been left to languish with no proof even that their gods existed, much less that they would have been able to cast the spells, to work the alchemies, to brew the potions that had been instinctive truths upon the world for as many centuries as we three moons have roamed the skies."

"Are you suggesting that we are done and defeated, then?" growled Nuitari, lightning and hellfire sparkling in the depths of his colorless void. "I will never admit to that! I will fight, and if I must die, then the world will see me perish in glory and devastation!"

And the black moon spewed forth a great storm in the night, lighting and assailing the world with crackling bolts, sending them searing into the crests of mountains, the tops of tall trees, the steeples and parapets of lofty buildings. Each hissing missile was composed of pure magic, but as these bolts smote the world, they were snuffed into nothingness, leaving no fire, no hint of smoke or char. Instead their magical power melted into the wild sorcery that held such sway in the world.

"Nor shall I acknowledge this foul adversary!" chimed in Lunitari, surrounded by a blazing corona of flames. "I will blaze my way into Krynn and once again claim my rightful place above the world!"

And she sent a cascade of meteors plunging from the heavens, arcane chunks that had been torn from the very fabric of magical power. These burned through the skies with terrifying majesty, streaking bright colors, thundering with crushing roars of sound, but when they struck the surface of the world, they vanished. They left no mark upon the ground, nor did the impacts create any sound audible to the awestruck humans, elves, draconians, and others who witnessed the essence of magic smash into the earth. Instead the magic was absorbed by the fabric of the world, and the core of wild sorcery flourished and grew.

It was white Solinari who voiced a plea for unity. "We cannot hurl ourselves against the world at random, disparate and competing in our aims. We must work together, a godly model for the Conclave we desire upon Krynn."

"What use, that?" Nuitari's voice dripped contempt. "My deepest might, thrown lustily and with abiding hatred and vengeance, caused not a blink among the peoples of the world!"

"We must focus our attention, combine our presence, and direct it at a single place in the world where we can reenter Krynn and form a base of power!" Lunitari declared. "A target we can empower utterly and completely."

"The tower of magic, of course!" Now the god of black magic understood, and he sounded delighted and enthused. "We must awaken the Tower of High Sorcery in Wayreth Forest!"

"Indeed," agreed Solinari. "That is the only thing that we can do."

CHAPTER

2

SORCERERS

Murk lay over the land in this place. A stinking miasma enveloped the skeletal remnants of trees, outlining the leafless branches, caressing the rotted, moldering bark. The mist ebbed and flowed, surged and receded. It was green and gray and sometimes a pale, sickly white, lying close along the ground, filling the shallow hollows, and now and again surging through the dead trees like a brackish tide billowing among the pilings of a ruined pier.

Many of the once-lofty pines lay inert, a forest of giant matchsticks tangled and tossed by gigantic or godly hands. Some of the timbers were invisible within the mist, while others rose starkly against the gray and sunless sky. No creatures dwelled here, not even rat or vulture or other carrion scrounger. Even the wind seemed afraid to intrude, to display any sign of vitality. Instead, the fetid air lay languid and suffocating over the ruined land, like a poisonous blanket that smothered all vitality.

Yet even in the lifelessness, there was noise. Bubbles of sulfurous gas percolated up through the soggy ground, bursting with the sound of gooey slapping. Branches and tree trunks snapped for no apparent reason; the sharp *cracks* immediately faded, as if the dead forest were acting promptly to absorb all sound into the corrupt bosom of its rotten soul.

Now and then a great rumble would shiver the flesh of the world, creak and groan forbiddingly, briefly raking the ground. Then trees wobbled and swayed, and brittle branches fell like stinging rain. One or two of the still-upright trees would lean too far, groaning like things that were dying in great agony. With a splintering snap, the ancient giant of the wood broke near its base and toppled to land amid the rotting corpses of its fellows.

The forest was decaying, dying everywhere, but it was not as dead as the lake. Across the vast expanse of poisoned wetness, the lake stood revealed in all its ghastly desolation. Fumes rose from the surface, thick tendrils of oily effluence that danced like wraiths above the fetid surface, slunk low toward the shore. These sinuous vapors coiled and twirled and reached toward the shore, forming the mist that thrust its foul fingers through the wasteland of wood. The vaporous tentacles caressed each rotted trunk, probed knotholes and stroked the splintered gaps, seeping into the very pores of the timber—and thus hastening its irreversible decay.

A spume erupted, violently, far out on the flat surface. Like a geyser, spewing steam of green and liquid caustic enough to burn through plate mail armor, the spire cast itself far into the sky. For several minutes it roared and pulsed, showering acid in a great circle while the steam that came after lingered, a toxic plume slowly settling toward the surface. For a long time that cloud expanded, adding countless additional tendrils to the vaporous emissions constantly poking and wending through the lifeless forest.

Far from shore, nearly invisible in the mists, the upper ramparts of a tower slanted skyward from the surface of the lake. Balconies that had once been crystal and silver were now corroded to a rusty gray. Gaps showed where sections of the wall had been rent by violence. Judging by the angle of its leaning, it seemed inconceivable that the spire could survive long without toppling into the waters and vanishing.

"That tower was a thousand feet tall."

The speaker was a tall man, gaunt and hook-nosed. His visage was concealed behind a massive spray of silver-black beard and a tangle of long gray hair. His eyebrows bristled, meeting thickly over his massive beak of a nose, shading a pair of deep-set eyes. Even sunken as they were into the almost gaunt face, those eyes gleamed, sparkling with intelligence, ambition . . . and perhaps a hint of madness.

"How can it still be standing?" asked a second man, much shorter and rounder than the first. His beard was neatly trimmed where his companion's was wild. His manicured nails somehow gleamed even in the murky haze. "The convulsion that wracked this place when the Green Mistress fell should have rattled it to pieces. It seemed as though every other building toppled! Beryl herself crushed a hundred great houses when her body struck the ground!"

"Ah, but the Tower of the Sun was not a structure made of mortal stone. Even among the elf-houses, which are enforced with crystal and gemstone on every side, that spire was a thing of ancient might. I am not surprised that it stands, even if somewhat askew." The tall man glared down at his companion as he gestured across the lake, waving his hand with disdain. "But that tower is insignificant to us. It means less than nothing."

"Very well, Kalrakin." The short man seemed to accept this with a shrug. He glanced over his shoulder, through the dead woods. The mist parted, slightly, revealing a glimpse of green, a living forest very far away. "But I am worried about pursuit. Perhaps now is the time for you to tell me what you plan for us to do."

"Did you not tell me, yourself, that in time our true path would be revealed to us? Luthar, you surprise me. I did not think you were the type to have doubts. If you wish, of course, I am sure the Dark Knights would be glad to take you back. Though, after the bloodletting of our departure, they may feel they have a score to settle."

Luthar snorted. "Did you have to kill so *many* of them? I told you, they were fully prepared to let us leave with the artifact. And they would not have been inclined to pursue their two most adept sorcerers, no matter what we took from them before our departure. Even before this morning, they had good cause to fear our power."

At the mention of the artifact, Kalrakin smiled, as a delectable memory was refreshed. His hand, a skeleton of long, slender fingers, crept into a pouch at his waist. They emerged, curled into a claw, holding a pearly sphere the size of a child's fist. Even through the cage of the tall man's fingers, the stone cast light bright enough to penetrate the midday haze.

"This is all that matters. They were insignificant men; their lives meant nothing."

"Still, we have no need of further enemies! In destroying so many, we leave others with a burning desire for vengeance.

"Luthar, you do not understand the power of fear. Those who witnessed our departure may mourn for their slain companions, and they may speak of us with hatred, but they are not likely to come after us—for they are afraid. And as to those who died, they had no reason to live," Kalrakin said contemptuously. "Their general is dead. The land they occupied, this place they once called Qualinesti, is a lifeless wasteland. The elves, their former subjects, are gone, and the green dragon is dead. Let the Dark Knights die, too, and this place might finally be forgotten. It deserves no better."

Luthar's expression turned sly. "But aren't we here, on the shores of the former elf realm, because Qualinesti was also the home of the Irda Stone?"

The tall sorcerer looked down at the pearly sphere. He squeezed and the light pulsed, brightening the spark in his eye. "The pathetic elves did not understand the power of the thing that they held in their treasury, locked away with a thousand other pretty baubles. And when the Dark Knights claimed those stones as part of their due tribute, Marshal Medan was equally a fool. It was not until *you*, my worthy helpmate, brought me to see the stone that I recognized its true power. Its true identity had been overlooked for thousands of years, but I have reawakened it. We claimed the opportunity, and we took it—the stone itself could ask for nothing less!"

The ground rumbled again, a tremor rolling through the dead forest, lifting the ground underfoot. Both men staggered, and Luthar leaned against his companion, bracing himself. Dead trees toppled here and there, and the tremor shivered up to the shoreline, sending a wave of ripples through the acidic brew.

No trace of amusement showed in Kalrakin's face now when he lifted his head and stared out across the lake of death. Vapors still danced and swirled, spires of lethal gas moving in uncanny synchronicity. Another geyser spurted, this one farther away but bursting upward to a nearly impossible height—as tall as the Tower of the Sun had once risen above the fair city.

"I fear this place," Luthar admitted. "That ruined tower taunts us, wards us away."

Kalrakin sniffed. "That tower is nothing to us, an insignificant piece of wreckage. Yet there is another . . . somewhere. It is calling us through this stone."

"Another tower? Where?

"The stone will show us the way. Now it is time for us to go," the tall sorcerer said simply.

Luthar nodded. "You are holding the key," he acknowledged.

Kalrakin raised his hand and struck a rigid pose. His left arm hung motionless at his side, but his right—with the hand still clenched into a fist around the pearly stone—he held straight out before him. Slowly, gravely, he called upon the wild sorcery of the world, the power that had brought him great, even exalted, status among the Gray Robes. He flexed the fingers of his hand, opening his fist, palm downward, spreading his fingers into a widespread spider of five golden legs. The artifact remained tight against his skin, held in place by an unseen magnetism.

Magic pulsed visibly, a flash of light beating along the shore, swiftly swallowed by the cloaking mist. The stone glowed warm, then hot—a thrilling, gratifying heat. The warm power surged outward and down, eager to do its master's bidding; tendrils of sorcery penetrated the ground, seizing hold of the bedrock.

The tall sorcerer remained rigid, except for his fingers. These flexed and twisted, each motion delicate, subtle, masterful. He played the wild magic as if it were a lute of infinite, invisible strings and Kalrakin were the musician summoning his melody from that instrument. The power arced downward from each of his fingers; crackling conduits of golden light stroked the ground. That same magic pulsed upward through his feet and legs, drawn by the force of his will and the skill of his spellcasting, amplified by the power of the precious artifact. He started to raise his right arm, his lips parting as, through clenched teeth, he uttered a sound that was half groan, half hiss, a mingling of desperation and pleasure.

Luthar shivered as the sorcerous magic began to respond. A ripple creased the surface of the flat lake, spreading outward from Kalrakin's position on the shore. The ground trembled underfoot and, back in the fringe of the forest, several tall trees toppled over, tumbling in splintering crashes that seemed shockingly loud against the backdrop of the dead land.

The power was truly great here, thought Luthar, for this was the site of a hallowed place of ancient sorcery and the grave of a monster of nearly unspeakable power. The great Tower of the Sun was a ruin here, the summit marking the gravesite not just of a city, but of an entire people. The mansions and manors of Qualinost, the crystal towers and silvery domes, had vanished; all had been swallowed by this reeking mass of putrid liquid.

But the ancient magic of this place, the ancient power of the elves and of the world itself, lingered, lurking beneath the brackish surface. Now that rich legacy of magic fulfilled its promise, as the tall sorcerer sent tendrils of his power into the bedrock beneath the lake, the city, the very world. Kalrakin's hand, still clutching the stone, was thrust nearly straight up in the air now, and the inarticulate sound of his casting grew in volume and intensity. Amplified by the power of the Irda Stone, wild magic seized the bedrock of the land, and began to twist, to pull, to lift.

Larger ripples splashed across the water. A breath of wind stirred the brackish pools, dispersed the thickets of mist. Tremors convulsed the ground.

Finally he thrust his fist straight upward, and a storm of spuming liquid boiled along the surface of the lake in a line extending straight away from him, and from the shore. Brackish, foul water spilled away to both sides, pouring off a surface that rose gradually into view. The fumes swirled more thickly now, and Luthar pressed a cloth to his mouth, coughed through his gag, his eyes squeezed tightly shut. Pools of acidic liquid steamed and hissed on the flat stone pathway, flowing off to the sides, trickling back to the lake.

If Kalrakin felt any hesitation or discomfort, he displayed no sign. He held his hand aloft, long arm extended over his head. Light flashed from the stone, cold white beams brightening the long, straight pathway that now stretched out before them on the surface of the lake. Gradually that trembling surface ceased to move, took on an appearance of permanent solidity.

A stone causeway had appeared, wide enough for two men to walk side by side, a smooth surface only a foot or two above the brackish surface. Connecting to the shore before them, the path extended until it vanished into the mists that still masked any attempt to see a far distance.

"Come—we have but minutes," Kalrakin said sharply.

"I can't see!" protested Luthar, blinking and wiping his eyes through another fit of coughing.

"Hold the tail of my robe," snapped the tall sorcerer, taking his companion's hand, giving him a fold of the brown cloth. Luthar clutched the material as if it were his lifeline, which indeed it was.

Kalrakin strode onto his magical causeway, ignoring the seething lake bubbling and churning to both sides. Luthar took a moment to get his balance, then stumbled along behind. In moments the two of them had started across the wild magic causeway through the great span of the toxic lake.

CHAPTER

3

A GIRL OF THE ICEREACH

Coryn pushed herself to her feet, and turned to retrace her steps back along the rim of the gorge. Her legs were weary after the morning's long climb, though she knew she was capable of many more miles of hiking. More burdensome than her fatigue was the disappointment of the fruitless hunt: To this point she had not even seen a deer track, much less caught sight of any prospective quarry. There didn't seem to be any point in probing farther into the highlands toward the Icewall, when there was probably just as much chance of finding game along the bluff near the village.

That would be just her luck, she thought sourly—to hunt all this distance and then find a huge buck and bring it down with a single arrow, within sight of her village! She resolved to follow the high path back to the edge of the bluff, where the view was good and she could still find concealment if she needed it. She'd hunt just a little longer.

When she reached the edge of the escarpment, she peered ahead, imagining that she could see her village, though it would still be a long, hard march of many miles before she would feel the warmth of her parents' hearth fire.

Her bow remained strung, suspended easily from her shoulder, though she hadn't used it once all day long. This after she had boasted—not just to her father, but to all the village elders—that she would bag a doe and a fawn today with her tough, sharp arrows. Why had she opened her mouth?

Umma was always telling her not to brag or boast. She thought of her grandmother with grudging affection. The old woman certainly had a lot of good advice, and wasn't the least bit shy about sharing it with her sixteen-year-old granddaughter. Why couldn't Cory do a better job of listening?

Umma was certainly the wisest person in the village, the only one Cory knew of who had ever been beyond the Icereach. People told stories claiming that, as a young woman, she had gone as far as the grand city of Tarsis, though Coryn had never known her to speak of that faraway place. But the girl liked spending time with Umma in her cottage. She would go there to wash her grandmother's dishes, to chop wood, tend the fire and the mending, and help out with the countless other chores that the old woman's frail fingers and failing eyes had grown too feeble to easily accomplish.

Part of it was purely for the pleasure of Umma's company, even if her tart tongue and irascible nature sometimes leavened that pleasure. But another part of her motivation brought Coryn a little flush of guilt, when she thought about it. Her grandmother had precious books, the only books in the whole village of Two Forks. Though she had warned Cory, waving her bony finger for emphasis, to stay away from those fascinating tomes, the girl was always tempted. When Umma drifted into one of her long afternoon naps, her graying head bobbing forward against her chest, long snores rumbling through her nostrils, Cory would sneak the books out of their hiding places. Some were in a jar on the hearth, others underneath the counter in the kitchen. One, the most fascinating of all, Umma kept under the mattress of her bed.

Over the years Cory had found and read them all. She wasn't at all sure she understood everything she was reading. Most of them seemed like recipes of some sort, though not for any kind of food Coryn could imagine. A few were collections of letters, missives that occasionally arrived in the village, carried by wandering hunters, trappers, or traders, over the years. Just last month Umma had gotten a new one, which she had snatched away from Cory's prying eyes. Usually the letters described far-off places—one of them even mentioned a wild forest! Coryn had often tried to imagine such a forest. Here on the Icereach there were occasional trees, cottonwoods and cedars clinging to life in sheltered river valleys. But these were sparse and scanty woodlands. What would it be like to see an expanse of woods, where the trees were so thick you couldn't even see past them to the other side?

Coryn sighed. It was not like she would ever get to see anything so exotic. Though even here, in the southern realm of the world, strange things were known to happen. She reflected, with a secret flush of delight, on the great phenomenon of this past winter. Her father and the other elders called it the Night of Two Moons. On that cloudless evening the bright silver moon Coryn had known all of her life had vanished, to be replaced by two smaller, but even brighter, disks. One of these was white and the other red.

Umma had been particularly excited by the appearance of those moons, at least for a few days. Then she had become increasingly cross, until she had taken to her bed with a high fever. Coryn had sat with her for much of the spring, until at last her grandmother had been strong enough to move back to the rocking chair where she spent so much of her time. Cory had pressed her for information about the moons—she knew that, in her parents' youth, those same orbs had ruled the night skies—but Umma quickly became contemptuous of the questions, referring to the new moons as nothing more than a taunt offered by dead, vanished gods.

With the coming of full spring, the tribe's needs had sent Cory outside again. She had always had a gift for helping her people. From her youngest days, she could remember feeling the power in the world around her, the wild sorcery that dwelled in the wind, in the water, in the wood of the trees. She knew that she had a unique gift, and she enjoyed sharing it, finding fish even when the most experienced net-men failed, or drawing up water from a spring that the elders had deemed worthless. Unfortunately, that confidence had led her to make a few misplaced boasts—like this failed hunt today.

Coryn froze suddenly, her thoughts and daydreams vanishing in an instant of alarm. Every sense tingled alertly. She looked around, saw nothing except the rock and snow of the landscape. Her nostrils sniffed carefully, but she smelled only the melt, the wetness of spring.

Yet she was certain that danger—an enemy—was near. She listened and smelled some more, turned her head slowly to look around, but saw no sign of the dread walrus-men. . . .

She had no doubt that she was in fact menaced by a band of thanoi. Concentrating, trying to quell her rapidly rising fear, she let her senses run free. The wild sorcery spoke to her in the wind, even through the water in the melting snow. She explored those avenues, and as the wind and water spoke to her, she formed a clear picture in her mind. Coryn realized that there were nearly a dozen thanoi lurking nearby. Some of them were at the crest of the gorge, hiding out of sight, while others crept along the upstream canyon wall, using the many rocky outcrops for concealment. All were stalking her.

A whisper of panic started in the back of her mind, but Coryn roughly forced it away. As coolly as possible she considered tactics: The thanoi were on two sides of her, the churning river on the third. That gave her one narrow route of escape, down the valley on this side of, and running parallel to, the stream.

Every nerve in her body screamed: "Run!" But that would only invite immediate doom—she needed to use the element of surprise. "Be patient. Be smart," she counseled herself, forcing her fear away, breathing slowly to restore her sense of calm.

Coryn stretched, arching her back, yawning as if she had no worries. She bent double, flexing her waist to the front and to each side, reaching her hands over her head as if she was working out the kinks of a long rest. Her bow remained ready, where she could snatch it in a second. All the while, she studied the terrain out of the corners of her eyes, picking out a path that would let her sprint at full speed, not too close to the precipice. She leaned over again, touching her toes, picturing the brutish, tusked walrus-men coiling their sinewy limbs, preparing to attack.

Never before had she been so close to these brutal creatures, the traditional foes of the Icefolk. Oh, she had seen a few of their tusked skulls, and once even the body of a bull thanoi that had ventured too close to the village, a predator that her father and the other hunters had killed with a volley of arrows. Even dead, it had been a vile and disgusting sight, with its thick and flabby skin, tiny eyes, and grotesque tusks.

Now real panic began to churn in her belly, and she could tell that the thanoi were pressing closer. Blunt, calloused fingers tightened around the wooden hafts of stone-headed spears, as webbed feet braced themselves for a lethal charge.

With practiced artistry, she shrugged the strung bow off her shoulder, her hand snatching a heavy hunting arrow from her quiver. In an instant the missile was drawn, the bowstring taut against her cheek as she aimed along the crest of the bluff. No thanoi was in sight, but here was where the young Icefolk girl might give her hunters a nasty surprise.

Coryn called upon the power of wild magic, the sorcery of the natural world. She felt the power surge with each breath, every gust of wind, and she drew that airy power to herself, shaped it with her will. That sorcery spoke to her, showed her the positions of the three thanoi closest to her. They lay just beyond the overhead crest. Already their limbs were coiled; their tusked faces were rising to attack.

In one smooth gesture she drew her bowstring back and pivoted so that she was aiming uphill. She let fly, the *twang* of the bowstring lost in the rumble of the churning rapids below. With her usual accuracy, she aimed just past a large boulder that jutted from the ground some twenty paces away, at the crest of the slope. In the same instant of release she cast the power of her sorcery into the wooden shaft, and the arrow immediately became three identical missiles, all soaring upward on parallel paths.

Her spell was not completed. Now came a gust of air, a blast of wild magic that spewed out of the gorge and swept across the precipitous ledge. The wind caught the three arrows like a trio of invisible fists, twisting, forcing them around, veering their flights. The wooden missiles, their heads razor sharp— and very precious—steel, reversed course as they crested the hill, swerving back down to drive out of Coryn's sight, vanishing behind the large boulder.

Immediately the young woman was rewarded by beastly shrieks of shock and pain. In her mind she could see the three walrus-men pierced, shot through their backs before they had climbed to their feet. In various stages of dying, they thrashed about in the snow, red blood staining the white slush.

Coryn took off, running at full speed. There was no magic fueling her flight, but her grace and strength carried her like a mountain goat along the steeply sloping side wall of the gorge. Behind and above her, the other thanoi uttered barks of alarm and agitation, but the pursuit had been delayed for precious seconds by her preemptive attack. A heavy spear, tipped with a head of sharpened stone, careened off of a rock as she raced by, while another flew past her ear and landed with a *splat* in the slushy snow. Ducking, the young woman turned sharply downhill then darted onto the traverse again, the maneuver throwing off the aim of the next couple of spears.

Snatching a look up the slope, she almost screamed at the sight of a hulking walrus-man loping into view. His face was ugly, with wickedly curved tusks jutting forward from overhanging jowls, and small, red eyes shining from pockets of droopy fat. He barked and woofed shrilly.

The mere glimpse of that horrible visage propelled Coryn to even greater speed. Her foot skidded in the wet snow, and she almost stumbled, catching herself with a hand on an outcrop of rock. She pulled herself up onto the boulder and sprang across a span of snow to the next limestone surface, then sprinted along a stretch of flat, dry rock. Grunts and pants came from above and behind her, sounding terribly close, but she dared not glance back—even a moment's distraction might send her tripping through a disastrous fall.

Behind her she heard a shriek of rage and the tumbling of a body through the snow ending in a loud splash. She knew that another of her pursuers had fallen, but that was little comfort as she raced along a precarious slope, snow sliding away beneath her moccasins with each step. She veered downward, following the curve of the gorge wall. Still she dared not look back—she could only run!

Too late, she saw the large wall of stone rising in her path, a twenty-foot barrier too steep for her to climb. The base of the precipice was a tangle of large, broken boulders, a tumble that dropped straight to the edge of the churning, surging stream. That whitewater torrent was death, she knew—even her wild magic would not protect her from being crushed against the huge rocks that littered the stream.

She had no choice but to turn upward again, scrambling to climb the snowy slope. Coryn clawed with her fingers, pumped her legs, kicked each foot as hard as she could into the cold, wet surface. The barks of the walrus-men erupted anew, with an unmistakable element of triumph to their noise.

Something hit her hard in the side, a massive body bowling her over as one of the thanoi hurled himself upon her, diving down the snowy slope. She cried out as she felt a tusk jab her shoulder, then turned and punched the bestial face full upon its blunt nose. She smell the stink of old fish, felt the cold snow on her back as the walrus-man pressed her down heavily. He was powerful, too strong for her to push him away. Those nasty tusks pushed against her chest as he leaned down over her, and she gasped in pain, struggling to draw a breath. Her hands, taut fists, pushed at the tusks, but couldn't budge them away. The leering creature pushed downward, driving the sharp tips harder against her skin.

Snow was all around, white and icy, so bright that she could barely see. Out of that whiteness, a surprising notion came into her mind, a picture of a word that she had read somewhere. She didn't know what it meant, had never said it aloud before, but somehow—right then—she knew it was a perfect word. She had just enough air left to bark the sound, the word exploding from her mouth.

Coryn felt a momentary disorientation, an exhilarating sense of freedom, and then everything changed. She woke to find herself still lying on her back, still wet and cold, but the sun was gone . . . vaguely she realized that she was in a hut, with a crackling fire nearby. She all but sobbed in relief when she looked up to see Umma peering down curiously, rocking in her chair.

"Dear girl!" said the old woman. "What on Krynn are you doing lying on my floor?"

CHAPTER
4

RED LADY

The sun was high in the sky, though the bright golden light of the fiery orb was obscured by a cloak of dust than hung like a veil in the air, casting a brown shroud over the brown landscape surrounding the brown city. It was good-sized, this city, marked by lofty minarets and sprawling palaces, by wide avenues of impressive homes as well as vast areas of teeming slums. A wall surrounded it, but the city had spilled beyond that wall, sprawling in tendrils of shanty-towns and tent cities across the parched flat ground that extended toward the horizon in all directions. In the far distance, ranges of mountains—brown mountains, of course—formed a jagged perimeter.

There was, however, a splash of unusual color in this city today, for this was the day of the Great Market. Once every moon, by decree of the caliph, the merchants came to the vast plaza in the center of the city, setting up their booths, their tents, their pushcarts. Throngs of people came from throughout the city. Others were drawn from the nomadic tribes of the desert, while traveling knights and adventurers also joined the vast congregation of humanity. All of them, merchants and buyers, with their multihued awnings and robes, the variety of people and their beasts, formed a confluence of vitality in the midst of this brown and dusty place.

The plaza was truly a vibrant place on market day. Pennants of bright silk flew above the richer booths, while even the poorest vendors managed to hoist some sort of attention-grabbing banner. Birds of brilliant plumage squawked from inside huge cages, while under short leashes, dozens of monkeys shrieked in mockery or indignation, a simian parody of the human throng all around them. Horses, some of them splendid and others shaggy nags, neighed and kicked in their corrals, while everywhere sheep bleated and goats brayed, adding their voices to the cacophony.

But mostly there were all types of people, thousands of them. They came to buy and to sell, sometimes to steal, to gawk and beg, eat and drink and talk and laugh, to do all of the things that drew the race of man together. They were bearded and robed for the most part, though some went about in bits of armor, leather tunics, or even the canvas leggings of sailors—though the nearest port was hundreds of miles away. All of them were eager with curiosity, and, judging from the noise, all of them were trying to talk at once.

One cloaked figure moved quietly through the crowd without drawing very much attention. The slight, bowed form of a person, wrapped within a nondescript robe, walked up and down the narrow aisles between the stalls, looking into the shadowy tents, peering down each narrow dead end, slipping knowledgeably among the sellers. The cloak the figure wore was a tan color and concealed the person's exact form, except for the eyes. Even the hands remained tucked within that anonymous cloak.

Those eyes were lively, however, searching, narrowing with interest here, scowling in scorn a moment later—but always watching.

In the center of the plaza a small black dragon thrashed and hissed within the confines of an iron cage. The wyrm's wings were flattened together above its back, held firmly in an unnatural position, because coils of wire were wrapped around its snarling, hateful muzzle. The cloaked figure's eyes brightened slightly, betraying at least a modicum of interest, and the mysterious shopper pressed through the crowd to get a closer look.

"This wyrmling is a true treasure!" hawked a fat merchant dressed in bright silk robes. He waddled back and forth before the cage, gesturing broadly to the onlookers and potential buyers who had gathered hesitantly before him. "Don't be afraid, good citizens of Neraka—his wings are immobilized by my spells of containment. Not to mention a coil of good steel wire! No, he shall not be released until I give the command.

"For now, it is enough for you to know that the bidding is about to commence! Who is to lay a claim to this unique and terrible beast? A claim paid in steel, with ownership guaranteed. Enough steel, a clever and timely bid, and you could take this rare creature home with you today!"

"What would anyone want with an evil brute like that? Why, it would snap your head off at the first chance!" snapped one bearded man, a tall fellow who had come over from his own booth where he had been attempting to sell pots of stinking brews. "These good customers would be better off buying a good, honest potion!"

"Bah!" The fat merchant waved off his rival. "True, you would have no use for the serpent, since you have nothing of value to protect! But for one who counts a vault or an armory among his possessions . . . or a dungeon, a fortress of ancient might . . . a secluded bastion, or an idyllic retreat? For one who has such a place to protect, this creature would make a splendid guardian! Bound by magic, it is, sworn to the service of the one I appoint. It will not bite your head off, unless you should give it that very command, fool! It is my true power, the spell of command I have placed upon the creature, that holds its power—not in check—but to place it at the owner's beck and call."

"I offer five hundred steel for the beast!"

The bidder was an old man, known to all as the primary agent for the caliph. That ancient ruler, wealthy beyond belief, was known to keep a harem of young maidens secluded in his mountaintop palace. Now nearing his dotage, his jealousy was fabled, and such a beast would surely prove to be a deterrent to any but the most determined of amorous adventurers.

The merchant's eyes flashed momentarily at this initial, respectable bid, then clouded with an expression of bemused disappointment. "Why, the collar alone—proof of the potent spells holding the wyrm in bondage—cost me nearly a thousand," declared the fat seller in injured tones. "Know that the ring around the creature's neck is the key to its bondage and obedience, a treasure of magic unavailable anywhere else upon Krynn. So, good citizens, worthy buyers, the bidding shall commence at twice the cost of that collar—two thousand steel pieces, for the most potent turnkey any jailer could require! Do I have a *serious* opening bid?"

"Two thousand, then!" cried the agent for the caliph.

"Two thousand five!" came another bid, this one from the slender cleric of a mysterious temple north of the city. His body was wrapped in a black robe, and his head—utterly hairless, even missing brows and eyelashes—gleamed in the desert sun. He cast the caliph's buyer a look of contempt, and that worthy noble all but sputtered out his reply, raising the thousands to three.

The robed figure meanwhile stood in the forefront, unnoticed by anyone in the crowd—which began to jeer and cheer as the bidding accelerated—and scrutinized the dragon, especially that allegedly enchanted collar. After several minutes, in apparent disinterest, the cloaked one stepped back with a barely audible sigh. The pair of intriguing eyes, wide and dark, with long lashes marked by a gentle shade of henna, turned to inspect the other booths and tents that made up this section of the vibrant market.

One hand, a woman's hand with several pretty rings—a hand that displayed the strength of maturity, apparent in a few wrinkles and lines of age, and tempered by the vanity visible in long, crimson-dyed fingernails—pulled a little of the robe aside from her face, enough to allow a breath of dry air to penetrate. But she was careful not to reveal too much of her features, nor to let any of the sellers or buyers look directly into those eyes.

They were mostly men, here, on both sides of the counters. The most visible females were in the slave quarter of the market, which was off in one corner. The masked woman could see these miserable wenches, dressed in filmy robes, huddled together in a pathetic lot. One of them was being dragged forward by her owner. Forced to climb the steps to a lofty platform, she was then paraded about, encouraged by the lash of a whip, followed by the prod of a blade, when she moved too slowly. Her owner pulled the robe away just enough to display the quality of the flesh underneath. Depending on the attractive nature of that flesh, the bidding would commence lethargically, or in frenzy.

The masked woman stared in contempt for a few moments but turned her eyes away from the slave quarter, knowing she would not find what she sought there. Instead she briefly scrutinized the bubbling potions at the alchemist's cart, leaning down to sniff, to stare, even probing here and there with those well-manicured fingers, touching and tasting. The vender, drawn by the bidding around the black dragon, had temporarily left his cart under the eyes of a hulking swords-man. That swordsman watched dully, without interfering, as the figure inspected each one of the dozen or so vials on display. The guard shrugged with boredom as finally the woman, unimpressed, pulled her robe tightly across her face and strode away.

She came next to a table shaded by a large awning, staked with flaps that extended nearly to the ground behind and to either side. Several men sat there on an elaborate rug, shar-ing a pipe between them. One, the hawk-faced vender, looked up at the woman and scowled. "We are discussing the sale of enchanted weapons here," he snapped. "Do not offer us the ill favor of a woman's presence during such manful talk!"

Ignoring him, the masked stranger stepped past the men to stand before a table where four swords lay beside their jeweled scabbards. Each blade gleamed slightly, casting just enough of a glow to be discernible in the shadows under the awning.

"Those are priceless treasures!" squawked the seller, bounding angrily to his feet, confronting the unwanted visi-tor. "You defile them with your very eyes!"

The woman sniffed loudly, the sound of contempt drawing the seller's eyes to narrow slits of fury. "How dare you—!"

He reached as if to seize her wrist then froze in reaction to something he detected in the woman's eyes, the only part of her visible through the masking robe. His face suddenly went pale, and he took a step away.

The woman flipped her hand above the four swords, a gesture of disdain. A gust of wind puffed across the table, sweeping a cloud of sparkles into the air. She turned to look at the other three men seated on the floor, all of whom had been watching the confrontation with narrow-eyed intensity.

"Faerie dust," she said contemptuously. "He could make his own nose glow, if he patted it onto his face. These blades aren't magic—and this scum wouldn't know a magic sword if it pierced his black heart."

"Eh?" One of the men was already on his feet, a heavy scimitar appearing in his hands as if by his own brand of magic. He waved it at the vendor while he examined the table. The four blades sparkled a bit, but so did the wood and the sleeve of the seller's robe where it had been near the dust.

"How did you know that?" demanded the scimitar-swordsman, but the woman had already left the tent. He showed no inclination to follow. Instead, with his two fellows, he closed in upon the cringing merchant.

Through still more booths she made her way, increasing impatience visible in her haste, and in the momentary carelessness that let the masking robe fall away to expose a smooth jaw, a curving cheek. One of the vigilant guards, seeing this, moved jerkily toward her, ready to rebuke this disgraceful display of flesh, but one reproving look from those blue eyes reminded him of some other, very pressing, business in the opposite direction.

Moving from stall to stall, the masked woman fingered a selection of rings and baubles, held faux jewelry up to the sunlight, rustled through the pages of several dark-bound books that one seller kept concealed in a locked strongbox. She watched a conjurer for several minutes, as he pulled smoking images from a cauldron then caused baubles, weapons, and even a goat to disappear. Her eyes gleamed briefly as the conjurer began to chant; then she snorted and turned away as he revealed, to her, that his skill was naught but sleight of hand. Nowhere did she find anything to pique true interest.

With a muttering of disgust, she stalked out of the last stall, seeing that several groups of bearded, angry men were huddled at either end of the narrow walkway. The agent of the caliph was walking away, being taunted by several other buyers, including the bald cleric who had competed with the caliph's buyer. With a great show of excitement, the crowd was pressing around the corral as the fat merchant, with two brutish henchmen hauling on the restraints, ceremoniously brought forward the young black dragon.

"Congratulations!" declared the fat seller to the bald cleric, with a look of cool triumph. "You have purchased a superior guardian for your temple, capable of securing your treasures against all who might come against you!"

The masked woman quietly inched her way to the front of the crowd. The gaunt cleric, noticing her, twisted his face into a sneer and advanced to push this insolent female out of the way of his trophy. He hesitated then, for her hood fell back a little, revealing a proud face, beautiful in spite of lines of age and worry, and a neat bun of gray hair. Beneath the masking cloak could now be glimpsed the shoulder, crimson red, of a neat gown.

"You'd better have a look at that dragon's collar," declared the woman in cold, contemptuous tones, addressing the thin, gaping priest. "It's no more magical than the pot you pissed in this morning."

Then she disappeared.

CHAPTER

5

MYSTERIOUS MISSION

Coryn was wrapped in a blanket, seated by the fire and sipping a mug of strong tea. Her grandmother had fussed about for a time, getting her settled and warmed. Now, however, Umma cleared her throat, looking at Coryn sternly.

"Tell me what this is about, young lady!" she demanded. "Showing up on my floor, soaking wet, scaring me out of a perfectly good nap? Why, the very idea!"

"I—I'm not sure, myself. I was hunting up on the bluff—I left the village . . . why, it was just this morning," the girl said, half in wonder, half stalling. Slowly, she reconstructed events. "There was a good deer trail, and I thought I could maybe get close to the herd. I promised Papa I'd bag a doe and a fawn, and of course, he told everyone else. I guess I went too far, farther than I should have."

Umma gestured, a command to "hurry up and spit it out."

"Walrus-men!" Coryn gasped, the full horror of the memory returning in a rush. "There was a hunting party of them, and they caught me against the gorge. I sensed them up on the ridge, knew they nearly had me in a trap. But I shot three of them, Umma—right away! Let me tell you how—"

"I'm sure you shot them, Girl. But the rest?"

Coryn frowned. Her grandmother was impatient, always cutting off her explanations. "Well, I started to run, down the valley. But the slope was too steep, and I was trapped against a big rock. One of them jumped on me, had me pressed into the snow. He was going to stab me with his tusks, right through my heart!"

"So how did you end up here, on my floor?" Umma's eyes narrowed suspiciously. "Like to scared the life outta me! Not to mention all this snow you tracked in—why, look at that mess! Who's going to clean that up?"

"I will," Coryn replied meekly, with the momentary thought that perhaps the thanoi were not really the most frightening thing she had faced that day. Not when Umma was frowning down at her with a look that seemed capable of summoning storm clouds into a clear blue sky.

" 'Course you will. But that can wait. Now tell me! No dodging and weaving, now. What happened to get you down off the bluff and here into this soggy puddle on what used to be a nice rug?"

"Well, I'm not really sure *what* I did," the girl admitted hesitantly. "I said . . . something. . . ."

She squinted, trying to remember while deciding exactly how much she should tell. "I don't really know the word . . . but I said it out loud, and I felt a strange flash, and here I am, on your floor."

Umma's bony fingers wrapped around Coryn's wrist in an iron-hard clamp. "Think, Girl!" demanded the old woman. Her dark eyes flashed, lightning brewing within that great storm. "What did you say? What word? Where did you learn this word? And what was the word?"

"I honestly don't know, Grandma! I thought of it right away, but now it's like the whole sound and shape of it is gone, wiped right out of my mind. But . . . I guess . . . I guess it was one of the words I read in your book. You know, the one you keep . . . um . . . under your mattress." Coryn braced for the eruption of the lightning, or—even worse—the searing lash of her grandmother's tongue.

She was surprised, however, when suddenly the steely clasp on her wrist eased, as Umma leaned back in her chair and regarded the young woman with a strange expression that Coryn could only describe as "amused." Suddenly conscious of her matted hair, her soggy shirt and leggings, and the chill that was soaking through to her bones, Coryn couldn't hold back a flash of irritation. "What's so darn funny?" she demanded.

To that, Umma cracked a single sharp bark of laughter. Then her expression grew stern and full of dangerous lightning again. "You mean to tell me you been sneakin' more peeks at my old tomes? Why, them books ain't got a lick o' useful writin' in them anymore. Not since the gods of magic went away, before you was even born, Girl! Why are you wastin' time like that?"

The question, Coryn sensed, was far more than rhetorical. It was some kind of test. She drew a breath, intended to take her time forming an answer that might get her into trouble, but she was ever impulsive. A rush of words exploded, seemingly unbidden, from her lips.

"I've read *all* your books," she admitted. "Over and over. They're the most interesting things I've ever seen. They take me places beyond the muddy huts of Two Forks, beyond the bluff, beyond the whole Icereach. I've read about other people—like elves and dwarves and draconians—and places like Sanction, where the mountains are spilling fire right into the city. Forests . . . with trees everywhere! What *that* must be like! And Palanthas! Oh Umma, how I would love to go there some day, to see the fine ladies in their gowns, the palaces and manors and fountains and statues! Lords and knights on splendid horses, soldiers with armor shining like silver."

Umma's eyes narrowed to mere slits now. She nodded, muttering ominously not to Coryn, but to herself. Coryn couldn't catch all the words. Finally she looked up, as if remembering that Coryn was there, and stared at her.

"Yes, of course. That's what books do, Girl." Umma gestured to a pile of tomes, leather-bound and well worn, teetering precariously on a table near her fireplace. "At least, *those* books. Those books, I daresay, will indeed lead you to such fancies about nobles and manors and elves and Palanthas." The old woman's eyes became two slits of darkness in a scowling mask of leathery skin.

"But you mentioned something about a particular book, didn't you? One I keep under my mattress, you said . . . one you know darn well I put there to keep the prying fingers of curious young girls off of it. But that didn't work, it seems. Now what made you to go poking around there? Tell me true!"

Coryn gulped. She looked at the stack of books, volumes that she had virtually memorized over the years. Yes, the *other* tome fascinated her more than any of rest, and again impulsively she blurted out the truth.

"Actually, Umma, I read your secret book for the first time a long time ago, even though it seemed like so much nonsense. I couldn't make anything out of it. But then, later, I felt almost like it was calling me. Last winter, it was, the first time it called me. You were napping out here in your rocking chair. You just had some of those winterberries I brought you, and a little nip of that bottle on the mantle—"

"You never mind that bottle, Child!" Umma said sternly. "That's an old woman's medicine, not for the likes of you!"

"No—I mean, I know! I've never touched it. Well, only touched it to pour some for you, I mean. But I don't even like the way it smells!"

"Never mind my bottle—tell me about the book!"

"Well, I started to tell you, if you would only let me finish! I felt the book calling me that day, last winter. I remember when—it was just after the Night of Two Moons. At least that's what the villagers called it. You know, when the big white moon changed, got smaller. And there was a red moon, too, one I had never seen before. But Papa told me they had been the moons when he was a boy, only they went away when the gods left. All the old hunters were talking about it . . . about the two moons coming back."

"Yes, yes, the moons. Stop dawdling, girl. Tell me!"

Coryn set her chin and spoke defiantly. "Like I was saying, if you'd stop interrupting, they all were talking about two moons. I didn't say anything to them, didn't want them to think I was crazy . . . again. But there are *three* moons up there now, aren't there? The red and the white. Everybody sees the two. But there is a darker one, too—a black moon? One that nobody can see."

"Nobody?" Umma's eyes, for the first time, glimmered not with irritation, but with concern for her granddaughter. "You are saying you can't see it then?"

"No, I can't see it," Coryn replied, surprised to see relief soften the old woman's visage. "But I can sense that it's there. Sometimes I watch the night sky, and see that stars blink out of sight for a little while. And I know, somehow I know, that's because the black moon is crossing."

"Get back to the book! What about the book? Tell the truth, and don't waste my time!"

"Grandma!" The young woman stared defiantly. Without softening her own gaze, Umma waited for her to continue. "It's . . . it's just the most fascinating thing I have ever seen," Cory admitted. "A lot of it doesn't even make sense to me— like it's written in a whole different language. But even when I don't know the words, I like reading them, thinking about what they mean, and trying to make the sounds."

"Surely you haven't read that whole book? Many a fool has tried and failed!"

"All of it," Coryn said, getting angry. "All of it! Twice. The first time, when I didn't understand a thing, and the second time, when it called to me."

Umma sat back in her rocker and looked at the girl with an expression as close to astonishment as anything Coryn had ever seen on the old woman's generally cross, stony, and inscrutable visage.

"All of it! Huh!" It was as if Umma were speaking to herself. She looked at Coryn, shook her head once, and snapped curtly, "Help me up!"

Cory climbed to her feet and extended both hands, taking her grandmother's thin but deceptively strong fingers. She pulled her up, and the old woman hobbled over to the crowded writing desk next to her small dining table. She fumbled through the stack of objects, pulling out a sheet of parchment that, while torn and ragged, seemed to be free of writing.

"My quill!" she snapped. "Where is it? And bring some ink, too! Hurry, Girl!"

Coryn hastened to obey, finding the writing implements on the hearth over the big stone fireplace. Umma sat down at the desk, uncapped the inkwell beside the flat sheet of parchment, and scowled at her granddaughter who stood, full of curiosity, nearby.

"Well? Shouldn't you brew some tea or something? And get out of those wet things—can't have you catching a chill! Not now, of all times! You're going to be needing all of your strength, you are. Besides, your hair's a mess—you'll have rats making a nest there if you don't take care. Move, Girl!"

Shrugging her shoulders with irritation, Coryn hurried to fill the teapot, stoke the fire, doff her soggy trousers, and run a stubby brush through her long, dark tresses. Every time she glanced toward the desk, she saw Umma busily scribing away. Every once in a while the old woman looked up and gave her a fierce stare, and Cory quickly went back to her combing. She had a particularly stubborn tangle, where her hair had picked up some burrs during her struggles in the snowbank.

"My stamp!" Umma snapped, looking up finally and rolling the parchment into a tight roll. "And don't forget the candle!"

Obediently, Cory lit a long wax taper with a coal from the fireplace then carried the burning candle and the small brass stamp over to the old woman. She tried not to show her burning curiosity as she peered at the scroll of leathery paper. Wasting no time, Umma melted a spot of wax and dropped it onto the edge of the parchment, then stamped it tightly shut.

"Here," she said abruptly, thrusting the scroll at Coryn as if it were a short, blunt sword. "Take this now!"

"Sure," the girl replied. "But, um, *where?*"

"Why, to Palanthas, of course," snapped the old woman. "Weren't you just telling me how much you wanted to see that place? 'Fabled city' . . . 'shining knights' . . . 'ladies in their fine gowns?' It's all kind of overrated, if you ask me, but I 'spect you young'uns have to find that out for yourself."

"Palanthas!" gasped Coryn. Her head was spinning, and she wanted to sit down and jump in the air at the same time. She settled for standing stock still and staring at Umma in disbelief. "Why, that's on the other side of the world! It's got to be a thousand miles away from here! I can't go to Palanthas! I can't even leave Two Forks! What will Papa say? And Mama—I have skins to tan, nets to haul. . . ." Her voice trailed off as a myriad of real obligations, boring and mundane to the last, rose in her mind. Was her grandmother going crazy?

"And what about the fish? You know how the men need me to tell them right before the salmon start running—I listen to the water, and I know."

"Bah, I'll talk to your Mama and Papa—remind your Papa of when he decided to take off for Tarsis, if I have to. Let the fishermen fend for themselves. Stop babbling, and get moving. You're going to Palanthas!"

"Why? Why am I going to Palanthas all of a sudden?" demanded Coryn, determined to get a grip on the conversation before her mind spun completely out of control.

"Why am I going to Palanthas?" Umma mimicked the question, her scratchy voice harsh with sarcasm. "Why, you were just telling me, Girl. Knights! Ladies! Nobles! Sounds like you know that city better than some folks who've lived there all their lives. Now, get cracking."

Coryn didn't budge, but now her face looked puzzled and worried.

Umma's mouth creased into a hint of a smile as she reached and lifted up her granddaughter's chin, stroking it with an affection she didn't usually show. The old woman gestured to the parchment scroll that Coryn was clutching very tightly in her hands. "You are going to visit an old friend of mine, one of those 'fine ladies' you're all hepped up about. You are to do me a favor and deliver her that scroll, and after that, you are to do whatever she tells you to."

"You mean, I'm to be her servant?" asked Coryn, aghast.

The old woman shrugged. "If that's what she wants, yes. Hear me well, Child—you are to do whatever my good friend tells you to do."

"Who is she?"

"Her name is Jenna. I knew her long, long ago—before the moons changed for the first time. Before your mama was born, even." There was a hint of wistfulness, and also of tenderness, in Umma's voice, that Coryn had never heard before.

"Jenna will take care of you, once you get there. But there's no time to waste!"

"B—but Umma!" Cory was nearing panic. "I've never been out of the Icereach. I don't even know where Palanthas is! And I told you, I have to check with Mama and Papa! I have things I'm supposed to do around here! I can't just go away, not now, not like this!"

"When *can* you go away, then?" The old woman's tone was as stern as ever. "I'm not going to be around here forever, you know. And don't you think your pop, and all them other brave hunters and fishers, might be able to keep their bellies full even with you off to the north? Fact is, it will do them old hook-baiters some good to get up and about, not leavin' all the chores to bright young girls who got more important things to do!"

"Huh! You think I'm bright?" asked Cory, inordinately pleased.

"Did I say I was talking about you?"

"No," she admitted, instantly humbled. "But then, how am I supposed to find Palanthas."

"Open the door," Umma declared.

Puzzled, Coryn crossed to the lone entrance to the small hut, and pulled open the wooden-slatted portal. She gasped in surprise as she saw a person—a *small* person, but most definitely not a child—standing outside. "It's a kender!" she blurted. She had never seen one, but she identified the fellow's race by his wizened features, long topknot, and the haphazard collection of pouches, purses, packs, and pockets dangling from every part of his frequently patched garments.

"Moptop Bristlebrow, at your service," said the kender, with a bow so deep that he tumbled through the threshold to fall in a heap a Coryn's feet.

"Who *are* you?" gasped the girl. She spun to face her grandmother. "Who *is* this?"

"He's your guide. I hired him. He'll be taking you to Palanthas—in fact, right to Jenna's house. So you don't have to worry 'bout a thing."

"Don't have to worry?" Coryn's eyes, wide open, took in the ramshackle figure who was clumsily climbing to his feet, stuffing various items—she noticed a teapot, a branding iron, a small frying pan, and her grandmother's brass stamp—into his pouches. Firmly the young girl reached into a leather pocket and retrieved the stamp. "This doesn't belong to you!" she said firmly.

"Well, of course not! I was just returning it to your grandmother. See that she gets it, won't you? Hey, who's in charge here anyway? I don't need young whippersnappers talking to me rudely—"

Umma cut in sharply. "I meant, you don't have to worry about finding the way to Palanthas. You'll have *plenty* to worry about, believe me. Why, there's bandits in the forests and thieves in the cities. You'll have to book passage across the Newsea—let's see, I have a few steel pieces stashed over there, should help you with that."

Coryn's head was whirling as she put the stamp back on the desk. Yet Umma's dark eyes were alive with amusement.

"I've packed some sandwiches, and a few slabs of jerky for you," Umma said, gesturing to a bulging knapsack near the door. Coryn hadn't noticed it before, but now it seemed perfectly natural that it be packed and ready for her departure. And where had that kender come from, so suddenly?

"I'd better get dressed," she said, blushing as she realized that she had greeted the kender in nothing but her knickers and shirt.

"Good thing, too," said Moptop. He pulled a sheet of paper from another purse and unrolled it, releasing a cascading scroll that spilled to the floor and then some. "I've got our route marked on my map. Let's see,"—he squinted, inspecting his notes—"if we start now, we should make it to the Icewall tonight. All due speed. Them's my orders!"

Coryn felt a glimmer of concern. "But—the Icewall is south of here! Isn't Palanthas in the north?"

The kender squinted, lifted his map, turned it around in his hands so that the voluminous top of the scroll was draped over his head. "Why, so it is!" came his voice, from beneath the makeshift shroud.

"Are you *sure* he knows the way to Palanthas?" Cory asked her grandmother.

Umma cackled, one of the few times her granddaughter had ever heard her laugh out loud.

"Well, he did okay when he took me there. That was fifty-seven summers ago, but I don't think it's moved all that much. Now, daylight's wasting. I'll see your folks know what's happening, count on that. Get going, girl, and you, Moptop, you'll know my wrath if anything goes awry."

The kender saluted stoically, as if indeed he did recall Umma's wrath.

"What will my parents say?" Coryn asked, suddenly feeling an intense wave of homesickness.

"Why, they'll say they love you. And they'll miss you like parents tend to do. No doubt they'll have a few special things to say to me, but don't you worry about that. I can take care of myself, you know. Now, good-bye, Girl, and good luck, and hurry! Hurry!"

Only a half hour later, the little cottage in its grove of cottonwoods was nearly out of sight. Coryn paused only long enough for one last squint, until she saw a wisp of smoke from her grandmother's chimney. The kender was hurrying along a dozen feet in front of her, showing no signs of slowing his pace for her benefit. With a sigh, and an unmistakable tingle of adventure, the young woman adjusted the straps of the heavy pack and turned her steps toward the north.

CHAPTER 6

A MASTER FOR THE TOWER OF MAGIC

Where are we going?" asked Luthar. "This woodland is strange, is it not?"

Kalrakin paused, drew in a deep breath though his beaky nose, and nodded in satisfaction, even anticipation. "Strange, perhaps. But it makes us welcome! See how the path opens—even the trees grant us passage!" The trail, indeed, was wide and smooth, though darkly shadowed by overhanging limbs and dense foliage.

Luthar hurried to keep up, a step or two behind the tall sorcerer. He couldn't help looking this way and that, wide-eyed, as they advanced along a path that was startlingly clear amid the flourishing underbrush and tall, gnarled trees.

Those trees stood back from them to either side, but loomed very high overhead, extending curving limbs over the trail like a series of shadowy arches. Beards of moss draped many of these boughs. Vines and stalks of dewy underbrush also leaned over the path, fingers of foliage brushing against the hems of their robes, but Kalrakin stalked steadily onward without taking notice. His eyes remained fixed on the path before him, and his long strides carried him forward determinedly.

"Wait! Did you hear something?" asked Luthar suddenly, stopping.

"The wild birds," Kalrakin replied, shrugging. His long fingers stroked his tangled beard as he cocked an ear. "Noisy little fools. All this shrieking makes it hard for a man to think!" He, too, had stopped and now glared into the woods as if to challenge the cawing, shrieking flyers. All the while he flipped his polished white stone back and forth from one hand to the other.

"That's just it—listen! It's more than noise."

Many crows and more exotic birds were calling, a cacophony of sound unlike anything in any forest Luthar had ever visited. There was a musical cadence to the notes, but something more . . . almost intelligible.

"This is not the woodland we woke up in this morning, my lord," Luthar suggested. "Something has happened here—listen, I beg you!"

The birds cried and cried again, with ever greater urgency, and gradually the swelling sounds took on a distinct meaning.

It was a summons.

"Come, wizards . . . come to my heights . . . come to my walls . . . come to my sacred site . . . ."

"The birds are speaking to us," noted the dour sorcerer, frowning so deeply that his bushy eyebrows nearly melded. "Calling us, it would seem."

"How can birds talk in a language men can understand?" Luthar asked, squinting and peering ahead, as he, too, listened intently. "This must be magic!" he exclaimed excitedly.

"Come, wizards. . . ."

"Could it be some kind of trick?" asked the shorter sorcerer. "An attempt by our enemies to lure us into an ambush, a trap?"

"Bah—who would dare?" sneered Kalrakin. "In any

event, we have no need to fear anything of magic. Remember, I carry the stone of Irda magic!" He raised the white orb in his hands, clenching it in one fist and waving it grandly, as if to ward away the mysterious presence of the forest.

In response, the birds cawed and shrieked with renewed frenzy. This time there was no mistaking the siren call of their words. Kalrakin bulled forward eagerly, leaving Luthar to sprint after frantically as the tall, gaunt sorcerer plunged down the rapidly forming pathway along the forest floor.

As he pushed through the last tendrils of trailing vine, Kalrakin blinked in a sudden wash of sunlight; a clearing had opened before him. His eyes traveled ahead to witness the great structure, a double spire of dark stone and elegant architecture, rising hundreds of feet toward the sky.

"Behold—like a black claw, it scratches at the heavens!" cried Kalrakin.

"Where are we?" asked his equally awestruck companion. "Surely there is no place in the Qualinesti forest like this?"

"My loyal companion, we have left the elven realm behind—no doubt we passed into Wayreth when we experienced the change in the woodland this morning. We are bid welcome to the Tower of High Sorcery—and this is Wayreth Forest. It all makes sense, now. Opportunity awaits!"

"Yes, it can be nothing else!" Luthar agreed, leaning an outstretched arm against a tree and breathing heavily. "And that must mean—"

"That we have been *invited,* here, of course," Kalrakin concluded. He snorted at the irony: this hallowed place of ancient godly magic, for some reason—a mistake?—summoning two practitioners of wild sorcery.

"Is the Tower dangerous?" There was a clear tremor in the younger mage's voice. "Perhaps we should move farther away from it."

But Kalrakin was already advancing closer, his long legs

swiftly carrying him toward the wall and gateway surrounding the Tower. The gate was a wispy thing, a spiderweb of magical strands, which swept open at their approach without any move on their part. Beyond the gate the Tower rose: two lofty, conical spires with a short, round foretower between them. The Tower thrust up from a flat meadow of neatly trimmed grass, the ground smooth underfoot. A single door stood in that smaller, central structure, a plain-looking barrier of weathered hardwood boards, banded by three stands of rusty iron. A large keyhole gaped just below a metal ring, which suggested use as both a knocker and handle.

The Tower rested upon a foundation that seemed to flow directly from the ground itself. It was all smooth black stone, almost glassy in appearance, which swept upward uninterrupted by any suggestion of a joint or seam. It was unmarred by cracks or blemishes. It was as though the bedrock itself had given birth to the Tower, magically extending toward the sky.

Kalrakin touched that cool, smooth black surface, pressing his white Irda Stone against the outer wall. He closed his eyes, shivering slightly.

"I see clearly that this foundation is set very deeply into the ground. The walls here are very, very thick. There are many levels in the Tower, chambers and stairways too numerous to estimate. I find at least one chamber that strangely seems much larger than the Tower itself!"

Kalrakin suddenly trembled, and his eyes opened, shining with excitement. "There is one room in the Tower, a chamber within walls of stone, masked by an enclosed barrier of solid metal. This is a special vault, a chamber of spectacular size built to hold unique treasures. The shell of iron masked my probing powers, but I could sense a quantity of magic there, magic in purity and potency that we have never before imagined."

He pressed his hands hard against the outer wall as if the

sheer force of his will would push them physically into the treasure chamber.

But soon, with a shrug, Kalrakin turned and made his way back to the door. As he reached the portal, it opened automatically, swinging inward to reveal a small anteroom with a floor of black slate. A rug of exquisite beauty lay just within the entry.

"How did it open?" asked Luthar wonderingly as he hesitantly approached.

Kalrakin shook his head. "I don't know. I had yet to raise a hand when it swung wide. Once again, we are made welcome. We are invited."

Without delay he stepped through the entry, looking down with amusement at a colorful rug. He wiped his feet then watched with interest as the scuffs of mud vanished a second later, apparently absorbed by the threads of the fabric. Luthar followed him closely, but Kalrakin had already moved on. The anteroom opened into a huge, circular chamber with three large, different staircases spiraling upward, and several closed doors suggesting other rooms around the periphery of this central atrium.

When the tall sorcerer turned his attentions to one of the nearest of the closed doors, staring curiously, its portal swung open. Pleasing aromas—fresh-baked bread, roast meats—emerged, and Kalrakin stepped into a small banquet room. There was a table large enough for perhaps a dozen guests, but now it was set for two, with silver candleholders holding long, burning tapers. A bottle of wine rested in a platinum dish filled with crushed ice; beside it sat a decanter filled with dark red liquid. A haunch of roast beef, steaming hot, oozed juices on a large wooden board, while a loaf of fresh bread and a dish of soft butter were positioned near both settings.

Kalrakin laughed out loud. He stepped forward, poured

a glass of the red wine into one of several crystal goblets on the table. He quaffed the drink, losing a few droplets into the tangle of his beard, then hurled the vessel at the stone wall, just above the dark, cool hearth. The glass shattered, shards exploding across the room, leaving crimson drops spattering across the wall.

"Was that necessary?"

The sorcerer whirled around at these words, his beard and hair flying wildly, eyes bulging in shock as a man in a long black robe entered the room from a discreet side door. He bore a staff capped by the golden image of a dragon's head, and his robe formed a hood that draped loosely over his head. His face was aged, but he moved with the grace of a younger man. His eyes were very deep set, and they flashed with challenge as he stepped into the dining room.

Luthar gasped in alarm, clapping a hand to his mouth. Kalrakin drew himself up to his full, imposing height, and glared at the Black Robe like a hawk ready to seize its prey.

"And just who are you?" Kalrakin demanded.

"I am the one who invited you here," said the newcomer. His tone was stern, yet not angry. "I saw that the gates were parted, the food was ready and available, for your pleasure. But I am surprised—and disappointed—that you do not treat this hallowed place with more respect. After all, you come with a legacy of magic; that much I could sense from a hundred . . . a thousand miles away. We should strive together to make this place alive, again!"

"A legacy of magic?" The sorcerer howled with laughter, and held up the Irda Stone. "*This* is what you sensed! My magic has fooled you. Yes, it has a legacy, but as different from yours as your three moons. As for me, I spit on your gods, your magic. I would spit on your three moons if I could!"

The Black Robe's face grew pale, and his knuckles tightened where he gripped his staff. "How dare you!" he hissed.

Kalrakin merely sneered. "I have no need to kowtow to you or your silly gods. Your era, and theirs, is through. It is time you made way for me!"

"You shall not dare to blaspheme the gods of magic, not here, in this most sacred of places!" declared the Black Robe in outrage. "Perhaps I have made a mistake. You and your friend must leave this place—now!"

"I have no intention of leaving," Kalrakin replied. With elaborate casualness he poured himself another goblet of wine, took a deep and messy drink, and hurled this second vessel against the wall so that it burst amid the shards of the previous shattered goblet. "No, I like it here," he declared with a bark of a laugh. "And you do not frighten me, Black Robe."

"Go!" roared the wizard, in a voice that rattled the windows and rumbled through the floor and the walls. His robe flapped as if in the midst of a gale, and the staff grew longer in his hand. The gold dragon head seemed to darken until it was blood red in color, and now flames flickered within the image's eyes. "Go at once, if you wish to leave here alive!"

"Let us leave, my lord," Luthar urged in a whisper, coming around the great table to tug on his companion's arm. "We should do as he suggests!"

"Be silent!" Kalrakin snapped, seizing Luthar by the face and pushing him down hard. The rotund sorcerer toppled back heavily to the floor, where he looked between the other two men with wide, frightened eyes.

"Do you not recognize this flesh?" demanded the Black Robe, stepping closer, stamping his staff against the stone floor. More thunder rolled, and his dark eyes flashed as if they might release the force of lightning at any second. Dark smoke spumed from the flared nostrils of the dragon head.

"I see a simple-minded mage," Kalrakin declared, sneering. "One who does not realize that his era is gone. One who is about to learn some lessons."

"I am Fistandantilus!" roared the wizard. "I am the most feared wielder of magic in the history of Krynn! I have consumed the souls of greater men than you, and I am always hungry for more! You are a fool if you do not flee now, running for your wretched lives! Or perhaps you want to feel the tortures of a thousand years—do you think I can't arrange that!?"

"Cheap tricks," Kalrakin said with an arrogant shrug. Once again he flipped the white Irda Stone between his hands. Then he laughed, a sound that brought an almost comical expression of outrage to the face of Fistandantilus. "I do not fear you. In fact, I doubt your power. Your impotence is proof that your time is passed . . . that *my* era commences."

"Doubt at your own risk, fool! Depart at once, or I shall unleash that might to your unending regret!" declared the Black Robe. "The black moon is high in the sky, and the power of Nuitari once again thrums in the world!"

"Power? You speak of power! *Here* is power!"

The sorcerer held up the white bauble. It pulsed, and a stab of light flew outward, a spear of pure energy. The white light made no sound, but the flash of brilliance lingered in the room almost like an echo, ebbing and flowing ominously around the form of the ancient, black-robed wizard. A corona that shone like the sun outlined the shape of the wizard; his staff glowed fiercely. And then the illumination began to grow even brighter, until it seemed that it must turn into fire—yet there was no heat.

Slowly, gradually, it began to wane, allowing the shadows back into the room, plunging everything suddenly into darkness. And when the light had finally faded altogether, the Black Robe was gone. There was no residue where he had stood, no mark to prove that he had even been there.

"Wh-hat happened? Where did he go?" stammered Luthar, climbing nervously to his feet. He had been holding his hands over his eyes so tightly that he left red impressions of his fingers in his cheeks and forehead.

Kalrakin shrugged. "What does it matter? He is gone and will trouble us no more. First let us eat. Then we will have a look around our new home."

CHAPTER

7

WIZARDS OF WHITE AND BLACK

Dalamar the Dark rode his magic steed through the skies of Krynn. Wind whistled past, flapping his black robe against his lean frame, streaming his hair into a long tail behind him. He squinted, leaned low, and looked down to study the forest of Qualinesti as it undulated past. To his right, the snowy peaks of the High Kharolis gleamed, a horizontal necklace of eternal ice. Dark thunderheads loomed over that great mountain range, though the air before the wizard was clear, lofting to a sky of pale blue.

The phantom steed he rode was a ghostly shape, sleek and horselike as it pulsed and shimmered in the air, vaulting the dark elf through the sky with speed approaching dragon-flight. For hours he had flown over a seemingly endless forest, but he knew that before midafternoon he would arrive at his destination—even though Solace lay hundreds of miles to the northeast, beyond the far border of Qualinesti.

A sense of growing urgency propelled him, allowing for no delay. He recognized that he needed help. For too long he had been alone. Since he had awakened, starving and weak in a small cave in Silvanesti, he had learned to relish his mortal flesh again, even those flaws, those proofs of life, such as the hunger that periodically gnawed at his belly. While he languished under the black power of Mina, those things had been gone from his existence.

Dalamar shuddered momentarily then sneered at the memory of Mina; it didn't matter. That was over now, her dark power broken. He flexed his muscles, feeling them ripple beneath his smooth, unblemished skin. He rotated his arms, flexed his fingers, leaned back, and relished the smooth and uncomplaining response of his muscles. Another treasure of life . . . another thing for him to cherish.

He had learned to cherish the bad along with the good. He remembered, upon awakening, that he had pulled aside the black robe covering his chest and looked down to see five bleeding sores. These had been marks of discipline, the punishment of his *Shalafi* many decades ago. They would never heal, not so long as he breathed—and for once, the presence of the oozing marks reassured, even pleased, him.

For, by all the gods, he *lived* again!

That life itself was a reward of sorts surprised him, but he was grateful that it had been granted to him. The greatest gift, the true blessing that the gods had bestowed upon him when they restored him to life, was neither the pumping of his blood, nor his complete control over the physical form of his body. It was something that he sensed in his mind and in his soul, a churning, growing power that bubbled there, percolating through his thoughts, permeating his very being. And he knew:

His master of magic had returned. Nuitari, the black moon, once again soared through the skies of Krynn.

Even before Mina had taken him, the dark elf had languished for long years, despairing of ever wielding his black arts again. Of course, he had dabbled in the wild sorcery, even learned some of the art of necromancy, but that had been a pale imitation of true magic, the blessed power of his god, Nuitari. Always there had been the taint of corruption around the wild magic. Now that the god Nuitari, and his magical cousins, had returned to the cosmos, wild sorcery was nothing less than pale imitation—no, blasphemy.

Indeed, Dalamar knew his destiny: He would be the leading prophet of that ancient magic, and he would drive the corruption of sorcery back into the shadows where it belonged. Lovingly Dalamar traced his hands over the silver runes embroidered into his robe, as the material fluttered and flapped in the wind of his passage. For decades the runes had been dull and silent; now they glowed and sparkled, and he could feel the warmth of their power in the mere touch of his fingers. They were potent again, and this robe was no longer a mere garment. It was his badge, his armor, his herald, all in one.

He thought of the great Tower of Sorcery where once he had been Master. Here the first taint of bitterness soured his mood. The place he most desired to see again, the place where his greatest treasures were stored, where he had collected the most remarkable library of magical books in the history of the world . . . that place was barred to him, forever. It had been the one condition exacted by those ever-jealous gods, Solinari and Lunitari, before they would allow Nuitari to restore his favored devotee to life. Dalamar had accepted the condition—to refuse would have meant permanent, irrevocable death—and at the time had not even regarded it as a very burdensome restriction.

In the past weeks, however, he began to understand the full cost of that banishment. He remembered not only his own spell books left there, but the night-blue tomes scribed by Fistandantilus himself, and the black, hourglass-sigil volumes that were the legacy of his *Shalafi*, Raistlin Majere. All those wonderful books were gone to him. Many contained enchantments unique in the history of Krynn, enchantments that were lost not just to Dalamar but to the world. Perhaps someday he could reconstruct—

No . . . the dark elf's lip curled into a sneer of contempt as he mouthed the word. Those spells would never be restored, for the world did not deserve to receive his largesse.

Even as his bitterness settled into a dull anger, Dalamar shrugged away any inclination to despair. As his homeland was merely a place, his spell books were merely objects. He had his life back, and even without those spell books he knew how to put his magical power to use.

His thoughts had turned to another tower, the one place in Krynn that might house an equal, perhaps even greater, trove of magical lore. The Tower of High Sorcery in Wayreth Forest was the traditional center of magical study, the place where aspiring mages—including Dalamar himself, in a time lost to the far, far past—went to learn the arcane arts. The most talented of the mages were granted an opportunity to take the Test, with those who passed being awarded a robe in the color—red, black, or white—of the god who most favored the apprentice mage. There, at the Tower of High Sorcery in Wayreth Forest, he had sworn allegiance to the Conclave, working on behalf of wizards of all three robes, spying upon, and eventually betraying, his *Shalafi*. Again he touched his chest, this time with a grimace—those five wounds now, and forever, the legacy of that betrayal.

Of course, the Tower of High Sorcery was not easy to find . . . unless it wanted one to find it. Dalamar had been more fortunate than most; in the past; when he had needed to go to the Tower, the path had opened before him. Indeed, though Wayreth Forest lay to the west of distant Qualinesti, the dark elf had entered that enchanted wood from places as distant as Ergoth and Solamnia. He saw no reason the path would not welcome him again, from here. So he had embarked, months ago, on a search for the Tower.

But, for the first time in his life, the Tower had refused to acknowledge him. After a long and fruitless search, he was now in the air, flying to visit a man he had never expected to see again. During the flight, he took note of the scope of devastation that had wracked that once pastoral land, the land the Qualinesti had lost to Beryl, the place where that massive green dragon had died. Villages were now blackened ruins, burned to ashes. Much of the forest was shattered, trees knocked down every which way, or languishing in a wilting that browned the leaves and left the stench of rot to rise through the air. Elven arrogance had been soundly punished, he observed with cool detachment. The devastation didn't affect Dalamar, except for a sense of mild regret that a once-pleasant destination no longer existed.

Finally he crossed the gorge of the White Rage River, and even the dispassionate dark elf was annoyed at the sight of the brown sludge that now passed for water in that formerly pristine canyon. More important, he was nearing his destination. His mere thought directed the phantom steed to descend, and soon Dalamar skimmed along barely above the height of the treetops. The ghostly flying horse followed the course of the river as it spilled from its rocky gorge to meander into the lowlands. The course grew wide, the water even more brackish and stagnant as it pooled in mudflats and eddies. Soon the elf recognized the tributary to the north, Solace Stream, and was moderately relieved to turn his magical steed up toward that unpolluted waterway.

Darken Wood lay to his left, but Dalamar ignored the attraction of those magical groves and mystical denizens. There was nothing for him there, neither any spell book nor colleague that could help him gain entry to the forest, or recover the mastery of his own spells. The dark wizard was acutely conscious of this weakness as he approached Solace, spotting the lofty crests of the great vallenwoods from many miles away.

Normally, Dalamar would have entered the town discreetly, seeking out Palin at some quiet and private place. However, the dark elf felt he was on an acutely urgent mission; each enchantment he cast that vanished from his memory was irretrievable forever, unless he gained access to the proper spell books. In light of that vulnerability, he opted for a more dramatic display of his power as a reminder to Palin, and anyone else who might be paying attention, that the black-robed wizard was still a force to be reckoned with.

He guided his phantom steed along Solace's main street, flying several dozen feet above the ground—well below the level of the tree-mounted houses, shops, and inns that were such a characteristic of the city of vallenwoods. It was still several hours until dinnertime, and that avenue, a curving route that meandered between the roots of the mighty trees, was fairly crowded by the standards of bucolic Solace. As soon as he dropped below the canopy of leaves, a watchman pointed up at him and shouted in alarm.

Dalamar smiled to hear gasps of fright from merchants and peddlers, shouts of surprise from shopping womenfolk, and cries of glee from a multitude of children. The children ran in a pack along the street, pointing up at him and shrieking in delight as the wizard slowed his eerie, vaporous steed. He flew across the town square then turned up the lane that would lead to Palin, leaving the band of youngsters behind with a sudden burst of speed.

He drew up to the great balcony surrounding the Inn of the Last Home, the structure located on the sturdy boughs of one of the greatest vallenwoods. Here the phantom steed came to rest, the misty apparition fading away gently to bring Dalamar's feet to rest upon the broad, sturdy planks.

"Hello, Dalamar."

It was a woman's voice, which carried not the slightest hint of welcome. Nevertheless, the dark elf smiled thinly as he turned around to see the speaker: a female with long straight hair, now white but still suggestive of vital, golden youth. He tilted forward, a formal bow that was only slightly mocking.

"Hello, Laura. I see that you are as beautiful, and gracious, as ever."

"What do you want? There is nothing for you here. Palin is through with magic—you, more than anyone, should know that!"

Dalamar sighed, having neither the energy nor the inclination for a confrontation with Palin's strong-willed sister.

"I need to talk to your brother. Can you tell me where he is? Or does such a conversation require advance approval from you?" he asked sharply.

She sniffed contemptuously and turned back to the side door of the inn from which she had emerged. "Wait here," she ordered, before she disappeared.

Dalamar scowled after her then turned his back. He rested his hands on the railing and breathed deeply, trying to get his bearings and relax. He could not allow himself to be agitated when he talked to Palin.

"Hello, my old . . . comrade. It is rather a surprise to see you," Palin said mildly, coming out and closing the door behind him.

"Not a pleasant one, if your sister's reaction is any guide."

Palin shrugged, offering a regretful smile. "Laura has never been shy about her opinions. I suspect she thinks you are a rather bad influence on me. But nevertheless, I did not expect to see you again . . . so soon."

Dalamar studied the former master of the White Robes. Palin looked healthier than he had in years: he was fit, broad-shouldered and held himself proudly erect. His hair, faded to a pale gray and thinned somewhat on top, was fastened in the back to a tail that hung down to the level of his shoulder blades. He advanced to clasp hands with the dark elf, their eyes meeting in appraisal. What do I see there, Dalamar wondered—and what does *he* see?

A serving maid came out the door with a tray. She set down a loaf of bread, a tub of butter, a pitcher of ale, and two mugs, and she wordlessly withdrew.

"Thank you," said Dalamar, his stomach rumbling audibly as the aroma of the loaf—obviously fresh from the oven—reached his nostrils.

"Actually, this repast comes from Laura," the man said with a chuckle. "Even at her sternest, she is an innkeeper at heart; she would not let a visitor stay thirsty or hungry." Palin settled into a chair, and Dalamar noticed the ease with which he leaned back, fully secure. This was a man who was utterly at peace with himself, the elf realized with some dismay.

The dark elf took an adjacent chair and allowed his host to fill the mugs in companionable silence. The sun was setting, sending dazzling beams through the giant, leafy vallenwoods, illuminating the forest city in a surreal glow. The cold drink went down easily, and the elf realized that he had grown quite parched during his magical flight. His mug was emptied in a surprisingly quick time, but he leaned forward, holding on to it with both hands. If he put it down, Palin would offer a refill, and Dalamar wanted to keep his wits about him.

He found it strangely difficult to begin. His host cut several slices of the bread, slathered them with butter, and handed one to the dark elf. It was excellent, of course: crusty and aromatic, firm and pleasantly chewy. After eating a couple of pieces, Dalamar did allow himself another mug of the ale. He sipped at the foamy head, then leaned back to look at the man who had been, in the dark elf's opinion, the second-greatest wizard upon Krynn.

"I went seeking the Tower of High Sorcery," Dalamar began.

Palin raised his eyebrows, not so much in surprise as curiosity. "It sounds as though you didn't find it," he suggested.

"I couldn't even locate Wayreth Forest," the elf said, unable to hold back the bitterness in his voice. "I searched the western border of Qualinesti, rode south from there ... but nothing. I have been traveling for all the months since my ... awakening."

The word hung like a noose between them. Palin, too, had suffered from Mina's curse, had been granted that awakening by his god. But it was not a thing they would ever discuss.

"The Tower is closed to you? Strange." Palin looked outside, where the white half-circle of Solinari was just visible through the upper terrace of a nearby vallenwood. The moon was setting.

Dalamar glanced toward the sky himself. He could see Nuitari, nearly full and still higher in his line of sight than the loftiest tree top. The black moon was a shiny orb to him, slick and glossy like a spot of oil.

"Is it up there? The black moon?" Palin asked.

"You can't sense it?" Dalamar responded, surprised. "I know that it is only the mages of the Black Robes who can see it, but you always knew where it was in the sky."

The human chuckled. "I guess I've stopped paying attention," he said. "Ironic, in a way—I spent forty years and more pining for those moons of magic. Now they have returned, and I hardly notice."

"Is it really true? You continue to foreswear your art, your gift?" The dark elf made the questions into a challenge.

Palin didn't rise to the bait. "As to 'gifts' ... well, you enjoy that bounty. And perhaps I have simply chosen a new art. This town—it needs a lot of help. Can you believe they've made me mayor?" The man laughed quietly in wry amusement, not without a hint of pride. "There are dangers in the wilds now—thieves, bandits and . . . darker things. Chaos looms on all sides. In any event, I have all that I can handle, right here, doing this job. And it is a calling that leaves me with a great peace in my soul at the end of every day."

Dalamar was silent, thinking, carefully masking his face to conceal his disappointment. His scheme seemed less than pointless, now. He saw clearly that all the compelling arguments and carefully reasoned points that he had formed in advance of this meeting were utterly toothless in the face of this man's bucolic contentment. The dark elf didn't even have the energy to plead his case—he had no wish to face the humiliation of Palin's polite refusal.

But his old colleague deserved, at least, an explanation.

"I came here to ask for your help, Palin. I thought that two robes might succeed where one was blocked, that the Tower might welcome us both, together. I will not ask that of you, though; I see now that you have come to the place where you belong." Dalamar grimaced. "Of course, if I thought there was even a chance I could change your mind, I wouldn't hesitate to use every kind of persuasion I could muster."

"You have some very persuasive techniques, I seem to recall," said Palin dryly.

"But nothing, I know, that could bend you, not here, not now. Palin, when you told me you were coming here, abandoning your robes, your spells . . . I felt only pity and contempt for you. I thought you were a fool, a weakling."

Palin eyed the elf, his face revealing no emotion. Dalamar continued.

"Now that I have seen you here, I confess it is not contempt that I feel. One might call it envy, even a trace of jealousy. I know I will never have what you possess, day in and day out, in this little village in the woods."

"Oh, there are times when I remember the power, with a twinge of longing," Palin admitted.

"And that power has returned, in full!" Dalamar spoke with sudden passion. "Palin, surely you can remember what it's like—to call upon the moon, to feel the pulse of sorcery in your heart, deep in your belly, your very soul! I tell you, this is a time of new magic, a historical cusp in the world!" The dark elf was clenching his mug, pleading after all.

"I can remember," the former white mage said calmly. "And that is enough for me. But I am glad that you came here—it is good to see you, my old . . . friend?" Palin couldn't help but turn the word into a question.

Dalamar laughed softly; he neither wanted, nor possessed, any "friends." Yet he realized that Palin was sincere, and that made the statement strangely touching.

"Thank you, but I should not have come. No doubt Laura is terribly worried about you. She has probably sent a messenger off to Usha already, urging your wife to come and rescue you from my clutches. So I will leave, and you can go comfort her." The dark elf tried to keep his tone light, though he knew his words were mocking. He felt the bitterness of his own defeat.

"What is the hurry? Where are you going?"

Dalamar shook his head without replying. There was only one place he could go, now, one person he must see, and he was not looking forward to either the journey, or the meeting.

"That was quite a steed that carried you to Solace," Palin continued genially, as if accepting Dalamar's silence as his answer. "The inn practically tilted out of the tree when everyone ran over to the south windows to see you arrive. If you would like to spend the night, and take time to study your spell book before you leave, you are welcome to stay. Laura will certainly give you a quiet room, with a good lantern for reading."

The dark elf set down his mug and stood up with a sigh. "Do you see me carrying a spell book? No, Palin, I have nothing to study. My spells are gone, and I don't even have an apprentice's scrolls to relearn them. Ironic, isn't it? I awakened with every one of my spells fresh and vibrant in my mind. I have used them—I teleported to Qualinesti. I used illusion and fireball against those who stood in my path. But each spell, when I use it . . . it is gone, as always. Only this time I have no book, no means to study, to relearn the spells. So the spells are leaving me, one by one, and it is like I am fast spending all the accumulated knowledge—the treasures—of my life.

"As for the next stage of my journey, it will be made on foot, or horseback . . . at least until I can board a ship for Palanthas. Then I will ride through the storms, puking my guts out, white knuckles on the railing like any tin merchant or coal shipper. There are still penalties I pay, daily."

"There is, perhaps, something I can do to help," Palin said. He leaned forward, conspiratorially. "You have to promise not to tell Laura—or Usha."

"You have my word," Dalamar said, irritated at the childish guise, even as he was fully intrigued.

The innkeeper rose and opened the side door. He called into the kitchen. "I'm taking Dalamar to the stables, Lar. I'll be back in an hour."

The elf heard several platters slam onto a tray, and an unpleasant snap of sound that he took to be Laura's dismissal. Palin turned back with an apologetic smile and led the dark wizard down the winding stairway toward the street. Dalamar felt good to stretch his legs. He supposed Palin was going to offer him a horse, and in light of the dark elf's current circumstances, that was something for which to be grateful.

The inn's stable was located against the bole of the great

vallenwood, and Palin led him through the barn, where a stable boy was forking straw into various stalls. The former White Robe went into a small office at the very back of the rambling structure, a tiny room that was actually a small cubby chiseled right into the trunk of the great tree.

Palin carefully and quietly closed the door after Dalamar followed him through, and only then did he strike a match to a thin candle. Dalamar watched expressionlessly as the man touched a panel in what looked like the solid wall at the back of the room. The dark elf was moderately surprised when that section of wood slid backward to reveal a small alcove.

When Palin reached into that hole, Dalamar felt an unmistakable tingle at the back of his neck. Despite Palin's vow to the contrary, there was some hidden magic here! Carefully, the former white-robed mage pulled out a heavy object—a large, square object wrapped in what looked to be a soft doeskin. The dark elf's heart pounded with anticipation.

"I guess you could say that I have hedged my bet," Palin said. "I saved my very first spell book. It has many useful spells, and it could have taken me anywhere I needed to go, if I ever felt that I had to return to the life of sorcery."

Without hesitation, Palin held out the heavy book to Dalamar, who took it rather more quickly and fervently than he had intended. Palin smiled, with a hint of sadness.

"No, I want you to have it. And I am glad that you came here. I am sure you did not intend to do so, but your visit has confirmed for me that I've made the right choice—for Usha, for our children, but even, and without question, for me. I am through with that life, Dalamar, and you should make good use of this last vestige of my magic."

"I understand," said Dalamar; meaning that he understood that Palin was freely giving him this book of spells. In point of fact, he could not begin to grasp how Palin, a man capable of wielding almost unimaginable power, could turn his back on that power. But that was not a riddle the dark elf needed to solve. His hands trembled as he took the tome, clutched it to his chest.

Palin smiled now in genuine good humor. "Perhaps you would take that room, now? Just for the night? It seems that, after all, you might have something to study."

Dalamar nodded his thanks. He could hardly wait to sit down, light a lamp, and start to read.

CHAPTER
8

PASSING THROUGH PALANTHAS

Jenna was already walking as the teleport spell faded around her. The lingering wisps of sparkling light quickly evanesced into nothingness. She crossed the anteroom of her villa, her temper foul and her skin clammy. Her assistant, Rupert, stood nearby, as usual having uncannily anticipated her arrival. He came forward to take the heavy cloak as his mistress sniffed in annoyance.

"Kendermore was even worse than Kothas," she declared haughtily. "Not a true wizard to be found in either place, though there are quite a few pretenders. Wild sorcery, on the other hand, is everywhere."

"The minotaurs, as you suspect, are making trouble?"

"Very much," Jenna said, with a shake of her head. "But that's not my problem."

"And the humans in the east, the caliph's realm?" inquired Rupert. "You had no luck there, as well?"

"They might as well be barbarians!" snapped the Red Robe. "Their women are kept locked away, or else put up for sale. And the men are so busy cheating each other that they wouldn't know real magic if it turned them into toads!"

"That is unfortunate, my lady. I do hope you will not lose faith."

Jenna sighed. "In truth, the people are as backward everywhere," she declared. "Simply ignorant of the ways of real magic. Perhaps our gods were gone away for too long."

"I trust that is not the case," Rupert said solemnly. "Keep heart, my lady! As I recall, this is no less than you expected."

"No, you're right," Jenna said, pulling the pins out of her bun, letting her gray hair—as soft and luxurious as a much younger woman's—cascade across her shoulders. "But I suppose I had my hopes up. After all, it's been more than half a year since the gods of magic returned to the skies—surely some of my order should have emerged, *somewhere* on Krynn!"

"The Tower of High Sorcery might hold your answers. You still have not discovered the key?"

She shook her head again. "The Master is as stubborn as ever—if he still exists. I have concluded that, by myself, I will be unable even to find the Forest of Wayreth, much less gain access to the Tower of High Sorcery."

"Undoubtedly you will find that secret, and in good time," said the dignified servant. "For now, you should know that you have received visitors in your absence."

"Visitors? When did they arrive?"

"Only this morning, my lady."

"Well, who are they?"

"A young lady . . . from the country, I should say, if not the wilderness itself. And"—Rupert sniffed audibly—"a kender."

Jenna chuckled for the first time all day. "Well, maybe things are about to get more interesting. Where are they?"

"I took the precaution of having them wait in the breezeway. I posted several of your men-at-arms there, as well."

Jenna crossed the wide hall and threw open the doorway to the outer porch, the balcony where she so often enjoyed the breezes coming off the Bay of Branchala.

"Moptop Bristlebrow!" she declared, immediately recognizing the diminutive visitor. She nodded at the two stout guardsmen who stood within an arm's reach to either side of the kender. "You two can go now," she allowed. Then she turned her attention to the second visitor, a dark-haired girl—or young woman—who regarded her with a strange mixture of curiosity and aloofness.

"Welcome to you both," Jenna said. "And what brings you the Red Manor of Palanthas?"

Coryn was staring at the most striking woman she had ever seen. This Jenna had graying hair that was nevertheless lush and full, and the smooth skin of her face belied her apparent age. She wore many necklaces, and an array of jewels, feathers, and precious rings dangled from them. More rings adorned her well-manicured fingers, and she wore a robe of deep red that swished easily as she walked, like soft velvet.

It took a second before the girl realized that Mistress Jenna—the lady she had been sent to meet—had asked her a question. Hastily she curtsied, at least insofar as she had guessed how to fake a curtsy, and replied. "I am Coryn Brinefolk, from the village of Two Forks in the Icereach. My grandmother is Scharon Fallow. She sent me to find you—she asked Moptop to bring me here from the Icereach, and she said that I should give you this—"

"Scharon Fallow!" Jenna practically shouted and reached for the scroll that Coryn pulled, still sealed by Umma's wax stamp, from her knapsack. She extended it to Jenna with a shaking hand, hoping that, maybe, Jenna would tell her what her grandmother had written.

Jenna inspected the seal for a moment then broke the wax. She unrolled the parchment and read intensely, stopping only once to look up and fix a penetrating glance on Coryn. The girl squirmed under the scrutiny, but felt no relief as the older woman returned her attention to Umma's note. When Jenna looked up again, it was to offer the kender a disarming smile.

"Thank you, Moptop. I appreciate the job you have done—go and help yourself to whatever you'd like from the kitchen." The smile faded to a more inscrutable expression, as she turned back to Coryn. "Come with me," she said.

"Yes, Ma'am," said the girl, hastily picking up her knapsack and following Jenna through the door.

The room they entered was, simply, the largest enclosed space Coryn had ever seen. "Oh, my," she murmured.

"You don't have houses like this in Two Forks?" asked Jenna, in a serious tone.

"No, my lady. Nor in any of the places we passed through on the way to Palanthas."

Cory's mind had been filled with wonders in the past weeks, during the trek that the kender had taken her on through ancient Tarsis, through a decrepit seaport and aboard ship to cross the Newsea, and, just this very dawn, into the crowded streets of Palanthas. Throughout the journey, Moptop had maintained a steady chatter. He cheerfully informed her of nearby places where terrifying monsters had lurked, the sites of horrific battles and massacres throughout history, scenes of wrack and ruin brought about by the First Cataclysm, and seemingly innumerable dangers lurking just beyond every hillcrest, each bend in the road, any given swell of the sea.

Yet the kender's account had been utterly fearless and entertaining, and this had helped Cory to keep her own fright in check. Without qualm, she had confronted the rowdy young men in Tarsis. She had held her tongue and maintained her pride in the face of rude questioning from the captain of a passenger ship at Newport, and when one of the sailors had proved overly bold, she had cut him with her skinning knife. The kender had escorted her through those forests she had once dreamed about, until the woodlands seemed to go on so far that she was afraid it would *never* end.

But nothing had prepared her for the splendors of this place, the wonders of what must certainly be the greatest city in the world. So far she had beheld marbled edifices that loomed like mountains to either side, gawked at the armored knights and gowned ladies of whom she had dreamed, seen horses and carriages and teams of great cattle. Dwarves and kender and elves—and even rougher types—mingled among the multitude of variegated humans. Finally they had come to the grounds of this splendid house, high on one of the hillsides just outside the great city.

And not even her view of that city had readied her for this elegant mansion. She had gaped at the gilded columns, rising to a height of two stories all around the anteroom. She had bowed clumsily to the haughty servant who had kept her and Moptop waiting on the balcony for several hours.

Now she gasped in dismay as she watched Jenna take the letter from Umma, the scroll Cory had carried across the breadth of Ansalon, and blithely drop it into the fireplace. No coals glowed there, but the dry paper instantly burst into flames. By the time the girl had followed Jenna toward the wide stairway climbing to the second level of the house, the secret letter, the message that contained the key to her journey, perhaps to her future life, was nothing but cold ash.

She bit back her disappointment as they climbed a wide stairway to the second floor. She became aware of the heavy weight of her knapsack, the strap digging into her shoulder.

"Um . . . my lady? Should I put my knapsack down somewhere? Is there a room where I might change my clothing?" she asked, surprised at her own boldness.

"A room? No, there won't be time for that," Jenna said curtly. "You can change here, in the parlor, and get a bite to eat in the kitchen. But we'll be leaving Palanthas before nightfall. As soon as you are ready, I need you to go to the market, down in the city. You'll have to do some shopping for the journey."

"Yes, of course," Coryn agreed, her weariness vanishing at the thought of another excursion into that exciting city. "What is it you want me to buy?"

"Mules. I should think three of them will be enough. But they must be sturdy, not too old, reasonably well fed. And take care not to overpay."

Mules? Coryn's head whirled. She had seen mules during her travels, along with all sorts of other beasts of burden, but she had no idea how to go about *choosing* one, much less three, of the creatures for purchase!

Jenna seemed to read her mind as she called out to Rupert, who lurked nearby. "Rupert? Is your son in the house? Perhaps Donny would be kind enough to go along with Coryn, show her where the market is—and help bring the mules back?"

"Of course, my lady. I shall summon him at once."

By the time Coryn had changed to a clean pair of trousers and gobbled down two pieces of the softest, tastiest bread she had ever tasted, a boy of about ten appeared in the kitchen. "I'm Donny," he said. "I guess I'm to take you to the market."

"Let's go get some mules," Coryn said, following him through the maze of the manor's sprawling ground floor. The lad proved to be quite a bit friendlier than either his father or Lady Jenna had been. The young woman felt no worries for her safety, only a giddy sense of wonder as Donny quickly led her down the wide avenue running past Jenna's villa.

She saw that the manor of the red-robed sorceress was, while quite splendid, merely one of dozens, a hundred or more, such grand domiciles. These structures sprawled across this dominant height to the east of the city, each commanding a magnificent view from its lofty perch. There were fountains and pools, gardens laid out in ornate mazes, formal clusters of blossoms organized with martial precision. Each of these grand houses seemed a miniature fortress, with walls and gates and towers. Guards in colorful livery were a common fixture, and she saw mounted knights—in one group more than twenty armored riders—making their way along the wide streets.

"This whole area is called Nobles Hill," Donny noted, as they made way for a group of knights. "The really rich people live here."

Soon they were passing through a gate into the city—or the Old City, as Donny explained, since many structures had been erected outside that ancient barrier. Here the streets were narrow and twisting, and though Coryn saw gardens and fountains here as well, she also saw tiny alleys reeking of filth. On the roof of one flat-topped building a half dozen men with crossbows looked menacing against the skyline, studying passersby in the street below.

"That's the Thieves Guild," Donny explained. "Those guys don't like people poking around."

His route took them past the waterfront, and Coryn quickly and vividly recognized the stench of fish guts from her own recent sea voyage. Even so, it was a wonder to see the bustling docks, fishing boats unloading holds full of the morning catch, silvery salmon flipping and thrashing as they were smoothly cleaned and wrapped in seaweed. Small carts waited nearby, and every minute or two one of these would be filled, and would trundle off to the nearby market.

That market occupied a broad plaza festooned with brightly colored awnings, small stalls, and a multitude of handcarts, the latter often shaded by a single broad umbrella. The fabrics in reds and golds, stripes and mosaics, greens like the emerald purity of winter ice in the heart of a glacier, or blue as smooth and vast as the summer sky, reminded Cory of a great field of chaotic blooms. People milled and thronged here, bought and bartered all around these makeshift stalls.

This was far more than a fish market, she saw. A weaponsmith had an array of swords laid out on a table in the afternoon sun, and one huckster was doing a thriving business offering nothing more than a glimpse of a scantily clad female dancer moving languidly in the center of a small ringed arena. Coryn recognized sheep and lambs, cows and calves, goats, poultry, and even a few horses confined in impromptu corrals. Finally she spotted a dilapidated little enclosure where a dozen mules stood, more or less contentedly.

"We have to bargain with him," Donny said distastefully, for the first time displaying a touch of hesitancy.

The "him" was a huge, pot-bellied mule skinner who wore filthy trousers and a leather vest that didn't begin to cover his hairy, sagging gut. When he spotted the pair of potential customers, he favored them with a wide smile, and Cory saw that his mouth was almost entirely devoid of teeth.

"I kin see the lady 'as a keen eye for mule flesh," he said approvingly, swaggering over to greet them. He smelled very strong, like a sour version of the liquid in Umma's special bottle of medicine. "These 'ere are splendid animals. You kin 'ave the lot of 'em for a hundred steel."

Coryn shook her head firmly. If there was one thing she knew, it was how to barter. "I want three—that one, that one, and that one." She picked out the only animals that seemed to be watching them with intelligence, a trio of black mules that continued to regard them with oversized and upraised ears.

"Like I said, you 'as a keen eye," said Bulge-Belly with a nod. "Them's my best three. Cost you seventy five for the set."

"That's ridiculous! You just said the price was a hundred for all twelve of them, and now you want seventy five for three?"

"Like I said, them's the best three."

Donny, off to the side, was shaking his head furiously. Cory drew up her chin, and glared at the man. "Twenty," she offered firmly.

He looked injured, but kept the bargaining going. She, in turn, refused to back down, and felt rather proud of herself when the deal was finally closed for twenty-eight pieces of steel. Another six pieces were required to buy harnesses, but within a few minutes Coryn and Donny were leading the docile animals back through the city.

"What does Mistress Jenna do? I mean, for a job?" Coryn ventured to ask the lad. "Or is she a noble lady, born to her manor?"

Donny looked up and laughed. "You mean you haven't heard of her?"

"No," Cory was forced to admit, embarrassed. "I mean, except from my grandmother."

"Well, she's just the greatest wizard in Palanthas, maybe the whole world!" the boy said proudly. "She is mistress of all the Red Robes!"

"A wizard?" Coryn asked wonderingly. "You mean, she makes spells from the wind, the stones, everything around her?"

Donny looked at her in pity. "Boy, you don't know much, do you? No, you're talking about sorcery. The Lady Jenna hates that. She practices *real* magic, the kind you learn from books, and get taught by teachers. At least, you can, now that the moons are back. That's what my pop said."

"And she is the leader of all the Red Robes? Are there many of them?"

For the first time, the youth looked unsure. "Well, there used to be. And when the moons came back—there are three of them, you know, 'cuz there's a black one you can't see—"

"I know about the three moons!" Coryn declared. He continued as if she hadn't spoken.

"But since the moons came back, Jen—I mean, the Lady Jenna—has been looking for other wizards. But she hasn't found any." His face brightened, in sudden inspiration. "I bet that's why we got the mules."

"Why?" the girl asked, wondering what mules had to do with wizards.

But Donny had already said too much, and by this time they were making their way up Nobles Hill to Jenna's house.

There she was rather surprised to find that the lady had already laid out three pairs of saddlebags, bulging with provisions. Her men-at-arms started loading them onto the animals as soon as they arrived. Coryn barely had time to run in and get her knapsack, which she lashed to one of the mules, before Jenna was saying good-bye to her servants.

"Rupert, please take charge of my affairs, as usual," she directed the majordomo. "We might be gone for a very long time."

"Of course, my lady. And may I wish you great success on your quest."

Jenna didn't offer any explanation to Coryn, but the girl was resigned to another long adventure on the road. As they started away from the villa, Jenna strolling easily in the lead while Cory led the three mules, the girl looked back at the placid animals and made a practical decision about the only thing where she seemed to have a little control.

She decided to name the mules.

CHAPTER 9

A MASTER ENSLAVED

The Master of the Tower had erred.

That awareness came very slowly, but it was an undeniable truth.

At first he had welcomed the Awakening, a return to cognizance after so many decades of dormancy. The gods had reached out to him, and he had grown vibrant under their touch, their urging. Quickly, over the course of little more than a single cycle of the black moon, Nuitari, the Master of the Tower had shrugged off the lethargy of the godless years. This eight-day sequence spanned in its passing the fullness of the other two moons, Solinari and Lunitari, so that upon the second rising of Nuitari as a complete, dark circle—the Master could sense this fullness as clearly as could any black-robed wizard—the great structure in the heart of Wayreth Forest began to pulse with a return of long-forgotten vitality.

It happened during the spring of the year, and the Master of the Tower felt fully, vibrantly alive. When all three moons rose into the sky, the power of the gods of magic flowed toward the world, bringing forth that fully cognizant awareness of life.

With awareness there came remembrance, and with those memories, unspeakable pain.

The Master remembered eons of greatness, when these halls had been home to the likes of Fistandantilus, Raistlin the Black, and Par-Salian of the white robe. Power beyond imagination had once coursed through this center of learning and of might. Within this tower the great Portal had glimmered and glowed, tempting wizards over the years with easy transport between the towers of sorcery—all the time serving the sinister purposes of the Queen of Darkness. The Portal had been closed and sealed years ago, and now that queen was dead, and still the Tower stood. It remained aloof from the world, lofty and alone . . . save for the wizards who dwelled here, and the forest that protected it.

The forest!

The Master's first conscious act in this new age was to seek the comforting presence of that vast woodland, the warm nest that had been its bower since the Age of Dreams. The forest surrounded and protected, barred the unwelcome from entry, and sealed away the petty troubles of mortal lives and lands. That wood was the Tower's cocoon, its bower, its nest.

Yet now, in this new age when the three moons once again ruled the night sky, the Master could not feel this familiar, comforting, surrounding presence. The Master feared that the forest was dead, vanished into the same void that had nearly swallowed the Tower itself. A sense of bleak hopelessness surrounded the Tower, and if not for the strength in the deep-seated foundation stones, the spire might have collapsed in ruin.

Then, faintly, there came a sign—not a word or a message so much as the faintest of impulses, a hint of comfort, a signal that the ancient strength was being stirred and restored. The forest, like the Tower, was alive!

The Master of the Tower strained to enhance that contact, to reassure, to invigorate, but the weakness and hopelessness were too pervasive. Long years, decades, of catatonic unawareness had sapped the Tower's ability to project strength, to wield the sorcerous fundament that was its reason for existing.

But that arcane power held on and began to grow, and the master felt the power of all three gods of magic begin to thrum through those stones, parapets, and foundation. That magical might flowed into the surrounding forest, and the trees and shrubs and grasses began to show small signs of life. Over the course of another moon cycle, limbs once withered and drooping began to grow straight and strong, brown and rotted foliage fell away to be replaced by green buds that, in the course of only a few more days, turned into leaves and blossoms, fruits and nuts.

Slowly that warm embrace encircled the Tower, and the Master felt the vitality of ancient strength build and grow.

But the world beyond remained a vast wilderness, a haven of wild magic and blasphemy, a dark blight of ignorance, of seeking based on false gods. There was no time for rest, or reflection. There was an urgency in the summons of the gods, an urgency that the Tower and forest felt and shared. They had important work to do, and time was the enemy; for, with each passing sunset, the chaotic force of wild magic grew stronger in the world.

The Master of the Tower was a bulwark against that surging tide, but he alone was not strong enough, nor vital enough. The Tower needed a wizard, a mortal master to return here, to take up the challenge. The pulse had gone out across the world, a vibration through the ether that would tickle the fabric of magic, to seek, and to bring such a wizard home, to the Tower.

And now a wizard had come.

Kalrakin stared at the door, his bristling brows tautly knit together by the force of his concentration. Wild magic surrounded him, energy surging through the stones of the floor, entering his feet, climbing his legs, suffusing his body with the force of imminent, inevitable explosion. The sorcerer raised his right hand, where the Irda Stone shimmered with its pearly glow. For more than a day, he had prepared this spell, using the artifact to draw the power from many parts of the Tower, gathering it for this powerful blast.

Kalrakin concentrated his powerful store of magic not at the door—that barrier had resisted all of his previous efforts—but at the granite frame surrounding this entryway. With a cry of exultation, he let the spell go, hurling all his power—and the power of the Irda Stone—at that smooth granite.

Pain wracked his hands, his arms, and his shoulders. A vise closed around his heart, and his cry became a shriek of pain. Kalrakin stumbled backward, smashing his back against the opposite wall. Fire tinged the fringes of his vision, and he choked in agony, straining for a single breath of air. But his lungs would not respond. Blackness closed in, and though he fought to keep standing, he could not prevent himself from sliding down to slump on the floor, shoulders flat against the wall.

Very slowly, he drew a ragged breath, precious air driving back the unconsciousness that threatened to overwhelm him. His legs twitched convulsively. He was drooling into his beard—yet Kalrakin was unable to raise a hand, even to wipe his lips. He groaned. Bracing his hands to either side, he forced himself to sit upright and wiped his mouth spasmodically.

Crimson streaked his hand—from a cut on his lip and from blood streaming from his nose. His fists clenched in fury, and he spat contemptuously at the stubborn door, a glob of bloody saliva that dripped slowly down the deceptively mundane-looking planks.

Finally, he stood, turning toward the opposite wall of the hallway, confronting his own reflection in a crystal mirror, in an ornate platinum frame. With a strangled cry, Kalrakin smashed his fist into the mirror, shattering the glass. Ignoring the shards on the floor, he stalked on through the Tower.

This was the second time he had assaulted the wizard-locked door. The first had been weeks earlier, shortly after he and Luthar had arrived here. The first time the sorcerer had smashed the planks with a great battle axe. The blade, heavy steel of dwarven manufacture, enchanted with ancient magic, had bounced off the wooden planks without making so much as a scratch. Kalrakin had exhausted himself banging on the portal, without making any progress.

This time, he had focused on the stone, holding it while he caressed a multitude of magical items that he had collected while ransacking the Tower. Thus he had drained away the enchantments in pitchers that never emptied, weapons of rare ensorcellment, doorknobs and saddles and lamps that had each been infused with potent magical power. They were mundane and lifeless now, the enchantments having been absorbed by the Irda Stone.

But even that potent blast of stored magic had been thwarted by the wizard lock.

Kalrakin spiraled down a long ways, past many other doors and landings, passages leading through the still-imperfectly mapped tower. He found Luthar in the great dining room in the foretower. The rotund mage sat at the big table, eating noisily.

"Come—I wish to try again."

"You can't wait for tomorrow?" Luthar said with a grimace.

"We have been waiting for too many tomorrows," snapped the tall sorcerer. His hawk-nose jutted angrily toward his compatriot. "We are making no progress—none at all! That door must be sealed by the power of the gods themselves! I sent a surge of wild magic that would have torn down a castle—but it rebounded against me, had no effect on either the door or its frame."

"That makes only five rooms, all sealed, in this whole tower," Luthar reflected. "There are a hundred times that many we are able to enter and make our own. Again, Master, I counsel patience. These doors will open to us, in time. In the meantime, think what we have: food of any variety, as much as we want, provided by the Tower; drink; and treasures galore!"

"Bah—I have no patience for petty delights! Or for fools, Luthar. We have discovered apartments both Spartan and sumptuous; galleries of rare art, pantries and cisterns and training halls. All of them are filled with silly trinkets and novelties—paintings with moving pictures, dishes that wash themselves, rings and bracelets of various natures. But where are the true artifacts: the library of scrolls, the laboratory of potions and elixirs? What of the treasures of the ages, those items that will pave my way to ultimate mastery?

"No, my slow-witted friend, these all-important relics are still hidden away from us. And those are the secrets of the five doors, the doors locked by the ancient wizards, doors that still resist our most potent magic."

"Every lock can be broken," Luthar replied plaintively. "If not with a spell, then with great force. You must collect a greater force.

"No, these ancient wizard locks require a clever solution." Kalrakin said. "Clearly they encompass all sides of these chambers, including the floor and ceiling—I have tried to warp the stones in all dimensions, but they resist every probe, every advance of my wild magic. I need to find another way."

"There are times, Master, when I feel as though this cursed tower is alive, is working against us—it's like a secret enemy, lurking around the corner of every hallway—watching, scheming. I tell you, I don't like it! It is dangerous here, and we don't *need* this place! The whole world is open to us—maybe we should just go somewhere else?"

"No. There is a purpose here, a reason that we were invited in. The Tower beckoned to us, drew us through the dark wood, brought us safely within. It *wanted* us to come."

"Now, perhaps, it wants us to leave," suggested Luthar.

The gaunt sorcerer shook his head and ran his fingers through the long tangle of his beard, turning a slow circle as he inspected the dining hall. "I care not what it wants. I am here, I like it here, and I intend to stay. Now, come with me," he said abruptly.

As usual, Luthar had to trot to keep up with Kalrakin's long-legged stride. They made their way to the great central stairway and headed up, the taller sorcerer taking the steps three at a time, while the shorter mage huffed and hurried behind. Passing the scattered remnants of plate mail he had earlier wrecked, the wild magic user returned to the stubborn door that had resisted his most potent casting.

"You dare to taunt me?" he declared softly, addressing that door. He did not expect a reply, but Luthar's words had pointed him toward a truth: There *was* some being listening, observing, watching him. The Tower was indeed a sentient presence who was testing him—and with this realization, the tall mage had determined a course of action.

Kalrakin kept his eyes on the locked room as he reached his gloved hand behind his back and pushed open the door to another chamber. Only then did he spin around and stalk into that room, one of several small art galleries that he and Luthar had discovered weeks earlier, upon their first explorations of the Tower. The sorcerer waved his hand, and light flared from the crystal chandelier overhead, illuminating a large, irregular chamber that was dominated by a life-sized statue of three humans, a trio standing back to back in the center.

Executed by a talented sculptor out of three shades of marble, the statues depicted archetypes of the three schools of godly magic—or perhaps, the three deities ruling those orders. One image carved in pure white displayed an elderly man, wrinkled and slightly stooped in posture, leaning on a knobby staff. His eyes were kindly, his smile beneficent, and if his flowing beard and hair bespoke great age, his visage had a benign aspect that, when he had first glimpsed this statue, Kalrakin found it patently absurd.

Next to him was the likeness of another man, cut from stone of ebony black. This was a younger wizard, smooth-faced and short-haired, with penetrating eyes. The third image was female, carved from some exotic version of marble that was nearly blood-red in color; the sorceress was of indeterminate age, stern-faced, and slender, and her hands were raised slightly, reaching outward in a gesture of encompassing embrace.

"Artifacts of the distant past," Kalrakin sneered aloud. He leaned back and crowed toward the ceiling. "Pathetic symbols of a time gone by—but they are part of you still, are they not?"

He glared at the trio of statues and raised his hands toward the female figure in red marble. Intertwining his thumbs, the gaunt sorcerer roared, making an animalistic sound of fury. With a sharp gesture he broke his grip and whipped his arms apart—and in that instant the statue shattered, scattering shards of crimson stone across the wooden floor of the gallery.

Kalrakin stood still, every sense quivering. He heard it first as a groan, a sound of nearly physical pain, followed by the faintest of tremors. The floorboards rippled slightly under his feet. "Feel the force of my displeasure!" he shouted to the ceiling, his voice exultant. "And know that there is no limit to the pain I can inflict!"

With sharp, brutal gestures, he then wove a spell of wild magic around the white and then the black statues, leaving them likewise destroyed. Shards of rock in three colors now littered the floor of the gallery, and the suffering of the Tower became tangible. The floor shivered more violently; an elaborately jeweled lamp, with a surface of carved turquoise, trembled atop its marble pedestal. With a flip of his hand, Kalrakin caused that precious treasure to slide from its perch; it fell and broke against the hard floor.

The sorcerer breathed hard, snorting like a bull through his massive beak of a nose. He glared at a shelf of crystal vases then turned to scrutinize a painting of exceptional age, depicting an elven patriarch from beyond the Age of Heroes. He toyed with the thought of further mayhem. But perhaps his point had been made.

With a growl, he exited the room, glaring across the hall at the doorway that taunted him.

"Do you dare to tempt me into further retribution?" he asked, his voice rising. Once more he rooted his feet to the stone floor—and felt the wild magic surge. Curling his hand into a fist, still clutching the Irda Stone, he aimed his strongest blow at the wizard-locked door, expended the full force of his magic in one mighty hammer strike.

This time the force rebounded against him so hard that he was hurled against the wall; his skull rang as he bit down, hard, on his own tongue. He was utterly unconscious by the time his insensate body hit the floor.

The pale, cringing Luthar crept into the hallway, and with a deep sigh, and a small snort of disgust, slumped down next to Kalrakin, to wait.

CHAPTER 10

SHADOWS IN THE WILD

Settle down, Dora!" Coryn snapped. Confronted by a familiar, stubborn glare, she whacked the mule across the snout and repeated her command. Turning more docile, the shaggy animal fell into pace behind Diva and Dolly until once again the three mules shuffled patiently along, following Coryn, who was following Jenna.

As Coryn had been following Jenna for more than three weeks, now. They were somewhere in the western half of what used to be called Qualinesti, Coryn was pretty sure. That much she had gleaned from Jenna's conversations with innkeepers, knightly patrols, and the occasional traveler they encountered. As to why they were here or where they were headed, Coryn had no idea.

Coryn had learned, quickly, about the mules: how to feed, load, unload, lead, and occasionally prod them to greater urgency. She worked hard, ate as well as Jenna did, and still had no idea why her grandmother had sent her to visit this unusual, and admittedly intriguing, woman. Certainly she had seen more of the world in these past three months than in the whole of her previous sixteen years. But there must be more to it than that.

At night, rolled in her bedroll near the fire, Cory would pretend to sleep. Through slitted eyelids, she would watch as Jenna went through mysterious routines. Often these involved reading—the girl knew that one of the mule's saddlebags bulged with books, more books than she had ever seen before. The older woman was very protective of these tomes, so Coryn had never been able to see inside them, but she stole compelling glimpses of the red leather covers, with their shiny binding and silver filigree inscriptions. She suspected the volumes were similar to Umma's little book, the one hidden under her mattress. Once she had asked Jenna about them, only to be told—curtly—to collect more firewood for the evening's cooking.

When Jenna read at night, she did so by the light of a medallion, one of the many pieces of jewelry that she wore on slender chains around her neck. Cory was fascinated by the nature of that illumination, brighter and more steady than any lamp. On one very still night, she had heard the woman whisper a strange word as she touched the medallion. It was one of the word's from Umma's book; of that Coryn had been certain!

That had been only yesterday, and now another long day of forest-track was behind them.

"Down there, in that hollow. We'll camp there tonight," Jenna announced, gesturing to a narrow trail descending steeply away from the winding forest track. "I remember a nice clearing near the stream. And nobody will be able to see us from the road. Take the mules down there and wait for me—I want to have a look around and make sure of our safety."

"All right," Coryn agreed, eyeing the narrow trail dubiously. They hadn't seen a single person since the innkeeper at the crossroads, at least ten miles and six hours ago, but she knew not to challenge the older woman's sense of caution. "Diva, lead the way."

She took the bridle of the lead mule and started down the path, which was more of a dry ravine than any kind of hewn trail. Still, the animals followed with surefooted ease, and they rapidly descended between the lofty, moss-draped trunks into an area of soft undergrowth. Sure enough, the little run debouched into a tiny meadow carpeted with small, white flowers. Nearby was a placid stretch of water. With the first sweep of her eyes, Cory spotted a least a dozen fat trout, and her stomach was already rumbling as she unhitched the mules and started to spread out their small camp.

With practiced ease, Cory removed the saddlebags and tack from the mules and tethered the animals near the stream, where they had ready access to a nice patch of clover-heavy grass as well as fresh water. Next she pulled the cooking gear and bedrolls from Diva's saddlebags. Dolly's load contained their dried provisions and extra clothing. Dora's bags, containing Jenna's books as well as many other mysterious items that the girl had yet to examine, were left to Jenna to handle, for Cory knew better than to open them.

Jenna, her red robe damp around the fringe from the wet underbrush, strolled into the clearing a few minutes later. The girl never ceased to be amazed that her companion, who was draped with bangles and chains and feathered gewgaws—as well as the golden medallion—could move so silently.

"This is a good place to camp," Coryn offered with a smile. "Really hidden down here. Did you remember it from an earlier visit?"

"Long ago I spent a pleasant couple of days down here," Jenna replied. "I wasn't much older than you, I guess. I was on my first trip outside the Tower, traveling in the company of a young knight—"

Abruptly, the older woman paused, her lips creasing. "Come to think of it, I *was* a little older than you are."

Cory would have liked to hear the rest of the story, but she had learned to take Jenna's snippets of conversation for what they were: tantalizing pieces of a personal history that, the girl hoped, she might someday put together to make sense. Whenever she asked to hear more, Jenna was likely to change the subject or, more likely, send her off on some errand.

This time she went and gathered firewood without being asked. In only a few minutes she had collected a plentiful supply of dry, hard wood. Jenna was going through the mysterious components of Dora's saddlebags, and, as Cory arranged the wood, she worked up the courage to ask a question.

"You mentioned you came here after you were in a tower. My grandmother used to talk about a tower, too—is that where you know each other from?"

Jenna looked at her sharply, carefully setting down a bag of jars that clinked musically together. "Yes, as a matter of fact. That was a long time ago. In fact, it was the last time I saw Scharon—that is, your grandmother."

Cherishing this tidbit of information, Coryn quickly built a cheery fire. The sky, viewed through the halo of surrounding tree tops, was still pale blue with late afternoon sunlight, and she looked toward the deep pool where the brook eddied near their camp. "How about fresh fish tonight?" she asked. "I could probably catch us a pair of nice trout before it gets dark."

"Good," Jenna agreed. "I have some reading to do."

Coryn went to the portion of Diva's saddlebags that had been given over to her few possessions. She took out her bow and strung the weapon. With one arrow in her other hand she went over to the bank of the stream. The trout were as thick as before, meandering through the clear water. The pool was only three or four feet deep, with a silted bottom, perfect for bow-fishing. Every few seconds the surface roiled as one of the fish struck at a careless fly or waterbug.

The girl studied the fish, picking out three of the largest.

Slowly she drew back her bowstring, holding it close to her ear. Tension thrummed in the taut strand, in the bend of the sturdy bow, in the quivering of the carefully aimed missile. Her eyes flicked back and forth, watching the fish meander, waiting until their paths drifted close together.

Coryn drew a breath in through her nose. She relaxed and felt the wild sorcery tingling in the soles of her feet, pulsing in the air around her. That power was reflected in the silky patterns on the surface of the water, in the dappled scales on the sides of the three trout.

It was time. She let the arrow fly as she exhaled, and with her will she drew the power of magic from her surroundings and channeled it, tightly, into her shot. In that breath the arrow became three, each missile slicing unerringly into the water, aimed slightly below the apparent location of the targets—Coryn had done enough bow-fishing to know that she had to correct for the bending of the light as it passed through the water.

The trio of missiles penetrated the water with barely audible splashes, and each drove through the body of a fat target. The fish thrashed and leaped momentarily, but the shots were true and, moments later, each floated lifelessly to the surface, pinned by identical wooden shafts. Since the late summer evening was warm, Cory had no qualms about stripping off her trousers and wading into the pool to retrieve her prizes. She was feeling rather proud of herself as she bore the trout back to the shore and climbed onto the bank. Only when she started toward the fire was she aware that Jenna had put down her book and stood to face her, hands on her hips.

"What did you think you were doing?" asked the older woman, no sense of amusement, or even tolerance, in her voice.

"Getting dinner," Cory said defensively. "I told you—"

"I am referring to *how* you got those fish! That was

corruption—you sucked the energy out of the very air! How dare you?"

"Dare I?" The girl was irritated by the stupid question. "I have been fishing like that since I first learned to use a bow. What harm did I do?"

"Harm?" Jenna drew a breath and made an obvious effort to control her—to Coryn—surprising anger. "Didn't your grandmother teach you *anything?*"

The girl bit back her growing temper. "Umma taught me a lot, nearly everything that I know!" she retorted. In the face of Jenna's stony silence she continued. "About that, what you call 'wild magic,' I guess I figured some things out for myself. But Umma knew and didn't care. Why are you so upset?"

"You wouldn't understand," Jenna said sternly.

"Of course not! You won't tell me anything! How am I supposed to understand anything?"

"Now is not the time. Throw those fish away—I will not eat them, and neither will you. We have plenty of flatbread and dried fruit for dinner. That will serve us as well tonight as it has for the past weeks."

Coryn stared at the older woman. Jenna met her gaze directly, but her eyes glanced down at the fish with an expression of real disgust. Slowly Coryn came to a surprising realization: Jenna was not so much angry as frightened!

Still reluctant, the girl went back to the stream, and dropped her catches into the flow. Swiftly the three dead trout were carried out of sight.

They ate their bread and fruit in silence, Cory stealing sidelong glances at the woman in the red robe. Jenna had stored her books away, and now she seemed distracted, looking into the surrounding woods with an intense, staring expression. Coryn cleaned up their few dishes, banked the fire against the morning's chill, and then sank into her bedroll with a strong sense of unease.

The tension lingered as she lay on the hard ground, staring at the small patch of stars visible through the ring of trees. She turned to look at Jenna, who was wrapped up in her own blankets on the other side of the fire, and who, from the sound of steady breathing, was sound asleep.

In the darkness and the silence of the deep forest, Coryn began to muster her defiance. Someday soon she would confront Jenna about her mysterious edict. Why did she fear the wild magic? The girl felt certain that Jenna was no stranger to magic! Jenna's lighted medallion was but one small example of things Coryn had observed. But why would one kind of magic cause her to react with such fear, when she willingly used her own powers with merely a whispered word, or the deft maneuvering of her fingers?

She knew such whispered words from Umma's books, the books that she had committed to memory years ago. One word, spoken by pure instinct, had saved her from the walrus-men as it whisked her, still wet from lying in the soggy snow, onto the floor of Umma's cottage.

She remembered the word Jenna murmured when she summoned the light from her medallion. Would that word work for her?

It was with a sense of rebellious determination that she rolled onto her side, her back toward the low fire and the sleeping woman beyond. Cory didn't have a medallion, but reaching out a hand, she felt around until she found a small stone, small enough that she could easily hold it in the palm of her hand.

As softly as she could, she whispered the remembered word, focusing the power of the magic on the stone cupped in her fingers. Immediately, to her delight, it came to light, spilling a surprising brilliance over the ground, across the clearing, and into the nearby fringe of woods. The girl listened for any disruption in Jenna's breathing. Convinced that the Red Robe still slumbered, the girl uncapped her fingers slightly and let the beams of light play across the trees, the moss-draped branches, and the trailing vines. . . .

And then she saw the black-cloaked figure standing there at the edge of the woods, regarding her with an expression of keen interest.

Coryn gasped and sat up, raising the stone so that its full light spilled wildly into the woods. With a grimace, the stranger—he was a rather handsome man, she noticed vaguely—raised a hand to shield his eyes from the rays.

"Would you mind?" he asked, pleasantly enough, as he strolled forward into the clearing.

"I—I don't know how to stop it," Coryn admitted, though she cupped the stone tightly to cover its brightness.

"Then your mistress is doing a poor job of teaching you," the stranger remarked. He was dressed in a sleek black robe, the fabric intertwined with silvery threads that picked up and reflected the light. He had an expression of mild amusement on his face as he looked past Coryn toward the sleeping Jenna.

"Mistress?" Coryn suddenly realized she needed to raise an alarm. "Jenna—wake up!" she cried. Her eyes remained fixed upon the robed traveler, as Jenna immediately stirred herself.

"Of all people—Dalamar!" she snapped, her tone angry. "What are you doing here? Get away from her—get away from both of us!"

"Not so quickly, mistress of the Red Robe," said the man dressed in black. He walked past Coryn as if the girl didn't exist, his eyes fixed upon the woman, his face still creased by that expression of mild amusement.

He was the most magnetic person Cory had ever seen. His eyes were wide and unusually large, shaped kind of like almonds, she decided. His face was so smooth that, though he was clearly an adult, his skin showed no signs of ever having been touched by a razor. The cowl of his black hood covered much of his head, but she could see enough of him to realize that he had light-colored, beautiful hair. He walked with a sense of utter assurance, and even as he crossed the grassy ground—littered with fallen twigs, as she had noticed when gathering firewood—his steps made no sound.

"You are a difficult person to find," said the one called Dalamar. "I have been seeking you for some time, but did not expect to run into you so far from your usual haunts. What brings you here, to wild Qualinesti?"

"I needed to get out of the city," Jenna retorted, without conviction.

"I suspect there is more to it than that. I think you are here for much the same reason that I am here. What I can't figure out—at least, I couldn't figure out until tonight—is why you brought this girl."

"You've been *spying* on us?" blurted Coryn. "For how long have you been hiding there in the woods?"

"It is no use asking questions of one wearing the black robe," Jenna interjected sharply. "His answer will be what he wants us to hear, but it will bear no relation to the truth."

"Tsk, tsk," Dalamar chided. "Leave it to the Red Robe to lecture about self-serving behavior." He turned to regard Coryn, favoring her with just a hint of a smile. "Has she been treating you well? Teaching you things, is she?"

"I—well, yes. She treats me fairly." Cory was confused, her mind whirling. She felt oddly compelled to come to Jenna's defense. "She is my mistress, and I try to serve her well. But you are wrong about one thing: She is not my teacher."

At that, Dalamar smiled broadly. "I see . . . you're just a humble servant girl who makes pebbles glow in the dark. Well, that certainly makes sense—can't have the servants stumbling around in the thick of the night. I don't know how many times I've heard Jenna say those very words."

"Who *are* you?" demanded Coryn. She was undeniably flattered when he bowed, deeply, looking out from the cowl of that dark hood to look her squarely in the eyes.

"Forgive me. I am called Dalamar the Dark, and I have long been an associate of your mistress." Startlingly, he winked. "You can tell by the warm greeting she has offered an old friend, after a long time apart."

"Get away from her—and me. I mean it, Dalamar," Jenna was saying. She stood now, wearing her red robe and glaring at the intruder. "She is the granddaughter of an old friend and has nothing for the likes of you."

Still those almond eyes lingered, making Coryn suddenly conscious that she wore only her nightshirt. She pulled the blankets up over her chest, but continued to meet Dalamar's eyes until, with visible reluctance, he turned back to Jenna.

"I have no ill designs on her, or yourself, for that matter," he said pleasantly. "But we do need to talk, and I have come a long way to find you. Perhaps your . . . 'servant' could add some wood to this fire, and we might make ourselves comfortable."

Coryn watched Jenna, who glared at Dalamar with an expression of furious distrust. Nevertheless, Jenna finally sighed and nodded in acquiescence. "Bring some more wood," she said to the girl. "And heat some water for tea."

Dalamar turned respectfully away as Coryn shrugged into her trousers. She looked at the dwindling pile of fire-wood—there was enough for breakfast tea, no more—and she knew she would have to plunge into the dark woods in search of more fuel. She looked at the pebble in her hand, which had now dimmed to nothing; and she didn't dare try the word again. She was reluctant to leave these two, and desperately curious to see what this meeting was about.

Dalamar crossed to Jenna as Coryn broke a log with a loud *crack* of dry wood. Placing the resulting two sticks on the fire, she picked up another branch, braced it on her knee. She listened, keenly, and from the corner of her eye she watched Jenna, who had all but forgotten her.

The woman in the red robe said one word—it sounded something like *shroud-yus*—and then all was utterly silent. Cory stared in surprise to see that Jenna was still talking, animated to the point of raising a hand and pointing a finger at Dalamar while she told him what she thought.

But she could hear no words, and there was no sound at all in the still forest clearing.

At length Dalamar raised his hands and Jenna's lips stopped moving. She planted her fists on her hips while the Black Robe began to—apparently—talk. More silent words; still Cory could hear nothing. Jenna glanced at her momentarily, glared, and turned back to Dalamar.

With a shrug, Coryn left the now lively fire and pushed along the little trail next to the stream, where she had gathered much of the firewood from the lower branches of a downed pine. She pulled more of the sticks, dry and brittle, off the trunk as she tried to make sense of this stranger in the forest carrying on a silent argument with Jenna. When she carried her armload of fuel back to the fire, she got another shock.

Dalamar had pulled back his hood to reveal, as Cory has suspected, long and beautiful golden hair. But it was something else that grabbed her attention: the tip of a slender, tapered ear that extended into view through the strands of smooth yellow.

He was an elf!

Even as she absorbed this shock, the two continued to converse while making no sounds that Coryn could discern. Kneeling at the fire, the girl took a little time to tend the blaze, thinking. That one word Jenna had uttered had triggered a magic spell, obviously, some sort of silence cloak that she had drawn over both of them to keep Coryn in the dark. Not a cloak so much as an invisible cone, Cory decided, wondering how large an area it enveloped.

She wondered what they were saying and why she was excluded—how their talk must involve her.

———◆·◆·◆———

"You're seeking the Tower, aren't you?" Dalamar noted with a triumphant sneer. "And you must think this girl will help you to get in."

Jenna snorted in contempt. "You know the Tower. It gives entry to those the Master wants to let in, and all others might seek it for a lifetime and never even see the entry into the wood. The girl is only a girl."

"Yes, I know the Tower," Dalamar conceded. "I think that the Tower is suffering . . . weakened. I think it needs help, the help of wizards from *all* the orders."

Again the Red Robe swatted his notion away. "What orders? Have you seen a wizard worthy of any of the robes, even since the moons have returned?"

The dark elf's expression grew grim. "I have been to see Palin. He's finished with the robe—it seemed like he'd barely noticed that his white moon was back in the skies. Tell me, Jenna—*you* feel Lunitari again, do you not? The pull of your red goddess, waxing and waning with that sacred circle in the sky?"

"Of course I do. And I know that Nuitari has returned as well, even though I cannot see him. Yet his presence, as it was so many years ago, is once again a thing I can feel."

"Humans are such fools," Dalamar snapped. "Do you know that they call it 'The Night of Two Moons'?"

"I should have thought such pridefulness was beyond your concern," Jenna said. "What does it matter to you, what the humans think?"

The dark elf shrugged. "You're right. It doesn't matter, not in the case of most humans, anyway." He turned his head, his eyes falling upon the dark-haired girl by the fire. She was staring at them with open curiosity, though when she noticed him looking at her, she turned and busied herself by putting another log on the fire. "She'll burn the woods down if you don't give her something else to do," he said wryly.

"Don't worry about her. I was telling the truth—she is a servant, the granddaughter of an old friend, a woman with little means. She rightly believed that coming to work for me might give her a chance at a decent life."

"Really? And what is this dear old friend's name."

Jenna hesitated. "She is Scharon Fallow of Two Forks, from the Icereach. We were friends very many years ago."

"A friend from the Icereach, met as a young woman. I don't believe you traveled that far south, not in those days. Nor would she be likely to come to Palanthas—the Icefolk are notoriously clannish barbarians, after all. So you must have met somewhere between . . . someplace where you spent some time as a young woman. Someplace like the Tower of High Sorcery in Wayreth Forest, perhaps?"

Jenna rolled her eyes. "You always did have an active imagination. No, Dalamar, not the Tower. There is nothing magical about Scharon Fallow, I assure you. Her father worked for a trader, and she traveled by ship to the north. My family took her in when her father died before he could return home. She lived with us for a year, until I went away to the Tower, as a matter of fact."

"Very well," the elf said, with a dismissive shrug. "In any event, know that I am here to stay. I have decided we should seek the Tower together."

Her eyes narrowed. "You have decided!" She paused, thinking. "You say that Palin has renounced the robes, any part in this quest?"

"He seems content to grow fat and happy next to his hearth fire, lording it over that pathetic village and letting his wife and sister cater to his every whim."

Jenna, for the first time, smiled slightly. "He stung your pride, I take it."

"I care not," the elf said with an elaborate shrug. "Except that we are without the use of our greatest potential ally."

"I am fully prepared to do what I need to do, alone," Jenna said sharply. "I don't need you."

"And I told you that I am not prepared to let you do that."

They stared at each other for several minutes. Neither noticed that Coryn was intensely staring at them; she had been futilely trying to lip-read their stalemate.

Jenna sighed and spoke more gently. "All right. You're right—we'll have a better chance together. So let's get moving." She turned toward the fire, stepping out of the invisible cone of silence as the magic faded around her. "We're going to get the mules loaded," she informed Coryn. "Leave the fire for now—we'll put it out before we get back to the trail."

If the girl had any surprise to spare over this sudden midnight departure, her stoic face did not betray her. Instead, she quickly went to the tethered animals and lifted the harness over the head of each.

"If you help," Jenna told Dalamar, "we'll get out of here faster."

"Your servant seems quite capable," said the dark elf with that slim smile.

Muttering to herself, Jenna bundled up her own bedroll and carefully checked the saddlebags on Dora, those containing all of her spell books, as well as assorted other tools she had brought along to help with the quest. She sent Coryn to take care of the cooking kit while she called angrily to Dalamar.

"At least give me a hand with these packs!"

He came over and helped her lift the big leather sacks over Dora's back, holding them in place while he watched Cory. With practiced gestures, the girl nested the plates and cups within the cook pot and brought them over to the mules.

Jenna was leaning over to buckle the snaps when the first arrow came out of the darkness. It *thwacked* loudly into the saddlebag, inches from her shoulder.

"We're under attack!" she shouted, spinning around and staring into the darkness. Light flared behind her as Dalamar barked a spell. In the surge of illumination she saw a half dozen scruffy, bearded men sprinting toward them. Others were unseen beyond them, and two more arrows came winging from the darkness.

"Deflectii—denius!" Dalamar cried, raising his clenched fists before him, crossing his arms at the wrists. One arrow struck the place where his arms were crossed and sputtered into nothingness; the other soared harmlessly over their heads.

Jenna peered into the darkness, past the men who suddenly hesitated at this clear evidence of magic. She spotted two figures in the shadows beyond, archers drawing fresh missiles into their bows.

"Braacius!" shouted the Red Robe. A crackling missile, like an arrow trailing sputtering fire, flew toward the dark stranger. She repeated the command and a second magical dart shot through the night. They struck the archers squarely and the two bowmen shrieked in pain, stumbling backward, swatting at the sparks that sputtered and flared from their clothing.

One of the bandits had a surge of boldness and came charging toward Jenna with an upraised sword. She ducked to the side, letting go of Dora's bridle as the sword *whooshed* through the air near her head. A bark of sound from Dalamar turned that sword into a striking viper—at least, that's how it looked to Jenna and, even more important, to the swordsman. He suddenly held a lashing snake by the tail, and—with fanged maw gaping—the serpent curled around, driving for a bite at that hand. With a shriek, the man hurled his weapon away, the writhing blade flying into the midst of the bucking mules.

Diva and Dolly pitched back, but remained tethered to the ground. Dora, her heavy saddlebags flopping, had been loosed from her hitch. With a neigh of terror she kicked up her heels. The mule surged forward and Jenna tumbled to the ground. She lay stunned, vaguely aware of the clattering hooves as Dora galloped away, following the demoralized band of thieves as they ran into the night.

"Dammit—Coryn, get the mule!" shouted the Red Robe. "She has my books!" Jenna pushed herself to her feet, and saw the dark elf striding into the woods, his black robe vanishing into the shadows. Jenna plunged after, listening for sounds of the mule's plunging passage through the woods.

She gave scant thought to the bandits, all of whom had run this same way along the stream bank. If any stood between her and her books she would kill them without a second thought. But the way the group had scattered, she expected they wouldn't stop running until dawn.

Branches crackled to her left, and she felt a surge of relief as she heard the nickering of a frightening mule. Dalamar was there, holding Dora and soothing the mule with gentle strokes on the long nose. The two saddlebags, still bulging with arcane treasures, remained securely in place.

Together they led the trembling animal back through the woods, to the small clearing. The fire was there, still crackling merrily.

But Coryn was nowhere to be seen.

CHAPTER
11

LORD OF THE WICKED

I suppose one of you louts thinks you can do a better job of leading this outfit—is that it?"

Captain Samuval sneered at the band gathered around him, his expression daring any one of them to take up the gauntlet. He knew that he cut a dashing figure with his gloved hands planted firmly on his hips, his cloak swirling as he stalked back and forth in front of the blazing bonfire. The longsword in its plain scabbard was mostly concealed by the cloak, but his bandits knew it was there, lurking.

The men among them looked down or shook their heads or otherwise signaled their acceptance of their leader's disdain. Samuval looked beyond the men to the group of hobgoblins and draconians gathered a little farther from the fire. From this bunch came hissing and chortling, a few muttered growls, but in the face of his unwavering glare no outright rebellion.

It was those on the fringe of the group that Samuval knew presented the greatest threats. He glared out at Bloodtusk, the one-eyed ogre, and was rewarded by a bored shrug of utter indifference. His gaze swept around the circle, to Lubbar, the other ogre, and finally to Rust-Knock, the gigantic half-giant, half-ogre. Sooner or later, Samuval knew, Rust-Knock was bound to make trouble.

"Rust, do *you* think you would make a better leader?" Samuval asked the half-giant, his tone expressing mild amusement mingled with disbelief. "You could hold this rabble together? Keep the Dark Knights, the dragons, off our backs? By all means, come forward and take charge—that is, if you can figure out which is your front, and which your back." The bandit lord bowed, smiling broadly, extending his hand in a gesture of invitation. He relished the appreciative chuckles rising from most of the throng.

Rust-Knock, however, only chuckled ominously. "I can figure more than front and back. I know who is my master, and who is my slave. I think I do not see a master anywhere around here!"

That bold statement produced a rumble from others of the gathering, especially the draconians and ogres who typically were impressed by such bombast. Samuval knew that here was his invitation to action, and he welcomed the excuse. Like his men, he had become bored with sitting around in the wilds, waiting for the all-too-infrequent caravan to traipse down any of the roads within the vast territory that the bandit lord had claimed for his own. Sure, they made occasional forays into the regions around their vast forest, but all knew that the pickings, in this chaotic postwar era, were very slim. In truth, there was not a lot for Samuval's bandits to do, very little to keep this restless lot busy, or amused.

It was time for a little entertainment.

"Come forward, then," Sam snapped. "I'll teach you a lesson about masters and those who serve them."

"It is *you* who will learn, human," grunted the massive creature, swaggering forward on two tree trunk-sized legs. "For too long we hide in the woods and attack only women and children. We are warriors, and we deserve more warlike fodder for our spirit!"

"Then eat this steel, you lumbering fool!" snapped Samuval. His longsword gleamed in his hand, red and orange flickers reflecting the glow of the surging bonfire. He meant this to be a fight with real stakes, for his men to see his utter lack of fear. He wanted them to be afraid of him, and this was the chance to remind them. He didn't want to kill the half-giant, but he was more than willing to if absolutely necessary.

Rust-Knock had his own weapon up. The half-giant bore a branch hewn from the trunk of a tall oak. The beam was as thick as Sam's bicep. At the head was lashed a massive block of stone, shaped very crudely like the blade of an axe. Even at its sharpest, of course, it was a weapon for crushing, not cutting, and many were the men who had known the weight of that bone-breaking force.

The huge cudgel swept through the air, the blow too low for Samuval to duck. He skipped backward, however, deftly sliding his blade out of the way. Balanced on the balls of his feet, he lunged as soon as the huge weapon had swooshed past. But Rust-Knock anticipated the move—already he was coming around, with the butt of his big pole flying up and out. Again the human backpedaled, evading the attack and holding his own weapon away.

In the periphery of his view the bandit lord saw his men sidle back, giving the two fighters more room. Many gathered around the simple plank bar established by an enterprising innkeeper named Fat Wally, who had brought a wagonload of kegs out to the camp. As the fight escalated, Wally worked hard to keep up with the demand, filling mug after mug.

Closer by, murmurs of appreciation and apprehension arose from Samuval's men, and more than one bet was laid, the flash of gold and silvery steel bright in the surging flames. Two draconians heaved more logs onto the fire, which blazed high and sent sparks even higher, glowing cinders that drifted away like fireflies through the summer evening.

Samuval beamed as he maneuvered. He wanted this to be just such a spectacle, a display that this rabble of men would not soon forget. He cried out and faked a frantic charge, his blade like liquid silver as it slashed through the air. Rust-Knock reacted immediately, smashing the stone club downward. The man danced to the side and again that steel blade flashed, drawing a howl from the half-giant, leaving a cut in the thick leather of his trouser leg.

More murmurs from the men, another shifting of coins as blood began to seep from the half-giant's cut. The brutish fighter's face tightened into a snarl and he raised his cudgel high, taking a menacing step closer to Samuval. The man slipped backward again, one, two, three steps as an increasingly wild series of blows swept back and forth, missing him. On the last of these, Rust-Knock's cudgel passed right through the fire, knocking a sparking, blazing log across the ground.

Both fighters sidestepped, moving away from the embers, the crowd moving out of their path. Samuval grinned as his opponent became increasingly reckless, advancing in a rush that carried him past the human fighter, who rolled to the ground, bounced to his feet, and stabbed a light but embarrassing thrust through the seat of the half-giant's pants.

Roaring, Rust-Knock whirled around. Flecks of spittle flew from his jowls, and his blunt, tusklike teeth gleamed red. His eyes were wild, shot through with blood, and it almost seemed as though he were having trouble focusing on his enemy. Instead his gaze swept across and beyond the throng of bandits, as though he sought succor in the vastness of the plains.

With a touch of impatience, Samuval darted forward and pricked the brute in his bulging gut. He needed an active, engaged opponent to make this duel the memorable contest he could tout. His goad served its purpose, and again Rust-Knock charged, flailing wildly, slamming the cudgel to the ground as the man darted right and left, evading each potentially deadly attack.

The bandit lord inched closer to his foe. Again that massive club came down, and this time Samuval crouched low as he dodged, looking up at the sweaty, bulging chest. The giant's vest was open, held only by a crisscross of leather strands, almost as if it marked the creature's heart for Samuval's next blow.

But that was too easy, and too quick; so instead of a killing thrust, the bandit lord contented himself with a slashing lunge, a painful gash that curved like a bloody, leering grin across the giant's huge belly.

Spinning on one heel, Samuval sprinted away, hearing his monstrous foe—now nearly sobbing grotesquely in frustrated rage—race predictably behind. Once again the crowd of ruffians scattered, making way for the combatants. Abruptly the man skidded to a stop and spun about, balancing himself carefully. Crouching, he raised his gleaming silver longsword.

Behind him men scattered, abandoning the plank stretched across two barrels, the resting place for numerous empty mugs and puddles of sticky beer. There stood Fat Wally, the keg-man with mouth agape, who nervously stood his ground before his still-loaded cart, a heavy pewter mug in each hand.

The half-giant had no eyes for the crowd, for the bar, for anything except the infuriating human. He roared in triumph at Samuval, seemingly cornered, and bore down on his puny opponent. The half-giant's club started its downward sweep, a blow that would have cracked the flagstones on a granite floor, as Rust-Knock's howling became tinged with mad glee. Both biceps bulging, he brought the huge timber through a tremendous swipe.

At the last instant, Samuval ducked away, rolling to the side and bouncing to his feet in time to see the club hit the ground and bounce upward from the force of the blow. The half-giant's charge carried him inexorably forward, through the plank bar and into the keg-laden wagon beyond. Rust-Knock lost his balance as he tried to swing himself around. The cudgel bounced into a keg, shattering the plank sides and releasing a foaming cascade—and a howl of indignation from Fat Wally.

The rest of the men, draconians, and half-breeds, pressed in now, sensing that the fight was coming to a end—and feeling protective of the remaining kegs. Having made his point, Samuval was content to accept the accolades of his band, waving cheerfully as the half-giant was assisted out of the wreckage of the cart. Soaked by blood and beer, he hobbled away, too humiliated and defeated even to glare at the victor.

"Who's going to pay for this?" squeaked Fat Wally, pushing through the crowd toward Samuval. "These are costly damages!"

"Put it down to the cost of doing business—or your business here is over," said the leader of the bandits breezily.

"Don't tempt me!" snapped Wally. "I have a good mind to do just that, to pack up the rest of my barrels and leave!"

Samuval blinked in surprise. "My dear beerman, you misunderstand me. Your business here might come to an end, but that doesn't mean there's any chance you'll leave here with the rest of these kegs." His tone was genial, but he wiped his bloody blade on a flap of the merchant's vest as he spoke.

"I-I guess I will make do with the losses," Fat Wally stammered, his face pale. "I still have two more, ready to be tapped."

"Well, what are you standing here for, then?" demanded Sam. "Tap one of them! And you men, put another plank across those barrels. The bar is open again!"

Even before the bandits could gather around the watering hole, there was a shout from the edge of the camp.

"One-Eye returns!" called a sentry. "And he has a prisoner!"

———◆◆◆———

Coryn was starting to wonder if it had really been that smart to let herself get captured. Not that she was worried for her life, not much, anyway, but she had to acknowledge that things weren't turning out exactly as she had planned.

What had she been thinking? Well, she had been irritated with Jenna, angry that the Red Robe was being so secretive about their purposes. And then Dalamar had appeared—he was, quite simply, the most intriguing and handsome person she had ever encountered. Yet Jenna seemed determined to keep her in the dark, right down to that ridiculous cone of silence!

When the bandits had attacked, Jenna and Dalamar had plunged into the woods after the wayward mule, Coryn had first considered simply running away. That had been a short-lived impulse: She was pragmatic enough to realize that she had no real place to go. And besides, Umma had sent her to Jenna and directed her to follow the older woman's orders.

Then had come a rustling in the bushes on the opposite side of the camp, away from the direction from which the bandits had attacked. Crouching behind Dolly the mule, Cory had seen four shadowy figures skulk through the darkness while their compatriots and the two wizards were blundering around in the dark forest. She could have sneaked away or even sprinted into the woods and counted on good luck to catch up to Dalamar and Jenna before the bandits caught up with her, if they even pursued at all.

But she had discarded that idea, and instead ventured boldly into the light of the fire, ordering the four bandits to leave before she turned them into knobby toads. They had merely laughed and one of them, his face grotesque behind a crusty, ragged eye patch, had grabbed her by the arms so roughly that he had left them bruised. She had been tempted right then to use one of the spells she had seen Jenna employ with such dramatic effects, but the bandits had immediately bound her wrists behind her, cruel lashes cutting into her skin. A filthy gag, tightly wrapped around Cory's head, had quashed any possibilities of magic words, and even prevented her from yelling for help. Apparently satisfied with their prize, the quartet of men had slipped into the woods, taking care to head directly away from Dalamar and Jenna.

Then they had made her walk for a very long time, and now they were approaching this well-lit, crowded compound in the middle of the nearly trackless woods. Already her little band had attracted the attention of the outer pickets, and soon her captors had prodded her into the reflected glow of a huge bonfire. The girl was footsore, staggering with weariness, and increasingly frightened as her one-eyed captor roughly shoved her toward the center of the circle of men who were gathered around the fire.

But these were not just men, she saw with a numbing chill. Several scaly creatures, reptilian snouts extended, snorted and snuffled as they beheld her. These were draconians, she guessed—but much larger and uglier and, well, *fiercer*-looking than she had expected. Others among the band had expressions so bestial and snarling she guessed they must be ogres.

Thus it was almost a relief when a man stepped forward to look down, with undisguised amusement, into her upturned face. He pulled her gag away and Cory drew a grateful breath. But the idea of a little crackling magic missile spell suddenly seemed inadequate for this unruly gang.

"What have you found for us, One-Eye?" asked the man.

" 'Ere's a little lady, maid-serve to the lady traveler, we thought ye might enjoy, Cap'n Samuval," offered the bandit cheerfully.

"Why, thank you!" said Samuval, waving expansively. "You are most correct." Effortlessly he spun Cory around. She struggled, and his grip only tightened. "Don't make me cut you, lass—hold still."

Her heart pounded as she felt the side of a cold blade against her wrist. The bandit captain thrust and twisted and the throng of ruffians laughed as Coryn flinched. Only then did she realize that he had cut away the bonds holding her wrists together. With relief, she brought her hands before her and started rubbing her chafed skin.

"Now, tell us about your mistress? We have been spying on her for several days. Why does she venture through such wilderness alone? Kind of rash, don't you think?"

"She has nothing to fear from the likes of you!" Coryn declared haughtily, a remark, judging by the chorus of hearty laughter, that the bandits found hilarious.

"Now, lassie. Don't go jumping to conclusions." Captain Samuval looked toward One-Eye questioningly. "Why didn't you bring the lady in, as well? And where are the rest of your men?"

"Well, Cap'n. . . ." One-Eye looked considerably less cocksure than before. "Seems there was two others, and both of 'em wizards! Why, one turned poor Snooty into a knobby toad, sure as I'm standing here. The rest—they might be kil't, so far as I could see. I judged meself lucky to snatch the lass here and get away. Brought her straight 'ere, I did."

"Wizards, eh?" Samuval's eyes narrowed in thought for a moment, and then he spoke loudly, obviously confident as he issued orders to his men. "Have the pickets doubled! Every other man on guard takes a sip of potion—can't have these sneaky bastards coming in here invisible! And string out the faerie bells, so we'll get a little advance warning."

"Aye, Captain!" Coryn was surprised as a dozen men ran to obey—such discipline was not what she had expected from such shabby brigands.

She watched with unabashed interest as several bandits unlocked a large chest near the makeshift bar, and carefully removed four large bottles. Each was carried, gingerly wrapped in a cloth, toward one of the points of the compass, the bearers quickly vanishing into the darkness.

"Be sparing with the potion!" Samuval called after them. "But make sure one man at each post has a sip! And that man had better keep his eyes open!"

Meanwhile, other men were removing what look like long spools of dark thread from another box. They carried these into the darkness, as well. Cory could only imagine that the slender string had something to do with the faerie bells. For the first time she considered the notion that her rash act would bring Dalamar and Jenna after her, and straight into the hands of these ruffians.

"Expecting a rescue, are you?" Samuval asked, studying her thoughtfully and, apparently, reading her mind. "I've dealt with wizards before. Don't like 'em much, but I've learned a trick or two over the years."

Coryn merely shrugged. "I didn't say they're wizards, your man did, and I don't think they'll come after me anyway. Why worry about a simple servant girl?" She felt a rising sense of fear, however.

Just then, over Samuval's shoulder, she spotted a blur of brightness in the evening sky. Shifting slightly, she realized that the white moon was rising. It was only about half full, but the cosmic brightness was somehow vaguely comforting—the same moon that she had seen in the Icereach, and the north, and everywhere else over Krynn. She didn't feel quite so alone all of a sudden.

"Now, what are we going to do with you?" He addressed her, but spoke loudly enough so that his men could hear his every word.

"You don't know? I got some ideas, Cap'n!" one of them shouted, to raucous laughter.

"Are you a girl, or a woman?" he asked, walking around her, looking down as if inspecting some commodity. He turned to his men with a flourish. "Perhaps a girl, tonight—and a woman in the morning?"

This remark drew howls of approbation, and Samuval, his face illuminated clearly in the moonlight, smiled with cruel pleasure. Cory felt her knees grow weak. This was crazy! How had she gotten herself into this? In a flash, she clutched at that one word—crazy—for a flash of inspiration.

"Papa!" she cried, forcing herself to sound flushed with pleasure. She threw her arms around the startled bandit's chest, shouting in delight. "It has been so long, Papa! I have so many stories to tell you!"

"What—stop that!" demanded the bandit captain, trying to pry her arms off him. "I'm not your pop, crazy girl!"

"Oh, Papa!" She held as tightly as she could, surprising herself with the strength of her grip. "There was a dance in the moonlight! And I made a doll, for you—but I don't know where it is. Oh, I have so much to tell!"

Finally he broke her hands apart and pushed her away, his face twisting in alarm. "This is a crazy wench! Get her away from me!"

"But . . . Papa!" she allowed herself to pout, reaching out, causing Samuval to recoil.

"Tie her up," he snapped to One-Eye. "Make it tight! She's not right in the head! Why did you bring me this lunatic?"

"I din't know, Cap'n," said One-Eye, looking askance.

"She din't talk crazy like this afore, at least not when she had the gag in her mouth!"

"Just get her away from me!"

She wept and wailed, grasping for the horrified Samuval as two or three bandits hauled her away and tied her securely to one wheel of the beer wagon. They didn't bother with the gag this time, just checked the bonds at her wrists and ankles. Then they made superstitious marks in the air between themselves and this lunatic, and hurried back to join their comrades at the fire.

"We could kill half of them with fireballs before they even know we've found them," Dalamar whispered to Jenna. They crouched at the edge of the forest, with the brightness of a large fire visible in the clearing.

"You used to prefer a little more subtlety," Jenna remarked.

"Bah," he waved her words away. "My subtlety is like my patience—thin. Come on, it has already been a long night."

"Consider this, then," she argued. "We kill half of them and, even if the fireballs miss the girl, someone cuts her throat before we can get to her."

The dark elf looked at Jenna, his expression one of calculated boredom. "So then you have to get another servant girl. That shouldn't be hard."

She glared back at him. "I told you, she is the granddaughter of an old friend. I will not let her die here. Now you tell me: What did you mean when you talked about her making a pebble glow?" she demanded.

He shrugged. "Nothing. It was just my imagination, a trick of the moon as I approached your camp."

Jenna snorted skeptically but turned back to their objective. Dalamar stroked his smooth chin thoughtfully. Perhaps she didn't know as much about the girl as he had been led to believe. Interesting. . . .

"All right," he said. "We'll do this your way. With subtlety." He murmured a word of magic and vanished from sight, utterly invisible; a moment later, she did the same. "I'll go to the left, and you take the right. Whoever finds the girl, send up a green flare. If you get into trouble send up a red one."

"Very well," she replied.

He saw the waving of underbrush as the Red Robe moved away from him, and moments later he, too, embarked in the opposite direction. Comfortable within his spell of invisibility, he used his natural elven stealth to slip silently through the woods, slowing making his way around the periphery of the camp.

Jenna, apparently, lacked some of his stealthy skills. At least that was his conclusion when he heard a loud jangling of bells, and shouts of alarm from the bandit camp. He ducked instinctively as several guards—posted in the woods—rushed past him. Then he shook his head at his own skittishness. He was invisible, by the black moon! Why was he hiding from a couple of bumbling thugs?

Pushing his way to the edge of the clearing, he saw sparks and flares across the way. Jenna was drawing a lot of attention to herself, this time on purpose, so he deduced she hadn't yet found the girl. As the dark elf scanned the compound, he spotted Coryn, lashed to the wheel of a small wagon, peering around the cart as much as her bonds would let her, anxiously watching Jenna's pyrotechnics.

Dalamar strode into the clearing, passed several bandits who were hastily buckling on their sword belts, and ducking out of the path of several more who were running toward the noise. None of them saw him, of course.

Nor did Coryn, as he drew close. He leaned toward her cheek, mindful of her reaction, and whispered: "Don't be frightened—it's me, Dalamar."

Naturally she was startled, but she impressed him by her restrained reaction. "I'm glad you're here," she whispered. "Is that Jenna over there? Is she in trouble?"

"She can take care of herself. Now, hold still." He reached out, felt for the knots, and in seconds her hands were free. A group of four bandits was rushing past as he knelt at her feet, ready to work on those bonds. Still confident in his invisibility, he merely held still so that his actions would not draw attention from the passing outlaws.

To his surprise, one of the men turned right toward him and lunged, sword pointing right at the elf's unprotected back. Dalamar couldn't imagine how the man had noticed him, but as he dodged, he was desperately aware that he was reacting too late.

"Braacius!" shouted Coryn, pointing at the lunging bandit.

A magic missile sparked from her finger and hissed into the attacker's face, drawing a scream of pain and sending him tumbling back. She repeated the command three more times, sending identical bolts at the fellow's trio of companions. Two of them were down, moaning, while the other two limped away, howling in pain.

"Nice," Dalamar admitted, standing up with a tight smile. "I don't know how he saw me."

"Their captain gave some of them a type of potion," Coryn admitted, breaking free from the last bonds. "So they could see my rescuers, if you came invisibly."

"Hmm. And the magic missiles?"

"Oh, I learned how to do that by watching Jenna, a few hours ago," she admitted, looking around in growing alarm. "Now, shouldn't we be getting out of here?"

"Indeed we should," the dark elf agreed. "Allow me to teach you a haste spell."

CHAPTER

12

MOONS OVER THE NIGHT

We're going to have to get the mules across this valley," Jenna announced matter-of-factly, as if she were declaring that they were going to have to put the cat outside before they turned in for the night.

Staring at the "valley," Coryn was dumbfounded. It looked like more of a gorge or canyon to the girl, from their vantage point at the top of a precipice some two hundred feet from the floor. The rocky face plunged straight down before them and extended as far as they could see to the right and left. They had been following this rim for most of the four days since the trio had left the bandit camp. The opposite rim remained only a stone's throw away, but might as well have been across an ocean, considering the obstacles.

No doubt, Jenna had some ideas. The Red Robe had seemed even more blunt and purposeful than usual, following the trio's retreat from the bandit camp. She had indeed tripped over the alert mechanism, the faerie bells, but had easily and noisily defended herself as sentries closed in, keeping them occupied until Dalamar and Coryn could get away—their exhilarating speed bolstered by a magical haste spell. Still, the experience had been plenty harrowing, though

Coryn was relieved that none of them had suffered any real harm.

The three of them, the mules plodding stolidly along behind, had pushed through the immense forest for hour after hour, and day after day. They had encountered the canyon, which seemed to surprise both Jenna and Dalamar—though it had clearly been a fixture here for ages. Still, Coryn got the idea that both of them had expected to reach some place called "Wayreth Forest," but that instead they remained disoriented, wandering around the eastern realms of Qualinesti. One forest had begun to look pretty much like another to the girl, and in fact, she found it ironic how, just a few months earlier, she had longed to see a great expanse of trees. Now she would give up her next day's food for so much as a glimpse of a broad meadow, dusty plain, or even barren tundra. But every step simply took them through more trees.

During this part of the trek she found Dalamar to be a much more engaging companion than the red-robed enchantress. She enjoyed a small sense of conspiracy with him—he had encouraged her to keep secret the fact that she had cast a magic missile spell in the bandit camp, and Coryn had willingly agreed, suspecting that his pride was hurt, since she, after all, had saved him from a sword in the back. She had told him about Captain Samuval, and been surprised when he recognized the name. "He used to be a well-known captain of knights," the elf had explained. "Ironic to think that he is now lord of a bandit horde. And proof, I should say, of how hard times are across the world right now."

Their often whispered conversations opened up new worlds, fresh ideas, for the girl, and had helped to pass the time as they moved along the seemingly impassable barrier of the canyon.

"How will we ever get the mules over there?" the girl asked Jenna, pointing across the gap.

"Well, for starters, we'll push them off this cliff. Let them float down."

She was serious, Coryn saw—not that Jenna was inclined to joke.

"The featherfall spell," Dalamar guessed, looking at Jenna. "I noticed you were reading up on it, last night."

"Yes. I read it three times—one for each mule. I myself will fly across." She looked at Coryn. "I trust you can find your own way down."

"All right." The girl frowned. During the past few days she had seen many ravines and gullies that she could have followed, carefully, down into the canyon—though no track that would have allowed the mules to descend.

"But how will we get the mules up the other side?" she had to ask, even though Jenna was intent on rummaging in Dora's pack.

"Levitation, I suspect," said the dark elf, winking at Coryn even as he addressed the Red Robe. "No doubt you read *that* spell three times, as well."

"Four." Jenna replied as she pulled a small pouch out of the saddlebag. She opened it to extract several small fluffs of down feathers. "The girl can climb down, certainly, but I am not as confident that she can find her way back up again . . . without a little assistance."

Coryn turned away to hide her irritation. She was getting tired of being "the girl" while these two talked over her head. Maybe she *should* tell the Red Robe that she knew how to use a magic spell or two!

"How are *you* getting across?" Coryn asked Dalamar.

The elf smiled his very handsome smile, but there was a hint of sadness in the expression. "Since I lack the resources of my crimson colleague, I shall climb down, just as you. Levitation, however, is one of the few spells in my paltry collection, so perhaps you and I can float upward together.

"I'd like that," Coryn said. She had learned through eavesdropping that Dalamar, while a powerful wizard in his own right, was seriously hampered, because he possessed only a very small spell book, one that an old friend had given him in an act of what the elf had described as "pity." Jenna tended to lord it over him, and though the elf took pains to conceal his deep frustration, she sensed that he was resentful. Jenna was very private and secretive regarding her personal magical trove—all of which was stored in Dora's saddlebags. She wasn't being very fair to the elf, Cory thought, especially since they were clearly very old friends.

Jenna was holding one of the mules—Diva—by its ear. The Red Robe said a word of magic and released a tuft of feathers over the animal's withers; Cory felt a tingle on her scalp and sensed that the enchantress had just cast the first featherfall spell.

Jenna was starting toward a second mule when Coryn asked her a question. "The levitate spell will cause the mules to float upward, right?"

"That's correct," said the woman cautiously.

"And featherfall—I guess, to judge from the name—will allow them to fall down to the bottom gently, without hurting themselves."

"Yes."

"But it will still be terribly frightening, won't it? For the mules? I mean, when we push them off the cliff, they'll buck and kick and just generally panic."

"It can't be helped," the Red Robe said with a shrug. "They won't be hurt, if that's what you're worried about."

"Maybe there's a better way. Why not tether the mules to our rope, and have two of us carry the rope across. Climb down and up again if we have to. But keep one end of the rope here, and get the other over there with two of us to pull. Then you can levitate the mules right here and we can tug them across—there's no need for them to go all the way down to the bottom of the canyon."

"Hmm. I think it's a good idea!" Dalamar said, clearly impressed. Cory was inordinately proud of his reaction, and she looked to Jenna.

The woman frowned thoughtfully and nodded. "Yes, all right. That should work. I agree, it's a better idea than mine—and it saves the casting of three spells. Though I daresay the mules might also panic to find themselves floating above a two-hundred-foot fall."

"It shouldn't take long to pull them across," said the girl.

A half hour later, Coryn was holding tightly to Dalamar's hand as Jenna cast a levitate spell upon her. She was unable to suppress a cry of delight as the ground dropped away below her feet. Looking down at the mules, at Jenna, she kicked her feet and whooped, utterly unafraid. She was flying!

Well, floating, if she wanted to be strictly accurate. After casting her spell of levitation on the girl, Jenna cast her spell of flying upon Dalamar. Coryn paid careful attention to the words and gestures used by the older woman, committing them to memory so she could repeat them, if necessary.

Coryn had the end of their long coil of rope securely wrapped around her right wrist and hand, with the left clenched in Dalamar's strong grip. Willing herself upward, Coryn drifted farther above the ground, pulling the elf along as she rose as high as the treetops. Dora, Dolly, and Diva stared at the strange sight with ears raised in alarm. Simply by thinking about it, Coryn floated back down to hover just a few feet above the goggle-eyed mules.

But when she tried to move to the side, or float backward, she learned that the magic gave her no such flexibility. The levitate spell was limited, as its name suggested, to transporting her up and down.

Dalamar, with his greater experience in magical matters, would propel them across the canyon. With a slight shift of posture he now angled away from Jenna, and Coryn felt herself pulled behind—even a little dizzy as they whisked away from the canyon rim, hovering over a sheer drop of two hundred feet. But she was not afraid—she *knew* she wasn't going to fall. She felt an exhilarating sense of freedom, and at the same time perfectly secure. The beauty of the view took her breath away, and she wanted to soar up and up!

"Can't we go higher?" she asked.

Dalamar smiled, squeezing her hand reassuringly. "Sometime we will—but for now"—he glanced over at Jenna, who was watching them intently—"I think we'd better stick to business."

All too soon they neared the far rim of the canyon. Dalamar finally released her hand, and she settled gently to the ground, still holding the length of rope that Jenna had been gradually paying out.

"I like that!" she declared, grinning.

"And you were paying close attention, weren't you?" Dalamar asked breezily, "when Jenna spoke the spells."

Coryn flushed. "Well, yes. Of course. Why shouldn't I?"

"Oh," the elf said with an easy smile. "I think you *should*. Now, let's see about pulling those mules over here."

Already the three beasts of burden were braying and kicking as Jenna's spell lifted them gently off the ground. Tugging hard on the rope, Coryn and Dalamar started to pull them across while Jenna took a drink from a small bottle and, moments later, took to the air with her own spell of flight.

The white moon rose, clear as a beacon through the intertwined branches of the trees. The moon was only half full, but it was as bright and beautiful as any that Coryn had ever seen. She had been sleeping, but when she opened her eyes and saw that gleaming semicircle, she sat up, her tiredness forgotten. Memories of her brief flight earlier today still thrilled her. And Jenna had actually been pleasant to her at dinner, engaging her in conversation instead of simply reading or talking quietly with Dalamar.

The fire had faded, though orange embers still gleamed here and there in a mountain of ash. The spring night was unseasonably warm, and she had no qualms about climbing out of her bedroll and walking away from the fire, the mules, and her two sleeping companions. The woods were quiet and peaceful, smelling of sweet pine, the stillness broken only by the rustle of an occasional small creature moving across the dry needles on the ground.

She made her way back to the rim of the canyon, through a fringe of pine forest. As she walked out onto the precipice— a smooth slab of stone extending beyond the shadows of the trees—she experienced the full glory of the moon. It was big, nearly as large as the moon of her childhood, and though less than three quarters full, it still cast Cory's surroundings in stark relief. She gazed at the beautiful moon and the starry sky in awe, thinking of Jenna's levitate spell, and momentarily tempted to try it on herself.

"Beautiful, isn't it?"

She gasped and spun around, relieved—pleased—to see Dalamar emerge from the trees. His hood was pulled back, and in the moonlight his face looked pure, almost godlike. "Y-yes. Yes, it is," she agreed.

He was standing very close to her, and she liked that. A little giddy, she turned her back to him and looked back out over the view, dry and still, with bright highlights broken by very murky shadows in the ravines and gullies, all the lower places where the moonlight could not penetrate.

"Nuitari is full tonight," said the elf. "Can you feel him?"

Coryn thought a moment, looking at the vault of the sky. There was a void there, well past its zenith now, and she did sense the invisible presence of the black moon.

"Yes—there, in the west, setting now." She looked to the east, saw the glow of red light beyond the horizon. "And here comes Lunitari, just rising." Earlier in their trek she had learned the names of the moons from Dalamar, and they sounded meaningful and powerful, rolling off her tongue.

"Do you sense the cycles, yet?" he asked.

She thought for a moment. "Nuitari has the shortest, that much I can tell. It seems that Lunitari takes longer, nearly a full month, and Solinari cycles once per month, like the false moon of my childhood."

"Very perceptive. Yes, Nuitari cycles in about eight days. And what does that tell you about the next full moon?"

Coryn did some quick calculations. "Why, Solinari and Nuitari will be full at almost the same time. And Lunitari—I can't tell for sure—will be close."

"Actually, the red moon will be full, too. Eight nights from now, all Krynn will behold the Night of the Eye. It is a fabled time of high magic—of profound power for the wizards of the three moons."

"I can imagine!" Cory declared, almost breathless at the thought. Three full moons on one night! She sighed, taking in the splendor of the scene, marveling at the things she had yet to learn.

Dalamar placed a hand on her shoulder, a hand that felt very warm, understanding . . . simply wonderful. She welcomed his presence as he took a step forward, welcomed the warmth, the soothing smell, of his soft black robe, and she allowed herself to lean back against him. She felt very grown-up tonight.

They stood in silence for several minutes, watching the moon and the rugged landscape. Dalamar finally spoke.

"There are not many people who can do what you do, you know."

Coryn was startled, simultaneously pleased and puzzled. It sounded like a compliment, but she wasn't entirely sure of his meaning. "What is it that I can do?"

"It seems to me as though you listen very carefully when you hear a magic spell cast. And then you are able to repeat the words yourself. Not just say the words, but *cast* the spell! I have seen you do that with the magic missile, and I suspect you were doing that with the light spell, also. Without study, reading, training. I don't know anyone who has ever done that."

"Oh, really? Huh! I guess I've always known I was a little different. As a child I could work magic with water, with wood—"

"That was not true magic!" Dalamar interjected, with startling intensity. He turned her around so that he could look at her, his hands on both of her shoulders. Her own palms were against his chest, but she wasn't pushing him away. His eyes burned with something that she didn't understand, and she wanted desperately to understand. But her attention was already drifting. He was so close . . . so warm. His robe surrounded her with comfortable smells, like spices and a pleasant kind of sweat.

"That was sorcery, wild magic," he explained. "A feeble balm, perhaps, while the moon-gods were gone from the world. I even dabbled in it a bit myself, to fill the time. But you should know that it is a poor relation, weak and corrupt by comparison to the immortal gifts bestowed by Nuitari and his cousins! I have cast it aside, forever, and you should do so, too."

"You're right—I'm sure you're right. I know I should. I guess I've been fortunate. My grandmother had a small spell book, and I read it after the Night of Two Moons. I found I could understand the words!"

"Remarkable. And still . . . Jenna doesn't know?" Dalamar asked, shrugging as if the answer meant little to him.

"I . . . I'm not sure." Coryn knew that she had been furtive where the Red Robe was concerned. "I guess she didn't see the pebble. And I didn't tell her about the magic missile in the bandit camp because, well, maybe because I didn't want to worry her. Didn't you give me that advice?"

That sounded foolish even as she said it, though Dalamar nodded calmly. In fact, she had been *hiding* her skill from Jenna, for reasons she didn't exactly understand. "I'm sorry—I guess it wasn't very forthright of me."

"Perhaps not," the dark elf said with a smile. "But it was smart. It is best to keep some secrets, when it comes to magic. Jenna is also smart, and she's very wise. But her goals are her own, and she is determined to achieve them. If she thought she could achieve them by sacrificing you, she would."

"No—she wouldn't do that!" Cory argued. "What do I have to do with her goals?"

"You don't know the history of the Red Robes," Dalamar said, not unkindly. "They are ever seeking to serve their own ends. I can't blame her, not very much, anyway. She's the last of her order, and she is desperate to continue that legacy. I suspect she intends to make you her protégé, the next Mistress of the Red Robe."

"What!?" Coryn looked flabbergasted, but she was quick with another question. "And what are the Black Robes striving for? What do *you* want?"

"A fair question. The Black Robes strive to further the glories of magic for our brethren, and for posterity. As for what *I* want. . . ." He leaned in, his face very close to hers, just a little above. There was a different kind of light in his eyes, now, a very warm and appealing brightness.

Coryn held her breath as his lips closed in, touching hers. She felt a fluttering in her belly as she pressed close to him, relishing his kiss. Her arms were suddenly around him, his chest broad and powerful against hers, and she more than equaled his passion with her returning embrace. She pulled him close, still breathless, and felt that warmth turn to genuine heat.

Abruptly, then, he pulled away from her, roughly breaking the embrace, and in the moonlight the expression of anger that flashed across his face chilled Coryn. He was furious—looking past her, furious with another. The girl gasped and stepped back as Jenna's voice lashed out of the darkness.

"I expected better of you—much better!" she snapped. It was she who had spun Dalamar around. Now she faced her rival, her tone like ice.

Dalamar smiled, almost a smirk. Coryn did not think it was a very attractive expression, nor did she like the vicious tone of his words.

"Haven't you waited a little too long to turn into a prude?" he asked.

Jenna spun to glare at Coryn, her jaw set, the sparks blazing in her eyes. "You silly twit! Did you let him charm you with Black Robe lies?" She turned back to Dalamar, her fury rising. Then she snapped out the command word to another magic spell, one that the girl had heard before.

It was the cone of silence. Once again Jenna was shouting at Dalamar, just a few steps away from her, but Coryn couldn't hear a word she said.

CHAPTER
13

CALL OF THE WOODS

Coryn's emotions churned between embarrassment, humiliation, and anger. She was mortified that Jenna discovered them, had interrupted her and Dalamar at such a precious moment. And she was appalled at the transformation in the dark elf as he turned to acidly confront the Red Robe.

Had he "charmed" her, as Jenna accused? She was certain he hadn't used magic, but had she been manipulated by his charm? Perhaps she had been foolish—but was she a "silly twit?" Those words still stung, as if they were echoing back and forth through the canyon, now and for the rest of the night. Coryn looked at the two wizards, ensconced under the cone of silence, their angry faces only a few inches apart. They gestured furiously, with mutually contemptuous expressions. Neither so much as glanced her way.

Of course they were talking about Coryn, so why shouldn't she at least be entitled to know what was going on? The answer: she *was* entitled to know. And how to find out was obvious; she already had the idea.

She turned the word for the cone of silence spell over and over on her tongue, felt the harshness at the beginning and the smooth, sibilant conclusion of its enunciation. She tried it back and forth, then discovered a breaking point, a place in the middle of the sound where the purpose of the spell was emphatically declared with a sharp, uprising "ee." Working from that, she shifted the shape of the vowel in her mouth, dropping it through deepening tones until she was at the bass end of the spectrum, making an "oo."

Then Coryn pronounced the spell—the cone of silence— staring at Jenna and Dalamar as she completed the word, then feeling the giddy rush of magic as it slipped away from her, and insinuated itself amidst Jenna's spell.

"—a slip of a girl, by the moons' sake!" the Red Robe was hotly declaring. "She's barely out of childhood! Were you so impatient that you couldn't wait until we reach a town where you could buy yourself a whore?"

Shocked at Jenna's words, Coryn felt her jaw clench with anger. A forceful denial rose within her throat, but with effort she quickly bit it back, remembering that Jenna didn't know she had penetrated the cone of silence. Instead, she turned pointedly away, even walked a few steps along the cavern rim. Her knees trembled and she wanted to scream. Instead, she kept listening.

"I was just having a little fun with the 'servant' girl," Dalamar said, his tone coldly mocking.

Now Coryn felt as though she had been struck squarely between the shoulder blades. She was afraid she would give her emotions away, she trembled so; she walked a little farther away, losing herself in the shadows beneath a huge pine. Her arms wrapped around her chest—now the night seemed cold—as she turned around and watched the two wizards argue.

Dalamar continued to speak in his cold, mocking tones. "She's rather pretty for a human, after all. I meant nothing serious, simply a little diversion. No harm was intended, nor done. Jenna, I should think a woman of your, um, appetites would certainly understand!"

Jenna hissed back in fury. "I never knew you to turn your head for just a pretty face—especially one so youthful! No, there's more to it than that—you want something from her! I know!"

The elf shrugged. "Maybe I've changed, and you can't recognize that. Elves don't age in the same way as you humans. Sad, they say humans inevitably forget their youthful passions as they wither and gray."

"Bastard!" Jenna shot back, as the elf went on, his voice darkening.

"I was in a very cold, very barren place for too long. Now I am alive again—and what makes a man feel more alive than a woman's embrace?"

"She's a mere girl!"

"Maybe, maybe not. Perhaps you underestimate her—I certainly felt her kissing me back. It was not as though she seemed reluctant. That is no child, Jenna! Besides, you continue to insult me. Anyone can see that she's no more a servant than I am a Knight of Solamnia. There are quite a few things that you are keeping from me, and I think you're keeping them from her, as well."

"I keep my own counsel," Jenna declared.

"Such secrets are at cross purposes with our quest! How are we going to find the Tower of Sorcery if we don't trust each other and work together? It's time you stopped pretending," the dark elf said. "Tell me, why did this 'mere girl' come to you? Did you really know her grandmother?"

Coryn took a step forward, taking care to remain in the shadows. She willed her heart to cease pounding, anxious to hear what the woman would answer.

Jenna drew a sharp breath then lowered her voice. "Yes. I sent a letter to her grandmother, right after the gods returned.

Actually, I sent dozens of letters, to people all across Ansalon. But Scharon was one of the few to reply, and to understand the situation."

"You were seeking wizards, new apprentices for your order?"

"Not really. I was seeking older wizards, those who might still be alive after all this time. And not just *my* order—any of the orders, even the black! Scharon was once a White Robe, if that makes any difference to you. Just a young apprentice at the time of the Chaos War, though she showed some promise. When the gods disappeared, she left the Tower and went back home."

"And in response to your letter, she sent her granddaughter?"

"Yes. She thought Coryn might take the Test, someday. And that I might help her prepare. But that is all premature. I simply brought her along to help with the mules! We can't even locate the forest, much less find any sign of the Tower! Until we do, I don't want to encourage the girl to do any magic. I must get to know her better. I need to find the Tower, first, to obtain the counsel of the Master. Then I will decide about her."

Coryn waited for Dalamar to spring to her defense, to tell Jenna that she *was* ready, that she could learn spells, could absorb them in ways that Jenna didn't even suspect. Instead, he seemed to *agree* with her.

"As you wish. Your secret is safe," Dalamar said. "She doesn't seem to know anything about magic anyway; nothing about the orders or the three robes. I have no wish to dispel her ignorance." He glanced over at Coryn, and she felt as though his eyes penetrated right into the thick shadow before he turned back to Jenna. "Besides, I was already bored with her when you appeared out of nowhere to cause a scene. She is, as you say, just a girl."

Cory didn't want to hear any more. The two wizards resumed their conversation, but Coryn was already making her way back through the woods, toward the dying fire in the middle of the cold forest.

———◆———

The moon was gone by the time Coryn got up again, though it was not yet dawn. Cool mists penetrated the trees, raising enough of a fog to limit visibility to a few feet. Jenna and Dalamar were now sound asleep, wrapped in their bedrolls on either side of the now-cold fire pit. First the girl cast the cone of silence spell over herself; then she rummaged through Diva's saddlebag, taking her bow and arrows and her small knapsack. She wondered if she should take anything else—after all, she felt as though she had earned some remuneration for all of her labor on Jenna's behalf. She was tempted by those spell books . . . but no, she was not a thief—and besides, there was nothing the Red Robe possessed that she needed.

She slipped into the woods, moving quickly, the sounds of her urgent passage swallowed by the cone of silence that moved along with her. Daylight started seeping through the murk about an hour later. And by then Coryn was more than two miles away, still moving with youthful speed. Much of her route had followed the stony rim of the canyon, where she would leave no tracks. She didn't know where she was going, but she knew she didn't want to be followed. Not by those two . . . not by anybody!

In daylight, the forest was pleasant. The path at her feet was wide, smooth, and clear of debris, winding through a bed of soft grass; broad birch trunks, alabaster white, jutted up from the ground. The canyon lay behind her now, as she moved steadily away from the precipitous rim. She followed a game trail that avoided the densest trunks of the woods, and it was nearly midday by the time she realized that she was getting hungry. Why hadn't she thought to take some of Jenna's food?

Because it would have been stealing, she reproached herself sternly. "But I don't *need* your food; I don't need anything!" Coryn whispered to herself, as if afraid that the Red Robe could hear her thoughts.

She came to a ravine across her path, and shimmied down a rotting tree trunk toward the bottom, crying out as she scraped her leg on a stub of a broken branch. Her eyes swam with tears as she cleaned the cut and wrapped a thin piece of cloth torn from her increasingly tattered shirt around the wound. She found an easier way out the other side of the ravine and limped slightly as she proceeded on the trail.

Still, she was making good time, and her long trek on the dry stone of the canyon rim would make it difficult for her former companions to pursue her. When she thought about the way they had talked about her, it made her so mad she felt like weeping. But she wouldn't let herself do that.

Coryn dropped to her knees to crawl under another large birch deadfall, wincing as her cut leg scraped along the ground. Climbing to her feet on the far side, she patted her hip, making sure that her quiver of arrows was safe. It was then that she noticed the sudden darkness of the forest floor in front of her, the closeness of the looming evergreens.

Indeed, she faced a newly darkened and murky expanse. The pines were so thick here they prevented any sun from penetrating, and the dense brush all across the ground was wet with dew. It would take only moments for Coryn's moccasins to be soaked; her leggings felt damp and chill all the way up to her thighs, and she didn't relish the discomfort.

Moss dangled limply from many of the low branches, and she did a double-take as she glimpsed one beardlike bloom—

she could have sworn that someone was watching her from behind impenetrable whiskers. But it was only the natural vegetation, thick and cloaking on all sides. She listened carefully for a long time, but heard nothing that indicated any person, or any other kind of animal, moving through the woods. Even the birds had fallen silent, however, and that realization made her feel very much alone.

Where were the birches, the open, grassy woodland? Coryn didn't remember the forest changing, but the transition was sudden, absolute. She looked behind, saw the birches and grassy terrain extending behind her as far as she could see. Should she go back and try another way? Could she even find her way back?

The thought was a little unsettling. Even more unsettling, however, was the clear memory of crawling under that big, dead birch. She had just stood up, a moment earlier, after making that tight squeeze, but when she looked back, now, that deadfall was nowhere to be seen.

The wood was changing before her very eyes. A shiver passed down her spine. She spun through a quick circle. She couldn't see any sign of danger—but all the same, this wood was darker, more ancient than before. She stood upon a wide trail, but couldn't see as far as a few steps away, where the path vanished around the bole of a massive, gnarled oak. Hesitantly, and limping slightly, she walked around that huge, white-bark tree, and found that the path continued, wide and smooth, before her. Yet there were shadows on every side of the path, and she sensed that *things* lurked in the shadows. She heard a noise and ducked, looking behind her. But she saw nothing except the oppressive, cloaking forest.

It was then that she noticed the birds; they were now crying strange sounds, raucous and strangely compelling. She sought to find the birds in the branches, but they remained just out of sight. A dark shadow flashed in the distance, and another whisked around the trunk of a knotty tree, but she couldn't be sure if they were mere shadows. Still, the sounds came so close, so clear, she expected to spot the feathered denizens around each bend of the path. Instead they seemed to flit ahead just enough to keep out of sight.

The cries of the birds then took on a note of urgency, and as Coryn pushed herself along, she heard the cacophony ebb and flow together, forming a melody that was repeated over and over. She chuckled wryly, imagining she heard *words* in the birdsong. No doubt the solitude was getting to her!

And then she froze, listening.

"Come, girl of the white moon. . . . Come, we will be there soon. . . . Come through the woods. . . . Come along the trail. . . . Come with us. . . . Come to your future, and your life."

She found herself unafraid, walking again, though she wasn't aware of consciously moving her feet. It was more like the pathway was gliding beneath her, as she effortlessly progressed. The song was seductive, and she felt a sense of wondrous curiosity—she just *had* to see those birds.

A bend in the trail, the pines and oaks parting with almost visible movement . . . and the vista opened to reveal a small clearing, and an astonishing sight: a lofty, double-spired structure. As she stepped forward, the birdsong ceased, and she advanced into the meadow with a sense of awe.

She knew instinctively that she had found the Tower of High Sorcery—the place that Jenna and Dalamar had been circling around without success. Then this ancient woodland must be fabled Wayreth Forest! The Tower itself was so tall that she had to crane her neck just to see the tops of the two main spires. She counted innumerable parapets and lesser platforms, some carved right into the Tower's smooth, stone walls, others suspended out from the main structure by a spiderweb of cantilevers and elegant, narrow walkways.

Only gradually did she sense something intangible about this tower. It was beautiful, lofty, and graceful . . . but more than that, it was suffering. There was no visible movement, yet she could sense tremors within the immobile shape. There was no wetness on the outer walls, yet she could discern tears along its marble facade. She didn't know how a building could feel, much less express, pain, but she knew that this structure was experiencing an awful agony.

For the first time since leaving Two Forks, Coryn was truly afraid. She quivered like a frightened doe, wanting nothing more than to turn and flee.

But she could not. She had embarked from home at Umma's command, and then had followed Jenna's orders uncomplainingly. Now she was on her own, and it seemed as though her destiny was here—as if she had been brought to the tower by some strange force.

She was startled by that thought: Could it be that the Tower had called to Coryn?

Starting forward, she noticed for the first time that the base of the Tower was enclosed by a long, plain wall. A single gate stood just before her, a shimmering structure of wiry-thin bands of bright metal; that gate swung soundlessly open as she passed through. The gauzy material was more like a spiderweb than any construct of metal. It was still glowing, and she made no move to touch those gossamer strands as she passed through the gate and found herself upon a broad courtyard paved with smooth, gray stones.

Now she could see that the bases of the two great spires were connected by a squat foretower, a smaller structure that melded the two halves into one sprawling building. There was a single door in the base of that foretower, and she approached it, noting without surprise that it swung soundlessly open when she was still twenty paces away. Without hesitation, she came up to the very shadow of the great spire and stepped inside.

Immediately an aura of warm welcome surrounded Coryn. The greeting was tangible in the aroma of fresh bread and the array of bright flowers in vases around the entry hall. She identified fleabane and columbine, daisies and willowbloom, and saw a host of unfamiliar blossoms. Some of these were huge and hooded, like cowls of deep indigo, purest white, and blood red, while others seemed to explode in bursts of yellow, orange, or purple petals. The light was subdued in the large, circular hall, but gathered into clusters of brightness around each arrangement, as if the air around the flowers breathed some enchanted illumination.

She found herself following her nose, and the scent of the bread, through an open, arched doorway. This room was rectangular, dominated by a long table large enough to seat a score of diners. One place setting lay pristine at the near end, plates and goblets shimmering like clear ice, utensils to either side—a multitude of forks, knives, and spoons, beyond anything Coryn had ever imagined. Just beyond the plates and goblets, still within easy reach, several silver domes formed a semicircle of small metallic hills.

And there was the loaf of bread, steaming on a board with a sharp knife beside it, and the bright yellow butter in one of those icelike bowls. It looked safe—and familiar—enough. She wasted no time in seating herself, sawing off a thick piece of bread, and layering on the sweet spread. The butter was melting by the time she took her first exquisite bite. She forced herself to savor the bread when every instinct told her to wolf it down, and by the time she had finished that first slice, her worst hunger pangs were past.

More slowly, she worked on a second piece, while looking around with an attentive eye. She lifted one of the silver dish covers by its ornate pearl handle and was delighted to discover a trout, grilled to perfection and presented on a bed of fresh greens. Another uncovering revealed fruit, sliced and chilled and arrayed in concentric rings of color; a third protected some steaming white grains—white rice, but rice of a purity and plumpness far beyond any of the tiny, nutty grains her people gathered from the summer bogs.

She ate, alternately sampling the fish, the rice, and the fruit. The tastes were so splendid that she could think of nothing else than the wonderful sensations in her mouth—until a terribly obvious question occurred to her.

Who had prepared this food for her?

For Coryn had no doubt she was the intended guest for this magnificent repast—since her first glimpse of the Tower, she knew she was supposed to be here, that the Tower *wanted* her to enter. Logically speaking, it was the Tower that had presented her with this meal, then. But how?

"Welcome."

She was so startled that she dropped her spoon with a clatter. "Who said that?" she asked, whirling around in her chair. A sad old man limped into the room, leaning heavily on a rickety cane. He had white hair, a beard of the same color, and a robe of such pure whiteness that she almost had to squint.

"It is I who offer you this food . . . and I who invited you. I am the Master of the Tower."

CHAPTER 14

A COSMOS UNBALANCED

Storms boiled and churned through the ether, spanning the void between worlds, swelling in the gaps among all the planes. Clouds of black billowed beyond all horizons, looming vast and dark and deadly. Immortal anger rumbled through all existence, fueled by the undying rivalry, the distrust, and the suspicion that ever marked the three colors of magic. Nuitari and Lunitari fumed and seethed, roared and spouted, and their fury coalesced in a storm that their alabaster cousin was forced to acknowledge and confront.

The three gods of magic met in the heart of the storm. They were the undisputed masters of the cosmic tumult, poised in balance atop the raging, seething force of the gale. Red lightning flashed and crackled, casting brilliant, flashing illumination across the trio of immortal visages. White light churned from a new sun, driving back the chill of the vast emptiness. And perfect blackness framed them all, a void that gave proof to their vitality.

"Foul!" cried Nuitari of the black moon, a gust of pure midnight blasting toward Solinari, surrounding him, welling up until it all but obscured him from their sight. "You betrayed our compact!"

"Betrayal!" boiled Lunitari the red. Red tongues of fire flared, embracing the white god, driving like blazing knives and swords against his immortal flesh. "Our trust is violated—our alliance imperiled."

The red and black violence surged, rising higher, surrounding them all, extending tendrils of destruction far beyond, into all the corners of creation. Other, lesser gods recoiled from the conflict, and those mortals who beheld the strife—they did so in their dreams, if at all—trembled and quaked, praying only for the daylight to come and soothe their fears.

"But for what cause is this most unjust protest?" asked Solinari calmly, his corona of white shielding him, for now, from the wrath of his fellows. "There has been no betrayal, no foul on my part. As ever, I seek to mend relations, to soothe the path of cooperation and friendship. Nay, if at all, these traits you accuse me of are hallmarks more of your own behavior."

His tone was reasonable, his mystification apparent, but even so, his cousins disdained his words, roaring closer in fury and vengeance.

"The girl who wears no robe has gone to the Tower alone! She meets with the Master, even as we speak!" cried Lunitari, her tone shrill. "While my devoted servant strives to find Wayreth, the Master comes to this child disguised as Par-Salian of the White Robe—what more proof do we need? You have tried to steal a march upon us, to maneuver the world into alignment with your favorite!"

"Not I!" cried Solinari, white beard quivering with indignation, raising his hands. "Cease these unfounded attacks! Lay back the furious tempest and let us talk about this calmly, with the dignity that befits our status."

"You deny it, then?" asked Nuitari viciously. "You claim the girl has not entered the sacred place, alone? I know that my own dark elf has, like the Red Robe, been thwarted in his great quest. Do you still claim that you have not given her the access that has been barred to both of our wizards? How can you make such a claim, when we can all see the proof through the lens of the Tower?"

"Well, of course she has arrived in the Tower of High Sorcery—have we not all observed that fact, through the eyes of the Master? And is this not proof that the Master of the Tower serves us all? I will have no further talk of treachery and betrayal—why, the very idea!"

The white god, his immortal reputation assailed, effected a tone of high dudgeon. Pure light pulsed in the midst of the storm, and thus the black clouds and the crimson lightning, eased back slightly. The corona rose higher above the dangerous storms, bright light striving for release.

But immortal rage still glowered and grumbled. The thunderheads of cosmic distress reared anew, and the brightness flickered and was muffled.

"Bah," Nuitari retorted. "Your servant has gone in before my own agent, or our cousin's. How is this not treachery? We both know what kind of advantage she seeks—she will infiltrate the Conclave, holding the other robes at bay. This is a betrayal that overrules anything that has happened in our immortal past! It is a treachery that cannot be allowed to stand!"

"It is not treachery, not betrayal, for a very simple reason. Because," Solinari continued, with an elaborate air of patience, as if he were lecturing stubborn and unruly children, "the girl does not wear the white robe. As you yourself stated, Fair Cousin—she is a girl of no robe, at the present."

"So she wears no robe at all, now, at the present? This matters not," cried Lunitari, "for she is your foil, your tool!"

"Your statement is proof of its own falseness. How can she be my tool, when she does not wear my robe?"

"She lacks but the Test, and you are arranging it so that she will soon have that chance. Do you deny that you seek to give her the white robe?"

Solinari shrugged his cosmic shoulders. "Of course not. But do either of you deny that you do not seek the same, with your own chosen colors?"

"I have my agent of red," Lunitari dismissed. "She has served me well and kept the faith of my creed even when the Dark Queen stole our world away. Now she seeks to spread the cause of magic around the world. I am well satisfied."

"As am I, with the dark elf who serves my own faction," Nuitari noted. His stormy visage darkened. "Though he labors from a position of weakness, since you both laid such a harsh condition on his return from the dead. Yet he is wily, and powerful in the ways of magic. He will remain my champion. As you well know!"

"Ah, but he *did* return from the land of the dead, did he not? And he does indeed seem to be on the way toward a restoration of his prominence." Solinari blew a cloud of steam, a billowing construct of cumulous that reflected the redness of Lunitari and brightened the aspects of them all.

"Besides, when have either of you, or any of us, been satisfied with that? If she is granted the Test, you will surely seek to steer her toward the color you wish her to wear. Is that not true?"

"We may steer, influence, guide. But her soul is free, and her soul leans toward the white," argued the black moon god.

"That much is clear. Furthermore, for the full Conclave to gather, we need wizards of all three robes. It is in our own interests to see that one wears the white," accused Lunitari.

"Then how may I be accused of treachery, if this serves the ends of us all?" inquired Solinari, with a great air of innocence.

"Enough of these word games!" spat Nuitari. "We concede, the girl must take the Test—and, as always, the Test will choose the robe. But we see your alabaster hand in this, Elder Cousin. And we demand satisfaction!"

"Satisfaction? In what way?"

"We will overlook the treachery that brought her alone to the Tower, leaving our wizards lost in the woods. But when she takes the Test, and earns her reward, let that reward be a gift that will serve all three robes."

"Hmm. Very well," Solinari agreed, easily. "That is only a fair condition. Should she succeed, she will be blessed with a boon for each of the orders. But let this be the result, no matter what the color of her robe."

And so it was that the gods of magic agreed.

———◆◇◆———

Finally the Master felt as though he could breathe again, as if a monstrous weight had been lifted from his chest. The human body was a remarkable vessel, and he never felt so alive as he did when he wore the flesh of man. But a cloak of flesh was a rare treat and had been so ever since his gods had been stolen away. There had been a glimmer of hope when the moons again appeared in the sky, until the Master's domain had fallen under the corrupting influence of the two sorcerers. The very stone of the Tower, his eternal body, continued to suffer and complain under their relentless tortures.

Then had come the arrival, like a blessing from the gods, of this mysterious girl. It was this that gave him hope, allowed him again to feel vital. There was new promise in her bright eyes and fresh skin, new hope in the vibrant power that he sensed lay untapped within her.

He would make her welcome and hope that she could help him. The food had been an easy first offering—just by looking at her, he could sense her gnawing hunger. Now he needed to talk to her, to learn, and to teach.

For this initial encounter he had chosen the guise of one of his favorites. He appeared as old Par-Salian, white-bearded and avuncular. He thought this shape would be less inclined to frighten the girl, than would the images of, say, severe Justarius, or lean and ever-hungry Fistandantilus. Par-Salian was a benign presence. And, too, the Master felt the girl would treat the esteemed White Robe with the dignity that he deserved.

At first, he was not sure that his benign intentions had been perceived. The girl's initial impression had been shock, and then she seemed to be afraid. But she gazed at the repast on the table, and then at the Master, and he could tell that she was not inclined to run. She had only eaten a little before his arrival, and he sensed her hunger, saw it in the longing looks she cast toward the food.

"I hope you like the bread," he said. "It is one of the classic recipes. I conjured it just as it was baked a thousand years ago, in the ovens of Ergoth."

"It . . . it is very good," she said cautiously. As if reminding herself, she tore off another large piece and chewed it vigorously, following the bread with a large drink of cold milk. Only after she had swallowed the food did she look at him curiously. "You said you are the 'Master of the Tower.' What does that mean?" she asked.

He sighed and allowed himself the liberty of sitting at the table near her as she slowly resumed her eating.

"In a sense, I am this tower . . . the presence, the sentience of this place, such as it exists. This flesh, this body you see"—he indicated himself, the elderly man in the white robe—"is something that I choose, that I can vary."

In that very instant he changed, for her benefit. Now he wore a red robe and sat tall, a proud man with black skin and a haughty demeanor. Then he became a female, garbed in a slinky black robe, with eyes shadowed in blue henna and a mouth that curled in a demure smile. In another blink he was Par-Salian again, holding up a liver-spotted hand to calm the girl—who was staring at him in amazement.

"I am the Tower, and I am all who dwelled here, all who served as the Heads of the Conclave and all who studied under their tutelage. This tower has stood for thousands of years, and in that time there have been many who have ruled the orders of magic. Mostly humans, but some elves . . . I can select the forms of any of them. But I chose Par-Salian, for you."

"Thank you," she said. "I—I think I like this one better than some of the other shapes you might have adopted."

He chuckled dryly. "Well, thank you for humoring an old man, in any event."

"But why am I here? I was traveling with two great wizards, and I know they were seeking this tower. Why did I find it, and they did not?"

"Because you, Child, are the one—the only one—who can help me, now."

"Help you? How?"

He sighed. "There are bad men here. Men who are killing me. I invited them in because the gods commanded me to find a wizard to take the Tower. I summoned them—well, not them, but a wizard. These two came under false pretenses, bearing an artifact of potent magic, wielding it as great wizards would. But they are not wizards. They are sorcerers, wielders of wild magic. They dwell here like a cancer in my flesh, slowly taking my life."

"How can I help you?" The girl seemed mystified but— this was encouraging to the Master—bold.

"You must take the Test of Magic," said the Master.

"A test of magic? Why? How could I?"

"The Test will know you, do not worry. But you must convince them to let you live long enough to take the Test. If they kill you, then all is lost."

"I daresay!" the girl said, her eyes widening in alarm. Where are they now?"

The old man shrugged. "Elsewhere in the Tower. It is a very large place. But no doubt they will find you, soon enough."

She was courageous, this girl, but couldn't help looking around in some apprehension. "How can I fight them?"

"Oh, you can't. They are much too powerful for that. Even *I* cannot fight them—especially the tall one, with the long beard. He is most dangerous. And he bears the Irda Stone."

"The what-stone? Never mind. Tell me, why shouldn't I run away, while I still have a chance? I don't want to be killed!"

"If you leave here now, then all is lost—for me, you, and others to come. No, you must stay, and you must survive, and you must convince them to grant you the Test!"

"And if I do?"

"Then you must pass the Test!"

"What happens if I fail?"

"Well, you will die, of course. Death is ever the penalty for failing the Test—either that, or ultimate, hopeless madness. But that's not the worst part."

"Really! Just what *is* the worst part?" The girl's face had grown quite pale, though her voice was remarkably steady.

"The worst part is that, if you die here, you will doom the future of magic on Krynn."

CHAPTER 15

A SUBJECT

We should carve out her eyes—then make her be our maidservant! Imagine her, tottering around through the Tower, groping about in the kitchen, unable to see a thing! And every time she breaks a dish or spills a drink, we'll cut off a finger. Yes, that would be diverting, don't you agree?"

Kalrakin's eyes glowed as he made the suggestion, all but licking his lips. "It has been too long since we have had real flesh and blood for our pleasure!"

"Well, yes, I rather think that would amuse us momentarily," Luthar replied tentatively. "But perhaps there is a more suitable use we can put her to. She might know some secrets about this tower, after all. It is rather startling that she came here like this, is it not? Quite unanticipated!"

"Bah, look at her. It's an accident of fate. She's a callow youth! She can know nothing of wizardry!" The tall sorcerer's eyes narrowed as he glowered at his rotund companion. "Or do you have baser desires, my old friend? True, she is an attractive morsel, but I thought you had given up entanglements with female flesh? Was that not part of our mutual vow?"

"Oh, very much, my lord! No, I do not want to take her, not like that. But see how the old man is warming to her, welcoming her. He is treating her like a queen, as if he seems to think she might be important!"

"That old man talked to us, too. For a moment, in any event." Kalrakin's laugh was a harsh bark.

"Well, he would have talked longer if you hadn't, uh, dealt with him! I still don't know why you couldn't have been more patient."

The two sorcerers were in one of the high chambers of the Tower of High Sorcery. A rubble of broken glass, ash, and other debris covered the floor of the large room. The one thing left undamaged was a window, a pane of dark glass mounted on the stone wall. It was a window with no view, barely revealing the face of the wall—at least so it had appeared originally.

Luthar, however, had discovered its true nature, after some contemplation. He had stood boldly in front of the window, when Kalrakin, in his fury, would have shattered it, flinging its parts across the floor.

"Look!" the short sorcerer had all but shrieked, waving his hands, using his own body as a shield. "Don't you understand? It is a magical window—it allows you to see beyond this place! Observe, my lord!"

Kalrakin, his massive beard twitching with frustration, had paused long enough for his fellow to demonstrate.

"Show us the dining hall of the foretower!" Luthar had commanded, nervously glancing at his companion, his lord. In a flash, the image of that chamber had appeared. It first displayed the empty table where they had grown used to taking their meals, in the vast hall that had once held countless priceless artifacts, talismans of ancient magic, squirreled away in numerous alcoves. With a little further experimentation Luthar had revealed a magical portal that allowed them to view any place within the Tower of High Sorcery.

Kalrakin had immediately seized upon the magical window with delight, commanding that it reveal to them the Hall of Mages—the huge, cavernous chamber in the North Tower where the twenty-one empty seats formed a circle in the center of the room. These stood silent and empty, and the sorcerer had mocked the power of the mages who had once ruled from their vantage. He had peered into the armories, the apprentice cells, the luxurious apartments where, presumably, these once mighty wizards had dwelled.

He had quickly learned that there were limits to the scope of this magical window. There were three rooms in the Tower that remained obscure to him, despite all of his efforts. Maddeningly, the window refused to grant him even a glimpse into these sacred precincts. His impulse, naturally, had been to smash the window, but Luthar had begged him to stay his vengeful fist.

Now, two weeks later, that restraint was finally paying off. Earlier, the sorcerers had observed, from a high window, the ragged-looking girl who emerged from the wilderness of the surrounding forest. They had watched with amazement as the magical gates of the compound parted for her, had watched her approach the door until their line of sight was blocked by the low bulk of the foretower.

It was Luthar who had suggested they continue to spy on her with the aid of the magical window, and so they had come here to enjoy the show. From here they had watched her find the food on the great banquet table, saw her sit down and eat like a starving beggar. And they had gasped in surprise when the white-bearded old mage had tottered into view.

"He's the man I killed—the first day we entered this place!" Kalrakin objected indignantly. "He wore black then, but I know him!"

"Well, certainly, so it seemed that he was dead," Luthar agreed diplomatically. "But if you recall, when you pierced him with that bolt of wild magic, his body disappeared. There was no corpse. At the time, we speculated that he might have been some sort of illusion. A magical phantom, as it were."

"*You* speculated. I saw a man die! I know that I killed him!"

"Perhaps he has a twin, then. For this appears to be the same person, now speaking to the lass." Luthar bit his lip, as if afraid that his tone had crossed the realm into insolence, but his master did not seem to notice.

"Bah—this portal is useless unless I can hear their words!" cursed Kalrakin, gesturing contemptuously at the window. "I am no lip-reader!" He turned and stalked away from the window, intending to confront the old man and the young girl in the dining room below, but Luthar, jogging behind frantically, urged patience.

"I beg you—don't attack her!" Luthar cried. "At least, not right away. She may be able to tell us something important, provide information. We may even want to leave her eyes intact, at least for the time being." Boldly, Luthar reached out to tug on Kalrakin's robe, bringing the gaunt sorcerer to an immediate, angry halt.

"How dare you?" the taller man spat, spinning furiously around.

"But think!" Luthar leaned in, whispering conspiratorially. "She may be the secret, the key to opening the treasure rooms—those chambers that have remained barred to us! Perhaps the doors will yield to her for some reason."

Kalrakin scowled. His long fingers stroked the wiry hairs of his bushy beard, tugging absently at tangles and knots. Eyes narrowed, he squinted down at his companion. "Hmmm. You might be right," he acknowledged. "At least, we will see what the wench has to say."

"Thank you, my lord—it is a wise decision!"

"But as for the old white beard, he dies again—and this time I intend to see that he stays dead!"

———◆———

Coryn took a bite of fish, followed that with another slice of delicious fruit, some sort of sweet melon, she guessed, and then washed the mouthful down with a swig of icy-cold milk. She felt as though she hadn't eaten in weeks. Besides, this was the most sumptuous meal she had ever enjoyed, and she was determined to take advantage of it, murderous sorcerers or not.

"Tell me more about this Test," she said, after another swallow, turning to query the white-bearded Master of the Tower. "Hey, where did you go?" she gasped, startled to see that she was, once again, alone in the large banquet hall. She was even more startled when a new voice, raspier and harsher than the Master's, came from behind her.

"He fled; he fears me, and with good reason."

She whirled to see a tall, forbiddingly whiskered person, standing in the doorway through which she had entered. He wore a tattered gray robe, the same nondescript color of his hair, whose eyes were the eyes of a madman, wild and staring and very frightening.

"What do you mean?" she asked, chilled by this newcomer's sudden appearance, and by the realization that he had seemed to be reading her thoughts.

"I killed him once, when I first arrived here. And I would have done it again if he had but waited for my entrance."

"Who are you?" she demanded as the man advanced into the dining room. His face was gaunt behind the massive effusion of his beard, and those crazed eyes were sunk into deep sockets, like wells in the face of his skull. From within those caves, his eyes sparked and glittered, fastening on Coryn's face with an almost physical intensity. She had never seen such a tall person, nor one so frightening. His hands twitched with nervous energy, and she saw that he was passing a white, smooth stone back and forth from hand to hand. She remembered the Master's words—the warning that there was an evil being in the Tower—and did not doubt that this was the evil.

He raised a long, slender finger, wagging it toward her. The pearly gem was tucked into the palm of this hand, and she saw that it glowed with a pale, sickly brightness.

"You are the traveler, come seeking sustenance and shelter." His tone was stern, rebuking. "You break in, stealing my food—"

I did *not* break in! she thought, then immediately did her best to control her thoughts. There was something edgy, unpredictable, about his man, and she did not want to agitate him any more than she had already. He loomed over her, glaring down, and she sensed a coiled violence, an evil barely restrained. "I did not mean any offense," she said calmly.

"And you dare to ask my name? Insolent child! It is I who should be asking for a name, a purpose," he continued. "Who are you?"

For the first time, Coryn noticed a second man, shorter than the first, short-bearded and rotund, looking at her almost apologetically as he slunk into the room behind the first. Remembering the words of the Master, describing one sorcerer who was far more dangerous than his companion, she had no trouble determining which was which. She faced her interrogator with her head held high—it was the only way she could look up into his unsettling eyes—and made her own tone as solemn as she could.

"My name is Coryn Brinefolk. I come from the Icereach,

the village of Two Forks. And I did not come seeking shelter—I was *invited* in. The door opened to admit me."

"I know of thieves who have been hung for less blatant infractions," said the man dourly. He took another step closer, allowed his eyes to sweep over the array of foods on the table. Coryn felt a stab of protective jealousy—it was her food!—but he made no move to reach for a morsel. Instead he looked at her as if she were just another item on the buffet.

The young woman fought her fear. This tall, lanky person menaced her in a way she had never felt before, not even in the midst of Samuval's bandits. A small, cowardly voice in the back of her mind urged her to turn and run, right through the anteroom and out the front door, never looking back.

She clenched her jaw, stifling that voice and stiffening her resolve. It wasn't just for herself that she was going to stay—she could feel an emanation, almost a plea, arising from the walls and the floor around her. She remembered the suffering and pain she had sensed within the Tower, which had been affirmed by the Master. She knew that this man, this interloper, was the enemy of the Tower. She was *needed* here.

"How did you get here?" asked the second man. "Oh, pardon me," he added hastily. "We don't get many visitors. Any, in point of truth. But our manners, I'm afraid, have lapsed. My name is Luthar, and my master, here, is Kalrakin. Perhaps you would care to finish your meal, before you talk to us?"

The tall man glowered at her—and Luthar—during this pleasant speech. Coryn could see that the one named Kalrakin was the real power, the real danger, here. She would not allow his compatriot to lull her with pretty words.

"I have had enough food, for the time being," she said. She saw Luthar's eyes widen suddenly, surprised; she spun around to see that the entire meal, including all the dishes and utensils, had soundlessly vanished.

"Perhaps you can now trouble yourself to answer our questions," Kalrakin snapped with a bored look. "What are you doing here?"

She drew a breath, deciding that boldness would be her best tactic. "I have come to take the Test of Magic!"

She wasn't sure what to expect from her announcement, but the contortion across the whiskered face of the tall man frightened her deeply—then it made her mad. Before he could speak, she lashed out.

"Who are you to make such a fuss anyway?" she demanded. "I was invited here, and I came!" She felt a growing sense of righteousness, certain that she belonged here as much as or more than this bearded maniac. However, he was powerful—she glanced again at that pearly gem and shivered inside.

As if sensing her wavering, Kalrakin flicked his hand. The floorboards under Coryn's feet rippled. She tumbled to the side, watching from a sitting position as three stout beams twisted and warped, snapping like twigs.

A moment later, she felt a surge of fresh agony, a thrumming of deep pain that washed over her through the floor, the air, the very essence of the Tower.

"Stop it!" she shouted, clenching her fists. Trembling with fury, she jumped up and faced him. Her mind flitted through the few spells that she knew. Somehow, however, she sensed that her feeble magic missiles would prove but sputtering fireworks in the face of this sorcerer's obvious great power.

She instinctively grasped the nature of the conflict in which she had become involved. It was wild magic that tortured the Tower, that had broken apart the floor under her feet—the same she had turned to her own purposes since she was a little girl. But she understood one more very important fact.

Wild magic was blasphemy here.

"I am here to take the Test, and I intend to do just that," she repeated, keeping her tone level, giving no hint that her knees threatened to turn into water.

"You dare to make such pronouncements?" Kalrakin sneered contemptuously. "You will not take this test—and your very life itself depends on my pleasure. Have a care with your tongue, girl!"

"My lord!" Luthar spoke urgently, immediately drawing the taller man's attention. Kalrakin lowered his hooked beak, which, Coryn saw, extended outward and down over the tangled nest of his bristling mustache.

"What?" he demanded.

"Please, let us confer discreetly." The shorter man stepped backward through the arched entryway, beckoning his companion, who, after another glowering look at Coryn, followed Luthar out of the room.

She let out a long, tremulous sigh, relieved to be alone again, even if it was only for a few minutes. Picking up her chair from where it had toppled onto the floor, she sat down heavily, feeling the trembling of nerves in her limbs as she tried to think what to do.

Coryn's plan had progressed no farther than an admonition to herself: "Be careful!" when the two men returned to the room. This time Kalrakin halted a few steps behind, and it was Luthar who advanced toward her. His round face was beaming, but she glared over his shoulder at the tall sorcerer, unwilling to be softened by charm or blandishments.

"Of course, you shall take the Test," Luthar said graciously. "And please forgive our initial surprise. In fact, you are the first visitor to arrive here since we made this Tower our home. You must understand that we are new to these duties—but of course, as you say, this is the Tower where the Test is given, and naturally this is what you have come here to do."

Coryn knew that this Tower was no more home to these men than it was to bugbears, but she decided to let the point pass, for now. A truce had been offered, she realized, and though the very thought was repugnant to her—and the Tower—she understood that she could buy some time.

"Thank you," she said, still watching Kalrakin.

"Now, it will take some time, perhaps a day, to make all the necessary preparations," continued Luthar smoothly. "There are several very nice guest suites in the Tower, and you are welcome to have your pick of them. Perhaps you would care to rest, refresh yourself, in readiness?"

"Yes," she replied, standing up. Her eyes never left Kalrakin's face; she could sense the emotions roiling inside the towering sorcerer, knew that he was forcing himself to go along with Luthar's hospitality. But why?

"I will look at the guest suites immediately," she said, speaking as she imagined a great noble lady would. She addressed Luthar but stared defiantly at Kalrakin as she walked out of the dining room.

"And I will take the one with the strongest lock on the door."

CHAPTER 16

A FENCE AROUND A FOREST

"She is a slippery one," Jenna said in a mixture of disgust and admiration. The red robe she was wearing was dusty and damp as the enchantress came wearily up to Dalamar. The dark elf was sitting on a moldy log, his head in his hands. "I thought she would be too frightened, too overwhelmed by the wilderness, to try to sneak away. Yet she has vanished utterly! Lunitari knows, we've looked everywhere up and down the trail. Where could she be? Damn it, what if something has happened to her?"

"Silly of her to run off like that," Dalamar said, shaking his head wearily. "You must have given her the scare of her life, with your heated outbursts—not to mention your invisible cone of silence."

"I'm not the one who tried to take advantage of her!" the Red Robe retorted. "Come on. She is hiding her tracks. We have to try to think like her and figure out where she went." She tugged on the lead, and the three heavily laden mules shuffled their feet with a barely perceptible shift in momentum. The enchantress cursed under her breath. "I never knew how good Coryn was with these mules. These animals are as stubborn as, well, mules!"

"We've already wasted a day searching for a trail that vanished on dry stone," Dalamar said, raising his hand to stop her momentarily. "If I were to guess, I'd say she went looking for the Tower. Why not? She heard us talk about it, over and over. She knows it's supposed to be in the vicinity. Why don't you give me access to your artifacts and see what I can find out?"

The red-robed mage narrowed her eyes. "You have nothing left of your old life? Not your spell book, not a ring, or a staff, or even a few bottles of potion? You don't have a lot of bargaining power, not much to offer me in return."

"On the contrary," Dalamar retorted. "We are partners in this quest. We are both looking for the Tower, but we both know that we will need the most powerful wizard of each of our three orders, working in concert, to restore the powers of godly magic. I know that you are the mistress of the Red, and I am the master of Black. And there is no White wizard anywhere, so far as we have been able to learn. But you and I both know that for some reason—perhaps he is losing his wits, in the wake of his return to our world—Solinari has appointed this naïf, this silly wench, as his own champion. She is destined to wear the White Robes!"

"Ridiculous! First of all, she is neither naïf, nor silly wench," Jenna replied tartly. "She does know some magic. True, it's mostly wild magic, but at this point I don't believe that she is destined for anything. Be careful, Dalamar, lest your arrogance lead you into another mistake."

Jenna was right: The dark elf could not afford to be wrong, but he suspected that Jenna still was not telling all that she knew or believed.

"Perhaps you are right. But have a care of your tone, Red Robe." Dalamar pushed himself to his feet and started to pace before the massive log.

The forest was gloomy and cool, even early in the afternoon of a sunny summer day. The ferns were wet, and

Dalamar looked down with distaste, seeing that the hem of his black robe was repelling the water that would have soaked a mundane garment through within a few seconds. "I still think she went looking for the Tower. Where do you think she went?"

"Her trail ends at the rim of this canyon," Jenna explained.

"Yes, on smooth stone. She's a hunter—she knows how to hide a trail. But I don't think she backtracked. Let's try pushing ahead, looking for the Tower ourselves."

Jenna agreed, and for nearly an hour they followed the stone ledge along the canyon, seeking signs that anyone had passed before them.

"There," said the dark elf at last, pointing to an almost invisible scuff where a branch had been smashed against a stone. "She went this way."

Dalamar started along the faint trail, noting a few crushed ferns where hasty feet had tripped. It was not long before he came to a pine tree standing at the rim of a small ravine. The brittle branches at the base of the tree were crushed, and when he knelt, he spotted dried drops of blood on the needles strewn along the ground.

"Hmm. She was determined to keep going, to get away from us."

"Well, we weren't very pleasant company," Jenna said, drawing a raised eyebrow from Dalamar.

"This way, then," the dark elf said. There was another crushed fern, then the footprint of a small moccasin in a muddy depression, and more signs of passage through the delicate undergrowth. The game path wound faintly among the lofty birches, meandering along the ravine, deeper into the forest.

Soon they came to a massive deadfall, a thick birch lying across the path. A bristling nest of stubby branches stood like a picket fence along the top of the log.

"Here's where she went down on a knee, broke those branches on the bottom so she could pass under it."

They struggled past the fallen tree. Squatting down on the other side, Dalamar could only see a stretch of muddy patches with a few deer tracks and some prints that belonged to either a small wolf or a large dog.

"We lost her," Jenna said.

"Or rather," Dalamar suggested grimly. "This is where Wayreth Forest found her."

Jenna looked shocked. "No, you go too far with your imaginings! Do you think. . . . It couldn't be possible!" She pursed her lips, frowning.

"But it is possible," the dark elf said bitterly. "Give me a better explanation." He looked up at the treetops, the sky, and raised his hands.

"What about us?" demanded Dalamar, furious not with Jenna but with the forest, the Tower, the gods themselves. "Where is *our* entry?"

"Perhaps," she replied dryly, "the forest prefers her for some reason."

The dark elf snorted, planting his fists on his hips, and glaring at the murk of the wood. He was mocked by the mundane trees, the rotting vegetation, the utterly unremarkable surroundings. "We could look all day and never find Wayreth," he declared in disgust, "unless it chooses to let us."

"Such is the way of Wayreth," Jenna said with a shrug. "But my senses tell me that the wood is near—or at least, it *was* here."

"So do mine," Dalamar agreed.

"The Tower only responds to the Master's will, and to the gods."

"I remember, when I took the Test," Dalamar mused. "I learned that there were caverns deep under the Tower. Several of them extending beyond the periphery of Wayreth. It was said that Fistandantilus created them, as bolt holes and secret ways. One of them, the Nether Path, was supposed to provide a secret entrance into the forest. Do you know what they said about it?"

"I've heard of the Nether Path," Jenna acknowledged. She scowled thoughtfully. "But I always thought it was just a legend."

"Well, perhaps. But the legend claims that the Nether Path exists as a hidden cave. The mouth of the cave should be near to the path into Wayreth. When the forest opens to allow someone in, the Nether Path is always nearby. And according to the legend, the cave will always linger for some time, even after the forest has done its business and disappeared."

"Hmmm, interesting. But how does that help us? What kind of cave is it? There are hundreds of caves in these parts." She stroked her chin and looked around thoughtfully.

"Not right around here. I'd say, let's try the ravine," Dalamar said with a sudden eagerness. "Down there is where I'd look for a cave."

Both made their way over to the rocky rim. The gorge here was nearly forty feet deep, only half that distance across, giving it the look of a deep and savage wound in the surface of the world. The floor was littered with large rocks, with murky pools of water collecting on the low spots between.

Jenna quickly cast a spell, featherfall, and stepped off the rim of the gorge to float gently downward, coming to rest on a large, flat-topped boulder. Dalamar muttered a curse—that enchantment was not in the slender tome Palin had given him—and instead was forced to pick his way slowly, and carefully, down the cracked and broken slope. Halfway down, a rock broke free and he almost fell, scraping his knee as he jammed his leg.

"Careful!" Jenna snapped, looking up in annoyance and ducking out of the way of the debris.

The dark elf was in a thoroughly foul mood when, a minute later, he reached the bottom and found the Red Robe on the other side of a steeply angled fallen boulder. "See anything promising?" he asked, trying to keep the irritation out of his voice.

"There's an overhang just past those rocks. I can't see all the way inside from here. And there are quite a few shadowy niches under these big boulders scattered down here—we'll have to check all of them out."

An hour later, they gave up. They had found holes, niches, and many small caves, but nothing that promised entrance to Wayreth Forest.

"Out of the gorge, then, and back into the woods?" Jenna asked. Her face was streaked with grime, and tangles of her hair clung to her cheeks and shoulders. She wiped her forehead with the back of her hand, leaving a streak of mud.

"Yes, that is our only option," Dalamar agreed. "But we should hurry. Sooner or later the Nether Path—if it even exists—will vanish."

Fortunately, the ravine became a little shallower as they progressed along the bed, and they found a tumble of rocks forming a makeshift stairway leading back up to the forest floor, on the opposite rim. For the rest of the afternoon, they plodded through the pines. Darkness settled around them, deepening the gloom until Dalamar found it necessary to cast a spell of continual light on the top of a tall, straight pole he had been using as a walking stick, and with this to light the way, the two wizards continued.

The forest began to close in, becoming a vast, smothering presence, lit only by Dalamar's staff, which danced and bobbed with his long strides. Caves were harder and harder to detect, but neither wanted to give up the search. The dark elf found himself pointing his staff and staring at the lightless depths of the forest, willing some rise or depression in the ground, some limestone irregularity that might give them some hope of success.

Just when he was ready to quit, however, he was startled to hear Jenna give a cry and point toward an irregular surface ahead of them. They came to a stop between two fir trees, with the light from Dalamar's staff washing across the lichen-encrusted face of a low, broken bluff.

"We're close!" he said with certainty.

"Don't be too sure!" Jenna warned, using one arm to lean against the nearest tree trunk. "All these rocks and caves begin to look the same."

"The ones in the ravine were limestone," Dalamar said. "But this is older. See how the face is pocked and broken all along here? And those lichens—they suggest nothing has been disturbed here for ages."

"Well, now what?" the lady asked, squinting.

"Water," the dark elf said, thinking aloud. "We have to find where water flowed out of here—that's our best bet for finding a cave."

Resolutely he started forward, still holding the light high. The top of the bluff loomed out of sight. Huge slabs of rock had tumbled from the crest in eons past, forming an irregular surface, but the dark elf began to climb the nearest steeply canted slab, noting the thick crust of treacherous lichens underfoot.

Jenna was forced to cast her own light spell, using one of the stone pendants on her necklace as a source, before hurrying to keep up. Dalamar climbed over to the next rock, working his way around an outcrop at the base of the bluff. His next step brought him to a halt. Before him were two looming shoulders of limestone, swallowed by a black void of indeterminate depth.

"This is it!" he declared.

"Are you sure?"

"Don't you *feel* it?" the elf asked.

Jenna paused for a moment, her eyes closed, her nostrils flaring with a long, slow breath. "Yes," she replied. "I believe I do."

Overhead rose a stone mantle that revealed smooth, water-scoured walls. The ground underfoot here had been swept clean by some force that had washed rocks, brush, and any other debris out of the way.

"Careful," Jenna hissed, coming up behind to touch the dark elf on the shoulder. "Do you smell something?"

Halting, Dalamar sniffed, wincing at the acrid, distinctive scent that was heavy in the tunnel. "Yes," he said bitterly, "I do." There was no mistaking the stench: chlorine gas, a stench that had only one source on all of Krynn.

"This might be the route into Wayreth," Jenna noted. "But it seems we'll have to get past a green dragon to go there."

<hr>

"The smell is strong. That suggests to me that the dragon is fairly mature. But the cavern isn't large enough to admit a truly ancient serpent," Dalamar remarked. He studied the mouth of the cave, overlooking it from a curving hillside no more than an arrow's flight away from the dark entry. He and Jenna had climbed up here to study their objective, and to hatch a plan.

"I agree—a mere newt wouldn't leave such an aura," concurred the Red Robe enchantress. "Should we explore the entrance? Maybe there is room to sneak past?"

"No," Dalamar retorted. "I'll simply kill the beast, and then we won't have to worry."

"Do you have the spells for that?" Jenna asked skeptically.

"I can burn the wyrm to a crisp," the dark elf replied. "That should take care of it. But I have to be careful, if it's tight quarters, not to burn us up at the same time."

"Good idea. I'll be right behind you . . . as far as possible."

"Or should we pinch this snake between fire and ice?" the dark elf offered.

"That might work better." Jenna looked into the cave thoughtfully. "I wonder how old the nuisance is?"

Dalamar shrugged. "Hundreds of years, probably."

Jenna shook her head with a grimace. "There was a time when I might have been reluctant to slay such an ancient creature—merely because it stood in my path. Now, I'm ready to cement our partnership with a kill."

"Let's not waste any more time. I will send an Eye to scout ahead, and we should follow at intervals, as silently as possible."

The elf raised an eyebrow as he studied Jenna's assortment of pouches, as well as her beaded necklace. "Silence is second nature to my people," he added. "You, on the other hand, will have to watch yourself—perhaps you might need another of your many cones of silence?"

She snorted. "Me inside a cone of silence, so you couldn't hear a thing I say? Don't forget, I'm the one using the Eye! And I know how to be quiet when I have to be."

She removed her necklace and gathered it and her pouches into a padded pocket. Jenna then removed a bit of fluff—bat fur, Dalamar recognized—from a pocket, and murmured a few soft words of magic. Immediately the Eye came into being, an orb about the size of her fist floating in the air just before her face. The pupil was a pale red, with thin lines of the same color scoring the entire surface of the grayish sphere. The Red Robe started forward, down the hill, and the Eye preceded her, floating like a wisp in the air.

When they reached the base of the slope, she made a gesture that sent the magical sensor ahead of them, disappearing into the mouth of the cave. Jenna closed her eyes and concentrated. After a few minutes she turned to Dalamar. "The first hundred yards is clear—a large passage, as you might expect. Pretty level, with a bit of a drop-off where the Eye awaits."

The two wizards entered the cave, following the slightly winding passage, feet moving soundlessly over the ground. The dark elf held his walking stick in one hand, carefully avoiding any unnecessary contact with the bedrock. They found the Eye floating at the rim of a ledge, where the floor slanted down for ten or twelve feet before it continued to a sharp bend.

Jenna sent the Eye floating ahead again. They waited. Jenna nodded, and Dalamar started forward, halting when he felt her hand on his arm. She leaned close; he lowered his head until her lips were nearly touching his ear.

"Big male, around the next bend," she breathed. "Coiled at the far wall of a large room, sleeping. To the right of where you will enter."

Dalamar smiled tersely. A large chamber around a bend meant that he could send a reliably lethal fireball spell against the wyrm, without having to worry about the two wizards being hurt by the explosion. The deadly blast would kill or incapacitate the monster, and then, if necessary, Jenna, with her follow-up tactic—ice magic—would finish the job.

The dark elf crept around the corner of the winding cavern, Jenna a few steps behind—still concentrating on the spell of the arcane Eye. The narrow confines of the cavern expanded into a vast realm of darkness. The stink of chlorine gas was powerful here, so much so that Dalamar had to restrain a sudden urge to cough.

Narrowing his eyes, the dark elf could just make out the shape of a massive green dragon, a coiled mass of serpentine scales, flanks moving ever so slightly in the steady respiration of sleep. Dalamar had seen many dragons before, but the sight always made him a little nauseated. The monster seemed simply too big, too powerful, to dwell in this world of men and elves. At least this one wouldn't be a part of that world for much longer. . . .

Angrily Dalamar raised his finger, pointing at the creature, and muttering the command for his incendiary magic. He was vaguely relieved when that low sound provoked no visible reaction from the monster, and he watched expectantly as a tiny marble of fire appeared in the air before his finger. Soundlessly he gestured, and that spot of brightness meandered through the vast chamber, floating right up close to the coil of green scales.

The dark elf then clapped his hands and closed his eyes, stepping back to safety. Even through his lids he saw the orange brightness, felt the wash of fierce heat on his face. He listened, expecting some howl of monstrous anguish, but heard nothing beyond the billowing roar of consuming flames. A second later the brightness faded, and he opened his eyes for a look at the flaming corpse.

But there was no corpse, no serpent, nothing in the middle of those flames—the dragon was gone. Dalamar blinked, momentarily wondering if his eyes deceived him.

"Where is it!" hissed Jenna, peering over his shoulder.

"It has to be there!" he replied, even as the words rang false in his ears.

Jenna was suddenly shouting magic words, the ice spell she had prepared to follow his fiery attack. Dalamar turned questioningly—and in that movement he saw the dragon. Jenna had already spotted it.

The green serpent was crouched in a far corner, like a cat preparing to spring. Its slitted yellow eyes and smug look told Dalamar it had never been asleep. Wizards were not the only ones who could cast spells—an ancient wyrm such as this would have a great command of magic, could easily create an illusion of itself to serve as a distraction, luring overconfident intruders to their doom.

The wyrm raised its blunt, crocodilian head; spread its jaws; and opened its moist, cavernous, fang-bracketed maw.

The lethal gas that erupted in a greenish blast of mist seemed to move in slow motion—roiling and expanding as it billowed closer—but Dalamar found he was unable to move his feet, to summon any reaction. He stood there, frozen by stark horror, waiting for inevitable death.

But Jenna completed her spell and now something new shimmered before them. Not a blast of ice, which Dalamar realized would have been ineffective again the monstrous beast, if his fire spell hadn't already done some damage, but a wall of shimmering crystal frost! It stood tall and broad, a translucent barrier. But it was incomplete—the cavern was too large, so it failed to reach either the cavern's ceiling or the distant walls. Still, the enchanted frost shielded them against the onrush of killing gas.

But the massive cloud of dragon's breath couldn't be denied. It churned up and over the wall, tendrils of green poison reaching down toward the two wizards. The dark elf stumbled and ran. He gagged on the toxin, staggering and dropping his staff from suddenly nerveless fingers.

Finally he tripped over a large stone and sprawled to the floor, scrambling to his hands and knees as he looked over his shoulder. The wall of ice shattered, then, as the dragon leaped right through it, its flaring snout smashing the barrier into crystal shards. Jenna, huddled to the side of the lingering cloud of dragon breath, fell back, shrinking against the wall.

The serpent batted her with a swipe of its huge forepaw, and she tumbled across the floor. She screamed once, slumping against a stalagmite, and Dalamar heard a snap that could only be her breaking bones.

She didn't move, didn't make any sound, as the dragon

continued its charge, bearing down on the dark elf. Dalamar scrambled and clawed against the hard stone of the floor, with his doom only moments away.

CHAPTER
17

THE TEST OF MAGIC

This door is protected by a powerful spell," Luthar explained to Coryn, indicating a normal-looking portal of wooden planks connected by iron straps. "The first part of your Test requires that you open it."

Looking over her shoulder, she noted the dour figure of Kalrakin staring at her intently. For the past day, while she rested and gathered her strength, she had not spied him, but she had felt his sinister presence in the Tower. Still, she had slept securely enough behind a stout, locked door. When she had awakened in the morning, there had been hot food in her room, and she had noticed with surprise that the gash where she had scraped herself against the tree was nearly healed. Luthar had eventually come to get her, leading her up flight after flight of steep stairs until they had come to this lofty hallway.

Kalrakin had been waiting here, and now she glared at him. "Are you going to stand there gawking? I don't think I'll be able to concentrate."

The tall, beak-nosed sorcerer stiffened visibly, but then turned and stalked down the hallway to the landing at the top of the stairs. "I'll stand over here if it helps your concentration in the slightest, which I doubt," he said, his expression twitching between smirking and glowering.

Coryn was already ignoring him, studying the blank door. There didn't *seem* to be anything magical about it, not even when she closed her eyes and tried to picture and explore any hints of sorcery in those planks, or around the small metal lock. Perhaps it was that this whole place was so magical that the mere spell on a door was lost in the haze. Certainly, she sensed unusual emanations surrounding her, encouraging her. The Tower still suffered, she knew, though she hadn't glimpsed the Master since Kalrakin's appearance. But she felt implicitly that her presence was a balm to that pain. Oddly enough, she was suddenly filled with confidence, and she viewed the door as an inviting portal, drawing her toward a world of wonders.

Safety awaited her there. Not perfect safety, to be sure, for the world was ever dangerous. But passage through the door would take her beyond the reach of Kalrakin's capricious violence. He would be left behind.

Her eyes remained closed as she walked forward, feeling her way. In her mind she saw the door outlined in white light. Raising her hands, fingers extended, she advanced one step, then another, expecting to feel the touch of smooth, cool wood. But she met no resistance. The glow expanded, encompassing her, and she felt a tingle of pure joy. Still nothing blocked her path as, with two more steps, the glowing aura completely surrounded and embraced her. In surprise, she opened her eyes to see that she was enclosed in a place of utter darkness.

At the same time, she heard an angry curse from somewhere behind her. Something smashed into a solid wooden barrier, pounding with a volley of repeated blows, and she had a vaguely satisfied image of Kalrakin throwing himself against the door, violently and futilely striving to follow her.

"Indeed, this must be *my* Test," she whispered, heartened by the sound of her own voice in the darkness. She felt a sense of ownership, of proprietorship. Though it was just a room, it was one of a very few from which the Master had managed to bar the trespassing sorcerers. And yet she had been allowed in. No, she had used her own magic to enter.

Coryn reached back to touch the door and murmured the soft incantation of a light spell. Immediately a soft, diffuse glow surrounded her.

She was in a medium-sized room, she saw at once. There was a single object, a large chest on a floor that was otherwise layered with a thick film of dust. Moving forward, she saw that the trunk was clean, as if it had just appeared in this long-disused chamber. Quickly she scanned the rest of the room, seeing no other exits or entrances. There was a round window in the far wall, secured by a wooden shutter so tight that no ray of daylight slipped through—if, indeed, it opened onto the outside of the Tower, as she assumed.

She focused her attention on the chest, kneeling before it, the knee of her torn trousers raising a puff of dust from the floor. A large clasp secured the lid, and there was a keyhole— but no key in sight. Coryn touched the clasp and a word came into her mind, one she had read in Umma's secret book.

She spoke it at once; the word made a strange sound, yet agreeable and even familiar on her tongue. A tiny light sparked, not at all unpleasantly, at her fingertip. She pulled the clasp upward, and it released easily. The lid was heavy, but with both hands she was able to pull it up.

Somewhat to her surprise, she saw the trunk was empty. Reaching a hand inside, she touched the bottom, comparing the depth of her reach to the outer dimension of the chest; there was no false bottom, so far as she could tell, yet she had reached deeper than the actual size of the trunk.

Puzzled, now, she got up, dusted off her pants, and went

to the window. The shutter was fastened with a simple clasp, which she released. When she pulled, the shutter swung away, and she found herself dazzled by the morning sunlight streaming across Wayreth Forest. She was about halfway up the tower, she guessed, above the tops of the surrounding trees, so she could see for miles. A rolling carpet of green extended to the far horizon; one view was dominated by a range of low, verdant hills. The blanket of trees extended uninterrupted in all directions, as far as she could see.

Her window was far above the nearest balcony, sheer wall extending above and to both sides, so this was clearly no way out—unless, of course, she was supposed to fly. The fly spell she had memorized from Jenna offered a possibility, but she had no intention of abandoning the Test.

Making a complete circuit of the walls of the room, she found no singular features other than a few torch sconces—which she pulled at, experimentally—and the door through which she had passed. Coryn had no interest in leaving the room yet—to face the hostile Kalrakin, waiting in the hall-way; besides, somehow she knew, just *knew,* that the next step of the Test had to do with something in this room. That seemed, pretty clearly, to mean the chest. She went back to the container, which was perhaps four feet long by three wide, and a little less than three feet deep. It was still empty, and that hollowness, that lack, made her a little sad all of a sudden—and in the swelling up of unexpected emotion she realized what she had to do. Stepping into the chest, she knelt and took hold of the lid. With considerable effort, she pulled it up and then lowered it, watching as the light from the window and her spell slowly vanished behind the descending cover. There was no terror in that darkness; instead it was like a warm blanket enclosing her.

The lid shut with a click, and with a start she heard the snap of the lock. In the next instant the floor beneath her dropped, and she found herself falling. In a panic she reached for the sides of the chest, but they had also vanished—or she had already plunged far away from them. A rush of air blasted her face, pulled her hair out straight, and loudly flapped the fabric of her tunic.

Another spell came into her mind, one she had heard Jenna use on this trip. Immediately she spoke the purposeful word of featherfall. In the next instant she was floating gently, righting herself, and quickly coming to rest on a flat, solid surface. She stepped to the side, slightly unbalanced, and her foot kicked a loose object on the floor. Coryn realized, with a chill, that another second or two delay, and she might have smashed into the ground and died.

For the first time, this Test began to seem like a very serious matter.

She needed to see better. Experimentally, she tried to mouth the command for her light spell, and was not surprised that she couldn't remember it exactly. Of course, it was an unfamiliar spell, and not at all an easy one; she would have to study and practice the spell some more before she would be able to cast it readily. But there were other ways to bring about illumination. She remembered the object her foot had bumped—it had sounded like a piece of wood. Dropping to her knees, she felt around on what seemed to be a floor of flat, mortared stones. Quickly she found a wooden shaft that seemed to be about the length of a club.

Another word of command from Umma's book brought a cheery blaze to the head of the shaft, making quite a serviceable torch. She held it up and saw she was in a very large chamber, so large that she couldn't see any sign of walls or ceiling within the dome of her flickering illumination.

Slowly she turned in a circle, trying to figure out which way to go; when she had completed the spin, she felt oddly certain that she was intended to head in the direction where she had begun the circle. Starting forward, torch held high, she tried to peer through that vast, surrounding darkness.

The sound came first as an indistinct roar, distant but clearly powerful. Almost immediately Coryn identified a surge of rushing water. Swelling in volume, churning so hard that it soon rumbled through the floor under her feet, the flood swept closer; already she could feel a change in the air, chill moisture sweeping against her skin, the noise a physical pressure.

She thought, momentarily, of the wild magic she had so long used to control water in all its forms; then instantly her gut lurched with a spasm of nausea. And suddenly she knew there was no place for wild magic in her heart, not now, perhaps never again. For a brief second, that thought filled her with sadness and sharp fear. Now she could see the huge wave, taller then herself, bearing down on her like a vengeful, white-haired hag.

"Gravitus—denii!" The levitate spell popped into her mind and out of her mouth in the same split second. Water surged against her feet, up to her knees, the white crest looming overhead—and then the churning maelstrom roared under her, as she rose swiftly into the air, above the surging waves.

She floated idly for a few minutes. The sensation of weightlessness was pleasant, as it had been when Jenna had cast the same spell upon her a few days earlier. How long had it been? She was losing track of time.

Staying low enough to see the surface of the water in her torchlight, but not getting her feet wet, she watched as the tempest settled into a placid lake and then, slowly, drained away. When she could see the wet paving stones reflecting back the glow of her torch, she lowered herself to the ground.

Continuing on her way she came to other challenges, meeting each with a spell. At first these came from her childhood reading in the hut, or from her eavesdropping on Jenna.

But then there were others, words and incantations that she had never heard before, enchantments that arose in her mind as needed. Where did the come from? Did they come from the Master? She wasn't sure. She wasn't sure she cared. She was filled with happiness.

She began to cast a variety of spells previously unknown to her. When a ball of fire exploded toward her, she summoned a protective globe that completely surrounded her. Invisible but strong, it held back the incendiary storm that would have charred her in seconds; and within the sphere she merely felt a mild, not even unpleasant, warmth. When, next, a deep chasm yawned before her, she delighted in crossing over it with the fly spell. When she came to another chasm a short distance later, she created a magical horse—a stamping, snorting creature of ephemeral mist—which she mounted. The steed surged through the air, carrying her to the far side. Making her way down a narrowing corridor, she then came to a wall of stone erected across her path; yet another new spell melted those rocks into sticky mud, and she tiptoed through the morass to continue merrily on her way.

Finally the corridor opened up to terminate in a small, square room. There was a door in each of the three walls—a red door to her right, a black door in the middle, a white door to the left. She thought of Jenna and Dalamar, their rivalry and hostility toward each other—and their contempt for her.

Without hesitation, Coryn turned to the white door and opened it.

She stopped in surprise when she spotted Kalrakin just a few paces away. The tall, bearded sorcerer was stalking away from her down a corridor in the Tower—it looked like the very same place where she had last seen him.

Abruptly Kalrakin stopped and turned, and Coryn suppressed an urge to back up and close the door. Instead, she stood there and faced him as he stomped toward her. Her eyes were drawn to his hands. Once again she saw that pearly stone as he flipped it back and forth. She was awed, and frightened, as the angry sorcerer approached; the ominous stone seemed to be wavering and dancing in the air. Her breath caught with a sudden jab of fear.

But Kalrakin walked right past her, without so much as acknowledging her existence. With amazement she grasped that he couldn't see her, and she felt a thrill of stealthy accomplishment as she fell in behind him, following the tall sorcerer along the hallway.

"You were a fool to let that little bitch live!" he snarled. Only then did she notice Luthar, standing outside the very door she had penetrated at the beginning of the Test. She had descended far from that place, and wandered a long distance through caverns and that vast chamber, yet she was not surprised to find herself right back at her very point of origin.

"I am sorry for the suggestion, Master," murmured the rotund man, his face paling. Coryn saw a bruise on Luthar's cheek, and a nasty sear of a burn that had blazed along his hand and wrist. Kalrakin had already punished his companion. "But it seemed our best chance of opening the wizard lock."

"Bah!" the dour mage turned again, startling Coryn who was just a few steps behind him. But once again he showed no sign that he was aware of her presence. His face distorted by fury, eyes blazing, he stretched out his fist, fingers clenched around the stone. White light pulsed and the sorcerer grimaced with the strain of casting his most powerful magic. Paving stones rose from the floor, shattered against each other, shards flew through the air; a whole section of the hallway was destroyed by Kalrakin's wrath.

But his wild magic was an abomination here, Coryn told herself. She could feel the suffering of the Tower, pain buzzing in the air all around her; every fiber of her flesh wanted to strike out, to stop the man's rampage.

But as the pieces of stone flew past her, and some, to her astonishment, right through her, she understood she was not really in that corridor. Some arcane means allowed her to see what was happening, to observe, hear, and even smell in that place, but she could neither come to harm nor lash out at Kalrakin. She found herself admiring the Tower's ingenuity—and its inherent courage, standing up to Kalrakin's destructive tantrum and still resisting the efforts of the wild mage to gain access to key locations.

Another white door gleamed, right in the middle of the hallway—though Coryn was certain it hadn't been there a moment earlier. She went over to it, opened it, and passed into a large cavern. The dank air stung her nostrils with a powerful acidic stench. It was dark, but even though she no longer carried her torch—she wasn't sure just where she had left it, but it was no longer in her hand—somehow she could see clearly.

Her steps carried her across an uneven floor, around great spikes of stone that jutted upward; curiously, she noticed many more of these strange formations on the cavern ceiling, dangling downward. Coming around a large shaft, where upward and downward spires had apparently merged into a column, she couldn't suppress a gasp of astonishment, and fright.

She had heard of dragons, but the creature coiled in front of her was much more of a *nightmare* than anything she could imagine. The mere sight of it made her knees weak, and brought a clammy sweat to her palms as she clenched and unclenched her fingers. The serpent was green, massively snakelike, and was watching her through hooded slits of eyes. Every instinct, every nerve of her being urged her to turn around and flee.

Instead she stood there and met that monster's lazy, disinterested gaze with a steely glare of her own.

"I have slain your comrades. You will find their corpses over there," indicated the serpent in an oily hiss of a voice. A forked tongue slithered from between the toothy jaws, jutting pointedly to the left.

"I do thank you," Coryn said. She was about to start along the indicated path when some notion caused her to hesitate. She faced the beast and curtsied. "Thank you, Sir Dragon," she added.

The wyrm snorted, but she thought that it was at least a little pleased by the gesture. As she walked past the dragon, toward a narrower continuation of the underground cavern, the beast spoke, almost a whisper in her ear.

"If you had tried to flee, I would have killed you."

"I know," she replied, speaking the truth. Somehow the words came out calmly, despite the terrified pounding of her heart.

Very frightened, now, Coryn hurried down the winding cavern, and quickly found Jenna and Dalamar. The woman lay twisted on her back, while Dalamar slumped back against the cave wall beside her. Though she walked right up to them, they, like Kalrakin, showed no awareness of her presence. But neither did they seem to be dead, as the dragon had claimed.

She saw immediately that the red-robed wizard was badly injured but breathing. Jenna's face was streaked with sweat, her jaw clenched in pain. Her leg lay bent outward at a grotesque angle, and a massive bloodstain, looking like black ink, spread out on her crimson robe. Tears rolled from beneath her closed eyelids.

Dalamar, too, had been hurt badly. He lay limply for a time, then rolled up and turned away from Jenna, coughing hard, slumping forward to lean on both hands, hacking until it seemed as though his lungs would burst. Finally, he shook his head, wearily wiped the sweat from his brow, and turned back to the sorceress. Jenna's face was deathly pale, her expression growing slack. The elf dribbled a few drops of water onto her lips, then lay back with a groan and covered his eyes with his arm.

Was this a real scene? Coryn felt a horrifying twinge of guilt—was it somehow *her* fault that the two wizards had been so grievously hurt? She had a sickening sense that the answer to both questions was "yes."

"I'm sorry," she whispered. And she knew that she had to move on.

Between the two wizards, Coryn saw another white door beckoning her. She couldn't help casting a lingering look at the black-robed figure. He looked weak there, and she wished that she could offer him comfort.

Instead, she touched the latch on the door, lifted it, and walked through.

The sun was shining brightly; it was hotter than she had ever known it to be, as she continued across the unending sandy waste. This arid flatland had been draining her strength for hours. No tree, no hillock, no ridge, not a single formation rose above the featureless plain. She wondered if this part of the Test was simply a challenge to her physical endurance. Coryn stopped and thought about her problem for a moment, but she could picture no spell to magically conjure up food or drink. Much less a map, she thought with a chuckle.

So she stumbled along, wearily, for more hours. Her feet were blistered, and eventually she became so exhausted that she almost slept as she walked. But she wouldn't allow herself to rest for more than a few minutes at a time—as soon as her eyelids grew heavy, and her head began to nod, she pushed herself to her feet and resumed her relentless trek. Her belly growled. And her hunger was nothing compared to the parching thirst that left her tongue feeling like a piece of dried leather in the arid cavern of her mouth. Water—what a precious substance, yet so easy to take for granted!

Certainly, the wild magic of her former life might have led her to a spring, or at least indicated where she might dig to discover moisture, but she never even considered employing those former powers; in her mind, she had already cast them away, forever. She would die of hunger and thirst before she would go back to that vulgar pathway, even if it held the means to her survival.

In the instant of that understanding, she was confronted by another door, a portal that suddenly materialized to stand upright on the ground before her, bringing her stumbling progress to an abrupt halt. Dazed, she studied the door. It was not in any of the three colors she had come to expect; rather, this was a simple panel of wooden boards strapped together with bands of iron. Come to think of it, it seemed identical to the long-ago door she had opened during the initial phase of the Test.

She had no doubt that she would open this door, and again pass through, but first she took a moment to gather her strength, to marshal her thoughts. A glance to the side showed her that the white moon, Solinari, was just rising above the flat horizon, a full white disk that seemed to smile upon her, shower her with promise, kindness, and love. Allowing that beneficence to fill her heart, she reached for the latch and pushed open the door.

Now she entered a huge, dark room, so vast that all the walls were lost in the shadows of distance. She was alone. Turning to look at the door she had entered, she was startled to see it was no longer there—indeed, the wall behind her was as far away as the other boundaries of the vast chamber. Her torch was in her hand and she raised it up, spotting a small table a few paces away. There was a pitcher of water on that table and she snatched it up, eagerly drinking down half the contents, with much of the rest splashing onto her dirty, dust-stained tunic.

It was then that she noticed the chairs some distance away, many of them arranged in a ring, all facing the center of the room. She approached, and studied the nearest chair. It, and all the others, seemed to be carved from black stone, as if they were part of the floor rather than resting upon it. There were twenty-one of these sturdy seats, arranged in three sections of seven.

"For the three orders," she murmured in sudden understanding.

She imagined a great meeting, a Conclave of the three orders, and she even saw herself, Coryn, sitting as the head of that great meeting.

All of a sudden she realized the chairs were occupied, not by people, but by empty, yet animated robes. The three sections were divided between the red, black, and white robes. The three different-colored robes filled the seats, turned and moved as if engaged in lively discourse, empty sleeves gesturing.

And then the hoods of those robes—with empty holes where the faces should be—all turned toward Coryn. They watched her intently, expectantly. She felt a momentary panic—what was she supposed to do now?

That is when the three moons came into view, rising with impossible speed until they loomed over her. Even the black one was visible, because it was actually darker than the darkness yawning above. The white was brilliant, the red like a spot of fresh blood, and all were full, round, and nearing zenith.

She heard a groan, coming from across the room, beyond the chairs. She made her way around the ring of ghostly robes, ignoring the gestures, the pantomimes urging her to stay. Instead she crossed to the far wall of the room. A spot of light attracted her and when she drew near, she saw that this was not a door, but more of a passage right through the wall of the room. She drew nearer and gasped as she recognized the familiar interior of Umma's little hut.

She stopped, pressing her hand to her mouth, stifling a sob of dismay.

Umma lay in her bed, wasted and frail. Her eyes were bright with fever; sweat streaked her brow. She turned her face back and forth, and her eyes were vacant, unseeing. A violent chill wracked her skeletal body, and she coughed and gagged, straining for each wheezing breath.

"Umma!" cried the girl, starting forward. The gap in the wall shimmered; there lay a free passageway that would take her away from the Tower, take her home, to this place where she was desperately needed.

"Wait!"

A command came from behind her, pulling her around. She saw the Master there, the white-bearded visage coming toward her slowly, holding up a restraining hand. He leaned on his staff but shuffled forward urgently.

"But she needs me!" she said. "I have to go to her."

"You don't understand," replied the Master of the Tower. "The Test reveals many truths, to you and about you. And this is the part that may doom you!"

"How?"

"You have felt the power, the magic, as you have wandered these past hours, have you not? And here, in the Hall of Mages, you saw the wizards of the Conclave all turning to you—honoring you, attending you, seeking your wisdom?"

"Y-yes. I saw that, sensed it."

"This has never happened before," the Master declared. "That one so young, so unprepared, has nearly emerged from the Test in a position, not just of learning, but of power, command, and influence! All this magic, the accolades of your fellow wizards, all will be yours if you but finish the Test!"

"While this hole in the wall you see before you, this escape from the Tower, is a cruel deception. For if you leave now, if you go to your grandmother and turn your back on the Conclave, your powers will be wiped away. You will have renounced the magic, renounced the world, and gone back to your miserable little village in the Icereach to live out your years. Until you, too, die as an old woman on a wretched pallet in a pathetic hut!"

"It is not a miserable village!" Coryn snapped, furious. "And you have no right to stop me! It is the place that made me what I am—the place where I belong!"

"No . . . I have no right," said the old man with a feeble shake of his head. "But I thought that you should know the very real stakes involved."

"My grandmother is truly ill?" she asked, knowing it to be the truth.

"Oh, most certainly. Probably dying—the Test does not deceive in these matters."

"Then I must go to her."

"The choice," said the Master of the Tower, "is yours."

Coryn nodded. She thought of the flight spell, of the tower of wonders, and the wizards of the Conclave. But she knew where she belonged. Her shoulders slumped under the weight of her decision, but there was only one thing she could do. She stepped forward, through the opening in the wall, and reached out to soothe Umma's fevered brow.

But Umma was no longer there. Instead, Coryn stood in a hallway—the same place where she had started the Test, she realized. There was a table beside her that had not been there hours—days?—earlier, when she had begun. Three objects rested there: a clear bottle containing a blood-red liquid, a small book of midnight black, and a slender wand of white.

She was obliged to take these things, she understood, and so she picked up the bottle first. But where to put it?

Only then did she realize that she no longer wore her travel-worn shirt and torn leather leggings. With a sense of awe, she looked down, felt the smooth, plush material against her skin, a cloth caress that felt wonderful all around her.

She was wearing a robe that was perfectly, immaculately white.

CHAPTER 18

A SLOW DEATH

Dalamar's eyes watered, and though he tried he couldn't seem to draw a breath. He could just die here ... that would be the easiest thing to do. He had been tricked, fooled, and defeated by a creature so much older, so much more powerful than himself. It was fitting rebuke, for the arrogance he had shown in recklessly entering the lair. By Nuitari, he didn't deserve to live!

Jenna, he guessed, was all but dead. Certainly she would lose her leg even if, somehow, she managed to cling to life. The dark elf groaned and leaned his head back against the unforgiving rock. He closed his eyes, with the events that had doomed them replaying themselves in the lightless shade of his mind.

He saw the dragon approaching, the reptilian head swiveling this way and that, jaws opening to flash teeth that were as long as swords. The dark elf was trapped, helpless, and terrified. He was appalled by the dragon's size—so much greater than the serpent he and Jenna had expected. This green was a very ancient wyrm, a monster that had somehow survived the Cataclysm, the War of the Lance, the Dragon Purge, and the War of Souls. Surely it had been alive during Huma's time and had survived the sundering of the elven nations thousands of years before! It was a beast from the lost ages of Krynn, and the two wizards and their magic were but feeble opponents.

Invisibility was useless, of course—the creature's sensitive nostrils would locate him more surely than its eyes. But deception? Drawing a breath, biting back his choking and coughing, Dalamar had lain on his back and summoned a spell of illusion. He whispered the words and then rolled over, directing the magic toward the far side of this cavern of doom.

Sorcery had shimmered for a moment, and then the spell took effect, in the form of a perfect image of Dalamar himself, black robe swirling as he stumbled back against the cavern wall. Dalamar added the illusion of a falling stone to his spell. The rock broke free under his perfect phantasm's "touch," dropping to the floor with a sharp crack, a sound that brought the dragon's head whipping around with a startled hiss. Those green jaws gaped wide, and then a roar filled the cavern to overflowing, breaking stones loose from the ceiling and rumbling the very bedrock underfoot.

In the face of that horrific sound, the illusory Dalamar had turned and fled, sprinting away as if under the influence of haste magic. The illusion was good, the dark elf knew—even the stink of his fear lingered in the air, so that even the dragon's nostrils affirmed the quarry, which was fleeing fast. With a roar, the dragon pounced after, great talons rattling on the stone floor.

The illusion of the black wizard disappeared into a narrow side cavern as the dragon lunged after. The sinuous forequarters vanished, followed by the long body, powerful rear claws gouging grooves into the stone floor. In just a few seconds, the phantom Dalamar was but a vanished memory, and so too the dragon, even its sinuous tail gone from the great cavern.

Still the dark elf had gagged and spit, convulsing on the floor as his lungs violently worked to expel the lingering taint of deadly gas. Knowing the urgency—the dragon would only keep up his fruitless pursuit for a short while—the dark elf pushed himself to his feet and staggered over to his red-robed companion. Kneeling, he saw immediately that her left leg was unnaturally twisted. But her chest rose and fell slowly, so she was still alive.

"Jenna!" he hissed. Her eyes fluttered open, blank for a second and then wide. "We have to get out of here," Dalamar continued. "Now!"

"Where . . . is the dragon?" she groaned weakly, struggling to sit up and then crying out in pain. "Ow, my leg!"

"It chased one of my illusion spells out of here," the dark elf replied. "But it'll be back—soon! Can you move?"

Weakly, Jenna shook her head. "You must go," she said. "Leave me!"

Dalamar grimaced, tempted by the offer. But he shook his head. "We'll need *both* of us to find the Tower," he reminded her, while reminding himself. "I'll help you walk."

"Can't . . . walk. Wait!" the enchantress reached for the bundle of her possessions, fumbled around for a second, then pulled out a bottle of liquid. "There's enough in here for both of us—you first," she said.

The dark elf quickly took a sip, recognizing the taste of the familiar potion. As Jenna grabbed the bottle from his fingers he felt the solidity of his flesh begin to dissolve and waft freely in the air. He looked down as the woman in the red robe also become diffused under the effect of the gaseous cloud. She soon was barely visible, like faint steam, hovering just above the floor. Her broken leg was no longer an immediate problem.

Together they had floated across the cave, making a slower progress than Dalamar would have preferred. Still, they made their way back up the entryway, along the winding subterranean corridor. Daylight glimmered around the next corner, when, within the depths behind them, the great green serpent could be heard roaring loudly in frustration. But it did not pursue.

And the potion wore off. Jenna collapsed to the ground, with Dalamar slumping down beside her. He could see that she was crippled, but he could only sit here, feed her a few drops of water, and sink deeper into gloom.

Jenna's world was pain, only pain. Agony rose like a tide, surging against her, pushing with hurricane force through the chinks in her soul. It swelled and overwhelmed her, drowned and suffocated her, pressing against her consciousness from all sides. She found no will to resist.

After falling to the stony ground, she felt such intense pain that she blacked out. She was vaguely aware of the dark elf staying beside her, giving her the few sips of water that were the only sustenance she craved. When her pain grew too great to bear, she cried out unintelligibly. They were not far from the dragon's lair, and Dalamar quickly cast a cone of silence, so that Jenna's fevered ranting could not be heard.

For a very long time, she slipped in and out of consciousness. She lost track of the hours, perhaps even days, during which the darkness claimed her. When she was awake, she prayed only for the mercy of healing oblivion. During these times she was keenly aware of Dalamar's presence, but she had no strength—or inclination—to acknowledge him. Of course, he had saved her life, but only after she had protected him with the ice spell, at terrible cost to herself. Protecting her now was uncharacteristic of him. She knew that, for the dark elf, her fate posed a cruel question: How long would he stay?

He was impatient, that much she could sense. It would not have surprised her to wake up and find him gone. But each time consciousness returned, he was there, dour and restless but there. She understood, of course, that he was staying not out of affection or guilt; rather, he was taking care of her because he needed her. He still needed her.

Her injuries were wrenching. Her right leg had been broken in several places, the bone poking through the skin of her thigh in an ugly, bloody wound. The bleeding alone should have killed her within the first few hours, except that Dalamar had stanched the wound with a crude bandage torn from his own robe. Something else was terribly wrong; she had no appetite, and the one time that the elf had insisted she eat a little dry cheese, she had violently thrown it back up, spasms of pain wracking her torso until she lost consciousness.

While lost in oblivion, Jenna's nearly comatose slumber was visited by a dream. She saw a vivid image of the red moon, knew that Lunitari was climbing high into the skies, outside and above this place—just inside the cave—and she heard the soft, musical voice of her goddess calling to her.

"I am here, Mistress," Jenna felt herself whisper, though her lips, her tongue, seemed utterly paralyzed.

"You must go on, my daughter," came the message from the red goddess. "You have made your way past death and mystery; you are close to your goal. You must not relinquish that goal to the one in black."

"But . . . Mistress . . . I fear you are wrong. I have failed," the wizard confessed, tears burning in her eyes. "I am broken. . . ."

"Listen, Daughter of the Red Moon!" Lunitari's voice was the lash of a whip, a dousing of chill water. The force of Lunitari's disappointment left Jenna shaking. "You *must* enter the Tower, and you *must* gather a Conclave. And then you must lead the Three Robes into the future . . . For you, Jenna of Palanthas, you shall become Head of the Conclave!"

Jenna couldn't argue with such a powerful will, even if she had wanted to. Instead, she quietly agreed, reaching upward in her dream toward that elusive crimson circle in the sky. She felt the goddess embrace her, warm her, bless her. . . .

And she slept deeply.

------◆◆◆------

Dalamar stalked out of the cave and into the woods, keeping the entrance to the underground shelter where Jenna slumbered just barely in his sight. He felt tied down by the wounded woman, and his frustration drove him to walk angrily through the lofty forest. She was a weak creature, no help to him in her state—in fact, a considerable liability.

His thoughts turned, of their own volition, to memories of his *Shalafi*. When Raistlin Majere had been burdened by the presence of a wounded woman, the cleric Crysania, he had not allowed that to hold him back. He had gone on to face his ultimate challenge, leaving behind his suffering ally. She had been key to his early success, but when he no longer needed her, he cast her aside, knowing her presence only hampered him and held him back.

But Raistlin had been prepared to make his final battle alone, and that was an important difference. Dalamar knew he couldn't reach the Tower on his own. He needed help, and right now, Jenna was the best candidate.

He was certain this cave was the path to Wayreth Forest, but now that path was blocked to them, and they needed to find another way. But Jenna would not be able to move for a long time given her leg wound; he wasn't even certain, given her strange stomach pain, she would recover at all.

Why hadn't the forest welcomed them, shown them the path? Why had the Tower made itself known to a mere slip of a country girl like Coryn?

"Have I been so unworthy, Nuitari?" he cried, his voice a hoarse whisper of despair. He shook his fists at the sky—in vain, for the only answer he received was the soft moaning of Jenna, as she stirred from sleep.

With a sigh, Dalamar turned back to the cave. Somehow it came down to helping Jenna in order to find Coryn. For some reason, it seemed the gods favored Coryn, and that she—and only she—could lead them to the Tower.

CHAPTER
19

THE WHITE ROBE

Coryn tucked the bottle, the wand, and the book into various pockets of her robe. She discovered an extensive array of pouches and other pockets on both the inside and outside of the garment, including several that were perfectly sized for her new possessions. Other pockets already had ingredients in them, and as her hands caressed the newfound materials she found that she could instinctively sense the difference between bat's eyes and dried blackberries, powdered ogre skull, and grains of fine sand.

She looked around, realizing she was still in the corridor where she had started and ended the Test. There was no sign of Kalrakin or his accomplice, but she sensed they wouldn't be far away. Tentatively, she started along the hall, heading away from the stairway.

That is when magic convulsed behind her. Coryn immediately sensed the explosive power of an attack. Kalrakin's sorcery exploded, sweeping down the corridor toward her backside in a wave of lethal power.

Her response came to her lips instinctively, emerging calmly and quickly, instantaneously guiding her out of the path of the violent blast of sorcery. This was not a teleport spell, however—though that could have carried her anywhere in the world that she wanted to go, she was not prepared to leave the Tower, to abandon it to this abominable intruder.

Instead, a newly confident Coryn chose to give battle.

"Arastia—disp—lasr!"

She found herself standing safely just a few dozen feet away and now on the other side of Kalrakin. He spun furiously, his beard and long hair whirling around with a contorted expression. He lunged for her.

"Bitch!" he snarled, the white stone glowing against his palm in his extended hand.

The command for the haste spell burst, almost unbidden, from Coryn's lips. Immediately the speed of the sorcerer's charge appeared to slow down. Though he still ran and reached for her, his limbs moved as if they churned through molasses or viscous oil. Meanwhile the girl sprinted down the corridor, her moccasins skidding on the smooth stones. Wind whistled in her ears as she flew like a rabbit, darting around the corner.

She heard Kalrakin screaming something behind her, the sounds deep and inarticulate—and then the stones under her feet started to shift and writhe, and she fell, slamming hard into the wall at the end of the corridor.

He followed her, moving in apparent slow motion, even as the haste spell helped her to react speedily. She shook off her pain and tumbled onto the stairway, rolling to her feet and running down the spiraling steps.

Abruptly, a stone flew from the wall, swishing past her head, exploding into shards when it smashed into the opposite wall. She had to dodge as another and then a third piece of masonry, shot outward. All down the spiraling stair, the curving wall erupted erratically, spewing out potentially lethal missiles. Kalrakin, despite his "slowness," was close behind—he must have somehow counteracted her haste spell with one of his own.

She whispered another magical word, cloaking herself in a blanket of invisibility as she shrank against the wall. Looking at her hands—or rather, at where her hands were supposed to be—Coryn saw straight through to the floor. Holding her breath, she pressed herself out of the way, though she feared the pounding of her heart would betray her. It took all of her courage not to flinch or scream as the maniacal sorcerer caught up to her . . .

. . . and raced right past, his face locked in that expression of insane fury, jaw clenched, teeth bared, eyes flashing hatred above his jutting nose and tangled beard. He moved with unnatural speed, now, his long legs covering four or five stairs with each stride. Howls of inarticulate rage exploded from his lips, and his gaunt body seemed to tremble uncontrollably.

Only when he had rounded the next bend and disappeared from view did Coryn dare to draw a breath. Then she heard more steps coming from above and knew the second sorcerer was coming. Again she froze as Luthar lumbered past. His movements were unnaturally slow, which confirmed that Kalrakin was being aided by a haste spell. It was more wild magic, and she hated the thought that Kalrakin was defiling the godly purpose of this tower.

With each act of destruction, each spell of wild magic, each and every stone torn from the floor and walls, the evil wizard willfully inflicted terrible suffering upon the Tower. The Master was right: Kalrakin was an abomination, a corruption, a cancer. More than that, he had become Coryn's personal enemy, the first person she had ever hated with a passion.

And now, clad in her pristine white robe, Coryn felt a flush of proprietorship about this hallowed place. Kalrakin was not just her enemy, he was the enemy of all that godly magic stood for, all she, newly confirmed by the Test, swore to protect. It was not enough to drive him out, she realized—he must be slain. Her fury coalesced into cold purpose, and she found another word entering her mind, an arcane command that brought with it images of incendiary explosion and searing, fiery death. She could cast that spell, watch the flames engulf the gaunt, bearded figure of her enemy, and know that this served a true, noble purpose. Her benign god, gentle Solinari, heartily approved her lethal goal and the deadly nature of her spell.

"Where did she go?" Kalrakin screamed shrilly. He was coming back up the stairs, now, snarling to Luthar, tramping behind. The wizard emerged into sight at the bend of the stairway as she inched back up the steps. Deliberately kicking at pieces of rubble scattered around her, Coryn sent pebbles cascading, and the wild sorcerer halted, staring ahead intently.

"There you are, you little fool," he sneered. "Did you really think you could evade me? Did you think that such a pathetic mask—invisibility?—could hide you, as wise in magical deception as I am?"

"I don't intend to evade you," Coryn said loudly and boldly, "or hide from you." She let the invisibility spell fall away from her like a piece of clothing she was shrugging off. She wanted Kalrakin to see her, wanted him to understand what was happening to him, wanted him to know his punisher.

"I intend to *kill* you!" she declared with cold fury.

The gray-robed wizard raised an eyebrow, and chuckled disbelievingly. But she raised her finger, pointed at him, and spoke the command word for the fireball spell. It rolled from her tongue, pulsed in the air around her, sizzled with the tremendous, fundamental power of godly magic. Kalrakin must have heard that word before—for his eyes instantly grew wide, and he threw his hands up to protect his face, tumbling backward down the steps. He screamed and writhed, trying to ward off the inevitable.

A bubble of fiery light appeared at Coryn's fingertip. The little sphere danced and drifted toward the cringing wizard. Suddenly, Kalrakin looked up, his eyes flashing, and his mouth curling into a cruel grin. He regained his poise, stood, and faced her, holding up the white stone that he had remembered was his advantage. It pulsed eagerly, hungrily. The talisman was firmly clenched in the sorcerer's grip, as the fireball exploded.

The release of power felt like a physical rush, to Coryn, draining energy from her body and channeling it into the lethal spell. Coryn expected to see the wizard, struck by such power, vanish within an incendiary cloud.

But he did not die, nor did any great fire materialize. Instead, the sorcerer howled in triumph, clenching his fist. Smoke billowed between his fingers as the surface of his skin took on a surreal, almost sun-bright, glow. And then the spell was over, and Kalrakin was leering at her through his beard, holding up his glowing hand in a gesture of scorn. The stone was hot and bright in his hand, taunting her with its superior might.

Coryn gaped in astonishment. For several seconds she could not believe her impotence; her magical powers had been so effective, so unfailing, during the full course of the Test, that she had never considered the possibility of failure. She had executed the spell correctly, but Kalrakin—or rather, his white talisman—somehow had thwarted the effect.

Kalrakin raised his fist. Pearly light gleamed between his fingers, as if the pale gemstone were afire. He climbed back up the stairs, toward Coryn. She pointed a finger at him, snapped out a command, and felt another rush of energy as a powerful, crackling lightning bolt erupted from her flesh, arrowing toward the wild sorcerer. Searing magic crackled— she smelled the heat and fire, felt her hair stand on end amidst the violent electric charge.

But amazingly, it happened again. Kalrakin actually laughed in the face of her foolishness. He held up that stone again—it was so radiant now that Coryn had to squint—and absorbed the full brunt of the lethal lightning bolt into the smooth, round shape. The yellow spear of electricity simply vanished, leaving the artifact glowing so brightly that Coryn could no longer look at it without being blinded—it was like trying to stare at the sun.

Kalrakin reached for her with maniacal fury. He grabbed Coryn's robe with those long fingers, tendrils of brilliant golden light emanating from the little stone in his right hand. What she did next was automatic: She spoke another word—a word she had learned from Umma's books, she recalled with a pang—the same word that had saved her from the thanoi in the Icereach.

She had no destination in mind, but once again the old tele-port spell served her true. Instantly she found herself standing at the edge of a meadow, with tall trees at her back, and a rocky bluff rising before her. The Tower was nowhere to be seen, and she sensed immediately that this wood was not Wayreth Forest. Or that Wayreth Forest had left her behind.

Nearby rose a low granite ridge, its face marked by lichen-encrusted rocks. A shady gap attracted her attention immediately, and Coryn realized she was looking at the mouth of a cave. Cautiously she approached the place, leaning forward, trying to peer inside the shadowy murk. As her eyes adjusted, she edged forward, coming under a lofty mantle of ancient rock.

From the darkness she heard—or perhaps imagined—a groan of unspeakable pain. Carefully she advanced, holding the folds of her robe off the floor, peering into the darkness as her eyes slowly adjusted. This place looked familiar—and there, on the floor, was a person she recognized.

"Jenna!"

The Red Robe lay on the floor of the cave, just as Coryn had seen her during the Test. Her face was pale and slick with sweat; her eyes, closed. Her breathing was ragged and shallow, like the panting of a wounded animal.

Coryn felt stabbed with guilt. She ran forward and knelt by the woman, touched her cheek, and found that she was burning with fever.

"Her gut is ruptured. She's dying."

Dalamar's voice, cold and brittle, startled her. She leaped to her feet and turned to look at the dark elf. He betrayed no surprise at seeing her. His demeanor was distant, almost contemptuous, as he looked her up and down. Coryn stood proud under his inspection, acutely conscious of her white robe—which was in contrast to his own garment of midnight black.

"We were following you, chasing you—you might say we were foolish enough to be worried about you," he said, his voice cutting like a knife. "But I see you had important personal business to accomplish."

"The Master of the Tower invited me in, and I came," she explained simply. Surely she hadn't done anything wrong—or had she? Why did she feel this stabbing guilt? She had *had* to run away from these two bickering mages.

"You and Jenna were determined to keep me in the dark, to use me as a pawn in your own struggles. I had to get away, strike out on my own—I didn't know where I was going, at first. But it turned out to be the way to the Tower, and I was invited by the Master to take the Test of Magic."

"Obviously," he said, his voice heavy with sarcasm. "So it appears I lose the company of one enchantress, only to be rewarded with the dubious presence of another."

"There's more at stake than you know!" she retorted. "And anyway, I'm a mage now. We need to help Jenna, not stand around talking. Maybe she doesn't have to die!"

"What—have you become a cleric, too? Even a high priestess of immortal Paladine—Paladine as he *used* to be—would be hard pressed to heal these grievous wounds."

"Be quiet." Coryn knelt beside the Red Robe and pulled the bottle of potion out of her robe. At the sight of the bottle Dalamar knelt beside her, his expression intent.

"Where did you get that?" he asked.

"At the end of the Test," Cory replied. "It was a reward, which I didn't understand at the time. Now I think I know why it was given to me."

Slowly, gingerly, she raised Jenna's head, cradling it in a strong hand. Placing the open neck of the bottle to the injured woman's lips, she allowed a slow trickle to run into the Red Robe's mouth. After the first small dose, she let Jenna breathe for a bit, and then repeated the process. Sip after sip, Coryn poured the precious liquid through the Red Robe's parched lips.

Slowly, imperceptibly, a flush began to appear on Jenna's clammy cheeks. Her breathing grew more measured, her temperature abated. The thrashing of her limbs gradually eased and by the time the potion was gone, she appeared to be miraculously well—and sleeping soundly, restfully.

"Impressive," Dalamar acknowledged, after a long silence. "You have been gifted with powerful magic. And you are right: The potion you were given was indeed a reward, which the gods in their wisdom evidently intended for Jenna."

"There is more . . . here is another of my rewards. And now I know that I am to give it to you."

She pulled the black book out of another pocket and was startled at the way Dalamar's eyes brightened at the sight of the unassuming tome. When she extended it, he snatched it from her hands almost violently. With exaggerated care he opened the cover and started looking at it, turning the thin pages faster and faster with rising excitement.

"Do you know what this is?" he hissed.

"A spell book, I should think," she replied.

"It is the key to my life, to the past I thought was gone forever." He looked at her with a new expression—a modicum of warmth but also respect, Coryn realized. "There can be only one reason these gifts were given to you. All three gods of magic must have joined forces for your Test, and all three wanted you to succeed. But why? Why?"

"Yes, I succeeded in the Test. But there is a greater challenge, one that I shall require your help to face. It is a challenge that faces all godly mages."

Jenna's eyes flickered open, looking around in wonder. The Red Robe sat up easily, under her own power, and reached down to feel the outline of her leg under the bloodstained robe. "What miracle is this?" she asked, gazing at Coryn as if she couldn't believe what she was seeing.

"It seems we have found our White Robe," Dalamar said to Jenna dryly, looking very intently at Coryn. "Or rather, she has found us."

After explaining to Jenna about the potion and the black spell book, Coryn told both wizards about the sorcerers who had taken over the Tower, the destruction Kalrakin had wreaked, and the evil he represented.

She told them about his unusually potent artifact. "It was a small stone, but it absorbed the effects of my most powerful spells. The Master of the Tower called it . . . an 'Irda Stone.' I fear it will make it impossible to attack Kalrakin directly, if he can render himself immune to magical blows."

"But we can't abandon the Tower to him!" snapped Dalamar.

"Of course not!" Coryn agreed. The dark elf glared to be addressed so sharply, but he waited for her to go on. "There was another part of my Test . . . I saw twenty-one wizards in the Hall of Mages, seven of each color."

"The Conclave!" Jenna exclaimed. "The last one was held more than forty years ago. When our gods had gone from the world."

"Well, the gods have returned now, and I think we need to hold another one," the girl explained. "A new First Conclave. We need to summon all the wizards to the Tower, and we need to do it soon."

"But I have been seeking wizards of any robe for months!" Jenna objected. "The only one I came up with was you! How can the three of us possibly hold a Conclave?"

Coryn removed the third of her gifts, the slender magic wand. "There is one last reward that I was given, an enchantment that will send the summons of our gods across the world. It is a spell that has never been cast before, and can be used only once—we will need a laboratory, a hot oven, and many unusual components."

"We can do it in Palanthas," Jenna offered quickly. "I have most anything we could need there—certainly my own laboratory is well stocked."

"And the casting of this spell?" asked the dark elf, his eyes glittering with excitement. "After we have done our preparations, how will we work the magic?"

"We must go to the top of the highest mountain on Ansalon," Cory explained, the words flying from her lips as if she had known the answer all her life. "The spell must be cast when the three moons of magic are all full, and all near zenith."

"The Night of the Eye, of course!" Jenna whispered. "The high conjunction of Krynn's magic."

"Tomorrow night," Dalamar said anxiously, "which doesn't leave us much time."

"No, and that is why we must hurry." Coryn climbed to her feet. She saw the mules were tethered nearby, and Dolly nickered familiarly as she went up and scratched the animal between the ears. "I see that the saddlebags are already packed," she noted cheerfully, nodding to Dalamar. "As you suggest, we will use work space at your house," she said to Jenna, who smiled her agreement—as if there was nothing unusual in taking such a suggestion from one who had, a few days ago, been her servant girl.

"Enough talk—let's get going!" said Dalamar, taking another moment to admire his book before he slid it into one of the pockets of his robe.

The other two wizards nodded as Coryn raised the wand, and the sparkling power of magic pulsed in the air around them.

CHAPTER
20

THE NIGHT OF THE EYE

The wand teleported all three of them, plus their mules, to the plaza before the great house in Palanthas. Jenna quickly rummaged through Dora's saddlebags, loading Dalamar, Coryn, and herself with an assortment of wooden boxes, pouches, and several of the red, leather-bound spell books.

Rupert didn't seem surprised to see them. With his usual dignified air, he held open the front door as the three wizards approached the manor.

"Please have Donny see to the animals," Jenna said to her longtime servant. "We have to get right to work."

"Very good, my lady. And welcome back."

"Thank you." Jenna was already past him and moving toward the stairway with purposeful strides.

"And to you, too, miss," Rupert said to Coryn as she closely followed Jenna. He bowed his head, apparently admiring the pure white material of her robe. "It would seem that congratulations are in order. Well done."

She smiled, embarrassed and pleased. "Thank you ... Rupert." She looked around at the sound of rapid footsteps to see Donny coming from the back of the house. He skidded to a stop when he saw her, his face slack with awe.

"You're a wizard, now?" he gasped.

She smiled at him. "Yes, but I'll still take your help, next time we need to go to the market."

"But"—he looked crestfallen—"you got a *white* robe? Not red?"

"Sometimes you get a better painting when you use more colors," Jenna called out obliquely, from the stairway. "Now stop staring and help us, Donny—we have important work to do."

Dalamar, a stack of Jenna's books teetering in his arms, staggered toward the wide stairway. Coryn, a box tucked under each arm and several leather pouches clutched in her hands, followed Jenna to the second floor. The girl was startled when, at the top of the stairs, she got her first glimpse of the Red Robe's grand laboratory. It was one very long room occupying two wings. Many arched doorways connected portions of the lab to the hallway, and a broad terrace flanked both outer walls, which were lined entirely by tall glass windows. The whole space was bright and cheery, even at sunset.

Dalamar, brushing by with his load, scolded her for gawking. Coryn set down her load and rolled up her sleeves as she followed the enchantress into the room and a far recess of the lab.

"Now, what can you tell me about this spell?" the older woman asked.

Cory took the wand from her outer pocket and held the slender reed of wood in her hands. It was pliable—she could bend it nearly into a circle if she wanted—but very strong. And she knew just from touching it lightly that the knowledge and power was there, contained within, ready to be used.

"We'll need high heat; we have to melt glass. And we also need to blow the glass. Each of us must make one globe. Let's

see . . . we'll need platinum dust, dried kelp—golden kelp.
And. . . ."

She rattled off a list, which Jenna scribbled down as
quickly as the younger woman could talk. On the list were
platinum, numerous coal- and charcoal-type components,
pure alcohol, and others. But each of the three brews would
have distinct characteristics—Coryn's required bat's eyes,
while Jenna needed those of a blindfish. Dalamar's recipe
didn't call for any eyes, but required something just as
rare—the stinger of a giant scorpion.

"Good," Jenna said in satisfaction as Coryn finished the
list. "Would you please help Donny with the books while I
start collecting everything? Besides what I have stored here,
we'll need most everything from Dora's load."

Coryn nodded and hurried back downstairs. The volumes
were heavy, but she and Donny went down and up several
times. Her face was red by the third trip. Dalamar had a
fire raging and now closed a pair of flat steel doors cut into
the sides of a cast-iron furnace—the largest firebox or oven
Coryn had ever seen.

Jenna caught her eye and indicated a large book on the
table, laid open to a page of arcane inscriptions. It was one of
her personal tomes, not one of the ones Coryn had unloaded
from the mules and carried upstairs.

"Hmm. I was just doing a little reading while you were
bringing things up," the Red Robe explained. "I learned a few
important things—unfortunately, though, nothing I learned
seems to be good news."

Coming to peer over her shoulder, Coryn noticed an illus-
tration of a small, pale stone on the open pages. The drawing
was rendered in black ink, but, using great swirls and arrows,
the mage who had made the drawing had indicated the power
of the artifact.

"Yes, that looks like the Irda Stone, the one that Kalrakin

had." Squinting at the strange symbols, she was surprised to realize that she could read the writing, though this was the first time she had ever seen such script.

"It is an artifact dating back to the Age of Dreams, isn't it?" Dalamar asked, coming over to join the women in examining the tome. His robe was already thick with coal dust.

"Yes." Jenna summed up what she had learned thus far for the other two. "It was created out of chaos—its power is very attuned to wild magic and has a parasitic effect. As you observed, it allows the one who holds it to absorb the power of any spells or magic—any enchanted weapon—that is used against it. Not only is the spell negated, but the Irda Stone actually draws from the spell and fuels the power of the one who wields the stone. And when Kalrakin wants to cast a spell, the energy stored within the stone will multiply the effect of his casting. To an unimaginable extent, depending on how much magical power the stone has had a chance to absorb."

"So I actually bolstered his magic when I cast the fireball, and the stone absorbed the lightning bolt? I made him *stronger?*" Coryn was dismayed to remember her losing battle with the sorcerer.

"You had no way of knowing what was happening, but yes, that's what transpired," Jenna said bluntly. "We're starting to understand what we're up against."

"Any clue in your book as to how he must have gotten the stone?" asked Dalamar.

Jenna shrugged. "Not really. It was held in the Tower of High Sorcery at Wayreth for thousands of years. But some time ago—the records are sketchy—it was granted to the Speaker of the Sun in Qualinesti, for him to use in combating the forces of the Queen of Darkness. There is no trace of it after that, but no doubt the Dark Knights expropriated it when they occupied Qualinost. Perhaps Kalrakin simply stole it from the knights, or the elves, as the elven realm was falling. Who would know to stop him?"

"He will be hard to defeat with magic," the dark elf noted. "But perhaps we can use uncommon spells to distract him, to get close enough to strike without magic, to slip a dagger between his ribs," he added coldly.

"We might," Jenna said cautiously.

"There must be *some* way to trick him!" Coryn exclaimed.

"If there is, we'll find it," Dalamar said fiercely, his words having a calming effect on the young woman. "We have much work to do."

"And time is wasting," Jenna added tartly, addressing Coryn. "Here—after you change your robe, put these on." The Red Robe indicated a rack of several leather aprons, sooty and worn. She handed the younger woman a pair of stiff leather gloves and some sort of bowl made out of the same material.

"No, it's a helmet—you don't want to burn your hair off, do you?" explained Jenna, amused at Coryn's obvious confusion. "Put it on and fasten it—I'll attach your face-plate before we open the furnace." She turned to Dalamar. "Bring more coal. The glass is almost melted, but we'll need to keep the heat up while we're working."

The dark elf had already removed his robe, Cory saw, looking trim and muscular in his trousers, boots, and suspenders. Like Jenna and Coryn, he, too, slipped into a leather apron and protective mask.

The leather bowl fit comfortably over Coryn's scalp, with a flap that protected the long dark hair she bound at her nape. Very curious now, Coryn allowed Jenna to attach a stiff visor at her forehead. When it fell into place, she could see out of two small, glass-covered holes; the rest of her face, from the helmet down to her throat, was protected by the barrier.

"Take one of these poles." Jenna said, sounding remarkably confident, Coryn thought, as she offered a long tube to the younger woman.

"This is platinum dust, powdered by dwarven smiths in the mines of Thorbardin," Jenna explained, removing a small vial from one of the many nooks and crannies over her workbench. "I obtained it at some expense years ago—this small bottle alone cost the equivalent of ten thousand pieces of steel. You will need three pinches of it, to start with."

Coryn had been about to reach for the vial; she looked up, startled. "These are such rare ingredients. How can you afford them all?" she asked.

Jenna's lips curled in an expression of wry amusement. "When you have magical powers, you find plenty of ways to get rich." She cast a glance at Dalamar, who was bringing several more buckets of coal to them. "You'll find plenty of ways to get poor, too," she added, with an amused shrug.

Hesitantly, Coryn took three pinches of the grainy, gray-colored powder, and dropped them into a clean bowl. In short order she added the other items as directed by Jenna, including talc, powdered charcoal, some crushed mint leaves, and a few shavings of hardwood. Dalamar, meanwhile, worked on his mixture, so that all of the spells would take shape simultaneously.

Next came the more exotic components: Cory painstakingly counted out twenty-five tiny black specks that, Jenna assured her, were dried bat's eyes. Then she broke apart a blue feather, from some bird called a parrot, and scattered the bits of fluff across the top of the odd-smelling mixture in the bowl. Finally came the tinder, dried bits of scrap purportedly made from seaweed that had been harvested from the *bottom* of the ocean, and then dried for ten summers in a desert climate.

"That, my dear, cost a sum of diamonds, twice as much,

by weight, as the dried seaweed." She looked at Coryn and actually grinned. She was enjoying herself immensely, Coryn realized. "I actually *paid* for that."

So was Coryn. "Who sells things like this?"

"I myself did, for a long time—many, too many years. Now that I have closed my shop, there are others—none so knowledgeable, nor with such a complete selection, as I was proud to maintain. I got this from an importer who brought it across the ocean from Kothas. Palanthas has more of such merchants than any other city in the world, though you will find magic-sellers in Sanction, Caergoth, Haven—even in rat-holes like Tarsis."

"Of course there are other ways to gain certain components," Dalamar interjected. "Go out yourself, snare a hundred bats, then dry them in a kiln so carefully that you can remove their eyes, their fur, and their feet, still intact. Takes a bit of learning, and time—but saves you the cost, and dealing with fools."

"I will learn how to do exactly that one day," pledged Cory.

She turned her attention to her glass, which had been heating up all this time. Following instructions, she gathered a medium-sized lump of the molten material on the end of one of the long tubes. Heating it carefully, she watched it soften, and turned the pole quickly to keep the gooey stuff from falling into the furnace. Soon it was soft and malleable.

"Now—we move to the well," said Jenna.

All three smoothly shifted to a depression in the floor where cooling white mists swirled. Coryn spun the pole as fast as she could, watched in amazement as the soft glass swelled into a small, perfect globe. She looked up, questioningly, as Jenna nodded. The Red Robe spoke a word of magic that kindled a spark into each of the three bowls of components.

Immediately, smoke began to churn upward, a thick vapor as pure white as any soft summer cloud. Dense and compact, it roiled and spun over the bowls. Coryn tried to watch the sputtering flames. She knew that she had only seconds to act from the last spark of the flame until the cloud started to disperse. And instinctively she understood what she had to do.

Judging her moment without so much as a glance at the other two wizards, who were busy with their own spell preparations, she exhaled completely and leaned down to touch her lips to the edge of that churning white vapor. Slowly, carefully, she inhaled through her mouth, drawing that mist into her lungs. She felt no shortness of breath—if anything, the pure white smoke was strangely invigorating. She inhaled for a very long time, until all the smoke was gone.

She started blowing through her pursed lips as she touched the end of the shaft to her mouth. The globe of molten glass hung loosely on the other end. Carefully she puffed, filling the soft globe with smoke, watching as it assumed a spherical shape and began to swell. Coryn felt a wonderful sense of release as the smoke rushed out of her, faster and faster, surging into the soft glass. The globe expanded, the glass pure and thick and clear.

She felt drained; the smoke had exhausted her, her limbs were weak and trembling. But she could not falter now. Cory twisted the pole, breaking the connection to the globe, and then she snatched up the cork Jenna had left nearby. She sealed the glass orb tightly and leaned down to pick it up. It was cool to the touch, and strangely light, almost buoyant. Gingerly, she carried it to the work table, setting it on the third wooden stand. Dalamar and Jenna had already placed their own perfect spheres to either side.

They rested there—three perfect globes of smoke, red and white and black murk swirling in their respective containers.

The clouds were impossibly dense, opaque, yet they gave the impression of massive depth, as if one could look inside them for a great distance. Each was a perfect color: red, black, and white.

Coryn didn't say anything—she was too weak to say anything, as she collapsed into the chair and drew deep breaths. But even through her half-closed eyelids she could see the three globes, and she was proud.

The white one was the largest of them all.

———————◆———————

Though it was invisible to the vast population of Krynn, Dalamar watched the black moon as it crested the eastern horizon. The cold, lightless presence filled his heart with sublime power—power that focused, and expanded through the smooth orb of glass he held in his hands. It was past sunset on the Night of the Eye.

Within that globe, black smoke churned and swirled, angrily pressing against the shell of its prison, desperately striving for release, while all around Dalamar was a vast gulf of space, with the steep slopes of the mountain falling away from him. He had teleported here by himself, impatient for the magic, and knowing that the women would soon follow.

"Not long . . . soon you will have the world," he whispered, caressing his creation, the churning sphere of black smoke.

He looked up to the heavens. Solinari, the white moon, was high in the dome of the night sky, the brightest object up there. Red Lunitari chased her alabaster cousin. The black, with its faster orbit, would soon close the gap, and indeed pass the other two before the dawn.

Dalamar felt a small rush of pleasure at the knowledge that he alone could actually see the black disk of Nuitari.

To Jenna and Coryn, it would be but a dark space against the backdrop of stars. To a Black Robe, however, it was the very pulse of life itself. Nuitari had the fastest cycle of all the moons, and though it was far behind the others now, by the middle of the night, it would arrive at zenith with Solinari and Lunitari.

And at that midnight, the Night of the Eye would reign over the world.

Suddenly impatient, the dark elf again gazed at the firmament. He stood at the very crest of Worldsmont, crown of the High Kharolis and the loftiest summit on all of Ansalon. Even in the midst of summer, the air was cold, the night breeze—while gentle—carrying a bite of late autumn. Yet Dalamar felt no discomfort; tonight, magic would warm them all.

He saw Jenna climbing toward him, coming along one of the ridges draping away from the summit. Carrying her orb of red smoke, she made her way steadily along a bank of snow, kicking her steps in the frozen slush as she ascended. In minutes she had joined the dark elf at the summit.

She did not meet the eyes of the other wizard, not at first. Instead she faced the east, head tilted back so that the red light of her moon washed across her face, bringing a bloody brightness to the smooth folds of her robe. "She is beautiful, is she not?" she asked reverently, after a time.

"Yes—though hers is a cold beauty," Dalamar said. "I feel the majesty of my own moon, burning hot as it courses through my veins."

"Where is Coryn—have you seen her yet?" asked the Red Robe.

"No. But I'm not surprised—she will arrive lower on the mountain than either of us."

"Of course," Jenna agreed. Since each of the two of them had been to this mountaintop before, they had been able to teleport unerringly. Coryn, however, had been forced to rely on the coordinates provided by her fellow wizards. For safety's sake, they had directed her to a broad, flat shoulder, where there was little chance of a miscalculation that might send her tumbling down the slope.

"There she is," noted the enchantress, pointing down the west ridge.

Dalamar saw the speck of whiteness, Coryn's robe, moving with painstaking slowness along the snaking crest. He cast a glance at the sky, worried. "She'd better hurry."

"Don't worry. She wouldn't dare let herself be late," Jenna replied.

Indeed, as the moons drew toward the zenith, they could see the young wizard increase her gait, stepping from rock to rock with lengthening and stronger strides, holding her large glass sphere cradled in her hands. She arrived at the summit with minutes to spare.

Plans had been made, the spells memorized and rehearsed during the long afternoon. Now, there didn't seem to be anything more to say. The trio of wizards simply stood and stared, as the three moons drew into very close proximity at the very zenith of the sky. The three gods of magic embraced the world, their power flowed, and the Night of the Eye was upon them.

Jenna began the casting. She held her globe high over her head and addressed the heavens. "Praise to Lunitari the Red. May the blood of life ever reflect your vitality and power."

As still as a statue, she maintained her pose while Dalamar hoisted his own orb.

"Hail to Nuitari the Black. May the perfection of your immaculate darkness ever shroud yourself from danger and threat."

Then he, too, held still, as Coryn raised her pale sphere.

"Honor Solinari the White," she chanted. "May the purity

of your essence bring balm to the very body of the world."

They turned in unison so that they were facing each other. On silent cue, they cast down their spheres onto the rock at the very summit of Worldsmont, the glass shattering simultaneously in a smoky explosion.

Wind whipped their robes. Dalamar blinked back the dust and smoke that stung his eyes, felt needles of icy wind lashing his face and his bare hands and arms. He kept his balance, staring upward, feeling as though he stood at the base of a cyclone. Howling noise surrounded them, colored vapors exploded, and rose boiling toward the sky. The tumult only grew, surrounding and enveloping them, but without menace.

The three pillars of smoke coiled together, rushing upward as if striving for the moons themselves. A hurricane gale now lashed at the wizards, but they remained in place, fixed like statues. The column of vapors suddenly whirled apart, high overhead. The smoke of each color diffused into tendrils, dozens or more of each of the three colors blasting across the sky with meteoric speed, trailing plumes of red, black, or white, flying to the far corners of Ansalon.

Chapter 21

Awakenings

The dwarf's eyelids snapped open. He could feel the chains on his wrists, recognized the pangs of malnutrition in his belly, and knew each scar the lash had scored into his back. These were echoes of suffering, insignificant details from a wasted, vanished time in his life. His empty sockets—his eyes had been torn out by the torturer's tongs twenty years ago—gaped vacantly, but a word of magic brought him a new eye, floating beside him, studying the surroundings, noting every detail of the filthy, wretched dungeon.

Now, tonight, for the first time in more than forty years, he remembered where he was—more important, *who* he was. That identity was a picture in clear, sharp focus, a stark contrast to the confused and tortured ramblings that had teased and tormented him for so many sunless years. That interval was over, banished into the past with the rest of his suffering.

Another simple spell snapped the manacles; the shattered metal brackets fell to the floor with a clang. He strode to the door of the cell, ready for more magic, yet the ancient door yielded to a simple push—it had not even been locked! He sneered at this proof that his captors had grown complacent. They would pay for their folly.

His arcane eye guided him down the dungeon hall and around the corner to the chamber where the two turnkeys gambled and were sharing a bottle of dwarf spirits. The magic of the spell showed him the room a split second before he came into view. One of the turnkeys, a grizzled Theiwar dwarf with a wildly bristling beard, looked up in surprise.

"Hey!" he barked. "Mad Willi's loose—did you forget to lock his chains?"

"Me?" snapped his counterpart. "I ain't been down there fer days!"

"Well, lock him up—I'll watch the cards."

"Like the Abyss, you will! Let the blind old fart find his own way back!"

"I am not Mad Willi," the former prisoner said calmly. Both dwarves gaped at him—they had been on the job for decades, and had never heard a rational statement out of the old wretch. The Theiwar reacted first, lunging for a short sword hanging from the wall. He died before he touched the hilt, his heart stopped by a terrible word of power.

"Hey, Willi!" pleaded the other dwarf, a Daergar. His milky white skin was slick with perspiration. "Take it easy!"

"I am not Mad Willi," he repeated, a moment before the other turnkey started to die—much more slowly than his fellow, as the newly freed prisoner cast a spell of strangulation, a noose that tightened gradually over the thrashing victim's throat.

"I am Willim the Black," he declared, feeling the sensation again: the song of the black moon coursing through his veins. Nuitari had returned, and the black moon's faithful servant had awakened to him in his cell. "I have business in the forest." He was speaking to a pair of corpses, now, but that didn't matter.

"Let all the dwarves of Theibardin know—when I am finished with that, I shall return, and they will pay."

The dungeon door exploded outward, the result of an exultant lightning bolt. Willim the Black strode through the streets of the dwarven city, toward the surface of Krynn, and toward Wayreth Forest beyond.

———◆◆◆———

"Rasilyss—get back in bed! Where are you?"

The old man's voice was trembling, in a mixture of age and concern. He held a small lantern up, yellow beams of light playing around the yard behind the small cottage. It didn't take him long to find his wife near the chicken coop, her skinny calves visible below the hem of her tattered nightgown.

"Come, dear," he said gently, hobbling forward on his own age-weary legs. " 'Twon't be dawn fer hours, yet. You need yer sleep, ya know."

"It is the Night of the Eye," said the old woman, a remark that drew her husband up sharply.

"What did you say?" he demanded.

"Look," said Rasilyss, pointing toward the western sky.

"Eh? You know I can't see beans on my plate without my specs!" the old man snapped. But, in truth, he didn't need his eyeglasses to see the two moons, red and white and both full, slowly sinking from the zenith. "Yer imagining things again. Now, come on, woman! You need yer rest."

"I have been resting for too many years," said his wife, in a voice that the man hardly recognized. Her voice was calm and reasoned, with an underlying hint of elation that brought a pang to his heart. There was no trace of confusion there, no sign of the age-malady that, as often as not, made her unable to recognize him, even unable to remember her own name.

"It's the magic, is it?" he asked in a tone of resignation. "Has it come back to you?"

"Yes, Hanc, my beloved. Yes, it has," she said tenderly. "I have felt the summons of Lunitari."

"So...." His heart was breaking. "So ... you'll be leaving, now."

She came to him in strong strides that belied her frail appearance, her stooped posture. His wife reached up to caress his stubbly cheek, with a hand that was steadier than it had been in many decades.

"You took good care of me, all these years," Rasilyss said. "And I'd love you for that, even if you hadn't stolen my heart when I was a young girl. If I can come back when I am finished, I will. But, you are right, I have to go."

"I understand," he said, shuffling behind her as she went into the house and pulled the red robe out of the trunk where it had been stored for so many years. She dusted it off while he found her old walking shoes, the ones she hadn't worn since her illness had confined her to the house six winters ago. "I hope your goddess watches over you," he said quietly.

"She will," said Rasilyss. "And I think she will watch over you, as well."

Hanc made no reply as she walked down the lane and turned onto the King's Road, the highway running to the west. He waited until she was out of hearing, and then he began to weep.

<hr />

"Are you awake. Have you seen it?" Adramis asked, speaking so quietly that—even if there had been others present—his words would have been inaudible to all, except Aenell. His twin sat up straight, her eyes wide, and she nodded solemnly.

"Yes. I can picture it in my mind," she replied in the same almost telepathic whisper. "A wondrous thing!"

"You have to come outside to see it for real—it's beautiful. The most beautiful thing I have ever seen!"

He took her by the hand, leading her from the tent she shared with several dozen other elf women. The two elves made their way through the sprawling camp, past the low fires and the multitude of slumbering refugees, many of whom were sheltered only by the blankets wrapped around their slim, shivering bodies. The two siblings avoided looking upward, in common agreement, until they were past the last of the fires and the full vastness of the night yawned before them.

Then they stopped and craned their necks, turning their wondering eyes to the vault of the sky. The three moons beamed down at them in the full zenith of the Night of the Eye. Solinari to the left, Lunitari to the right . . . and between—keenly sensed by the twin elves even though they could not see it—the shadow of Nuitari in the middle.

The moons seemed to be dancing up there, pulsing and shimmering in a strangely compelling pattern. There was no sound in the night, but in the hearts of the two elves—both of whom had been apprentice wizards more than forty years earlier—the rhythm of the night rang out as a hypnotic song.

"Sister, we must go," said Adramis.

"I know," Aenell replied. "I have what I need, right here."

He looked at her and saw that her thin cotton sleeping gown now gleamed with the brightness of Solinari. It had become a full robe, warmly enfolding the elf woman's slender body. When Adramis looked down, he saw that he, too, was wearing the garb of their order; his simple sleeping tunic had likewise been transformed.

"I had thought never to feel this white cloth against my skin again," he said, reverently. "It is a blessing."

"A blessing, yes. But I know that it does not come without cost. We are needed, my brother—let us depart."

The two elves, still hand in hand, walked past the sprawling camp, the makeshift city forming a crude shelter for thousands of their Qualinesti cousins, all driven from their homeland, now come here in poverty and ruin to the Plains of Dust. As Adramis and Aenell passed, many of those elves came forth from the tents and huts and lean-tos, and gathered at the edge of the camp, watching in silence as the twins walked past. Solinari shone bright upon them, and their white robes gleamed like a flare, the reflection casting shadows through the camp.

Before them loomed mountains, the massive barrier of the High Kharolis. They would cross those mountains, for their destination was the forest beyond.

The old woodcutter emerged from the thicket, his bow and arrows slung easily across his shoulders as he entered the yard around his little hut. The three dogs came out to greet him, tails wagging, ears flapping, all of them barking delightedly. They frolicked around him as he pushed open the unlocked front door. The man raised a hand and pointed, and the wick of his oil lamp immediately flickered into life.

What a simple pleasure that spell was, and the next one was, too—he snapped his fingers and a fire blazed in the stove, heating the water for his tea as he sat down in his solitary chair, idly scratching the head of his favorite hound as he pondered. It was the Night of the Eye, he knew, the first since the gods had returned to Krynn.

He had been using his magic, quietly, privately, here in the woods ever since the gods returned, but in those months he had never viewed the renewal of magic as having any significant impact on the remaining course of his life.

It had been such a fleeting joy, for, as a teenager, he had first learned the ways of magic; then the gods had vanished from the world—taking their powers with them—just as he was beginning to master the ways of his new craft. The pain of that loss had been so great, that he might easily have perished; certainly he knew of other young wizards who had died chiefly from grief or madness. At length he had grown used to a life barren of that joy. Still, his early dalliance with magic explained why he had never taken a wife. No woman, no relationship with anyone could replace that thrill.

When the magic had gone, he had moved here, and for forty years had lived his life in the forest; he had grown used to solitude, so much so than now he craved it, disdaining the company of fellow human beings. For the greater portion of his life, he had made a simple life in the woods, with only his dogs for company. When the gods had returned, he had seen no reason to move. The few years that were left to him would be eased, slightly, by his magic. But he had had no desire, not the slightest wish, to mingle again with the rest of the world.

Until tonight.

He had heard the summons while he had been nighthunting in a glade a mile from his home. The spell had come from far away, in the east. His reaction had been instant and instinctive: He had hurried home as fast as his old legs could carry him. Now he rose from his chair and pulled open his wardrobe. There it was, tucked in the back, where it had lain folded for more than forty years.

With loving hands he removed the red robe, dusted it off, and put it on. It still fit him. Perfectly.

"Come on, dogs," he said, throwing a few possessions into a small knapsack and pulling the door shut behind him as he left. "We've got a long walk ahead of us."

The crowd was cheering wildly, now, and Sirene could tell from the noise that the steel coins were piling up in her little dish. She danced around, taking stock of the marks, deciding which deserved an extra smile or shimmy—and which she could afford to ignore. A few draconians in the near corner fell into the latter group. They weren't tipping, and one of them had pawed her leg so aggressively he left a mark. With a bump of her hip and a sneer, she knocked their table over on her next pass around the room.

"Make way for some paying customers, you louts," she said over her shoulder as she danced past.

The reptilian warriors leaped to their feet, ready to fight, but they were quickly pushed out of the way by a number of customers eager to claim their coveted spot so close to the stage. Two ships from Ergoth had docked that very afternoon and their crews had spilled ashore, eager for an evening's entertainment. They hadn't seen a woman in months, and their pockets bulged with money.

Sirene was pleased to see a band of these sailors claim the newly righted table, elbowing aside the outnumbered draconians. Sullenly, the reptilian warriors skulked to the bar in the back of the room.

Sirene slithered back up onto the stage, undulating, dropping yet another of the silky veils that barely served to conceal her charms. She knew that the males found her exotic looks attractive. The slender half-elf wondered how they would feel if they knew that this nubile wench they were drooling over was more than a hundred years old! For decades she had been dancing here at the Barnacle Bar, and she knew that her appearance hadn't aged more than a few years—to human eyes—during that whole stint.

Dancing was all she had, now, but it hadn't always been like this. Decades ago she had studied magic, worked hard over spell books and laboratory tables, developing an art that she intended to guide her toward a great future. That dream, like so many others, had been shattered in the wake of the Chaos War, with the departure of the gods. She had heard the talk of the moons coming back, but she had paid little attention. The teeming city was her life, and she had no time for ancient games of magic.

Now the music was building, the drummer and flute player giving it all they had. Sirene dipped and swirled across the stage, dropping the last veil to a chorus of cheers A steady rain of coins poured into her cup. Another minute to let the frenzy run its course, and then she would be done for the night.

She was striking a final pose, peering enticingly at a happy drunk sitting behind her, when she felt the summons. It came through the air, from far beyond this bar, this city, this desolate realm, thrumming in her heart, awakening passions in her belly that she thought were gone forever.

And it brought tears to her eyes.

She was in such a hurry that she left her tips on the stage, drawing an amazed look from Fairie, who was due to go on next. Sirene went straight to the little cubby that served as her dressing room, glaring so fiercely at the protesting innkeeper that he had to step aside. In her tiny cubicle, she pulled out a gown of black fabric, all that was left of her ancient robe. It would have to do, she knew—she wasn't going to wait around for a tailor shop to open in the morning.

Putting on the black robe, she vanished into the night.

He smelled puke—his own vomit—but didn't have the strength to roll over. After all the whiskey he had drunk, he should have slept through till mid-morning, yet he could see a pale hint of dawn along the horizon. For a time he simply lay there, head pounding, nostrils and whiskers clogged with the stink of his own bile.

Groaning, he at last pushed himself to his hands and knees, feeling the usual trembling in his limbs. Where in the Abyss was that bottle? He groped around until his hand closed around the familiar, smooth neck. Shaking it, he felt the weight of just a small amount, a few precious sips of bitter rotgut, sloshing around in the bottom.

Carefully he shifted around to a sitting position, expecting his guts to start heaving at any time. Yet, strangely, his stomach felt all right, and even the throbbing between his temples was fading rapidly.

Finally he stood halfway upright, leaning against one of the shacks that formed this secluded alley, the place where he had been drinking too much and sleeping it off for so many years. He raised the bottle, brought the mouth to his lips—

And then he glimpsed the moon.

Solinari was setting, full and white and even larger than normal because of its proximity to the horizon. He could see that white orb clearly, as he had since its return to Krynn some months ago, but now, for the first time, he sensed that it was calling him.

There was a second's pause as he looked at the bottle, then decisively, he cast it away. Slowly, carefully, he pushed himself to his feet, ready to lean on the shack for balance. But his legs were feeling strong, his breathing grew steady—he wasn't even drunk anymore!

His eyes fell upon the dirty brown rag of his garment, and he felt a crush of shame that brought tears to his eyes. Again, he looked to that moon, and made a silent plea for forgiveness.

The blessing of Solinari flowed around him, a shower of cool white light encircling, washing, and warming him.

By the time he started toward the end of the alley, he was fully awake, and his robe, though still tattered, was a gleaming, ivory white.

———◆———

And so the smoke from the three globes fanned out across the world, serving as beacons of the gods of magic, seeking, searching, and finding those few magic users who had survived, who had lived through the long twilit years when their gods had been absent from the world. The vaporous tendrils spanned mountains, pierced the deepest jungle, and scoured the deserts. They reached deep into the ground, through caverns and dungeons, and penetrated to the upper vaults of the loftiest castles. Mostly the plumes flowed past, but every so often one found a latent coal, an ember of magic that was kindled to life, fanned into a renewed flame.

For more than four decades the followers of the three gods had known only a painful absence, gaping holes where the cherished part of their lives had cruelly stolen away. There was nothing to reward the faith and the skills of those lost souls—no power, no hope, no future.

Many of their number had died, as often as not in wretchedness and despair. Others had turned to wild magic, seduced so fully that they would never be called back. Indeed, there were many sorcerers who cowered and cringed under the Night of the Eye. They felt in that prominence of moonlight the presence of an enemy, an intractable and revitalized foe.

As to those whose magic was kindled, be it black, red, or white, they were awakened, they knew resurgent hope on the Night of the Eye

And they turned their steps toward Wayreth Forest.

CHAPTER

22

THE BASTION

"Will this cursed night never end?" demanded Kalrakin, stalking through the largest room in the Tower, the Hall of Mages. The ceiling was lost in the vast black space, obscured by shadows; the sorcerer's words echoed as he threw back his head and shouted skyward. "Those moons taunt me, vex me. If they would but come closer, I would smite them all!"

Wild magic pulsed suddenly, a flash of light emanating from the white stone he perpetually held in his hand. In that blink of time, he teleported, coming to stand again in the banquet hall where he had first encountered the Master of the Tower. He found food on the table, as usual, but the wizard disdained the splendid feast, knocking over a pitcher of milk in contempt, tumbling a bowl of fruit so that apples and melons rolled across the floor.

"Come to the door, my lord. I see the pink of dawn in the east." Luthar called from the anteroom. "This night is ending, at last!"

"It is about time!" snapped Kalrakin. "And Luthar . . . ?"

"Yes, lord?"

"I have been thinking. I want you to call me 'master,' not lord," Kalrakin declared haughtily. "It seems more fitting, somehow, since I am the new master of the Tower of High Sorcery."

"Very well, my lo—Master," answered the other sorcerer, glancing nervously over his shoulder as Kalrakin approached. Luthar stepped back from the open door to let his companion see the fringe of light coming into view above the eastern horizon. "It is welcome, the sun, is it not?" he asked.

"Welcome in that it signals the conclusion of this accursed night!" snapped the sorcerer. "And the departure of those three moons that so vex my thoughts and my dreams!"

"Do they worry you very much, those moons?"

"No! They insult me—that is all. Of course, they signal their wizards who will come here, soon enough. The white-robed wench I chased away will certainly return, with all the assistance she can gather. But when they come, they will die. The moons taunt me, and for this insult I shall exact keen revenge!"

"How, Master?"

"When the wizards come, I will meet them with a surprise."

"What do you have planned?" Luthar asked, looking around nervously.

"Come!" Kalrakin seized the shorter man's shoulder in an iron grip. Wild magic swirled around them then they vanished, appearing in another second far above the ground level, standing side by side on the outer parapet of one of the tower's loftiest balconies. This was one of several perches supported by cantilevered beams, outcrops that jutted to the sides of the spire like a multitude of short, stubby branches. This platform was a small half circle, surrounded by a crenellated rim of carved black marble near the top of the north spire. Behind them a single door made of the same black stone as the tower's surface offered entry back into the spire.

"Please, Master—you frighten me!" Luthar gasped, cringing from the edge, pressing against the stone door that would allow passage back inside.

"I shall kill them slowly when they come—the red and the black will certainly die as painfully as possible. The white wench appeals to me—I think I may keep her alive for a time . . . after I cut the little bitch's tongue out, of course." He laughed dryly. "I will not have her casting any foolish spells."

"No, er, of course," Luthar said, with a sideways look at his master. The pudgy wizard looked a little pale. "But she seems like such a child—a mere girl! Surely her spells are foolish, as you say—and she is no threat?"

"Don't be beguiled by her appearance," warned the tall mage.

"I'm not beguiled!" Luthar insisted. "It is you that has an eye for her, after all!"

Kalrakin snorted. "I might find a use for her, that is all. Even you have your uses, old companion."

Luthar looked stricken at this remark but bit his lip and remained silent.

"You need more sun!" declared Kalrakin. "Come out here in the open, and savor my work."

"I can see very well from back here, Master."

Turning his back, contemptuously, on the other man, the master of wild magic studied the broad vista. "When these wizards of the three moons come to challenge me for this tower, I intend to greet them properly—in the form of a guardian at our gate. That should put them at their ease. And with a little fortune, all of them will be dead before they even reach our tower."

Stepping forward, Kalrakin placed his hand against the smooth, sun-warmed black marble forming the parapet of this high platform. He closed his eyes and drew upon wild magic, pulled it up from the depths of the world, summoned it through the foundation and walls of the Tower. He called that ancient sorcery to him, imbibing it like a powerful drug—even as its toxicity shook the tower. The ancient structure shuddered and writhed, and this brought a fierce grin to Kalrakin's face. The Irda Stone was like a hot ember, a powerful pulse in his hand. He squeezed and caressed the stone.

The stone barrier began to soften and the wizard pushed slowly, bending the rock to his will, changing its shape, cracking it loose where he wanted it to break. He watched in glee as the entire rim of black marble tumbled away, leaving only a thin fragment of the original balcony. Kalrakin now stood at the very edge of a smooth platform, nothing between himself and a drop of several hundred feet. Luthar gasped and shrank back, but Kalrakin relished the sight of the marble tumbling below. He saw the stone crash into the ground far below, felt the tremor through the soles of his feet.

"That is a start," he announced. "Now, to the next."

He turned and entered the Tower with the still-trembling Luthar close behind. The corridor here was a ring surrounding a plunging well of space, with doors to a pair of similar balconies on the right and left, spaced evenly a third of the way around the outer wall. Shards of stone were scattered across the floor, rubble that marked where Kalrakin had torn a section of railing away in an earlier outburst. Here stretched a perilous drop of several hundred feet, a yawning gap plunging into the central atrium of the north tower.

Ignoring the potential danger, Kalrakin made his way to the closest of the doors on this level, leaving Luthar to edge slowly behind. The stout sorcerer inched along the wall, as far as possible from the broken railing, arriving at another, red parapet, surrounded by a ring of rose-colored marble.

His eyes wide, Luthar watched as Kalrakin strutted back and forth across the parapet.

Again, Kalrakin called on the wild magic, which surged through the sorcerer's flesh, expanding and destroying the stone, until this platform, too, tumbled to the ground. In a few moments he had destroyed the third crenellated wall, tearing the white marble cleanly away from its seamless black foundation.

And still the magic flowed through him; it had become a surging torrent of power quickening his heart, tightening his sinews. His jaw remained clenched, teeth bared in a rictus grin that terrified his comrade—who continued to watch from a cowering safe distance.

Kalrakin now turned his magic to the stone walls of the tower, leaping from a parapet to cling to the smooth outer surface of the spire like a human spider. The wind whipped his beard, his tangled hair, and his filthy robe, as he clawed his way down the wall. The wild magic was strong, and he never lost his foot- or handholds. Halfway down he paused, dangling by one hand as he admired the broken stones scattered on the ground below.

Luthar peered down. In less than a minute Kalrakin had climbed to the ground. Standing below, once again Kalrakin summoned the destructive wild magic, focusing it on the rubble. The stone in his hand glowed especially bright in the daylight as the sorcerer drew the shards of red, black, and white marble together, bending their shapes with his will, assembling them in what first looked like simply a chaotic pile of multicolored stones. Now the master of wild magic began to sculpt with care, precision, even affection. From large wedges of black stone he created a pair of massive, knobby stone boots—boots that each stood five feet high.

Next he shaped other chunks of black stone into a pair of massive, trunklike legs. He worked not with his hands, which remained outstretched and motionless, but with the carving skill of his wild sorcery. The white stone shone like a beacon in his hand, and whatever it touched was shaped.

Moments later Luthar pulled open the tower door, gasping and flushed, having taken ten minutes to run down the tower stairs. The shorter wild mage gaped at the torso of white marble which was taking form above the stone legs and huge black boots. Already the half-built creation loomed high over their heads. In a stir of whimsy, Kalrakin had placed a gash of red marble across his creation's "chest"—just where the heart would be in a mortal giant. Next came the arms, a mixture of some of the red and black marble he had remaining, and finally he was ready for the head.

For this crowning touch, Kalrakin took special care. His golem would be a manlike being, glowering and shelf-browed, with a square rock for a jaw and two deep, lightless caves where the eyes should be. But of course the thing had no organs, no sight, no flesh. This was a guardian connected by wild magic to Kalrakin himself. Luthar stared, speechless. When it was all done, Kalrakin stationed it at the door of the tower, facing outward, standing with arms hanging at its sides. It would never sleep, never rest, never tire.

And when the wizards of three robes came calling, it would destroy them.

——◆◆◆——

Later, Kalrakin stood atop the rampart of the south tower. He was alone, but his spoken word thrummed through the stonework, the flesh, of the lofty structure, reaching the ears of his cohort many hundreds of feet below. The answer returned via the same medium, tremulous but quick.

"Yes, Master? What is it?"

"How long has it been since I have slept?"

The wild mage closed his eyes, not in fatigue but in sublime ecstasy, as he awaited Luthar's reply. The power of the world pulsed in Kalrakin's veins, and his sinews felt as taut, and as strong, as steel cables. His ears tuned to the faintest sound. When he looked out he could clearly see the pattern and shape of every leaf on every tree within a mile of the tower.

The Irda Stone had become a part of him. He admired the object in his hand, flexed his fingers, saw the pulsing of his blood and the fiery veins of wild magic intertwined among the delicate pearly surface. That maze of energy flickered as, from somewhere far away, Luthar's voice reached him.

"I do not know precisely, Master. But I believe it has been many, many weeks—since shortly after we arrived in this tower."

"Yes. I know that it has been four months and five days since I became lord here. And in that time, the Tower has done my sleeping for me. It suffers, it weakens, it fades—just as the three gods do themselves—and I claim all of their collective power for myself. Luthar, this structure *sustains* me—and this stone is the vessel through which I now drink life!"

The mage scrutinized one of the lower platforms on the north tower, a hundred feet away. With a scream of delight, like an eagle surveying his mountaintop domain, Kalrakin sprang into the air. His powerful leap carried him across that space, his tattered robe flapping around him as he landed lightly. Approaching the north wall, where a gaping hole marked a door he had earlier smashed into kindling, the sorcerer placed his hand on the stone frame of the doorway, murmuring an incantation. Immediately the stones parted, creating a narrow gap limned in blue light. Ducking his head, the tall mage stepped into that gap, his gloved hand extended before him. In two steps he emerged—only now he was at the base of the Tower, entering one of the luxurious studies where he knew his companion awaited him.

Luthar, who had been seated before a roaring blaze in the deep fireplace, leaped to his feet in consternation.

"I wish you would stop doing that!" sputtered the shorter wizard. "I can never get used to you just popping in and out of sight like this!"

"Your wishes are insignificant," Kalrakin said, striding to the hearth, extending his hands, absorbing the warmth of the fire for just a second. Magic pulsed from the gauntlet in his hand, sucking the heat and energy of the fire, which was instantly doused into a mound of smoldering logs. When Kalrakin turned away, his body was smoking; wisps of gray vapor swirled from his filthy robe, and rose amid the tangled whiskers of his beard.

"There is something I am just beginning to understand," he added meaningfully.

Luthar knelt nervously at the hearth, putting more logs into the fireplace, casting a quick puff of wind with his own wild magic to draw yellow flames from the coals. "What have you learned, Master?" he finally ventured to ask, turning away from the once more roaring blaze.

"This tower has become the foundation of my being. It is slowly dying, and with each shattered block, each fresh hole in the wall, every blasted stone or swath of ceiling plaster, the power abandons these ancient stones and flows to me. As this structure, raised from the very bones of the world—as the wizards were once so fond of claiming—yields its power to me, it rots away, just as old bones rot. It is dissolving around us even as we grow stronger because of it. When it passes from the world of Krynn, I will take its place . . . strong, even indestructible, and everlasting."

"Do you mean you are becoming immortal?" In spite of his best efforts, Luthar sounded skeptical, and the shorter mage sneaked a close look at Kalrakin, wondering if he might glimpse a glimmer of derangement.

"*More* than immortal!" Kalrakin crowed. "I am becoming not just godlike, but *mightier* than the gods! Those three pathetic moons who created, who watch over this place—they are my puppets, my toys, my bread! I *consume* them, and they deliver me ultimate power!"

With a gesture of his hand, Kalrakin swatted at the fire and a great explosion pulsed through the room, knocking Luthar to the floor. The great force of the blast rushed outward, smashing right through the outer wall of the tower, leaving a gaping hole in the stones and sending the logs, embers, and coals plunging downward to the courtyard forty feet below.

"I am feeding, Luthar, and I grow stronger with every meal!"

The tall mage strode right into the smoldering ruins of the fireplace, placing his hand on a shattered stone, leaning outward through the hole in the wall to admire his handiwork. The larger logs, sooty and still burning, were scattered like matchsticks; a smoky cloud lingered in the air.

Abruptly Kalrakin turned and stalked from the wrecked room, heading for the main hall. All around him were shattered doors, scorched walls, and rubble. The alcoves between each apartment once were magically illuminated and once had displayed the treasures of history: a scepter from Silvanesti sparkling with gems excavated during the Age of Dreams; a vase of icy crystal, permanently chilled, reputed to have come, a dozen centuries ago, from some land far across the sea; a pair of bracers that had been worn by Huma himself when he flew against the Dark Queen. Now the alcoves were empty, the enchantments drained away, the ground was strewn with shards of broken glass and scattered jewels gleaming weakly in the sunlight that spilled through the various breaches in the outer wall.

This had once been a level of luxuriously appointed apartments, quarters for the mightiest of the wizards who had studied, taught, and convened here. Paintings from the old masters of Krynn had decorated each anteroom, with many of the canvasses predating the first Cataclysm. Now the frames were broken, the images stained and distorted and shredded by wild magic.

Kalrakin paused to admire one of the ruined paintings. Once it had been an intricate moving painting, a ritual display of elegant dancers performing their stylized steps at a grand ball in the grand manor of the Lord of Palanthas. The sorcerer snorted in amusement—the painting still moved—but now the lord in the image was dead, impaled by a decorative halberd, while the dancers moaned and writhed on the floor, their faces pocked by plague, blood running from their mouths and ears.

He placed his hand against the wall, and a blue-lit doorway opened. Two steps took Kalrakin through the outer wall of the Tower, emerging at ground level. He advanced until he stood just within the gates in the outer courtyard. Here his golem stood silent watch, its marbled brows tiered in a constant frown, the boulders of its fists dangling at its sides. Those fists, at the low terminus of two long, powerful arms, hung high above the tall sorcerer's head.

"Keep a careful watch, my stone sentry," Kalrakin said, tracing his hand over the craggy outline of one of its massive boots. "Be ready to smite the lackeys of the three gods—I know they will be here soon."

Of course there came no reply, but the wild mage nodded serenely, utterly reassured by the emanations of readiness he felt within the stone sentry. When it was needed, the golem would be ready.

Then Kalrakin was back in the Tower of Sorcery, this time in the hallway outside that vexing door that still resisted his most determined efforts. He stood on one of the damaged floorboards, staring at the barrier contemptuously. He toyed with the thought of another convulsive blast of magic, but decided the contemptible chamber was not worth his efforts; instead, he turned and stalked away, following the broken boards like a rickety bridge toward the stone stairwell at the end of the hall.

Halfway there he halted, frozen in his tracks. His mind churning with pent-up frustration, he whirled, his long finger extended toward that vexing door. An inarticulate cry exploded from his mouth, and wild magic shimmered in the air. That power lashed out, smashed into the door—and then burst backward against the spellcaster, slamming Kalrakin down onto the remains of the floor, rolling him along until he fell between two support beams, barely catching himself with a desperate grab of one lanky arm.

He pulled himself back and staggered toward the stairs, growing stronger every minute. Lost in thought, he opened another dimension door in the stone wall. His next step brought him back to the anteroom.

"Luthar! Bring me drink!" he called, his voice booming and echoing through the empty chamber and its towering adjacent hallways.

"Yes—of course, Master!" Kalrakin heard footsteps from the direction of the kitchen and, moments later, Luthar hastened into view. He carried a crystal pitcher, the outside of it slick with condensation.

"Chilled water," offered the short mage.

Taking the pitcher with a swipe of his hand, Kalrakin leaned his head back and poured the ice-cold contents into his gaping mouth. He ignored the spillage, though in fact much of the water splashed through his beard, soaked his robe, and fell into a growing puddle on the floor. When the pitcher was empty, the mage sent it flying across the hall; it shattered against the stone hearth, and joined the wreckage on the floor.

"Would you like something to eat?" asked Luthar.

"Hah!" Kalrakin sneered at the very idea. "Wild magic is my breath, and the body of this tower is my bread! I have no need of sleep, and I have no need of food, not while this ancient totem still stands."

"Dare I ask—how long will that be?" said the shorter mage somewhat wearily. "I am ready to go away from here, Master. There is a sense of doom about this place that allows me no peace."

"We do not need peace, my friend—for we have power!"

Magic sparked from Kalrakin's slender fingertips, arcing through the room in repeated, visible streams. The stone over the door began to melt, flowing like mud, seeping right across the wooden panel that had allowed access into and out of the tower. Pieces of black stone tumbled to the floor, sparking and flaming, rolling around the room, trailing plumes of thick smoke. Luthar cried out and fled from the room, though not before one of the rolling chunks of molten rock scorched the hem of his robe.

Kalrakin took scant notice. He flexed his fist and his voice rose in a keening, bestial cry, and still the very substance of the Tower broke apart and flowed down and added to his magic. Deeper and deeper the molten stone piled, sludgy waves of darkness rolling down across already-cooling base elements. By the time he was finished, the door was gone, buried under a sheen of hard black stone.

CHAPTER

23

PATHWAY AND GUARDIAN

"See how the forest is thick against the slope, there in the foothills?" Coryn asked, pointing toward the foot of the mountain.

"Yes," agreed Jenna, pausing and leaning on the staff that she was carrying. Dalamar too came to a stop, resting on his haunches as they looked down the steep slope.

"It wasn't there last night," the White Robe pointed out. "Last night that was a dry plain for as far as I could see."

"Then Wayreth has, at last, come to us," Jenna said, with a surprising rush of relief. "We have no time to waste!"

Coryn looked back at the lofty ridge they had descended. The summit itself was already out of sight behind the mountain's shoulder. She knew that they had negotiated the steepest parts of the descent, which had so far taken much of the Night of the Eye and half of the following day. The sun was slipping into the afternoon, and the air was growing more humid, and warmer, as they came down from the lofty elevation.

Though they had gone without sleep for a whole day, none of the three had wanted to rest on the mountaintop. Now, the sight of the forest they sought, the wood that surrounded the Tower of High Sorcery, infused them with new energy. They worked their way down the slope as quickly as possible, stepping sideways, Jenna leaning heavily on her staff while the more agile Cory and Dalamar skidded ahead, waiting just long enough for the Red Robe to catch up.

As they neared the ground, they could see the full vastness of the forest and smell the verdant wood—a mixture of pollen, foliage, and rot. Coryn recognized with certainty the forest that had provided her with a path to the Tower. The trees were tall, gnarled, and majestic. Those strands of moss still looked like beards, as if venerable old men formed a great congregation in the thick of the woods. Occasional birds hooted and cawed, though she did not hear the distinctive avian summons that marked her first visit. This time, though, she thought she imagined a layer of mist or vapor deep in the woods, lurking between the trees, collecting as a miasma in the hollows.

A path became apparent as soon as they reached the edge of the wood. Jenna seemed to find a renewed sense of youth and vitality as she strolled along, and Coryn found she had to hurry to make sure she didn't fall behind.

"How long has it been since we treaded these pathways?" mused the Red Robe, regarding Dalamar with an almost affectionate sidelong glance. "It feels as welcome and familiar as ever, I admit."

"Certainly there were many times I felt we would never be here, never find this place again," Dalamar acknowledged. He smiled wryly. "Even as recently as a few days ago."

Coryn was content to follow her two companions in reverent silence. Birds cried out familiarly in the depths of the woods. But that mist was an oppressive intruder, she sensed, growing thicker and ever more poisonous as the Master of the Tower lost his battle with the sorcerer Kalrakin.

The trail was not long, and though it seemed to grow

dark, that was only the effect of the dense canopy overhead. After perhaps an hour of steady progress, the wizards saw a brightening in the twilight murk. Another hundred steps brought them to the bright, sunlit clearing where the twin spires of the Tower of High Sorcery clawed their way into the afternoon sky.

They saw at once that the Tower had suffered physically—was pocked and scarred in dozens of places—and even more, they felt its pain.

"It's suffering—more than ever," Coryn said quietly, looking at the lofty structure. In several places balconies had been torn right off of the outer walls, leaving splintered remnants of beams and gashing, angry wounds in the smooth face of the black stone. In her mind's eye she saw the Tower trembling and shivering with agony.

"Such appalling savagery!" Jenna said sadly. "And this tower has withstood the ravages of the world for thousands of years!"

"It has been damaged badly since I took the Test," Coryn said.

"The wild sorcerer is a tumor, rotting it from the inside," the Red Robe declared.

"We *must* cut this tumor out," said Dalamar determinedly.

Jenna took the lead, Coryn to her left and Dalamar to her right, as they strode purposefully into the clearing and approached the spiderweb glow of the magical gates, the golden and silver wires looking feeble and frail. Through the airy barrier they could see the foretower between the great spires. But something else was different, and with a gasp of surprise Cory realized what it was.

"The door where I entered—it's not here anymore!"

"It looks as though the stone of the foretower has been melted down to cover it up," Jenna observed through a tight, angry grimace. "That was the only door on the ground level of the Tower."

"I will kill that sorcerous bastard, so help me Nuitari, if it's the last thing I do." Dalamar's words sent a shiver down Coryn's spine.

She had a strong feeling they were being watched, and she glared up at the structure, scanning every aperture, looking for the brooding, hateful visage of Kalrakin.

Instead, her attention was drawn to an ominous stone sculpture standing just off to the side, screened by the courtyard wall. All three gasped in unison as they realized they were looking at a giant-sized stone statue.

"What *is* that?" she asked, feeling a stab of fear.

"A golem—of stone. He made it from marble that he tore right from the body of the tower," Dalamar explained, his words clipped, his voice cold. "It is further blasphemy—if I could send that cursed sorcerer to the Abyss for ten thousand years, it would still be inadequate punishment!"

"Be careful!" Jenna warned sharply as the dark elf strode forward.

Dalamar didn't appear to hear; certainly, he took no heed of her warning. He raised both hands straight out before him, uttered a word of command, and spread his arms quickly to the sides. Immediately the feathery gates parted, opening the way into the Tower's courtyard.

At the same time, the golem moved. Coryn could scarcely believe her eyes as the stone giant stepped forward with a smooth, fluid stride—just as if it were made of supple flesh and not rigid stone. The great arms swung easily, while the block of a head turned to regard them with impassive majesty, like the cliff of a mountainous summit acknowledging some puny, insolent climber. The overhanging brow shaded unseen eyes within twin caves underneath. Coryn could feel them boring into her, appraising and menacing.

The dark elf, meanwhile, seemed undeterred; he had already advanced through the opened gate, with Coryn and Jenna scurrying after.

"Spread out," Jenna urged Coryn, as soon as the two of them had entered the compound.

The White Robe needed no urging. She sprinted to the side, casting through her mind for a spell, some incantation to smite this giant. Fire? Ice? She discarded these as useless—how could they hurt stone? Strangely, the next thing that came into her mind was mud—yet how would mud be helpful?

Dalamar showed no hesitation. He was already spellcasting, his right hand extended like a pike, finger pointing at the golem's marble chest. In the next instant, a bolt of lightning crackled, sizzling outward from the dark elf, lancing into the body of the stone creature. Coryn smelled the acrid tang of charged air even before she saw the brilliant spear of light. She watched in awe as the bolt seemed to wrap itself around the guardian, tearing at the hard rock of its flesh, searing and burning with thunderous force.

The golem took a step backward and shook itself, and just like that, the lightning bolt was gone. It had torn out a chunk of the monster's flank, leaving a black, smoking scar. But the magical creature was not visibly hurt—instead, it lowered its head and sprang toward the dark elf, landing with a ground-shaking thud right next to where Dalamar was standing.

Except that now the Black Robe was a dozen paces away. He had used an instantaneous escape spell to buy himself a few seconds. Jenna—limping along the inner wall of the courtyard, moving away from her fellow wizards—took advantage of that interval to cast her own lightning spear.

A violent explosion of fire engulfed the golem, knocking it back a step as the Red Robe's spell smashed home. The creature slumped to one knee, several shards of stone breaking from its rocky body. Again that acrid stench permeated

DOUGLAS NILES

the air, and the noise of the blast left everyone's ears ringing. Coryn shook her head to clear the buzz, saw Dalamar waving to her. The dark elf was pale, his face slick with sweat.

"Your turn—now!" he shouted.

Coryn raised her finger and pointed, remembering the words to one of the spells she had gained in the Test. The golem, lurching unsteadily, pushed itself up to a standing position, shedding several more large fragments of stone as it moved. The young sorceress aimed for its wound, felt the surge of magic, and cried the words of command that would unleash the spell.

The magic flowed from her and assailed the giant—but it felt as though her power were being resisted by a strong barrier. She strained, her gut tightening under the effort, and the spell was reinforced; a bolt slammed into one of the giant's hands. Coryn grimaced, clenched her fists, concentrated, and felt the magic penetrate, turning the hard marble into dripping goo. The monster shook its great arm and the fist fell away, falling to the ground as globs of mud.

But the stone creature seemed undaunted; it was only a very small fraction of its total mass. The young White Robe slumped to the ground, gasping for breath, her face slicked with sweat. Never had the casting of a spell drained so much from her—and she had barely wounded the massive construct! She could sense the wild sorcery of the golem's maker, imbued in the stony body, actually gaining strength from their magical attacks.

The golem took a step toward Dalamar, and the dark elf turned and ran toward the Tower, drawing the creature away from Jenna and Coryn.

"Cast another spell—now!" cried the Red Robe.

"I can't!" It was terrible, but true: Coryn had no spell ready, and could think of no magic with which to smite this lethal foe. Furthermore, she was too weary, too drained,

240

even to *think*. She groaned aloud; then a spark flickered in her subconscious. Pushing herself to her knees, she struggled to recall the words to a certain spell, focusing on her hatred of the foul—*blasphemous*, Dalamar had said, and he was right—being before her.

Her thoughts were gathering, as Dalamar turned to face the advancing golem. The dark elf raised his hands, twisted them through a pattern in the air as he chanted the words to a spell. With one of those great fists, the creature wrenched a piece of stone from its own wound, and hurled the missile at the Black Robe. Coryn gasped as she saw the rock, as big as a human skull, strike Dalamar and send him sprawling to the ground.

Jenna, leaning on her staff with her left hand, gestured with her right as she called out a spell. The words boomed, reminding Coryn of the great cracks that periodically scored the Icewall and sent lingering echoes for miles across the tundra. At the sound the golem spun around with surprising agility, raising another block of stone to cast at the wizard— but the Red Robe's spell blasted outward before the creature could finish.

A storm of ice assailed the stony giant, hailstones as big as fists smashing against the rocky visage in a whirlwind gale. Wind howled, chilling the entire area. The staccato pounding of the icy bombardment drummed like an avalanche, powerful enough to knock the golem off its feet. Great pellets of ice bashed and pounded, swelling in force and power.

More and more hailstones piled up. Ice draped the frowning brow of the stone giant, gathered in white heaps in those cavelike eye sockets, limned the entire form in a cocoon of rigid frost. For many seconds Jenna kept up the bombardment, until the golem was nearly buried. Finally the storm ceased and the older woman slumped back against the courtyard wall, drawn and trembling from the exertion of the mighty casting.

Coryn skirted around the now motionless, ice-caked guardian and raced to Dalamar. His face was utterly white, and his eyes were shut. He showed no sign of awareness as the White Robe leaned over him, gently probing at his scalp. He had lost a lot of blood, but she could only hope that his skull was not fractured. The elf's teeth chattered, and he cried out in pain when Cory gingerly touched his injured right shoulder. Suddenly he reached out and took her arm with his left hand, his fingers tightening like a vise around her. His eyes opened and came into focus, his gaze burning into the woman's with searing intensity as he pulled his head up from the ground.

"Forget me! Destroy it!" he hissed, then released his grip and fell back. He drew a deep breath, and his eyes clouded. Coryn felt a horrible sense of helplessness. She turned, despairing at the sight of shuddering and slowly increasing movement within that massive drift of ice. Chunks of frost broke free as one marbled arm thrust upward; then the whole mound shivered and came apart as the golem forced itself slowly to its feet.

But her lightning bolt spell was coiled and ready now. She pointed a finger and cried the words, the sound of her own voice strange to her, like the shrieking of a powerful storm. She felt a joyous release, watched as the electrical spear crackled outward, searing into the golem's face. Stones blasted loose and the creature took another step back, driven by the unusual force of the spell. Coryn leaped to her feet, still casting, forcing the lightning into her foe as if she were driving a blade deeper into its hateful flesh.

But once again she felt a powerful barrier deflect much of the power of her magic. Her power was being sucked from her and then rechanneled into her enemy. Her hand began to burn. Coryn shouted in anguish, a pitiable sound lost in the shattering of ice and the groaning of the great rocky golem. It stood once again, shrugging off the mantle of frost that draped from its broad shoulders; its face, revealed as the lightning faded away, was pocked and scarred, but its sightless eyes once again focused on the wizards.

In addition to the wounds on its face, one of the creature's arms had broken off, the stub jutting upward like a small monolith in the slushy melt. But the golem displayed no real signs of hindrance. It turned slowly, those gaping sockets in its face falling upon the motionless black-robed wizard, and the young woman in white who stood before him. Coryn frantically looked for Jenna and saw the Red Robe drawing herself up again, leaning on her staff while forcing herself to stand. Her face was pale, and when she started to chant, her voice was so weak the younger woman couldn't discern the words.

The golem heard the chanting, however, for it turned toward the Red Robe then smoothly reached down and pulled the remnant of its broken limb—which was still a pillar of marble some four feet long, and as big around as a man's torso—free. Raising the thing like a missile, it poised for a throw that would have crushed Jenna against the courtyard wall.

"No!" Coryn cried—and that exclamation started her mind whirling again. She still had potentially powerful spells, vibrant and alive with white magic. Perhaps she could protect her friend. The young wizard stood, glaring at the back of the golem, and held her cupped hands before her face.

"Palmis denni!"

Immediately the form of a massive hand appeared, disembodied and translucent—right behind the golem. Coryn reached with her right hand and the huge magical apparition matched her gesture perfectly. The massive hand reached for the stone guardian with grasping fingers. She squeezed, and the magic image grasped the broken arm just in time to interfere with the stone giant's throw.

Instead of flying toward Jenna, the chunk of marble simply shot to the side, pulled downward by Cory's spell, smashing ineffectually into the ground. With remarkable swiftness, the construct turned and took a long stride toward the white- and black-robed wizards, its gait incongruously supple and life-like. Coryn held up her hand, palm outward, the universal gesture commanding *stop* even without any spoken word; and the massive magical hand interposed itself between the wizard and the golem, pressing against the marble torso and stopping the huge creature in its tracks.

The heavy brow furrowed in a look of confusion. It swatted at the apparition with its remaining arm, but the magical hand blocked the blow. Then Coryn mimicked a backward slap, swatting aside the mighty cudgel of the golem's fist. The creature tried to step to the side, and once again the wizard held up her hand and parried the maneuver, holding the monster at bay.

Now the golem paused, its marbled visage raised to focus on Coryn. She pushed her hand forward, and the magical fist met the torso of the creature with powerful pressure; though she was unable to drive it backward, it could not advance. She felt the force of its great tonnage coming to bear against her, such pressure she feared her arm would break.

Countering rapidly, she drew her hand back, and the magic arm followed suit, pulling away so quickly the golem lost its balance and fell forward, its lone arm propping up its massive body precariously. Coryn felt the earthshaking thud of its fall, and knew she had but a few seconds to act before it recovered. A downward glance showed that Dalamar's eyes had flickered open; his hand was pressed against the bleeding wound on his scalp.

"Use it!" he hissed.

Coryn turned away, still wielding her magical hand, bringing it to bear against the creature's face. She punched and pressed, trying to twist it backward, to keep the stone giant from rising.

"Use what?" she gasped to Dalamar in despair.

With a lurch and a moan of straining rock that sounded like a cry of determination, the golem rose to its knees and swatted at the disembodied image. The White Robe tried to adjust, but she was too slow; the monster caught the image in its massive fist, drove it to the ground, and tried to crush it.

The pain was horrible, as if her own hand were trapped in a vise. Coryn cried out, twisting around, and fell to the ground, rolling over to cradle her wrist. Instantly she dispelled the magic—the enchanted fist disappeared. Her pain began to ebb. But lying next to Dalamar, she felt defeated.

"Your wand—*use* it!"

Of course! She grasped at that hope and leaped to her feet, pulling the wand from its sleeve in the front of her robe.

The golem smoothly rose to its feet, close to the two prostrate mages. If it stepped fast, it would crush them. Coryn reached for Dalamar's arm, ignoring his groan of pain as she tried to yank him out of the way.

Jenna took a step forward. She had recovered enough of her strength to cast another spell. The golem swung down, aiming its massive fist at the white-robed mage, but that stone fist struck an unseen barrier just inches from Coryn's face. With the terrible screech of grinding rock, the creature attacked that invisible wall again and again; then it spun, lowered its head toward Jenna, and charged. Almost immediately it crashed to a halt, blocked by the same invisible force.

Coryn looked at Jenna, who was inching forward, a look on her face of courage, but also of desperate pain, as she concentrated on her spell.

In a frenzy the golem thrashed around the confines of what looked to Coryn to be a large, and utterly invisible, cage. With its single fist the creature smashed at the wall that hindered it on every side. Jenna continued to advance slowly, leaning forward on her staff, clutching the wooden rod in a white-knuckled clasp, maintaining a low, almost inaudible chant.

The golem ceased its fruitless struggles, crouching on the massive pillars of its legs, its one arm cocked back, poised for one last mighty blow in the Red Robe's direction. Jenna halted a dozen paces from the cage. Coryn could hear the words now, the steady repetition a monotonic drone.

"Ammm . . . harrarr . . . moot. . . ."

Jenna shook with the effort to maintain the stone giant's confinement, staggering from weakness, leaning both hands upon her staff. Dalamar groaned, trying to stagger to his feet, but crumpling back down.

"End this! Destroy the thing!" he urged Coryn weakly. His black robe was stained with blood, soaking the shoulder and arm of his right side.

Coryn gazed at the golem's knobby back. Images danced in her mind—she saw swarms of great meteors plunging from the sky, magical missiles arcing from her fingertips in great barrages, blasts of heat and ice and fire all exploding simultaneously toward her foe. She extended the wand, unsure of what to say or do, not knowing what to expect.

Jenna staggered and slumped to a knee, only her hands clutching her staff keeping her from a headlong fall. Its cage suddenly weakened, the golem exploded into action with a speed that belied its huge mass, flinging itself toward the Red Robe. The wall of force crackled and bulged against the onslaught, and Jenna shook her head and tried to rise but stumbled.

As Jenna went down, the spell dissolved, freeing the golem. It lunged, the hammer of its fist raised above the enchantress, pounding downward. There was a flash of red as the woman rolled desperately to the side.

"No!" cried Coryn.

Solinari was with her. The wand thrummed in her hand, vibrating with concentrated power. She was abruptly surrounded by whiteness, a storm of magic drawn from the forest, from the air, from the lingering essence of the white moon. The swirling power coalesced around the young woman, exploded through the tool of her slender wand, and wrapped the golem in an irresistible grip. Its stone body cracked and crumbled with a force that shook the ground. The swirling and the noise and the stone-crushing seemed to go on forever.

But when the spell at last faded, there was only a pile of multicolored rock pieces where the golem had stood.

CHAPTER

24

WEARERS OF THE THREE ROBES

There is no door—so how can we get into the Tower?" asked Coryn. She stood in the courtyard, glaring up at the twin spires.

"We could fly up to one of those balconies and try to get in that way," Jenna suggested, "as soon as Dalamar is fit to take part in the attack."

"I won't hold you up," growled the dark elf. He had finished wrapping a piece of dark cloth around his scalp, where the wound had ceased to bleed. "But I'm not certain that would be the best tactic—a wizard who is flying is extremely vulnerable. Kalrakin could strike at us in the air, and we couldn't do much to stop him."

He pulled up his hood and draped it over the top of his head, concealing the makeshift bandage almost completely. "Still, I'm ready to go," he added in a tone of grim determination.

"Wait," Jenna said, suddenly holding up her hand. "It's almost dark. The moons will be rising, and the spell we cast on the Night of the Eye will not take long to show results. Let us look to the forest before we attack. We may find assistance there."

The sun had already dropped below the level of the courtyard walls, casting the whole area into purple shadows. Coryn looked out through the gates, saw that the face of the forest was glowing with emerald vitality, brilliantly lit by the nearly horizontal rays of the sun. In the frenzy of the battle, she had almost forgotten the spell they had cast on the previous night. Now she felt curiosity and hope: Had wizards heard the summons, and how long would it take them to get here?

Solinari was just beginning to rise, while Coryn sensed that Nuitari was already high in the sky. The very memory of the beautiful white moon, pure and full as during the previous night, nearly took Cory's breath away. For a moment she felt a dizzying rush of power, release, escape, and freedom—all embodied in the white sphere. How long would it be before she saw it again? She strained to see through the trees, even as she told herself that it wouldn't crest into view for several more hours.

Then, side by side with Jenna, she strode across the courtyard; Dalamar lingered behind to watch for any sign of Kalrakin on the ramparts or balconies. The Red Robe raised her hands as they neared the gate, uttered a magical command that was both reverent and exultant. She spread her hands to the sides and the shimmering gates vanished, opening the passage from Wayreth Forest into the courtyard.

"Can you sense them?" Jenna asked. "Coming through the woods?"

"I don't know," Cory admitted, straining for a glimpse of a robe of any color.

"Come, cousins under the three moons!" Jenna cried. "Let us reclaim our birthright!"

Coryn saw a glimmer of white, flashing between two massive, gnarled trunks. A moment later an old, old man in a clean, unadorned robe of white emerged from the fringe of the forest. He tottered weakly, leaning upon a staff as he walked slowly. The young wizard was about to hurry forward, to give him her arm as a support, when Jenna touched her on her elbow.

"That is Bernardus," she whispered, her voice strangely taut. Coryn glanced at the Red Robe and saw that tears were welling in Jenna's eyes. "He has been blind drunk, living in the gutters of Palanthas, for years, sleeping in filth and eating . . . Solinari only knows what. I have tried to reach him many times during those dark years, most recently a few months ago, after the moons returned to the skies. Always he pushed me away with scorn and fear. He was lost for all that time. Your casting on the Night of the Eye, even if his presence is all that it has wrought, still, it has worked a miracle."

Coryn studied Bernardus. His hand on the staff was bony, tightly wrapped with papery skin. His nose was inflamed, his eyes rheumy and watering, and grinning at her he revealed only two or three brown stubs of teeth.

Yet those bony arms embraced her with undeniable strength, and his breath smelled sweet as he whispered into her ear. "May all the gods rejoice, child, that a true daughter of Solinari has come forward to lead our order out of the darkness."

"Thank you, Grandfather—" She lapsed into the honorific of her tribe without thinking. He seemed touched. "And welcome back to our tower."

"Aye, lass. Let's see what can be done about this place." He frowned as he scanned the damaged facade. Still leaning on his staff, he hobbled across the courtyard, muttering and shaking his head.

By this time other figures, one or two at a time, were emerging from the woods and approaching the gates with various degrees. Coryn was taken aback at the sight of one dwarfish figure, swathed in a black robe with the cowl pulled low to mask the hateful sun. He limped grotesquely, and when he reached the shadow of the gates, two bent, crooked hands pulled the hood back.

Coryn gasped aloud as she beheld a scarred, eyeless face, surrounded by a thin patch of scraggly beard. A wide gash of a mouth gaped in a leering grin, and as that horrid face looked her over, up and down, she drew her robes more tightly about her breasts, and took a step backward.

"A young one, huh?" wheezed the dwarf with a harsh, breathy bark—a sound that Coryn only recognized as a laugh after several seconds. "Dalamar knows I sure likes 'em young! So where is that dark elf scoundrel?" The dwarf's sightless sockets swept across the courtyard. Clearly he could not "see" anything, yet he grinned in satisfaction when his "gaze" fell in Dalamar's direction. "Ah, there he is!"

The dwarf shuffled into the courtyard, toward the blank face of the foretower. He stopped and turned to face Coryn, enacting an elaborate bow.

"Willim the Black, at yer service," he said with the same hacking chuckle, lewdly emphasizing the last word. Coryn watched, speechless, as he limped toward the foretower.

By this time, Jenna was warmly hugging another newcomer, a red-robed woman, smaller and much older than the Red Lady of Palanthas.

"Rasilyss, my old teacher," Coryn's companion murmured. "May Lunitari be blessed—I never thought to see you again!"

"Bah, girl—you know I never sleep on the Night of the Eye. Yet it has been many years since those moons gave me a thrill such as this one past. I had no choice but to come."

"I know, dear. And thank you," Jenna said before reluctantly breaking the embrace. "Do you remember another of your students, Scharon, of the Icereach?"

"Of course," Rasilyss replied as her eyes fell upon Coryn. "I see a resemblance before me that quite takes my breath away."

"She is my grandmother," Coryn said with a stab of worry. "At least, she was. I have not seen her for many months. I fear her health is failing."

"Have faith, girl. We old grandmothers can be stronger than you know."

"Thank you for the kind words," Coryn said. "And welcome back to the Tower of Sorcery."

There were many more of them coming, now, representatives of all three robes. Most were humans, and the great majority of these were aged, appearing to be considerably older than Jenna. Those who were not old were surprisingly young, in their early twenties or teens, and they gawked around them in wide-eyed wonder as they filed through the gates and bowed to the two robed wizards who met them.

"Ah, these youngsters are the legacy of the previous Head of the White Robes, Palin Majere," Jenna explained. "Many are the students who passed through his academy in Solace—before it was destroyed in the darker hours of the age."

Coryn glanced with interest at some of these fresh-faced students, all of whom met her inspection with expressions approaching awe. A young man, with a red peach-fuzz beard, hastened to kneel at her feet and take her hand, thanking her for the summons. A stout woman in an oversized white robe bowed formally to Coryn, and she batted away the tears in her eyes—tears of gratitude, Cory knew. She was a young person, but twenty years of age or so—old enough to make the White Robe feel acutely aware of her youth in the presence of all of these more experienced magic users.

Two elves came up to her, a surprisingly youthful-looking male and female bearing more than a passing resemblance to each other. "I am Adramis, and this is my sister Aenell. We heard your summons, Mistress, and it has brought us more joy than we have known in four decades."

"Thank you, and welcome," Coryn replied.

"Solinari, in his wisdom has chosen well," offered Aenell, holding her brother's hand in one hand as she reached out the other to clasp Coryn's. "Bless you!"

All the arrivals looked at the Tower with horrified expressions, and soft comments of disapproval and distress could be heard. The wizards in the courtyard spread out to look upon the Tower from all angles. They were growing angry, Coryn realized, and their numbers made her feel much more hopeful.

Here came another dwarf, also a Black Robe, who was followed by several more elves in a small band, a mixture of red and white. Now they were appearing in droves, shuffling by and murmuring their gratitude.

"The Tower has suffered terribly," said one elder White Robe, a tall and slender man who introduced himself as Galarant. "Even in comparison to the suffering inflicted upon the whole of Ansalon, this is blasphemy and desecration. Bless Solinari and all the gods, that we may take this place back."

"Yes, Grandfather," Coryn said. "With his help, we will prevail."

Just then, something exploded in the courtyard. Coryn heard shouts of alarm and saw a residue of dust floating in the air, marking the spot of a violent impact. Two wizards, a White and Red Robe, lay near that place. The Red Robe was twitching and groaning; the White Robe, her garment stained with blood, lay still.

"Damn him—not the slightest warning. A blast of wild magic came from up there," said Galarant, pointing toward a lofty parapet. "I saw the sorcerer for a moment; then he cast the spell. Then he disappeared."

"Spread out!" someone called—Coryn thought it was Jenna—and the wizards were already instinctively obeying.

"There!" cried one of the elf twins, pointing toward a different parapet. Kalrakin stood there, glaring down at them from perhaps halfway up the tower. Several wizards were taking to the air, spells of flying lifting them quickly skyward. Others cast quick spells of attack: lightning bolts, magic missiles, and other violent magical onslaughts, which surged upward.

The wild sorcerer laughed aloud. He held up his right hand, where the Irda Stone glowed brightly. One lightning bolt, lancing through the shadows of twilight, blasted into Kalrakin and simply vanished, causing the stone to pulse briefly brighter. The other spells slammed home and each one disappeared, sucked into the powerful enchantment of the ancient artifact. With each attack the stone shimmered and glowed even stronger until, after the volley had faded away, the object gleamed furiously in the sorcerer's hand.

By this time several of the flying wizards had closed in. A Red Robe was in the lead, a man who lunged for the sorcerer with his hands outstretched. Kalrakin laughed loud again, and his wild magic pulsed; a stab of brilliant light flashed out, tearing through the flying wizard's flesh with brutal violence. Immediately the man fell backward, smoke and flames trailing from his ruined robes. Coryn hoped the poor mage was already dead before he violently struck the unforgiving paving stones.

Other brave flyers veered away. One White Robe—Cory recognized old Bernardus—cast a series of potent missiles that vanished, one after the other, into the artifact. The attack served one purpose, at least, in that the rest of those wizards who had taken to the air were able to dive and swerve out of the sorcerer's line of sight. Bernardus pressed home his onslaught, but then Coryn moaned with horror as a well-aimed bolt of wild magic ripped into his frail body. He, too, tumbled, smoking and charred, out of the sky.

"Fall back!" cried Coryn. "Back to the gates!"

Kalrakin disappeared in a blink. Coryn looked around wildly, expecting him to appear somewhere in the courtyard. Apparently he had retreated back into the Tower, however, for there was no sign of him on the ground.

One by one the wizards drew back from the area just below the Tower walls. Some were limping and several—old friends of those who had been slain—were sobbing quietly. Others glared in fury and hatred at the now vacant balcony from which the sorcerer had launched his vile attacks. Slowly they gathered around the gates, still within the courtyard but, they hoped, out of range of their enemy's attacks. Even if they were in danger here, none were willing to leave the courtyard. After coming this close to their hallowed hall of learning, they were unwilling to quit and retreat.

By now it was almost full night, and the black spires loomed like ghastly tombstones. Black and White and Red Robes mingled within the gossamer gates, muttering and cursing. "How can we fight this?" someone asked.

"It's impossible—he is too strong!" another replied.

"The artifact—" yet a third wizard started to say.

"Silence!" Dalamar snapped, and all of them obeyed him. "We will have to change our tactics, and be more clever than this if we are going to take back our tower."

"The Black Robe is right," Jenna said. "The sorcerer has an artifact that protects him from our strongest magical attacks. So gather under the moonlight, my cousins, and let us make a plan."

CHAPTER

25

MUDDY FLAGSTONES

The moons were all high in the night sky. Lunitari and Solinari, just past full, were approaching zenith, while Nuitari was beginning to set. Two cast their light on the world, and all lent their might to the practitioners of the three robes.

But would that might, the power of those three moons, be enough?

Dalamar pushed himself to his feet. He had been sitting with his back against the courtyard wall, studying his spell book and thinking about their formidable foe. Coryn had been sitting nearby, also reading, studying the incantations she had used in the battle with the golem. After a long time she had closed her eyes, and Dalamar noticed she had fallen asleep.

Other wizards were all around, and they, too, were resting, restoring their spells, meditating, or praying. He himself felt no need of rest. There would be time enough to gather their numbers, and that time would be very soon.

The dark elf shook his head to clear away his fatigue. He felt sluggish. He was surprised to see Jenna standing beside him—she had come up completely unnoticed.

"Do you think we should wait until tomorrow?" the red-robed woman asked. "The three of us haven't slept for two nights. And I'm certain those we summoned under the Eye have had no rest since then, either."

Dalamar pointed to the moons. "They are nearly full tonight. Tomorrow they will be fainter, our power weaker. I think we should attack as soon as possible."

"Yes, I agree," she said.

"And I," Coryn said. She had awoken and now climbed to her feet, her expression serious, glaring at the tower as if it were a personal enemy. With visible reluctance the white robe broke her stare to meet the eyes of Jenna and Dalamar, as the other wizards slowly gathered around them.

"Do you have any ideas as to what we should do?" asked the young woman.

"Yes," Dalamar replied. "I suggest we do something unexpected. We should use teleport spells to teleport ourselves into the Tower. Working in pairs or threes perhaps, we can spread out through the interior. When someone encounters Kalrakin we'll rush to that wizard's signal, and perhaps we can take the sorcerer by sheer numbers, if nothing else."

"Other spells are useless against him?" asked a young-looking woman in a black robe. She had large eyes and a very exotic, attractive appearance.

"Yes, Sirene," the dark elf replied. "At least, any spell he can absorb with the Irda Stone. But I don't see how he can counter our teleport spells."

"Here. These will help," Jenna said. She had drawn a small pouch from the depths of her red robe, and now poured the contents into her palm, revealing an array of small, sparkling gems. "Everyone take one of these," she said, handing them around. "If you spot Kalrakin, drop it to the ground. It will alert the rest of us, and we'll come as quickly as possible. Even if the one who drops the stone is killed before others arrive, you will have delivered a key warning—and your life will not have been lost in vain."

Dalamar took one of the stones as Jenna finished passing them out. "Are we all prepared? Let's team up, for safety. I will go to the Hall of Mages with Willim—if that's agreeable to my dwarven comrade?"

"Aye, elf. We go together," growled the eyeless dwarf. "Let's get on with it."

Swiftly the other mages paired up, Jenna joining her old teacher, Rasilyss—they would go to the aerie in the North Tower—while Coryn agreed to ally with old Galarant, the two of them teleporting to the anteroom in the foretower. As best as possible they divided up the inside of the Tower.

"All right," Jenna said. "Good luck—may the gods of magic smile upon us. And let's go."

Several dozen wizards simultaneously spoke the command word for the teleport spell. Magic sparkled and swirled around them. The spell flared and faded, leaving its familiar and slightly disorienting sensation.

After Dalamar cast his spell, he looked around, fully expecting to be standing in the Hall of Mages. He cursed when he saw he was still in the courtyard, with all his comrades. All of the wizards were muttering in dismay and looking around, showing surprise and outright disbelief.

"What is this?" demanded an elder Red Robe.

"Some sort of wild magic curse!" growled Willim the Black. "Bars us from the Tower—we can't even teleport through his damned walls!"

"Ignominy!" declared another mage. "All of the spells failed?"

"All save one," said Galarant. He had been standing beside Coryn; now he was conspicuously alone. "The lass, alone among us, seems to have managed to cast her spell properly and has made it into the Tower."

"That means she's in there alone with that monster," Jenna cried, turning to look at the lofty structure, strangling back her fearful gasp.

"And we're stuck out here," Dalamar said. He wondered how Coryn had succeeded and how much she could accomplish on her own.

He realized, with a frown, that if she prevailed, the future of the Conclave would be white.

❖

Coryn's teleport spell indeed succeeded and brought her unerringly to her chosen destination: the hallway connecting the great anteroom to the nearby kitchen. Immediately she turned through a circle and was relieved to see no signs of activity. She was puzzled when she didn't see Galarant and wondered if he had misunderstood this destination for their spell.

Stones lay on the floor, rubble so thick that it was difficult to take a step without having to kick some rock or gravel out of the way. Gaping holes yawned in the walls. Everywhere the light was dim and murky.

At the other end of the hall, the kitchen seemed quiet and dark; Coryn quietly stepped that way and peered through the door. The place seemed empty, though everywhere there were wreckage and piles of broken dishes.

In her hand Coryn clutched a small gem—the talisman Jenna had given her. Carefully stepping around as much of the rubble as possible, Cory made her way back to the main hall. It was shadowy and still, except where garish beams of light glowed in their alcoves and spilled into the rest of the room.

Three steps into the room she felt her foot sink right through the floor, as if the solid-looking stones were in actuality soft mud. Quickly she tried to spin away, but her feet were suddenly mired. She felt cold, viscous material tug at her ankles and close around her calves, and she made a desperate lunge back toward the hallway. A gleeful voice cried out strange, vulgar words.

She was stuck fast. The gummy stuff hardened around her legs, pinioning her just below her knees; gradually, the material became solid stone. Coryn twisted and pulled, but neither foot could wiggle free. Instead, leaning awkwardly, she was trapped in the midst of her lunge. From behind her came Kalrakin's unmistakable rasp; he almost cackled with delight.

"Ah, my trap has caught a mouse . . . a most fetching little rodent, indeed!"

She turned her head toward the sound of the voice, but saw nothing—until, an instant later, the tall sorcerer materialized, looming over her, his beard practically quivering with self-satisfied delight.

"Invisibility. Such a splendid little spell—simple wild magic, I assure you! Much better than one of those tedious little spells you are forever squinting at? I was standing here all along, watching you tiptoe around."

Coryn felt sick to her stomach as she realized her utter vulnerability. She whirled in panic.

"Why are you doing this?" she cried, raising her voice in a demanding tone—not because she wanted or expected an answer, but to disguise the noise of the gemstone as she dropped it. "You don't belong here!"

In the next instant her bravado wavered as she watched Kalrakin raise his hands and drop them quickly back to his sides. A web of hazy smoke spun from the golden fingertips of his right hand then spread out overhead, before descending from the ceiling with thin strands of magic woven into a fine mesh. In two places that net glowed with an eerie light, and the bearded mage looked up at them with a smile of pride and cunning.

"Oh, is that supposed to be a little warning? Or—oh, of course!—this was a summons to your pathetic comrades, wasn't it? A call to all of those in red and white and black to race to your rescue. How imaginative!"

"You're mad," Coryn said coldly. Her mind was flailing wildly. Their careful plan was a shambles, and she had never been more helpless than she was now, with her feet imprisoned in the anchoring stone of the floor.

"I may be mad . . . or I may be a genius. Perhaps I will yet embody all the future of magic upon Krynn. Unfortunately for you, my girl, you will be long dead by the time we find that out."

Kalrakin was clearly enjoying himself, flipping the Irda Stone between his hands with practiced gestures. Abruptly he slipped it into a pocket and made a simple gesture, placing his hands together and then slowly spreading them apart. Coryn gasped in pain; she couldn't budge—she was anchored by a heavy weight—yet her legs began to slide apart, stretching her muscles until they hurt. The sorcerer continued to expound.

"This tower . . . you claim it as your own, the symbol of your gods. But you must understand, those gods are pathetic remnants of the past. This tower is now a bastion of wild magic, a monument to the glory of myself!"

Coryn saw one chance to free her encased feet. She glared at the wild mage while at the same time trying to send a message to the foundation rock.

Help me!

Just as Coryn was sure that she was going to be rent in two, the slowly moving stone ceased its grinding progress. Kalrakin frowned and gestured sharply with his hands, but still the rock refused to move any farther.

"What feeble sorcery do you thwart me with?" he demanded. He pointed a bony finger at her, and though he was half a dozen paces away she could feel the pressure of that digit, like a sharp spear point, pressed against her chest. "I could tear your heart out with a single twist of my hand!"

Instead the floor underneath him buckled sharply, sending him toppling backward against the wall. He cursed and flailed, falling down hard. The Master had heard her, was giving her such aid as he could!

Coryn murmured the same spell she had used against the golem. This time the magic flowed without resistance, into the solid stone encasing her feet. The cramps in her legs eased at once, and she pulled first one, then the other foot, free from what had become a sticky ooze. Collapsing to the side, she kicked, sending gobbets of the mud spattering into Kalrakin's face.

The sorcerer shrieked, an inarticulate cry, causing a huge piece of rock to break from the wall behind him and fly toward Coryn. She was already dodging, and the boulder merely slapped at her robe as it went flying past.

The young wizard cast a haste spell to keep out of the way, then sprang to her feet and dashed across the anteroom and into one of the parlors beyond. A stone, flying very slowly, lumbered through the air and struck the wall behind her.

In the momentary safety of the next room, she pressed her back to the wall and tried to think of another spell. Where were the others? For some reason, it appeared the wizards were not in the Tower. She needed to improvise.

She heard Kalrakin coming, kicking his way through the rubble and crying out in rage, and she cast another spell. When the wild-magic sorcerer raced through the door of the parlor, he was confronted by the sight of *five* Coryns, each running away in a different direction.

The tall mage had obviously cast some sort of haste spell upon himself, for he was moving equally fast as the White Robe. Now he spat furiously, directing a rain of stones against the quintet of images that were all scattering away from the wall. The mirror images of Coryn each darted toward a different exit, and though two of them puffed into nothingness when they were struck by Kalrakin's missiles, the wizard herself was able to escape into an adjacent chamber. Darting around a corner, Coryn found herself entering the kitchen by one of the rear doors.

And here she came face to face with Luthar.

The rotund magic user held a cleaver in one hand.

"Stop!" he cried. Coryn felt the wild magic pulse. A whisk of her hand before her face broke the force of the lesser sorcerer's spell. She charged forward as he stumbled back, raising the big butcher knife.

Coryn grabbed a large bowl on the counter and threw the heavy piece of crockery, striking Luthar in the head and knocking him backward. She raced past him and down the hallway, back into the main anteroom.

The muddy swath where she had cast her spell had already hardened, leaving the surface pitched and roiling—like a stormy sea with the waves frozen into place. Coryn started across carefully, watching her footing on the irregular slabs. Once past, she broke into a sprint, heading for the last place she had seen Kalrakin, hoping to come up on him from behind.

Beware.

She felt the warning from the Master, but she was moving too fast. Before she could change course, she slammed into an unseen barrier. The force of the impact knocked her backward and down. Stunned, gasping for breath on the rough floor, she looked up to see Kalrakin looming over her.

He waved the pearly stone toward her, and Coryn felt the wild magic surge around her. The floor moved, opening a wide gap that swelled wider and wider, threatening to swallow her whole.

CHAPTER
26

STORM OF WILD MAGIC

D id you hear that?" Jenna asked, staring at the Tower.
 Around her the wizards stared in horror, watching
the clawlike shape of the giant edifice, listening to the terrible
sounds emerging from the black stone spires.

No answer was necessary from the gathered wizards: All
heard the creaking, agonized sounds as flagstones twisted,
and thick walls were warped and corrupted. The outer shell
of the tower seemed to waver in the air like a reed blown by a
powerful gale. A collective gasp rose from the throng of magic
users as the black spires appeared to sway back and forth.

Some wizards sobbed and others wailed piercingly. All of
them had studied, been tested—and passed their Tests—here.
Now, many of them cried out in anguish as this hallowed
place seemed on the brink of destruction.

"It is suffering—but it is *not* dying!" Jenna cried, trying to
rally the broken spirits. "Not yet—do not lose faith!"

"What can we do?" asked Rasilyss. "How can we fight
this?" Her skinny hands planted on her hips, she glared in
vexation at the Tower.

"We must get inside—Coryn's in there alone right now.
I'm going after her!" declared Adramis, the white-robed elf.

His twin sister Aenell quickly vowed her support, and they were joined by the other White Robes. Adramis pointed toward the high summit of the North Tower. "Each of those balconies has a door, and one of them may be vulnerable! If we can't teleport, so be it; let us fly up to each of the doors and find a way in!"

In seconds the elf White Robe had cast his fly spell, and he started up into the air as his comrades launched their own spellcastings.

"Wait!" Dalamar barked, holding up his hand. "We all have a stake in this. All three orders must act together. We'll have a much better chance."

He nodded at Adramis. "But the Qualinesti is right— Kalrakin can't protect every one of those doors. So let's go in unison, and spread out, explore balconies and outer walls. Spread the word if you find a way in!"

In seconds the wizards of all robes took to the air. Those who knew the flying spell cast it, while some who were limited to levitation floated upward, until a fellow wizard grabbed them by the hand and led them toward a balcony. They fanned out, some heading toward the north tower, others to the south, spiraling and climbing in the light of the rising moons.

Jenna, too, flew upward, her eyes on the other wizards. She watched Willim the Black, his eyeless face locked in a joyful grin, his magical Eye floating before him and guiding him magically along; he glided toward a wide balcony on the north tower—facing the gap between the two spires.

Dalamar flew just behind the dwarf. They both settled to the flagstones just before the solitary door leading into the Tower. The Red Robe hovered a slight distance away, watching as the dwarf approached the door.

"I'll blast the damned thing off its hinges!" the dwarf growled.

Willim put up both of his hands and chanted a spell. His fingers touched the unassuming wooden surface of the door as he tensed, preparing for the final command of his enchantment, but when he made contact, he disappeared.

"Willi!" Dalamar cried, lunging forward to snatch at the air where the black-robed dwarf had stood only moments before. The elf raised his hand, as if to drive a fist into the door, when Jenna alighted beside him.

"Don't!" she urged, grabbing him by the shoulder. "It's some kind of trap—under Kalrakin's control! It took Willi, and it will snatch you, too!"

"Yes—of course, I know that," the dark elf snapped bitterly, lowering his fist. His face was distorted. His whole body shook with rage. "That bastard has turned the entire Tower into a weapon to be wielded against us."

"Let's try somewhere else," Jenna suggested.

They took to the air again, making a circuit of the north tower. They learned that several other wizards had vanished when they tried their magic on the doors, just like Willim the Black. In other places the doors had been securely bound, locked by wild magic, so even the most potent of the wizardly spells proved futile. And some doors had been melded into the structure of the walls by the same kind of flowing stone that had obscured the front door. These formed smooth, impassive barriers, which no magic seemed able to penetrate.

Magic users continued to swoop and rise and circle around, but none reported any viable means of entry. Though she didn't stop to count, Jenna knew their number was dwindling, and she wondered how many had already been captured—or killed—by Kalrakin or his sorcerous traps.

"Look!" cried Dalamar suddenly, putting a hand on Jenna's arm, bringing them both to a halt in the air very near the summit of the spire.

"What is it," she asked, looking around.

"I don't remember that door being there," the dark elf observed. "And there's no platform, no balcony outside. If it opened from the inside, a person could step right out into the air. Doesn't that strike you as odd?"

Jenna studied the plain door—so plain, it was barely visible from the outside—high in the smooth side of the structure, apparently leading nowhere. Like Dalamar, she had no memory of seeing this portal before.

"Odd, indeed. It's worth a look," Jenna said, tucking her shoulder and diving nearer as Dalamar sailed close behind.

She approached the door, which, as the elf had observed, opened in the sheer outer wall of the Tower over a drop of some two hundred feet. It was a simple barrier of wooden planks, with a small golden knob and no visible lock. Jenna scowled as she flew closer, shifting her posture to slow her flight—for she was startled to realize that she seemed to be accelerating, drawn by some powerful force right toward the solid wooden barrier.

"Look out! I can't stop!" she cried, twisting herself, exerting all the force of her spell to try to get away from the magnetic force drawing her to the Tower. It was like trying to swim upstream—whatever limited progress she made was easily overwhelmed by the force that was drawing her in.

"It's got me, too!" Dalamar was kicking and thrashing nearby, reaching with his hands, as if he might be able to grab a tree branch or cloud and pull himself away. But he, too, was clearly overpowered.

Overcome, both were being sucked with increasing force and speed toward the high stone walls of the Tower.

Jenna threw up her hands to protect her head. She gasped, anticipating the impact, but instead was immediately enveloped by darkness. She tumbled to a hard stone floor, quickly twisted around and struggled to regain her footing. Something brushed past; it was Dalamar, who, she observed with some irritation, leaped to his feet while she was still fumbling with her staff. With a curse, she brought a light spell into being on the top of her staff.

"Where are we?" the dark elf cried, quickly stalking the circumference of what appeared to be a small, dark, enclosed room. "And where's the door? I swear we crashed straight into it!"

"It's gone—maybe it was never there in the first place. But we're somewhere high up in the Tower, I should think," Jenna replied, looking around in the cool light of her spell. "At least, judging from the small size of the room, and the curve of that wall, that's my best guess."

"Do you think Kalrakin lured us here, trapped us?" the dark elf mused aloud.

"*I* brought you here."

The word was spoken by an old man who stood in the corner, wearing a tattered robe of white. The old White Robe certainly hadn't been there a moment before.

"Par-Salian?" the dark elf declared, shocked by the recognition. "It is you! Though I fear that the passage of time has not been kind to you."

Jenna looked and also recognized the man who had been the Head of the Conclave when she had taken her Test. Age had ravaged him cruelly, as evidenced by the rheumy film over his eyes and the dark spots that marked his hands. His beard and hair, once lush and full—even though steel-gray—were now sparse and bedraggled. Even his robe, the pure symbol of his order, he had allowed to become dirty, torn, and unkempt; he leaned on a cane, his posture so feeble that he seemed likely to fall forward on to his face.

Only Par-Salian was long dead; he had perished during the Chaos War.

"You can't truly be Par-Salian. So who are you?" Dalamar demanded. "I would kill you in an instant if I thought you were the sorcerer Kalrakin in cunning guise, but there is no hint of wild magic around you."

"I am the Master of the Tower," said the image of Par-Salian. "I brought you here—it is the only safe place, for the moment. The sorcerer has ensorcelled all the other doors with dangers and traps."

"What's happened to the other wizards who disappeared?" asked Jenna. "Are they slain?"

"No . . . not yet. He holds them in the Hall of Mages. Of course you recall that there are no doors to that chamber, and his wild magic has secured the place. None may teleport in or out. As your wizards enter the Tower, they become his prisoners."

"What of Coryn? The Head of the White Robes?" Jenna prodded.

"Ah. That is why I brought you here—she needs your help. As do I." The aged White Robe pointed across the room, where appeared a sheet of glass suspended on the stone wall like a window. "Use the scrying glass. You will see her; she is down below, near the anteroom of the foretower."

"Look!" cried the dark elf, pointing to an image that began to glow in that reflective surface. Jenna stepped close, and she and Dalamar both immediately recognized Coryn. Her white robe was torn and stained with blood, and she was lying prone, trapped in a gap that had opened in the floor. As the two wizards watched, that narrow space started to squeeze shut. She struggled frantically, clearly overpowered in the vise of wild magic.

"What can we do?" asked Jenna desperately, whirling to confront the Master.

But he was no longer there.

Coryn pushed and pushed, but the viselike pressure resisted her puny strength. The gap in the floor was like a wound closing, shaping itself according to Kalrakin's wishes. The White Robe was caught in a brief slit that felt disturbingly like a coffin, just long and wide enough to accommodate her body. As soon as she had fallen in, it had begun to squeeze shut.

Watching her, Kalrakin smiled and held up his hand; the stone gap immediately stopped closing. Coryn was tightly trapped—she couldn't so much as wriggle—but at least she was able to draw breath.

"What a pretty little rabbit I have snared," declared the sorcerer. To Coryn, from her position lodged beneath the floor, he seemed like a giant covered with smudges of dirty cloud, which trailed off his craggy visage.

"You thought you were pretty clever, I suspect . . . when you tricked us into letting you live. That is not a mistake I shall make again. Not that your death will be overly speedy, of course. These things take time!"

"No—I wasn't being clever," Coryn said. She searched for words, ideas, anything that would distract Kalrakin and give her a chance to stay alive.

"I was foolish," she said quickly. "Now I am curious. I came here to learn about this place—and it took me a while to understand that you have become the master. I am in awe of your power—I wanted to learn from you!"

"Master . . . yes. I am Master here. I didn't think you appreciated that."

"Oh, it's obvious," Coryn said. "I should have known it right away. And I'm sorry about taking your food. That was an honest mistake."

"Hah! My food? I have no need of food! This tower is my sustenance." As he spoke he flipped the white stone in his hand, and Coryn found her eyes drawn inexorably to that pearly artifact. It was terribly bright, and created a hypnotic flash of light when he alternately covered it up and revealed it.

Kalrakin looked down at her, clearly enjoying himself. He grinned at her and twisted his hands, drawing the vise of stone just a bit tighter around the White Robe. Coryn strained to breathe, but her elbows were now trapped against her sides, and the pressure was crushing her lungs.

She saw movement out of the corner of her eye, and apparently the sorcerer did, too. Kalrakin whirled around, white lights flashing all around him, and he shouted.

"I destroyed you once—you have no right to be here!"

Wild sorcery flashed and the floor shook against both of her shoulders, squeezing Coryn even harder. She saw a Black Robe flash past the wall, a haggard old wizard she had never seen before. She blinked, and the wizard's robe had turned to white.

And now it was the face of Par-Salian she saw, looking down at her with a kindly expression. The Master of the Tower nodded once, surprisingly calm in the face of Kalrakin's frenzied cries. Then he vanished in a convulsion of wild magic.

Coryn found herself lying on a bed, alone in a room. She heard an echo of Kalrakin's disbelieving scream, but that faded almost immediately into blessed silence. The wild-magic sorcerer was not here, however, and could not possibly know where she was. For one thing, she didn't know herself.

She sat up and looked around, crying out as her back and hips creaked in pain. Gingerly she moved a bit, realizing with some relief and surprise that she didn't seem to have any broken bones. But where was she?

This room looked vaguely familiar; she guessed she was still in the Tower of High Sorcery. This was a simple sleeping chamber, with a table, desk, wardrobe, and this comfortable bed. And there was a door, with a big lock, secured with a key from the inside.

Of course! This was the room she had slept in on her first visit, the night before she had taken the Test of Magic. But that seemed too easy. She stood up on shaky legs and walked across to the desk. There was nothing on it, nor on the table, which was just as before. Of course, she had thrown a few of her belongings in the wardrobe, things she hadn't taken with her when she had left the Tower rather precipitously. It contained nothing that would help her. She pulled open the wardrobe: There was her water skin, her bedroll, and a few extra pieces of clothing. And then she saw something else, which she had left here and all but forgotten.

It was her stout hunting bow. Beside it rested her plain, but serviceable, quiver of arrows.

The wizards circled through the air outside the Tower. Many of them had vanished, by now, having attacked one of Kalrakin's locked doors and simply disappeared. There was no way to know the fate of those comrades, but Adramis and his sister were rapidly despairing.

"I can't fly much longer," Aenell warned her brother. "My spell is fading."

"Down to the ground, then?" he asked dismally. He would be able to stay in the air for only a few more minutes at the most.

"No, not to the ground," his sister demurred. "We've seen these trapped doors work their magic. But so far no one has followed up after one of our number has vanished. What if the trap is good for but a single use?"

"Interesting. . . ." Before he could say anything else, she dipped away, swooping toward the balcony where Willim the

Black had disappeared. She came to rest on the flagstones just outside the door. Adramis hastened after, landing next to her on the balcony, which was about halfway up the north tower.

"Be careful!" he advised

"I'll be careful, but you have to admit we don't have many options left."

"Yes. But I will not let you risk your life—stand back, and see what happens to me."

Nodding at his gallantry, Aenell stepped out of the way. She knew better than to try to argue with her brother, and anyway, she would be close by, ready to help him or follow him to death, if necessary.

"Now you be careful!" was all she could say as she fidgeted anxiously, spells of attack and defense tingling in her fingertips. She watched her brother approach the door. He reached out slowly, gingerly put a finger to the wooden surface.

And the portal exploded inward with his touch, vanishing in a shocking display of violence. The force of the blast apparently sucked Adramis inside, for the elf vanished from his sister's view instantaneously, pulled just like the others to some unknown fate inside the Tower.

So she was wrong, Aenell thought bitterly, preparing to follow.

CHAPTER

27

GRIEVING OF GODS

Kalrakin stared disbelievingly at the empty space where Coryn had been caught in a vise, just moments before. He kicked and swore and frothed at the mouth. Where had she gone? How had she escaped him?

"Bah!" He stalked across the room, calling out, "Luthar!"

"Y-yes, Master?" The other sorcerer nervously appeared.

"I was mistaken to let you talk me into sparing the wench. She continues to taunt me, and I do not intend to tolerate this insolence!"

"Surely you have terrified her to the point where she will never return here!" Luthar argued. "If she has vanished, she had doubtless gone back to her own land, her home. She was a simple child—we should forget her!"

Kalrakin snorted contemptuously. He planted his hands on his hips, the Irda Stone still gleaming brightly in the clasp of his right hand. "Luthar, you give me a very good idea. There are two ways to make sure she never comes back here," the sorcerer declared in a supremely pleased tone. "The first, of course, is to kill her, which I surely will do, when I catch up to the bitch. And the second is to make sure that this place ceases to exist."

He lifted his hands over his head and spread them apart, a gesture that sent ripples of wild magic convulsing through the air. The chandelier, a crystal-and-silver masterpiece that had lasted more than a thousand years, broke free from the ceiling and fell to the floor, smashing into a million glittering shards. Great chunks of stone broke from the ceiling, and the top of one wall collapsed in a loud explosion, smashing half of the banquet table.

"Master—stop this noise and destruction! Please!" Luthar shrieked, recoiling against the wall of the anteroom, pressing his hands to his ears. He slipped down haplessly until he was sitting on the floor; then he turned and crawled in order to huddle under the other, still-standing half of the banquet table.

Kalrakin paid no attention to his cringing comrade. Instead he sent a fresh blast of wild magic through the hallway and up into the vast stairway ascending toward the south tower. The magical force tore into the solid onyx of the steps, shattered many of them, and heated others so that the stone began to run like black ink, pooling in puddles in the landings and halls. Cracks appeared all along the great hall, scoring their way up the ceiling. Several ornate columns toppled like dead trees, and a choking cloud of stone dust billowed everywhere through the tortured chambers.

The sorcerer cast another bolt in the opposite direction, searing away the columns and railing that curved along the outside of the north tower's stairway. A thunderous cavalcade of rubble rained down as a whole section of the ceiling gave way, dropping much of the second floor right into the broken heaps of rock that more than half-filled the once majestic hallway. Kalrakin gestured and another bolt of magic exploded upward, crackling through ceilings and floors, bringing down another mess of debris.

"Wait!" cried Luthar piteously. "You'll bring the place down on our heads! We'll be killed!"

"You may be killed. I assuredly won't. Besides, I grow tired of your complaints and distractions!" declared the sorcerer, turning to glare at Luthar. He raised the white stone high in his hands, flipping it back and forth.

"No!" cried the chubby henchman, cringing, throwing his hands over his face as crackling tendrils of sorcery surged toward him, engulfing him in white heat. Fire swept over him. Luthar defended himself as best he could, taking hold of the writhing, wriggling heat-blast like it was some kind of snake, screaming in pain as he burned his palms and face. Frantically he wrestled with it, falling to the ground, shrieking as the burning sparks poured over his skin, flashing into his eyes.

"Please, spare me!" he shouted.

But Kalrakin, with a bored look, had already moved on. The tall sorcerer was gazing upward, as if studying the supporting beams that he would have to tear away to wreak final destruction upon the Tower.

Behind his back, Luthar, with a final convulsion, managed to cast the wriggling, magical serpent away. The bolt of white magic hissed and spit sparks, as it struck a crag of fallen stone. The block shattered into gravel, several of the shards pelting Luthar. Other bits of stone cut into Kalrakin's clothes, hair, and skin, but the sorcerer took no note of the trivial barrage.

Luthar shrieked and rolled on the floor, thrashing around in horrific pain, batting frantically at the flames still spreading across his gray robe. His palms were bloody, his face pocked with angry red burns. The flames finally dying out, he got on his knees to make one last plea to Kalrakin.

But the tall sorcerer had stalked away, scrambling over any rubble that blocked his path. He was laughing loudly as

he launched another blast of wild magic through the anteroom and into the foundations of the south tower.

"Do you feel that, wizards?" he cried shrilly. "Your doom
gathers around you!"

Luthar covered his head as more rubble cascaded down on
him. When he looked up, he was horrified to see that a huge
section of the ceiling, a solid mass of stone, was teetering
crazily on the verge of collapse.

Everything around him began to spin. Kalrakin didn't
care, he intended to pull down the ceiling and the walls. The
tower could not stand for long, and all would be buried. But
Luthar was not ready to die.

Sobbing, pulling himself along by his burned hands,
Luthar crawled from the room, back toward the quiet, small
sanctuary of the kitchen.

Kalrakin didn't notice his escape.

———◆◈◆———

Dalamar and Jenna emerged from the room into one of the
high hallways of the north tower.

"She's all the way down to the foretower. Can you cast a
teleport spell?" asked the dark elf.

Jenna quickly shook her head. "No, that spell's gone for
now. I cast it when I first tried to enter the Tower. I'll have to
go back and study it."

"Me, too," Dalamar said bitterly. "Looks like we're taking
the stairs."

There was no more idle talk as they started down the
steps, winding down levels of the Tower. They could feel
the frequent tremors and occasionally were forced to grasp
the railing as the whole structure wobbled ominously.
It seemed to take a maddeningly long time to make the
descent.

"Do you think any of the others made it inside?" Jenna whispered to Dalamar, as at last they reached the lower levels of the Tower.

"We must assume we're alone," Dalamar replied softly. "And that the Irda Stone protects him against our spells. We can't use magic to kill him."

She nodded in grim agreement, as he whipped out a narrow-bladed dagger. "I'll do what I can to distract him—you'll have to get in close to use that.

They came down the last flight of stairs close together, edging toward the inner wall of the steps. A great section of the railing and portions of several stairs had been torn away. The floor of the hall was a terrible mess, and Jenna had to suppress a gasp of dismay as she took in the full scope of wild magic devastation. It was nightmarish, a horror to behold, a sight that made her all the more determined to succeed—or die.

Somewhere not terribly far away they heard a crash. They started across the floor, trying to pick a clear path, but almost immediately had to climb over a small mountain of debris that lay across their path. They pushed through the rubble, with Dalamar grunting as he pushed one of the larger chunks out of their way. Jenna looked up, appalled to see the ceiling of the second story training rooms teetering above her. Almost the whole floor of that large chamber had been ripped away. More cracks spread along the floor, and small cascades of rubble fell with each fresh tremor.

"Why are you here? You should be in the hall, with the others!"

Kalrakin's voice, a petulant screech, reached them from the shadows in the long hallway. He seemed to emerge from a cloud of dust. To Jenna he looked wild, insane. His long hair stood out from his head, and his body and robe were covered with dust, highlighting the madness in his staring eyes.

Without a moment's hesitation, Jenna raised her hand and cast a magic missile spell. Sparkling bolts of fire flashed from her finger, tearing through the air toward the sorcerer. Kalrakin laughed wildly, raising the Irda Stone. One by one the missiles hissed into the artifact and disappeared, as his laugh rose in shrill volume and the Irda Stone grew hotter and brighter.

Jenna scrambled over a section of broken stone and readied another spell. Dalamar had disappeared—she could only trust he had found concealment and was making his way unobtrusively toward their enemy.

The ground shook underneath her feet, momentarily staggering her, but she steadied herself and didn't fall. A great slab of wall fell down behind her, but she ignored it, shaking her head to clear the billowing dust away from her eyes. She cast one spell after another, holding her ground, though she knew her spells could not really harm the sorcerer; she opted for spectacles and distractions, determined to keep the sorcerer's attention.

Great blossoms of fireworks exploded through the hall and dancing images of draconians and ogres charged at Kalrakin, issuing bloodcurdling screams. Shrieking with laughter, he swatted them aside contemptuously. The image of a red dragon materialized into the hall, slithering out from one of the side rooms. Crimson jaws spread wide. The sorcerer held up the white stone to meet a great gout of fiery breath. Like all of Jenna's attacks, the seemingly lethal fireball was snuffed into nothingness by the Irda Stone.

Jenna looked around frantically. She knew Kalrakin would quickly grow bored with such diversion. How long could she keep this up?

Then she spotted something that gave her a flash of hope.

The dark elf had burst courageously from the shadows, the knife gleaming in his hand. Quickly and silently, he charged the wild sorcerer.

But Kalrakin saw him coming, must have known all along that he was lurking nearby. The sorcerer merely flipped his hand in a gesture, and a crackling bolt of fire exploded toward the dark elf. Jenna felt the searing heat even from down the hall. She watched in horror as the wild magic tore at the right side of Dalamar's head, peeling back the skin of his face, tearing at his eyes, ripping away one ear. By the time the spell faded, crackling and hissing into nothingness, the dark elf lay like a corpse on the floor.

It looked like half of his face had been burned away.

The god Nuitari cried out in anguish. He howled his grief like a storm through the known planes of existence. He felt the terrible pain of his favorite son's grievous injury, as though his own flesh had been ravaged. Thunder broke around him, and great storms of rain fell through the cosmos.

The black moon was shedding tears.

"The Master of the Tower is failing," Solinari noted glumly. "And all our pawns fall." His visage was wan, a pale approximation of his usual silvery brilliance.

"The wild magic is too powerful," Lunitari declared, equally dejected. "The sorcerer will slay them all and leave the wreckage of the Tower as their tomb. Our children are trapped, defeated, doomed."

Even as they spoke, the blood of the dark elf Dalamar drained into the Tower of High Sorcery's broken stonework. The gods felt the slow ebbing of his life.

"His life slips away, and with his death our hopes perish," Solinari said. His tone was gentle, even sympathetic toward his black cousin, who was experiencing such grief and failure.

But Nuitari raised his head. Thunder and lightning flared in the black sockets of his eyes, and when at last he said something, it was not to pronounce a message of defeat.

"Yes, if time advances, he will die. But there is one way he can survive," the god of the black moon said. "Let him cast the spell that will bring time to a stop."

———————◆◆◆———————

Far above the dying Dalamar, Aenell gingerly approached the door on the high platform that had been destroyed at her brother's approach. The broken entryway gaped like a wound. Only darkness could be glimpsed within.

None of the other wizards were in sight. All of the ones that had been drawn into the Tower were apparently dead. Never had the young elf maid felt so alone as she did at that time, in that lofty place. There was really no choice, no alternative. She had to follow after her brother.

Hesitantly she reached a hand forward, feeling the abrupt tingle of magic. She pulled back, tried to break away, but it was too late—a powerful spell had trapped her, was catapulting her through space, a teleport spell that was overruling her own will. She fought it with all her might, and lost.

She found herself lying on a cold, stone floor. Other wizards milled about in distress and agitation, including a young Red Robe who was kneeling at her side, asking if she was hurt. The Red Robe repeated her question.

"Can you hear me? Are you hurt?"

"N-no, I don't think so," Aenell replied, dazedly. Sitting up, she looked around. The elf maid recognized, first, that she had been teleported to the Hall of Mages, and second, that her brother was here, too.

He laid on the floor just a few steps away, alive, but gravely wounded.

CHAPTER 28

THE SCAR

Luthar! Come here! I forgive you! Come and see the great red-robed enchantress! She is on her knees, begging for her life!"

But Jenna was not yet ready to beg—she had more important things to do. She tried to get up but fell roughly to the side as the ground shifted under her feet, and strong waves rippled the solid stone of the Tower's floor.

The wild magic made the floor twist and writhe beneath her, jolting her from one side to the next, preventing her from gaining any equilibrium. Somehow the sorcerer kept his balance, like the captain of a pitching ship during a violent storm, though the floor continually rose and sank. He laughed crazily.

When she tried to push herself up again, the floor heaved wildly, and she fell roughly onto her face. She rolled over, feeling tremendous pain, wondering if her nose was broken. Once again the floor buckled, and she was slammed against a slab of rock.

"She dances; she prances!" Kalrakin crowed. "See her cavorting about the floor—Luthar, you must witness!"

Though there was no sign of Luthar, Kalrakin seemed

to take no notice of his lackey's absence. He was too busy enjoying his victim, toying with his wild magic just enough to keep the floor lurching unsteadily. The white Irda Stone flashed as he tossed it back and forth from one hand to the other. Jenna was tossed like a rag doll from one place to another.

At last she managed to grab hold of something and sit up, her hands spread to the sides in anticipation of another lurch. Her staff lay nearby, and so, too, Dalamar, who lay on his back, motionless and probably dead. The right side of his face was a gruesome sight, flesh torn away and awash with blood.

Kalrakin's attention drifted for a moment as he raised his head, looking as if he heard something. He shrugged then waved one hand. Instantly another wave of violence wracked the Tower. Crashes and bangs echoed everywhere. Streams of rubble and dust fell from the ceilings. The foundation groaned. The floor lurched sickeningly, and Jenna's heart faltered. The whole place was about to come down around her.

But Kalrakin, head thrown back as he cackled with crazy laughter, was momentarily preoccupied with his spellcasting.

The Red Robe drew a breath. Her hands were raw, scraped, and bruised. Her stomach lurched unevenly. Magic spells roiled in her mind—spells that might conceal her, possibly even let her escape—as a last resort.

Kalrakin seemed to remember her then, glancing down at the Red Robe. "All of your great wizards have fallen into my trap, now. Ironic that they will all perish in the Hall of Mages, don't you think? Like pathetic rats, drowned in a little cage? But still, I can't decide—is that how I should kill them?

"Drown them, perhaps, with a storm inside a closed room? Or should I simply bring it all down on their pathetic little heads—an avalanche of black stone, so that the Tower dies along with them? Symbolic and appropriate, of course, but perhaps a little too sudden for my tastes. What do you say?" he asked, looking at her with his eyebrows raised mockingly.

Jenna watched him warily, her attention focused on that stone, which he was flipping back and forth between his two hands, so casually. By Lunitari, how she wanted to tear that thing from his grasp. Yet she knew that before she could reach him, he would destroy her with the simplest spell.

He smiled coldly, as if reading her thoughts, then continued to speak conversationally.

"The flaw in that plan—destroying them along with the Tower—is that I won't get to see the last looks on your colleagues', my victims', faces. Tons of rock fall, they die, and it's all over. No, I might prefer a more measured approach." He extended his hand before him, made a simple gesture, and two heavy chunks of stone rolled together, pinioning Jenna's ankle.

"Such as this!" Kalrakin squeezed his hand and the enchantress gasped in pain as the two blocks of stone slowly began to move together, squeezing her ankle so tightly that she cried out. Slowly the two stones began to grind closer together; the bones of her ankle began to be crushed.

"Yes, that would be much better." The sorcerer seemed pleased with his experiment. "A gradual approach. More fun to watch."

Then the stones stopped moving, though Jenna was still trapped. Pain etched on her face, she looked up, sensing that Kalrakin wanted to toy with her, torture her; anything, she thought, if it would help buy a little time.

"I can pull in the walls on all sides of that chamber, just like those stones now pinning your ankle." He seemed oddly eager to explain his brainstorm to her; she had the bizarre sense that he was seeking her approval.

"I could do the same with all the little wizards. Gradually shrink the room, so to speak, until they are all pressed into the center. Like fish in a net, they will splash around, wriggling and wiggling. Perhaps some will even climb atop their companions as the space grows smaller. Oh, they will know they are going to die, but it will take some time for them to get it over with. Yes, perfect—I will kill them all that way, so they die with a sense of style!"

Kalrakin chortled, absently fondling his artifact, pacing back and forth as he imagined his lethal spell. "Of course, by the time I've finished, the tower will be in too sad a state to stand. It must come down—it *must* be totally destroyed! How fitting—a perfect monument to mark the graves, not just of a few dozen feisty wizards, but a tomb for all godly magic upon Krynn!"

Despairing, Jenna looked over at the dark elf. The rocks pinning her ankle ground slowly closer to each other. The pain was unbearable. She thought of a spell that could relieve the pressure, and she murmured it quietly. With great relief she felt the stone on the inside of her leg soften a bit, becoming almost rubbery. But she kept her expression grim.

She glanced again at Dalamar, and her eyes widened for a moment, before she turned quickly back to the sorcerer, hoping that her surprised reaction hadn't given her away. But she was sure of what she had seen.

Dalamar's hands were twitching, and the bloody mess that remained of his lips had started to articulate a spell.

The pain was a distant thing now. Dalamar knew that his face was badly torn, suspected he might even be blinded, but that was no matter to him now. His flesh was finally responding to his will, and he would allow no weakness to restrain him now. He called upon his hand, his might, his magic.

He drew a quiet breath, ignoring the blood that gurgled in his throat as he filled his lungs with precious air.

As awareness returned to his flesh, his every nerve seemed to scream out from the highest peak of agony. But he also heard the whisper in his ear, Nuitari counseling him, soothing him, acting as immortal balm.

Serve me, my elf—serve me as you never have before. This is not just your life at stake, nor even the lives of all the mages. You strive now for the survival of godly magic upon Krynn—and if you fail, my cousins and I will be forever banished from the world.

And he knew that it was the truth. Dalamar had to survive, had to fight, had to prevail.

The spell took time to build in him. The gift of his god, given to him through the medium of this tower, was not something that would smite the sorcerer. But it would allow Dalamar the chance to slip away; to make a tactical retreat; and to form one last, desperate attack. Vaguely he sensed Kalrakin taunting someone—it could only be Jenna. She must still be alive, fighting on. He was relieved by that knowledge. Now he needed to do his part.

Words choked thickly in his bloody mouth, but he gritted his teeth and forced the torn muscles to give shape to the necessary sounds. And then the power exploded from him in a god-nourished burst of magic, one of the most potent spells he had ever devised. It was not a spell of warmth, but of absolute, irresistible cold. The force of it shot out; surrounded; and embraced the room, the Tower, and the forest, clamping down on movement, on life, and on vitality with irresistible force. It coalesced through the air, the ground, the very world, imposing the will of the dark god on all creation.

And time stopped.

Dalamar sat up, his body tingling. He felt numb, removed from his surroundings, aloof even from his flesh—and this was a good thing, for that numbness held his pain in abeyance. Gradually he pushed himself to his feet, with a sense he was pushing through air that had the viscosity of cold syrup.

His first thought was Kalrakin, as he pushed himself to his feet, and he kept his eyes on the stunned sorcerer. Dalamar felt a red haze across his vision, and he thought it was an effect of the spell. Only after he touched his face did he realize that it was blood, smearing across both of his eyes.

The dark elf's legs staggered weakly. When he tried to raise a hand, he found that he could barely extend his arm before him. He was disoriented, and realized that he was in shock and had lost a lot of blood. If time had flowed on, he might well be bleeding to death at this very moment.

But time had stopped, and this was keeping him alive.

Kalrakin stood in the rubble-strewn hallway like a statue, hands on his hips, his bearded face twisted into a leering grimace as he stared down at Jenna. The Red Robe was likewise still, in the thrall of the spell. To the sorcerer and the enchantress, Dalamar knew, nothing was happening right now—this was merely a nonexistent space between two instants of time.

The dark elf slowly approached Kalrakin. The wild-magic sorcerer was trapped in the moment, but his fist was still wrapped tightly about the Irda Stone. Dalamar would have to leave him alone—if he touched the sorcerer or the stone, the spell would be broken, and time would start flowing again; if that happened while he and Jenna remained in this corridor, he knew they were as good as dead.

Still, the gods had given him the power for this spell, and he would not waste the opportunity. Wrapping a strip of cloth around his head, he tried to stem the worst of the bleeding, though he knew his jaw and shredded cheek were still exposed. There was nothing to be done about that, not for now.

He went to Jenna, saw that she had melted one of the large stones that had pinned her ankle, using a spell to soften the rock. Gingerly he reached down to take her by the arm, and as he pulled her free, she began to respond to the pressure of his touch. She rose to her feet by her own power, though her eyes remained blank, nor did she show any signs of breathing or speech.

But she followed his lead willingly enough as he led her away, through the rubble of the chaotic mess. He guided her down the long passageway to the south tower, carefully taking her around the shattered stones on the great stairway. They climbed until they reached the great circular hall, making a full circumference around the Hall of Mages.

That great chamber occupied most of the interior of the south tower, at least here on the ground level and for nearly a hundred feet above. There was no door into the hall—the mages who gathered there had always used other means to pass through the stone walls that enclosed their most sacred chamber. But the ones there now were trapped by Kalrakin's wild magic.

Teleporting inside was useless, he knew—Kalrakin had said as much, and besides, Dalamar had already expended that spell when he had first attempted to enter the Tower. But there were other means of penetrating stone barriers, other ways a wizard could gain access to a place he needed to go.

But he could only wield one spell at a time, especially in this condition. With a twinge of fear, he waved away the stop-time spell. Jenna woke up, cried out with a shiver, clinging to his arm, gasping in surprise.

"Where are we?" she asked.

"This is the wall surrounding the Hall of Mages," Dalamar explained. "And I need to open a dimension door."

Coryn was ready. This small room, as it had once before, had provided her with a quiet haven, where she could collect her thoughts, gather her courage, and make a plan. She had recovered her nerve. And she had found her favorite, familiar weapons, the simple bow and arrows that had helped her to put food on her family's table for so much of her life.

She decided to start with the teleport spell, and once again the word came to her lips, though it had been a long time since she had studied the enchantment. But that fact didn't seem to matter anymore. Just when she needed the power, it was there, waiting, ready. She arrived unerringly near the second floor landing of the great central stairway of the north tower.

She could see down to the bottom of the great stairway, though much of the flight had been torn away by the blasts of wild magic. Still, the arched hallway leading to the anteroom was visible, from the base of the staircase.

Holding her breath, she started down the steps, listening for signs of Kalrakin or Luthar. She heard a violent commotion some distance away, more walls breaking, stones cracking, and supporting structures collapsing.

Her bow was ready, the string taut. She had an arrow in her hands as she made her way carefully down the steps. As she neared the bottom, she nocked the missile on the bow-string and started to pull the weapon back. She thought of the sorcerer's artifact, and for the first time, the memory of that stone brought the hint of a tiny, hopeful smile to her lips.

She knew the Irda Stone could not stop a sharp, steel arrowhead.

CHAPTER
29

WILD MAGIC

Dalamar stared at the stone wall. The spell was ready to cast; indeed it was pulsing in his mind, anxious for its release. He raised his hand to make the sign of the dimension door against the side of the great hall.

But the words emerged thick and slurred. His tongue felt like a useless piece of swollen meat. Air escaped through the torn fabric of his cheek, while his lips could not seem to articulate the most basic of sounds. His eyes watered with frustration.

"Here, I'll do it," Jenna said with surprising tenderness. The dark elf watched bitterly as she made the sign and smoothly cast the spell.

Immediately a passage appeared through the thick black stone of the wall. It was a shimmering doorway outlined in blue light, magical but also real. The wall here was some six feet thick, but the dimension door was flat and thin as a piece of paper. It was also visible to those on the other side of the wall.

"Who's there?" growled a thick voice from within that great chamber as soon as the dimension door shimmered into view. A burly dwarf squatted close to the door, his eyeless face cocked in an expression of listening.

"It is I, Willi," Jenna shouted, "coming to get you all out of here."

"A dim door?" The dwarf sounded skeptical. "Don't ya think we already tried that in here? Wit' no luck!"

"The sorcerer's spell bars you from getting out, via teleport or other spells. It doesn't stop us from opening a door on this side of the wall," Jenna explaining, raising her voice in urgency. "And Dalamar is here with me. Now come, all who serve the Three Gods—there is no time to waste!"

Quickly the wizards massed before the door. Willim the Black was the first to step through, nodding to Jenna and Dalamar. "Where is that bastard? I want his spleen for breakfast!" he growled. The half-elf woman in the black robe came next, gliding past Willi. She looked shocked to see Dalamar.

"By Nuitari! What happened to you?" gasped Sirene, her face going pale as she beheld the dark elf's horribly scarred visage.

"Never mind about my petty injuries!" Dalamar snapped, tugging the cowl around to obscure the right side of his face as much as possible. "Get on through the dimension door— and hurry the others behind you!"

"We'll have to leave Adramis," an elder elf, a White Robe named Suwannis, said as he appeared. "He's badly hurt, and we don't dare move him."

"Very well. But the rest of you, hurry!" urged Jenna. "Through the door—quickly! Spread out through the hall!"

One by one the wizards pushed through the blue-tinged door, the younger and faster going first, the elders following with as much alacrity as they could muster. Their numbers had been thinned by the battle; there were maybe twenty left, not counting Adramis, who was all but unconscious. Led by Jenna, and with stealthy, over-the-shoulder glances at the scarred Dalamar, they hurried down the hallway toward the foretower.

They had to make their way around patches of rubble, fallen columns, and other destruction. They had collected in the alcoves along the broad corridor when Jenna called for a volunteer to scout ahead for Kalrakin.

"I'll go," said Aenell. "For my brother." Her eyes were burning in her pale face.

Dalamar nodded to Jenna. The Red Robe turned to Aenell. "We last saw him at the base of the north tower. And beware of using magic to find him—he senses any spellcasting. We'll wait here until we hear something."

"I'll do my best," the elf maid pledged grimly. "If something happens to me . . . help my brother as best you can. And tell him I died honorably."

Aenell slipped away, moving soundlessly across the rubble-strewn passageway. She crouched behind the next broken pillar then darted down the hall connecting the south tower to the anteroom and the foretower.

Dalamar was acutely aware of the other wizards stealing sidelong glances at him. The hilt of his knife was cold comfort in his hand. When he noticed Sirene staring at him, horror apparent in her eyes, he pulled the cowl of his robe down around his face and leaned, fully masked, against the wall.

———◆———

Luthar stared at the wall of the room where he was hiding. Once more he summoned his limited wild magic, clawing at the stone, but could not break through to the outside. This tower seemed as impervious to his escape as it had been to the wizards who had so desperately tried to gain entry.

Abruptly he heard someone moving around in the room behind him, and he fell to his knees, cringing against the wall. He was only slightly relieved when he saw that the newcomer was a white-robed mage, a small, slender female. At least it wasn't Kalrakin, which is what he had feared.

"Who are you?" he gasped. "Please, don't hurt me!"

"I am an elf maid seeking vengeance for the suffering of my brother!" declared the woman. "Give me one reason why I should not kill you!" She might have been young in appearance, but she sounded very dangerous to Luthar.

"But I seek only escape!" he cried piteously. "I simply want to leave this place! You can have it, you and your friends; I don't belong here!"

"If I let you leave, will you tell me where the tall sorcerer is?"

"Yes! Yes!" he blubbered eagerly. "Just let me go!"

She spoke a few intricate words of magic, gestured subtly at the wall, and abruptly the blue outline of a passage appeared there. An opening, outlined in the pale blue light, shimmered in the wall of the Tower.

"Oh! Oh, my!" Luthar exclaimed.

The verdant expanse of Wayreth Forest, pale green in the early dawn, beckoned from beyond the walls of the courtyard. But there was a film across that tantalizing aperture, and when Luthar reached out a hand he found his way still blocked by a magic curtain of some sort.

"Tell me!" the White Robe demanded.

"Kalrakin is in the north tower. He is bent on destroying all the foundations of the spire and soon plans to bring it crashing down."

"Very well," said the angry elf maid. The screen faded, leaving the dimension door open to the outside of the Tower. "You may go now. But hurry before I change my mind and kill you anyway, fat one."

Luthar was already gone.

Kalrakin was finishing his inspection of the base level of the north tower. He was satisfied that everything was in place for the final destruction—he wasn't sure if the tower would crumble straight down or tip to the side like a toppling tree. He very much looked forward to finding out.

All of a sudden he spotted a flash of white, something moving in the connecting passage. Wild magic fueled him and he teleported instantly to block the figure's path, finding himself confronting a female wizard in a white robe. For a moment he recalled the dark-haired wench who had earlier escaped him. But this one had golden hair and the slender build of an elf.

"Hmm. Unpleasant surprise. How did you get out of the hall?" he demanded, momentarily bewildered. "Or are you new to the Tower?"

His eyes widened in surprise as she threw herself at him, fingernails clawing like a tigress. Unfortunately, she was too far away, too far to have any chance of reaching him. She died midway through her lunge, blasted by the power of his stone, an explosion that echoed loudly through the Tower.

And continued to resonate. He was startled, though not displeased, but the ruckus caused by her death. Strange, it was as if the mage had thrown herself upon his power, just so that her death could make a lot of noise.

The sorcerer whirled at that thought then laughed out loud as he observed the wizards of three robes rushing forward from the south tower like a bunch of alley ruffians. They were charging him! Attacking!

"Come, children of the god-fools!" he cried in delight. "Let us play together!"

The Irda Stone was blindingly bright as he lifted his right hand. Energy exploded from the artifact. The first blast of sorcery knocked an elderly White Robe down and tore his chest open when the old man was still forty feet away. Others got closer, but then more sorcery erupted, multiple bolts of wild magic spreading into the throng of wizards with deadly results.

During the past months, Kalrakin had stored considerable might within the artifact, and it was now at the height of its power and effectiveness. Like blasts of lightning, lacking only heat, the powerful magical energy exploded outward, slashing and stabbing and choking the attacking wizards.

A Red Robe screamed and fell, her slender body torn nearly in half. Next to her one of the black-robed dwarves howled and died as sorcery tore at his face, searing away his beard, his nose, down to the bone of his skull.

Some of the fools stopped to cast their spells, and these Kalrakin confronted with particular relish, using the Irda Stone to suck their fireballs, swarming meteors, and hissing lightning bolts out of the air, and draw their magic into his artifact. Some lurked there, harmless for the moment, while others rebounded against the casters, the many explosions wracking the hallway, sending all the pathetic survivors scrambling for cover.

There was that Black Robe, the one Kalrakin thought he had killed already. The dark elf, gripping a pathetic knife, had tumbled to the ground in the wake of one explosion. As he rose now to a fighting crouch, Kalrakin laughed loud at the sight of that once-handsome face, half-swathed in blood.

"You look dead already!" crowed the sorcerer. "So die twice, stupid elf!" He raised the stone high in his fist, the artifact pulsing with power.

———◆◆◆———

Coryn heard the sounds of battle and raced as quickly as she could through the ruin of the north tower's ground level.

Nearly all of the interior walls had been destroyed and she had to jump over piles of rock, leap over gaps in the floor, and climb over huge fallen statuary. Coming around the corner into the wide hallway, she had her bow up, its string tight, and a single arrow quivering in her grip when she spied the sorcerer just ahead.

He was under attack from a small army of the wizards and tossing bolts of wild magic as if they were snowballs—fatal, crackling snowballs. The spells burned and sizzled through the air, burning the wizards, searing their flesh, igniting robes of white, red, and black. Smoke lingered in the air; blood covered the stonework; she heard the moaning of the wounded.

It had been a while since she had used this weapon. But the wood felt smooth and supple in her hand, and the string was steady and taut. Without hesitation she drew the string back to her cheek, took aim, and let the arrow fly.

At the same time, the old words of wild magic sprang to her lips, and she cast the spell that had served her so well on so many hunts. The arrow split into three identical missiles, and Cory quickly blew a strong gust of wind to guide them home. The three arrows diverged as they flew, one heading straight ahead, while the others arced outward and around.

Something, perhaps the soft twang of the bowstring, drew Kalrakin's attention. He turned, eyes wide, and raised the stone in Coryn's direction. He was grinning. Sorcery flared—a blast that knocked one of the hurtling arrows out of the air. He cackled and raised the stone higher.

That is when the other two arrows took him, one in each side, puncturing each of his lungs, driving inward until both steel arrowheads—they weren't strictly magical, but Umma herself had sharpened them for hours—lodged in his heart. With an expression of astonishment, he looked down at the blood that was starting to stain his filthy tunic.

Kalrakin staggered backward. The stone fell from his nerveless fingers, rolled across the floor, and came to rest against a stone heap.

And then the dark elf was upon him, the sharp knife doing its bloody work.

CHAPTER

30

CONCLAVE

The Red, White, and Black Robes all took their places in the Hall of Mages, sitting apart from each other in their stone chairs. There were twenty-one of these chairs, though only sixteen of them were occupied. The silence in the dark, lofty hall remained vast, broken only by the soft rustle of a robe or an occasional, whispered phrase between members of an order.

The ringed chairs were arranged as always, facing the center, with three wide gaps marking the boundary between orders. Jenna sat in the center of the Red Robe section, with her four surviving colleagues, two to each side. Dalamar and Coryn were in the center of their respective orders. Counting the three Heads of the Orders, there were five Black Robes, five Red, and six White—counting the weak but determined Adramis—present.

Coryn felt acutely aware of her youth. She was the youngest mage in this august gathering. But she had much of which to be proud, she reminded herself. She had come all the way from the Ice Folk village of Two Forks to pass the Test. Along with Jenna and Dalamar, she had made the sphere of glass and filled it with smoke, then sent that crucial signal out across the world, awakening her order, summoning them here to retake the Tower. And she had shot the arrow that finally brought down their greatest foe.

This was the greatest conclave of magical power the world had seen in many decades. Though the white moon had set, Solinari seemed to rest a comforting hand upon her shoulder. Lunitari was low in the west, and Nuitari was coming up in the east. Godly magic, once again, soothed the world.

Coryn well understood the portent of this night.

And finally, in a moment of pure clarity, she knew what she had to do.

She listened with an expression of grave solemnity as Jenna welcomed all of the members of the orders to the Tower, gave thanks to them all, and to their trio of gods, that they had been able to respond to the summons issued by the three wizards on the Night of the Eye.

"Aye—like a splash of cold water, that was. Woke me from quite a restless sleep," said Willim the Black, the eyeless dwarf's voice a raspy chuckle. Then his voice turned menacing enough to send a chill through Coryn. "Took only time fer a bit o' retribution—don't ya know what I mean?—before I was out o' T'orbardin and on the road t' Wayreth."

One by one the others acknowledged the importance of the summons. Two of the surviving elves—white-robed Adramis and a slender, even gaunt-looking female who wore the red robe—had come from among the diaspora of Qualinesti, the scattered refugees who had been driven from their homeland in small groups and now sought sanctuary wherever they could find it in the world. These two Qualinesti mourned Aenell, whose body had been found near Kalrakin's. Her chair was empty for the Conclave.

Another, a white-robed elderly male from Silvanesti named Suwannis, had journeyed all the way from the borders of his own native land. His voice choked as he recounted the plague of minotaurs enslaving and slaying those of his people who remained. Coryn felt a shiver of sadness, realizing that the most ancient peoples on all the world were now left without a homeland.

There were two human Black Robes who were sisters— elderly women of stooped posture and skeletally slender hands. But their voices were strong and steady as they coolly acknowledged Dalamar as their leader; his black smoke had awakened them both on the Night of the Eye. In a relatively easy journey, they had teleported to the edge of Wayreth Forest at the exact same instant from their widely separated homes in Sanction and Caergoth.

One was the beautiful, young, black-robed woman Sirene. Coryn had thought she wasn't much older than her, until Jenna had whispered to her that Sirene was a half-elf, and already well over a hundred years old.

One by one the sixteen wizards recounted their origins, with a succinct declaration of homeland and a description of their journey to the Tower. There were elves and humans and besides the cackling Willim the Black from "T'orbardin"—a second dwarf from the Khalkist Mountains.

"We are gathered here to restore the orders of magic to their proper stature upon the world of Krynn," Jenna announced as soon as the roster of introductions was completed. She stood up, leaning on her staff, and stalked with a firm stride into the center of the circle. There she pivoted slowly, allowing her eyes to meet the gaze of each of the other fifteen seated wizards.

"There is much work to be done. Our tower has suffered grievously, and we are the ones who must make this place right once more. It will be work that will last for years, possibly a lifetime. Undoubtedly it will become the labor of the next generation of wizards. But it is work that must begin."

"Aye, it will begin," exclaimed Suwannis and Rasilyss in unison. The other wizards echoed those words, like a prayer.

Jenna continued. "Our procedure must, in a sense, be unique in that the first matter of any Conclave is a vote of confidence in the Head of the Conclave, so that she—or he—may lead the Conclave in matters of wisdom and practicality."

The Red Robe let another stern look sweep around the ring of faces. "But we all know that the most recent Conclave was many years ago, held in the absence of our gods, and was viewed by all as the last that would be held in the history of the world. Our last head, Palin Majere, dispersed the orders of magic at that time, and withdrew from the practice of magic in his own life. There was no expectation that the gods, and their magic, would ever return."

"So we have no official head of the Conclave. This, we understand," Willim the Black snorted impatiently. "Let us choose one, then. Obviously, the matter falls between yourself—the Red Lady of Palanthas," he cackled with a leer, "and our own admirable head, Dalamar the Dark. Make your speeches, and we shall decide with the spell of consensus, as always."

"Wait."

Coryn spoke up. The rest of the wizards looked at her in shock, mixed with suspicion on the faces of the Black Robes, skepticism writ in the expressions of the Reds, and pride in the visages of her own order—even from old elf Suwannis, who sat back with a satisfied, even smug, smile.

"There are *three* heads of the orders here," Coryn announced. "Three of us who cast the spell of awakening on the Night of the Eye. And I make my bid, not as an equal to the esteemed masters of the Red and Black Robes"—she nodded coolly in the directions of her two counterparts, both of whom were watching her with their own mixed, wary emotions—"but as the one who brings the most promise to leading the orders into the new age."

"But—you're still a child!" Jenna finally found her voice, with an edge of anger. "You have only known the power of godly magic for a matter of weeks! True, you accomplished much in that time, but the Head of the Conclave must be one who has studied for years, has dedicated a lifetime to the pursuit of magic!"

"Tell me, where is that written?" The Red Robe was condescending to her, and Coryn's temper flared. "I am no longer a child. I am Mistress of the White Robes. I have passed the Test in the Tower of High Sorcery—"

"As have we all!" Dalamar interjected sharply, the robe falling away from his scarred face. Seated to his right, Coryn had a view of the half of his face that had suffered the worst; it looked grotesque, yet oddly compelling.

"—and, indeed," she continued calmly, as if she had not been interrupted, "I emerged from that ordeal stronger than when I began. That, alone, you may all take as a sign of my worthiness. I have stood beside the two of you, mighty wizards both, and cast my own spells of might and power. I studied in my own way before the Test, and I continue to study; but the spells I needed during battle came to me when I needed them, even without study.

"Remember," she concluded, taking the time to meet every pair of eyes in the room. "I am the one who first learned the secret of the Tower's corruption, and it was that revelation that brought us here—first to cleanse the Tower, and then to gather in Conclave. I have seen the hostility and division between the Red Robes and the Black, firsthand, traveling with Jenna and Dalamar." She stared at the two of them, who eyed her stonily. "It is fitting that I should preside over the healing that will occupy us all, as Jenna states, for the foreseeable years."

"Hmm. The lass has a point," declared Rasilyss from the Red Robe section, her aged eyes sparkling. Jenna cast her a sharp look, but she didn't withdraw the comment.

"A point, but it is moot."

This was a new voice, a man's, and he spoke not unkindly.

Coryn whirled in surprise. The man came from the shadows around the edge of the hall. As he approached the circle, Coryn saw that he wore a red robe. He was tall, bearing himself with immense dignity as he pulled back the red hood so that all could see his handsome face. Murmurs of recognition, even awe, arose from the older members of the Conclave.

His eyes fell upon Coryn, and she noted the great depth of wisdom there. But she was not intimidated, nor would she be so easily denied.

"Why is it moot?" she shot back, trying to keep her tone even. "Why shouldn't I become Head of the Conclave?"

"Perhaps none more deserving. But that, too, is beside the point."

"Who *are* you anyway, old stranger?" snapped the young enchantress. But she had gone too far, and the others gasped at her disrespect.

"This would appear to be Justarius, one of the most renowned of the Red Robes. Once Head of the Conclave, himself," Jenna said. She smiled slightly, a wry look. "Though we older and more experienced mages happen to know that Justarius, like Par-Salian, is long dead."

For a moment the red-robed stranger's visage wavered, and Coryn saw the avuncular image of gray-bearded Par-Salian, as he had first welcomed her to the Tower. The image shifted again, and she gasped in surprise at the sight of a Black Robe, his bearded face looking at her with a look of pure, unadulterated hunger. These were all variations of the same figure.

"And dead, too, is Fistandantilus," Jenna said, explaining the black-robed image to Coryn. "May the gods of magic be praised."

The stranger settled back into the face and form of Justarius, but now Coryn knew him for who he was: the Master of the Tower.

"These fleshly incarnations wear on me," the Master admitted, sinking with obvious relief into one of the vacant chairs—a chair in the Black Robe section of the circle, Cory couldn't help but notice. "Indeed I am weary. And indeed I am grateful for this Conclave, grateful there will soon be a trusted mortal presiding over this hallowed place, as in times past."

"Yes, a mortal—but not me?" Coryn pressed. "Why?"

"Because there exists a reason—one reason, but one that is ultimately binding—that prevents you from ever becoming the Head of the Conclave."

All the wizards watched the Master with keen interest. Coryn felt a stab of apprehension—what did he know? What had she failed to do?

"Would you please describe for us your first experiences with magic?" he queried softly.

Hesitantly, she related the stories of her girlhood—her first experiments with wild magic, using the tundra's water in creative ways to help her fellow villagers, hunting and fishing with spells. And as she spoke, a light dawned in the eyes of some of the older mages.

"Thank you for your candor," the Master said. He turned to address the whole Conclave. "This young woman is undeniably powerful. She has earned the right not only to wear the white robe, but to sit as the head of that order. But she can never be selected as Head of the Conclave, in part—though only part—for the reasons you have just been told."

"Surely I am not the only one who dabbled in sorcery while the gods were gone?" the young White Robe argued.

"I know that Jenna and Dalamar, both, sought to draw magic from the fabric of the world. Is that not true?"

But the Master waved off any answer by either the Red or the Black Robe. "I said that is *part* of the reason."

"I have renounced that power!" Coryn insisted. "The true magic of the gods, of Solinari, is all the power I need now."

"To destroy Kalrakin, you employed wild magic here, in the Tower of High Sorcery. That is the other, more important part of the reason."

"But—I had to! It was the only way to save the Tower!" objected Coryn, shaking her head in disbelief.

"Yes, quite true. And we are grateful that you did so, to be sure. But the fact remains. And it is inviolable. The gods have spoken."

"You have come far from the wild magic you learned as a girl, before you knew of the three gods," Jenna said consolingly, and her voice, too, was unusually gentle. "But it is clear that the temptation remains within you. Renouncing wild magic is sacred to the mages of all three orders, while using that which you have renounced, violates that which is inviolable."

"I ask again: Where is this written?" Coryn demanded angrily.

Still, the red-robed sorceress spoke kindly, and this to the young woman was almost more painful than if Jenna had delivered a furious rebuke. "It does not have to be written . . . you know it yourself, Coryn, in your heart. And if you still doubt, you have only to ask the one who has guided you, has taught and sheltered you through this long ordeal."

Jenna nodded to the Master of the Tower.

Coryn's knees grew weak, and though she did not have the strength to ask the question, she nevertheless heard the answer through the fiber of her being. The Master's next words concluded the matter.

"You are great, White Robe, a promising leader of your order. And I predict you will rise to higher greatness. But you can never rule the Conclave."

One by one, the others nodded solemnly. Coryn, numb, sat down while trying to hold her head high. She was painfully aware of Jenna's sympathetic look. Dalamar, in contrast, was aloof, coolly arrogant as he surveyed the Conclave, turning his head so that all could observe the gory smudge that was the right side of his face. By Solinari, she hated him!

But there was nothing more to say. She could only wait, as the wizards settled in their chairs, preparing to resume the pressing business.

Dalamar then rose. "As for me, I have paid dearly for this chair. I have paid in pain and in blood. Long ago I paid dearly." He tore open his robe to reveal five holes, still moist and weeping, in his chest. He turned in a half circle to display the ghastly wounds, so that all could see his badges of honor. "This is the mark of my *Shalafi*, and it marks me forever."

His hands went to his hood, and he pulled back the cowl, turning his face so all could see. "Now, again, here in this place during this historic battle, I have paid, with this horrible wounding, this scar, that shall mark me for the rest of my days. But I have paid in pursuit of an honorable goal. If the consensus spell soon to be cast by you, my fellow wizards, installs me at your head, know that I will sequester myself in this tower for years, for the rest of my life if necessary, to restore the dignity and strength of our orders. I shall rebuild, with my own hands if necessary, this tower. I will erase the physical scars of the sorcerer's reign, for those are scars on stone and foundation. *Those* are scars that can be healed!"

There was silence as the wizards absorbed the impact of Dalamar's stirring words, even as some shrank from his scarred countenance.

"But if the consensus should fall to me, instead," Jenna spoke, rising smoothly as Dalamar slowly took his seat, "know that I will send our agents, yourselves, into the world again—and I shall lead them. We will work to restore the Tower, of course—we must. But we will also see that the honor of our three orders is once more known, respected—and yes, feared—in the realms of man and elf and dwarf."

Her brief but impressive speech concluded, Jenna sat, and the consensus spell began. Coryn felt the choice probing at her mind, as she knew it probed all those gathered here. She made no conscious choice, but let her instincts guide her. Others sat quietly, undergoing the same process.

Finally a corona of light appeared around Jenna, outlining the Red Robe in a soft brilliance, like the trailing of a glorious sunset. She nodded her acceptance, and then stood and turned first to Dalamar, paying honor to him. The dark elf, though, glowered at them all from the depths of his black hood.

"You, my old . . . friend, please stay here and do the work you declared necessary. I beg this of you on behalf of all the orders. For though many of us will come and go into the world, one must stay here, keep the records and treasures, and supervise the efforts to restore this tower. Will you do so?"

"Aye," he said in a low mutter, after a time. As he said this, he grimaced—or perhaps smiled. It was hard to tell with that death's-head visage.

"And Coryn," Jenna continued her diplomacy, turning to the White Robe. "There is much you can do, my eager young friend, and much you have to learn. Studies and experiments in the Tower of Sorcery await you. But there will be time for that. The tower will always be here, when you return."

"Return?"

"I think there is a place you must go right away, is there not?"

The little hut was just as she remembered, though the grass had grown tall around it. The teleport spell had brought her just outside the small, familiar place, at the front door. She hesitated a moment, smelling the scent of the Icereach, listening to a vast flock of geese winging past overhead. Finally, she drew a breath and approached.

"Umma?" she asked softly, pushing open the door.

At first Coryn feared she had come too late. The old woman lay on her bed, still and pale, just as she had appeared during the Test. Only when the young enchantress sat beside her and took her frail hand, did Cory feel the flicker of a pulse. Her grandmother opened her eyes. She looked at Coryn carefully, her gaze lingering up and down on the beautiful white robe.

"You have made me very happy, and very proud, my child," Scharon whispered.

Then Coryn's grandmother smiled, closed her eyes, and drew her last breath.

The War of Souls is at an end,
but the tales of Krynn continue...

THE SEARCH FOR POWER:
DRAGONS FROM THE WAR OF SOULS

Edited by Margaret Weis

After the War of Souls, dragons are much harder to find, but they should still be avoided. They come in all hues and sizes and can be just as charming and mischievous as they are evil and deadly. The best-known **Dragonlance** authors spin tales of these greatest of beasts, in all their variety and splendor.

May 2004

PRISONER OF HAVEN
The Age of Mortals

Nancy Varian Berberick

Usha and Dezra Majere find that a visit to the city of Haven might make them permanent residents. The two must fight both the forces of the evil dragon overlord and one another in their attempts to free the city—and themselves.

June 2004

WIZARDS' CONCLAVE
The Age of Mortals

Douglas Niles

The gods have returned to the world of **Dragonlance**, but their power is far from secure. Dalamar the Dark, together with the Red Mistress, Jenna of Palanthas, must gather the forces of traditional magic for a momentous battle that will determine the future of sorcery in the world.

July 2004

THE LAKE OF DEATH
The Age of Mortals

Jean Rabe

Dhamon, a former Dark Knight cursed to roam in dragon form, prays that something left behind in the submerged city of Qualinost has the magical power to make him human again. But gaining such an elven relic could come at a terrible price: his honor, or the lives of his companions.

October 2004

Follow Mina from the War of Souls into the chaos of post–war Krynn.

AMBER AND ASHES
The Dark Disciple, Volume I
Margaret Weis

With Paladine and Takhisis gone, the lesser gods vie for primacy over Krynn. Recruited to a new faith by a god of evil, Mina leads a religion of the dead, and kender and a holy monk are all that stand in the way of the dark stain spreading across Ansalon.

First in a new series from *New York Times* best-selling author Margaret Weis.

August 2004

Long before the War of the Lance, other heroes made their mark upon Ansalon.

Revisit these classic tales, including the *New York Times* best-seller *The Legend of Huma*, in these brand new editions!

THE LEGEND OF HUMA
Heroes, Volume One
Richard A. Knaak
January 2004

STORMBLADE
Heroes, Volume Two
Nancy Varian Berberick
April 2004

WEASEL'S LUCK
Heroes, Volume Three
Michael Williams
May 2004

KAZ THE MINOTAUR
Heroes, Volume Four
Richard A. Knaak
July 2004

THE GATES OF THORBARDIN
Heroes, Volume Five
Dan Parkinson
August 2004

GALEN BENIGHTED
Heroes, Volume Six
Michael Williams
November 2004

Strife and warfare tear at the land of Ansalon

FLIGHT OF THE FALLEN
The Linsha Trilogy, Volume Two

Mary H. Herbert

As the Plains of Dust are torn asunder by invading barbarian forces, Rose Knight Linsha Majere is torn between two vows— her pledge to the Knighthood, and her pledge to guard the eggs of the dragon overlord Iyesta. To keep her honor, Linsha will have to make the ultimate sacrifice.

September 2004

CITY OF THE LOST
The Linsha Trilogy, Volume One

Available Now!

LORD OF THE ROSE
Rise of Solamnia, Volume One

Douglas Niles

In the wake of the War of Souls, the realms of Solamnia are wracked by strife and internecine warfare, and dire external threats lurk on its borders. A young lord, marked by courage and fateful flaws, emerges from the hinterlands. His vow: he will unite the fractious reaches of the ancient knighthood— or die in the attempt.

November 2004

The Ergoth Trilogy

Paul B. Thompson & Tonya C. Cook

Explore the history of the ancient **Dragonlance®** world!

THE WIZARD'S FATE
Volume Two

The old Emperor is dead, sending shock
waves throughout the Ergoth Empire. Dark
forces gather as two brothers vie bitterly for the
throne. Key to the struggle for succession are
the rogue sorcerer Mandes and peasant general
Lord Tolandruth—sworn enemies of one
another—and the noble lady Tol loves, whose
first loyalty is to her husband, the Crown Prince.

February 2004

A HERO'S JUSTICE
Volume Three

The Ergoth Empire has been invaded on two
fronts, and the teeming horde streaming across
the plain is no human army. As the warriors
of Ergoth reel back, defeated and broken, the
cry goes up far and wide, "Where is Lord
Tolandruth?!" Banished by Emperor Ackal V, no
one had seen Tol in more than six years. To save
Ergoth, Egrin Raemel's son rides forth to find Tol
and forge an alliance between a kender queen,
an aging beauty, and a lost and brilliant general.

December 2004

A WARRIOR'S JOURNEY
Volume One
Available Now